NOVELS

The Life of Jesus (1976)

Seaview (1982)

POETRY

Maps (1969)

Worms into Nails (1969)

The Brand (1970)

Pig/s Book (1970)

Vectors (1972)

Fishing (1973)

The Wrestlers & Other Poems (1974)

Changing Appearance: Poems 1965–1970 (1975)

Home (1976)

Doctor Miriam (1977)

Aesthetics (1978)

The Florence Poems (1978)

Birdsongs (1981)

We Are the Fire (1984)

THE WOMAN
WHO ESCAPED FROM
SHAME

TOBY OLSON

THE WOMAN WHO ESCAPED FROM SHAME

A Novel

Random House New York

All rights reserved under International and Pan-American
Copyright Conventions.
Published in the United States by Random House, Inc.,
New York, and
simultaneously in Canada by Random House of Canada
Limited, Toronto.

Library of Congress Cataloging-in-Publication Data
Olson, Toby.
The woman who escaped from shame.
I. Title.
PS3565.L84W56   1986   813'.54   85–18389
ISBN 0–394–54715–2

Manufactured in the United States of America
First Edition
9 8 7 6 5 4 3 2

Typography and binding design by J. K. Lambert

For
EDDIE, SEYMOUR, *and* WALTER:
lights in the tunnel.

The author wishes to thank Temple University and the Pennsylvania Council on the Arts for their aid and support, the Corporation of Yaddo for the space and time in which this novel was completed, and Julian Olivares for his Spanish.

If we can arrive at authenticity by means of lies, an excess of sincerity can bring us to refined forms of lying. When we fall in love we open ourselves up and reveal our intimate feelings, because an ancient tradition requires that the man suffering from love display his wounds to the loved one. But in displaying them the lover transforms himself into an image, an object he presents for the loved one's —and his own—contemplation. He asks her to regard him with the same worshipful eyes with which he regards himself. And now the looks of others do not strip him naked; instead, they clothe him in piety. He has offered himself as a spectacle, asking the spectators to see him as he sees himself, and in so doing he has escaped from the game of love, has saved his true self by replacing it with an image.

OCTAVIO PAZ
The Labyrinth of Solitude

PART I

NACO

Chapter 1

S everance from the past was handled with a little pay. We
never grew up, and so the shock of separating was as if from
family; we were kids again, and all our careful plans seemed foolish.
Mine had been to head back to Chicago. I even had my ticket. But I
cashed it in, needing to stay awhile, and got a small apartment over by
the base, close to Mother Navy.

There was really nothing in Chicago but another past, and I suppose
I had thought to go there because of remembered images: to walk the
streets and playgrounds of my childhood, to see some of the old houses.
But there were no people there any more, and so I stayed in San Diego
and went to movies. I drank in bars along the strip, watching the B-girls
who had thrilled me, seeing my lost self in the tight pants of young
sailors they hit on. I read books and went to the Shakespeare theater in
Balboa Park, rented clubs and played a little golf at Torrey Pines. I even
went back to the base twice as a visitor.

I was twenty-three and old enough to know about decisions, but I
was young enough not to have to make any until I got restless. San
Diego was a Navy town, and I was still Navy. I had to wait to cut that
past off gradually, to get into something other than civilian clothes. It
took me a month of settling in before I began to read the paper and
a little longer before I started to check the want ads. I must have been

ready when I came across the job. I went for an interview and got it.

There was only a little work at the tissue bank, and I suspect now that the hospital had been premature in its enthusiasm when it hired us for a night shift. We were hired together, Marv, Morales and I, each coming from the same background as surgical technicians in the Navy. We were all freshly discharged, and I learned in conversation in the first week that this was to be a period of moratorium for the other two as well.

Marv was a farm boy from Kansas. He had been a football player in high school, and though when he could be held to the subject he had interesting things to say about farming, what he wanted to talk about was football, what high school had been like, and the girls he had gotten as a sports star. He had enough to say so that he did not repeat himself in the first few weeks, and there were times when the conversation deepened as he was brought to recognize that his past was most probably gone and that his dwelling on it was a kind of avoidance of facing the unknown future. He would laugh when things like this came up, would shake his head and bend it toward his portable radio. He always had it tuned to cowboy stations, and when he winked at us and smiled we'd laugh too, and he'd get back to high school.

Morales, on the other hand, seemed fundamentally opaque, and in the beginning it was easier for Marv to talk with him than it was for me. Not that he wasn't talkative. He had much to say, but when it came to talk about his past he would become slightly inarticulate, a little reticent and vague. He too had been raised on a farm it seemed, and for the first few weeks we believed that the place of his origins was Texas. Our discovering only after much conversation that he was from somewhere deep in Mexico says something of the way he was. He had a way of dropping startling new facts into his talk, facts that would warp the picture of him that we had firmly gained, and as time went by I had an odd sense that the more information I got the less I knew. I felt that if I went on I would know the whole story and yet know nothing, would know only the details and not the tale.

Morales had told us that he came from a large family and that his father had raised horses and was very successful at it. This was when we thought he came from Texas, and I remember he gave us the information in a rather gratuitous circumstance, having to almost yell above the

4

music while we were drinking in one of the shit-kicker bars Marv had insisted we go to on a night off.

Later, when we were eating our lunch one night at the tissue bank, we found out that he was from Mexico and had only a brother and a sister.

"But I thought you said it was a large family," Marv said.

"Yeah, well they were both older. I had to do the scut work. Shoveling horse shit, polishing the stone. My father had an attitude about work. It was just that they were older, I guess."

"What's that? The stone."

"He got into marble after the horses, table slabs, cutting surfaces and ashtrays."

"How old was your sister then?"

"When?"

"Christ! Down in Mexico, with the horses, the marble!"

"My brother was older than she was, a couple years. He didn't get along with my father. I had to do the work."

"What about your mother, then?" I asked.

"When?"

"Oh, Christ," Marv said.

"At the same time," I said.

"That was another thing altogether. That was in Texas, where I was born. Maybe my sister was fourteen; it's hard to say."

The weeks turned into months, and still there was little work to be done. What tissue was prepared and banked was handled by the two day shifts, and we knew our jobs couldn't last long. This was not the Navy but a money-making proposition, and when the time for auditing came we'd be gone.

It was the beginning of the San Diego fall, a good time to get out and around and a good time to get ready to leave as well. When we got our letters, the pathologist himself came down. He apologized for having to let us go and he shortened our shift by a couple of hours and told us to call in sick when we felt like it in what time remained. He told us that it was he who had gotten us the month rather than the regular two weeks notice we had coming.

"Sally was so sweet. I hope she'll be around when I get back. She was Homecoming queen attendant. We were pinned for a while."

5

"Haven't you written to her?" I asked.

"Yeah. In the beginning, when I was in boot at the Lakes. One of us quit, though."

"There was a lake close to the ranch, a few miles over," Morales said. "In Mexico, right?"

"That's where my father told me the story."

"But where was the fucking lake?" Marv said.

"In Colorado."

"But you never told us about Colorado," I said.

"Jesus, now it's fucking Colorado!"

"Part of the story took place in the Rockies."

"But where the fuck was the lake?"

We toured Coronado Island, wandered aimlessly around La Jolla in the crisp, fresh air, and spent an entire day at the zoo. Marv had Sally and home on his mind, but he started to touch us, something he hadn't done before, slapping Morales and me on the back, taking our arms to show us things. He even developed a wistful look. He was trying to find ways of saying goodbye. Morales too seemed a little changed, and I suppose I showed my share of it. I had given up on Chicago and would be heading north to Portland. I'd remembered pleasant family talk about the place and thought there might be distant relatives there. It seemed a place to go.

When Morales saw the beach at Coronado he mentioned the story again, saying that the place was not unlike the one where his father had first told it to him. Marv and I looked at each other blankly; it was hard to see how the two places could be alike. But we didn't press, and Morales dropped the subject and only began to parcel out bits of the story later in the hotel bar. What we got then was something about traveling and some veiled talk about pornography. We also learned that the story was probably not his father's, but something his father had gotten from somebody else.

It was while we were at the zoo that Marv brought up the idea of a trip to Tijuana, a kind of farewell party. It was not surprising that he should suggest it, but both Morales and I were a little surprised at the preparation he had put into it. He knew a place, he said, a good place where we could spend time with some women. It was kind of private, but he had a name that would get us in. He had to call and set it up

6

in advance. He was excited about it, and though I think Morales was no more interested in the trip than I was, we went along with Marv's enthusiasm.

We were standing in front of the zebra pen when he brought it up, and after we joked and pumped him for information, we fell silent and watched the animals: two families of zebras, four adults and I think three small young.

"I must have been about twelve years old, and something had happened between me and my brother. My father had been away for some reason, and when he came back I was glad to see him. Or maybe it was after my sister left; I'm not sure. Anyway, we were at the lake."

"Oh, that fucking lake again!"

"Never mind that; go on, Morales."

"Wherever he had been, he had run across a friend at a bar, an old friend he hadn't seen for a long time. This guy was in horses too, and he had gotten the story from a trader he had dealings with I think, not somebody he knew very well at all. If I remember right, the trader got it from the source, or at least said he did, or at least I think that's what my father said. I'm not really sure at all. But that part didn't matter much to me. It was that my father told it to me, and I still don't quite know why. When he started I thought it was some kind of lesson or other, but once he got going he just seemed to need to tell it."

He stopped then and looked away from the zebras, and then pointed to where some antelope were grazing.

"Right, antelopes," Marv said. "Go on."

"That's it," Morales said.

"That can't be *it*; what about the story?"

"My sister never rode the horses, but my brother did; he used a riding crop when my father wasn't around."

"Right. Fine," Marv said. "I suppose in fucking Hawaii."

The days went by, and we were in our last week at the tissue bank when the Saturday came up that Marv had set for going to Tijuana. It was to be our last weekend together; we'd be heading out at the end of it.

There was a chill in the air and gusts of wind, and it was dark, like evening, although it was only five. We headed out of the city, and before we hit the shore road that would take us south to the border we could

7

see blue sky ahead of us. Marv kept up a constant chatter, most of it having to do with going home, with how he would show the car off and the things he would do with his buddies when he got there. Neither of us could have gotten much in had we wanted to, and though we both interjected comments when we could, Morales soon became quiet and a little withdrawn.

By the time we had reached the border and had managed to make our way across it, the sky had cleared and the beginning of real dusk had started. We could see the first lights in the city on the other side of the short, humped bridge. The dirt road leading into Tijuana was dark from a recent rain, but there were no puddles in its ruts. It was just after six. We were two hours early, and we decided to get something to eat.

We ate lightly, at a small restaurant Morales knew of on a side street not far from the center of town and the nightclubs and strip joints. The fish was poached in a sweet, buttery sauce, and the vegetables were fresh and not overcooked. I was curious about the quality, and Morales said it was a hangout for performers, shopkeepers and politicians. When I looked around I saw there were no tourists or anyone who looked like a sailor in the place. The waiter spoke only to Morales, and all their transactions were in Spanish.

We stayed as long as Marv could stand to, and before we went to the car we stopped at a liquor store and got a bottle of good tequila, sipping stuff. Then we drove to the place. Marv had careful directions, and Morales checked them against the map as we drove. The place we headed for was in the foothills, a good distance from the town.

As we walked up the drive, we could see dim lights through curtains in a window to the right of the heavy front door. A man dressed in a suit and tie, a butler of some sort, ushered us into a small alcove just beyond the entrance. He asked softly for a name, and Marv gave him one we didn't know and his own as well, and the man bowed and left. He was gone only a moment, and when he came back he bowed again and gestured and led us into a large Victorian room, complete with comfortable couches, overstuffed wing chairs, a large fireplace and chandelier, and with a worn Oriental carpet on the hardwood floor. There was no one else in the room, and after we were seated we looked at each other in an embarrassed way. At least Marv and I were embarrassed. Morales seemed to fit in where he was, to be at ease in the chair, his legs crossed and no gesture of discomfort visible. Then the women joined us.

They managed to enter in a way that was not obtrusive or surprising; they more or less drifted in, not together but singly. The first one glanced at us and smiled, then went to the mantle and lit the candles that stood in silver sticks at either end of it. When she turned back to us, it was Marv on whom her eyes came to rest, and she crossed to him smiling and sat down on the couch beside him. I moved a little closer to the couch arm on my side, to give her room and to separate myself from their engagement. She half turned in her seat, her hand on the couch behind Marv's head, and they began to talk. She was younger than the other two, had blond streaks in her hair and her body was full.

The one who came over to where I was sitting had her hair up and fixed in place with a bone comb. She was dark, only lightly made up as I remember, and older than I was then, maybe thirty. She had a long, lovely neck, and she wore a thin gold choker at the base of it. As she crossed from door to couch, I saw the third enter from another door and move to sit on the chair arm where Morales was. I remember his looking up at her face, his beginning to speak to her in quiet Spanish, the fact that he was serious and not smiling.

The six of us stayed in that room together for only a brief time, and when Marv and I and our two women left and went to separate rooms on the second floor, Morales remained where he was, the woman beside him on the chair arm, talking. I remember her nodding, her depth of involvement in the conversation, the way Morales spoke without gesture.

What transpired in those rooms on the second floor that night was nothing beyond what I take to be the ordinary. We were with women of experience, and we were guided. And both Marv and I needed that guidance; we were young men, and the Navy had really given us nothing to prepare us beyond the technical. I remember a certain release and the fact that when it came I was freed from some anxiety that I did not know I'd had. I remember falling asleep, which seemed odd to me even as I drifted off because I was used to the night shift. I remember waking to the sound of water running, and I think I remember a very large free-standing bathtub and a lighted mirror.

It was midnight when I left the room and met Marv on the stairs.

He was a little shy and quieter than usual, and the two of us went down into the parlor we had left three hours before. Morales was sitting there, in the same chair; he was alone, but as we entered the woman he had been speaking with earlier came into the room with a silver tray with a bottle of brandy and our tequila and some glasses on it. I remember looking at Morales in a questioning way, and that his smile was enigmatic. I could not be sure whether he had left the room at all. Then the other two women joined us, one carrying a tray with crackers and cheese and fruit.

We talked a little in an awkward way, and it was not long before the three women were engaged in their own conversation and the three of us were talking of things we had in common. Marv seemed to want to speak of or at least acknowledge the experience he had had upstairs, but he was shy about doing so in the presence of the women and could only manage an odd smile at times, one that intended to cut through our talk, but did not have the power to do so.

After a while, the woman Morales had been with disengaged herself from the company of the other two and came over to his chair. She leaned close to him, speaking words I could not hear into the side of his face. He closed his eyes, listening. Then he opened them and looked at us for a long time. I saw him nod, and the woman rose and went back to her companions. His eyes followed her, and when she was seated, he turned to us. His eyes were a little milky now, his smile tentative.

"We're staying," he said. "Are we staying?"

===

They were down the shore, not quite to the curve where the rocks ended, and we knew from the way the boats with the colorful sails tacked that there was some breeze past the bend. They were close enough to it so that the edges of their blanket curled and fluttered. They wore modest swimsuits, with open backs. I could see the spine of the one I had been with, straight as a rod from her neck to the bowl of her hips, fixed and in no way erotic, where she sat at the blanket's edge in tight conversation with the other two; they formed a circle, their heads leaning into the center and only the slight animation of hands and arms moving occasionally, pushing points in discussion.

We were at Rosarita, an hour's drive from Tijuana, at the big hotel with the windowed bar that curved onto the beach itself, the place that had been a play spot for Hollywood in the forties and was now almost elegantly seedy, awaiting a new wave of success. We had passed the money discreetly, and they had wanted to come because they liked us, I suppose. Marv had gone for it before I had. It may even have been his idea. But I was easy to convince; I liked her spine and the shape of her mouth, and I was in no hurry, and besides I was beginning to get a sense of her life a little and was feeling as it came to me in our broken conversation that as I got bits of it I wanted more. Morales seemed passive in the whole thing; it was Marv who arranged it.

The waiter brought the tray of guacamole and tequila to our blanket, and when I pointed to the women and called out, they waved, and he took the tray with the tall drinks down the beach to them. We had played in the water, had talked and laughed together for a good portion of the day, but then either we or the women needed some time alone together, and they had gone exploring beyond the rocks and then come back, a little away from us, and spread their blanket out.

Morales looked at the quiet water. "Reminds me of the lake," he said.

"Here we go again," Marv said. He was squinting and looking hard where Morales looked.

"When did it all take place?" I asked.

"I don't know what you mean."

"Christ!" Marv said. "He means the fucking lake, the story. Whatever."

"Well, it was over ten years ago that my father told me, probably another ten when the things in the story ended. It begins maybe thirty years before that. That would be the late twenties. But there are things that go way back, at least to the last century."

"Can you get down to it?" I said.

"Not yet. Pretty soon maybe."

"Christ!"

We had a very late lunch. We ate in the bar, and the women joined us for it. Marv hung close to the one he was with, touching her on the arm and hand often. She seemed really to like him, even beyond the arrangement, and that was good to see. It was the arrangement itself that kept Felicitas and me in consort, and I felt a certain odd respect for her because of this, a certain shame too, I think. She was not really pretty in the daylight, but she had a bearing that made her attractive. She was very smart and a little cold and self-contained, and I think I feared her a little, and there was something about this fear that aroused me. I knew I could never really reach her and that she didn't care to reach me. The sex was mechanical and as such unintimidating, and I liked that, although not in any final way. It was good to have, knowing it would soon become memory and in no way something I would have to carry forward as a weight from the past. It would be nice to think about, but only as a thing completely gone. The woman Morales was with was named Verta. They were like strange friends together, as if reacquainted after many years.

There was a balcony beyond the bar, its weight supported by pillars in the sand, and we had drinks out there at dusk, at a glass table, and watched the sun set. Morales seemed ready to begin, and it was Felicitas, not the woman he was with, who urged him softly in Spanish.

He mumbled something about a horse then, calling it "she," but before he could get his words together and begin, Marv interrupted.

"Lakes. And now horses," he said. "There were always, you know, jokes about that kind of thing. Like about sheep, you know, farm boys getting off with them. I remember . . . "

Morales and I laughed.

"Go on," I said.

"Oh shit, you guys, we didn't even *have* sheep. I was thinking about something else."

"Maybe it was cows, then?" I said, and Morales and the women laughed, Felicitas tentatively, until Morales translated quickly for her and she winked at Marv and laughed again.

"Oh, come on, okay, you got me, I give up!"

"Okay, okay," Morales said.

"Go on," I said.

"There was a time I had a horse, a good Morgan mare, when I was a kid. And, well, the thing was she died, she died trying to foal. The foal was breech, but it came out all right, but it killed her getting born. I liked that mare a lot. I was fourteen and already involved in football and beginning to get involved with girls; that's older than most kids out my way staying close with horses, and really I wasn't spending much time with her, what with football and school, when she died, but, Jesus, her dying that way really turned me around. I felt weird afterwards. I guess I knew I was acting extreme."

"Afterwards?" I said.

"Yeah."

"Go on," Morales said.

"After I killed the foal."

"You killed her?"

"That's right. But not her; it was a male. And I caught hell for it, too. Drowned him in the lake."

"What lake?" Morales said.

"We called it the lake; really it was a pond, spring fed, and bottom land that rain fed. He was only a week old. I remember I carried him under my arm and got in the lake with him, with all my clothes on, and held him under until he stopped kicking. Shit, to think of it, the poor bastard. I must have been crazy. But the thing of it that still gets to me is that I wouldn't have thought the mare meant that much to me anymore. Something about his killing her. That I *owned* her. He was like the worse kind of thief."

"Can a horse be a bastard?" I asked.

"Not a good question," Marv said. "When horses get it on, *that's* the marriage. I don't know who the father was, but we were careful with our horses, my father was, so I probably knew or just never paid any attention; I was involved in school, and there was football and girls. I remember I lifted him out of the lake and put him on the bank and didn't feel any guilt at all, just didn't feel bad about it. He was spread out and silent and relaxed, and I felt relaxed too. When my father got after me for doing it, I remember that I understood that I had done wrong, but I couldn't *feel* it, you know; I still can't feel it. Strange about the mare; it was just a horse, and I thought I had outgrown her. But I felt I owned her; he was a thief."

We were silent for a while. It was as much the fact of Marv's talking, of his telling a story in such an extended and reflective way, as the story itself that I think got to Morales and me. We were touched by his talking. The women, though they had not gotten the whole story from Marv's midwestern English, seemed to feel the effect of it on the two of us, and they were subdued also. The moon was out now, and full, and it was only when Marv joked about the sheep again and the woman knew that they could smile and laugh that I saw the way the moonlight struck against their teeth, making them seem to protrude and gleam. Their eyes too seemed hard, like thick glass, as the light reflected off them, and when their hands moved on the table, their painted nails shone like colored stones. Marv and Morales saw this too, I think; at least I remember we looked at each other, that they seemed unnerved.

—————

Morales was ill.

"Could it be the clap?" Marv said.

"Oh, hell, I don't think so; it couldn't come on that fast, could it?"

"And anyway," he said, "Connie says they probably aren't making it."

"What do you mean, probably? Wouldn't she know?"

"Well, I don't know; she'd tell me if she did."

After the day and night in Rosarita Beach, we had taken the toll road down to Ensenada. What began as an evening's farewell celebration had now lasted three days, and with Morales ill I could see no immediate end to it. On the toll road he had made a fitful start at his story again, but soon he grew reticent, allowing that he was feeling tired, something with his stomach, maybe a little fever. He sat in the middle in the back seat, between Verta and Feli, Verta ministering to him, wiping the sweat off when it started to come to his forehead. Marv insisted that Connie be beside him in the front, and I sat by the door.

"I really don't know Mexico, at all," Marv said, and Connie chuckled and leaned her head against his shoulder. Verta spoke in Spanish in the back.

"She say he's hokay now, but to get there soon," Feli translated.

"Morales?" Marv said after a while. "How's it going?"

"*Está durmiendo,*" Verta said.

"Let him sleep," I said. "Can you drive a little faster?"

I don't know why the women had agreed to come with us or how, exactly, it had been arranged. I wasn't even sure how it was that we ourselves had decided to go further. Morales had talked about it with Verta, and in the end he was the one who had made the financial arrangements. That had seemed a little touchy, both for the women and for us. The money wasn't a problem, and it was surprisingly little that

14

they wanted, but Connie and Marv seemed especially awkward about it. It was Connie who initiated it, and I think Marv had thought up the idea. They were talking a lot and spending more time apart from the rest of us. She had more English than either Felicitas or Verta, who had close to none. Marv, to my surprise, was picking up a little Spanish, and was using the few words he had as often as he could.

Verta brought a blanket from the room and Feli brought a pillow. They got Morales in a beach chair and covered him and sat beside him on the sand. The whole lovely bay was open to our view. There was a dock far down on the right, with fishing and sailboats, and far out on the water we could see clusters of boats trolling, others at anchor. It was a weekday and the motel was half empty, the beach as well. Morales looked smaller wrapped in the blanket in the sun, and while we walked the beach he was a landmark for us. His cheeks were drawn in, his forehead wet and creased and his eyes a little milky and sunken. We tried to get him to talk, but it was clearly an effort, so we let it be and hoped that the medicine Verta got from a local *farmacia* would do the job. He seemed to want to be in the sun, at least he did not want to stay in the room, wanted to be outside. We had a late lunch on the beach, some tamales that the women said were all right, and in the late afternoon we were still there, watching the boats come back to dock, the shadows shift and lengthen and the sun sink. The temperature dipped some, but it was still warm at five. Morales didn't seem to be getting any better, but Verta told Feli she thought he wasn't getting too much worse either. Marv had a medical kit and took his temperature from time to time. It spiked about noon, and between three and five it leveled off, a bit surprisingly, two degrees below normal. Marv said his skin felt too cool. He had wanted water earlier on, but later he had wanted nothing. He wasn't moving, and his head stayed fixed on the pillow, his eyes on the water, the rest of him wrapped in the blanket.

"What the fuck do you think it is? It couldn't be something we ate, could it? I mean, we *all* ate it. Could it be he's just tired? Some bug or something?"

"What about you and Connie?"

"What do you mean?"

We were getting close to the dock, the riggings beginning to appear distinctly on the boats' masts. When we turned to look, Morales was only a dot. The tide was out, and we were walking on the flat sand at the quiet surf's edge.

"I mean I don't hear you talking about Sally too much."

"Oh, shit, well that's later. Connie is okay, you know. She's sweet. She's helping me with Spanish."

"Where does she come from?"

"Pretty far south I think. I don't understand Mexico. She told me the name of the place, a small town. But not a poor one. She has family there, ranchers or farmers I think. They think she's here for school, in San Diego. She did start, but her English didn't get good enough, and she quit."

"Is that what she told you?"

"Yeah, that's right. What do you mean?"

"Go on," I said.

"Well. I couldn't get it clear how she got herself into being a prostitute, they call it *puta*; her family would call it that if they knew. She said she was a virgin when she came North. It was something about a first experience she had, something that made her cold, *frío*, and she's only been at the place a few months. She's helping me with a proper Spanish, not just the street kind."

We started back, Marv closer to the surf now, and as we walked we saw Morales grow in size. When we were a few hundred yards away, we saw all three women gather around him and help him to his feet and adjust the blanket over his shoulders. They were starting back up the beach toward the motel, and we quickened our pace some. We reached them when they walked under the canopy that fronted the patio running between the rooms. They had Morales by each arm, and Connie walked to the side, watching him closely.

"*Está* weaker," Feli said, when we reached them. "We got to take him in."

They were indeed supporting him, his walk was slow and a bit dream-like, as if he were not totally aware of himself.

"What is it, Morales?" Marv said, but he only turned his hanging head slightly and lifted a hand in half gesture.

"*Más tarde*," Verta said sharply.

" 'Later,' she says later," Marv translated, and we followed them into their room in silence.

16

We helped get him into bed, but we didn't really help much. The women were short with us, telling us we were in the way and clicking their tongues. We moved back to a corner of the room and watched Feli and Connie bustle about getting water, washcloths and towels. Verta took up station on the bed beside him and wiped his damp brow. His face was still sunken, and there was now a kind of vague chalkiness under the skin. He needed a shave, and there were faint drops of sweat in his stubble. His mouth moved, as if in preparation or rehearsal, before he spoke.

"Got to sleep a little," he whispered. "We can talk . . . "

"Never mind that," Marv said. "You rest now; we'll see you later on."

We lingered, and Marv leaned toward me and mentioned that he looked pretty bad, that he needed a shave, that maybe we should get a doctor. The women were tight around the bed now, leaning over him; Connie held his hand, and Feli was touching against Verta's shoulder. Connie heard Marv, though he was whispering close to my ear, and looked over at us sharply.

"¡No digas tonterías! she said.

Marv looked at me a little blankly. "I think she's telling us to get the hell out," he said, and when he looked back at her, she said, "Go, go!"

We left then, watching them as we crossed to the door. We couldn't see Verta or Feli's faces, but their bodies seemed set, their attention focused, and there was a kind of tough rigidness about their postures. We could see Connie's face, a little in profile; it had hardened into a kind of severe tenderness, and we weren't really sure that it was the aftermath of her sharp words to us. I think her look bothered Marv a little; I saw him glance away before I did and go ahead of me to the door. But when we got there, it was he who turned back to look at her again, and I think I remember a certain fascination in his eyes.

In the morning Morales was better. Verta shaved him; the chalkiness was almost gone and his eyes were clearer. But he was still a little weak, his cheeks still sunken in, and his nose seemed to protrude slightly.

After breakfast we got him out on the beach again. He didn't want the blanket, but he kept his clothes on. We walked him up and down, close to the shoreline. He rolled his pants legs up and waded in the water. At noon, he didn't want lunch, but we got him to eat some fruit, and he took a nap until two. When he got up he was considerably better, far less tentative in his step, but his face had not changed.

"Let's go into town," he said. "I could sure use something to eat."

We ate a late afternoon meal, a light one. The rest of us were not hungry, and we thought we'd eat again at night. Morales was careful with his food, but he ate with some interest, and we were all heartened to see him recovering from whatever was wrong with him. When we were finished, we went shopping, and Marv bought a very nice and expensive jade bracelet for Connie. She laughed and clutched it to her breast when he gave it to her, and I could see him watching her response carefully and with a strange intensity. He seemed to be watching for a remnant of that look we had seen the day before at Morales' bedside. It was almost as if the gift were a kind of testing, not so much of her but of her attitude toward him. His face brightened after the first few moments; I think he had satisfied himself in some way, a way that I was not at all sure of.

Feli held my arm, lightly and formally, as we walked the streets and went in and out of the shops. She pointed out the finer objects that we came across: good pre-Columbian replicas, the rugs with the best vegetable dyes, examples of crude and powerful local art (painted wooden fish with heads of tigers emerging from their tails), death objects used in the fiesta of the local patron saint. Her discourse, like the way she held my arm and guided me, was formal, almost professional in its warmth. Verta stayed close to Morales, watching him as we all did, but in a while she relaxed. He seemed all right now.

When dusk began and the first lights came on in the city, the shops closed up, and we headed back to the motel. When we got there, Morales said he felt fine, but he thought he'd take another nap.

"Don't want to overdo it," he said.

"Right," I said. "It's five. How about we meet in the bar at eight?" And we split up and went to our rooms.

Feli and I got to the bar early, at a quarter to, but Morales and Verta were already at a table, and as they saw us coming Morales waved his arm at the waiter, who was at the table when we got there. We sat down, ordered and asked Morales how he was feeling. It was eight-twenty before Marv and Connie arrived. Marv was grinning, and Connie tucked her chin down shyly.

"What took you so long?" Morales said, smiling.

"We were busy," Marv said. He was still grinning.

"I'll bet," Morales said, and we all laughed.

We decided to go to a good place to eat, and Verta and Feli compared notes. The place we went to was dark, elegant and half empty. It was expensive, but not in American money, and we had two waiters and a captain. When we finished, we had brandy in a garden to the restaurant's rear, a place carefully and beautifully landscaped, with comfortable chairs and modern steel-and-glass tables.

"Can you start the story now?" Marv said.

His asking surprised me, and I think it surprised Morales as well. It seemed to come from nowhere.

"Do you want that?"

"Yeah, well, we can't just leave it."

"What do you mean?" I said.

"Wait a minute," Morales said, and he got up from his chair and went back into the restaurant.

"Where's he going?" Marv said.

"*Al servicio,*" Verta said.

"Oh, she says the toilet, the men's room, the head," Marv said.

"What did you mean?" I said, "Can't leave it?"

"I guess I mean *I* can't," he said. "I guess it's that lake, his father, and the horse."

"*You* told us about one," I said.

"It was a pond, we only called it a lake. It was near some trees, in bottom land. You couldn't see it from the house. My father, well . . . "

"Go on," I said.

"It had a mud bottom, but it was a good place for swimming, if you didn't stir it up. When I drowned the colt I stirred it; I couldn't really see the colt under the water, could only feel it struggle, and it wasn't strong enough to struggle much. My father was a stern man. He didn't like it that we swam there, and we had to be careful not to get caught at it. It was in the trees behind the pond where, well, my sister showed herself to me. We were only kids then. And that reminds me of the time I went to a county fair with her.

"We were in the eighth grade I think, and it was in another town, and for some reason we decided we'd pretend we were dating, to give the impression to people we saw there that we weren't brother and sister, but were on a date. And we did it, and it was easy to pull off, silly really, but the thing was that I met a girl there who I had seen at a football game. I was already good in grammar school, and she was from a school we had played, and at the party afterwards we didn't talk, but we looked at each other a lot. And the goofy thing was that I wanted to get next to her at the fair and wound up having to pretend to have a fight with my sister so that it looked like we were breaking up, so that I could take up with this other girl. It's interesting, because this is the first girl I ever made it with, oh, not then, but later, when we were in our junior year. Not many guys were making it with girls then, and we, well . . . hey! Morales, about time. You okay?"

"Go on," I said.

"Well, I was saying about a time . . . but, hey! Connie, don't look at me that way!" He laughed, but his laugh was a bit forced, and his voice broke a little. Connie had a smile on her face, but it seemed tighter than it ought to have been given the circumstances.

"Morales, come on, get me out of this, man!"

"I don't understand," Morales said.

"It was a story Marv was telling," I said. "I think he'd like it if you could get on with yours. He got himself into a little trouble. It was about some girl."

"I get it." Morales smiled, glancing at Connie, then at Marv.

"But look, seriously," Marv said, leaning forward a little. "Are you up to it? You still don't seem too good."

Morales settled back in his chair then, lifting the glass of brandy to his lips. Then he looked for a moment at each of us.

"Well, maybe not," he said. "We'll just have to see." And then, finally, he started.

Chapter 2

The car moved through the curves in the mountain, leaving the town and the altitude of the Continental Divide, where it dipped into Mexico. Paul brought it up to speed as the landscape flattened, and headed for the border.

The crossing at Naco was a perfunctory matter only. He knew there would be difficulties coming out; there always were with the instruments. They'd examine the hemostats and the more exotic retractors, would want papers and then not be convinced by them. But, going in, the American hadn't even left his windowed enclosure in order to wave him through, and the heavy Mexican in his dusty gray uniform, though he came out of his hut, only asked, "How far you goin' in?"

He passed into the wide dirt streets of the town, remembering the low adobe buildings that lined them. The place seemed almost empty. There were a few women and children on the broken sidewalks, some looking into shop windows, others on their way somewhere, but that was all there was. He knew that come the weekend the soldiers would be there from Fort Huachuca, visiting the Casa Blanca and the Green Door. He himself had been to those places fifteen years ago when he was in high school in Bisbee, the copper mining town in the mountains with its clean and cooler air, only six miles away on the American side. Even then they had known not to come down on weekends when the soldiers were there and the houses were busy. Wednesday had been the best day; they had the houses to themselves, and the women liked them because they were young and inexperienced and not demanding. They would just go there to drink mild Cuba libres, to dance and to pretend they were dating. The women were perfect for them; they were their own age, but unlike high school girls they were wise and knew how not to tease them, and they themselves were naive enough to be able to romanticize the women's poverty away.

He turned into a side street that was narrower than some, more rutted and bumpier. The car was almost on its axles from the weight his trunk carried, and he had to slow to a crawl. Even then he bottomed out and his wheels stirred clouds of dust behind him, allowing nothing visible through the rear view mirror. A weak horn blasted behind him, and a ragged pickup bounced by and passed him, throwing up so much dust he could see nothing and had to almost pull to a stop. When the dust cleared, he saw that he had reached the corner where they said they'd meet him.

He had received the message at the reception desk of the clean, small hospital he'd visited in Bisbee the day before. It hadn't come through Pfeffer. It was a phone number, a Mexican exchange, and the message: *please call*. When he'd called he'd spoken to a very articulate man, a functionary of some sort, with only the slight hint of an accent. He had been asked to meet them, to bring whatever instruments he had available, and brochures and order forms as well. And now he saw the car at the corner, a long black Lincoln, and he pulled up behind it and stopped. Two men got out. They were both large and Mexican and dressed in suits; the driver had a thin mustache, was taller and had his hair slicked back. The other was stocky, looked strong, and his suit was a little tight and ill-fitting. They talked to him at the curbside briefly, decided that there was too much in his trunk to transfer easily, and asked him to follow them out. Just a few miles, five perhaps, they said.

The first two miles were only a little less bumpy than the streets of Naco. When they left the town they left it completely; there was nothing but low hills of desert scrub and a few broken-down houses set well back off the roadway. He had to stay a good distance behind so he could see the cloud of dust he followed. He couldn't see the car at all. But then the car turned left and became visible; the dirt road became black top; a private road, he thought. There was no white line, and the black top was no wider than a driveway with room for only one car. After another two miles, after the road had lifted through higher hills, it bent to the right and began descending into a low valley. There were a few trees now among the brush and cactus, and after the road had wound around a hill and straightened they came somewhat suddenly upon the house.

It was a very large house, stucco with a Spanish tile roof. It looked almost like a mission. There was a kind of courtyard with a stone fountain in it and a half-moon drive around the fountain where the car pulled up and stopped before stone steps leading up to high and heavy oak doors. Above the doors and the second story there was a bell tower, and to the left and right of the central structure there were wings running back at slight angles. When he pulled up behind the Lincoln and got out, he could smell the rich scent of the roses that were in the beds running along the wings. They were numerous, large and fleshy, and they bobbed and moved a little even though there was no real breeze.

＝＝＝

"¿El caballo?" It was the small, nattily dressed man next to Parker who had spoken in a quiet and deferential way. Paul thought him a medical doctor and not a *veterinario*. His hair and thick mustache were dyed, and Paul could see the edges of his face makeup where it feathered out against his earlobe; he seemed in his mid-fifties. He appeared to have little English, and his question had been addressed quietly to Parker, the words entering to the side of the conversation they were involved in.

They had finished eating, a rather good lunch of stuffed avocado, olives, cheese and wine, and were sipping strong coffee. They had driven the Lincoln and his own car away to be parked somewhere. The taller of the two men he'd followed had taken him through the vaulted entranceway, down the wide-tiled corridor to the staircase at the back of the house and up it to a sunny room on the second floor. The man had suggested that Paul might want to freshen up, saying that Mr. Parker would await him for lunch in half an hour.

The windows of the room overlooked a lush flower garden and beyond that a small stable with a fenced-in enclosure attached to it. The fence was circular and made, somewhat oddly, of wrought iron. It seemed to Paul a little *over*wrought, too embellished and fancy in its twists. It was spiked and very heavy looking. To the far right of the flower garden was an extremely modern building. It was white and constructed of poured concrete. Its roof was domed and Paul could see no windows in it.

"¿El caballo?"

"Yes, of course, the horses," Parker said.

The fourth man at the table was the Mexican with the ill-fitting suit, the one who had taken the Lincoln away when they'd arrived from Naco. Parker was an American, or at least most of him seemed to be. He had light-colored hair, almost blond, but his skin was dark. Paul thought he was about thirty-five years old. He was casually dressed, but his shirt and pants were raw silk, his jewelry—a neck chain and too many rings—was real gold. He looked strong and fit. It was obvious that even the doctor was his servant.

"Paul" (from the beginning he had called him by his first name) "you see, we have a few horses here, good horses, a few fine *palominos.*" (He pronounced the word with Spanish inflection and smiled.) "And around here the *veterinarios* are not too good. Do you know horse anatomy?"

"Not well, I'm afraid."

"Well, no matter really. *Mi amigo,* Gabriel here, he knows something of it." He gestured toward the doctor without looking at him.

"So. There is what I've told you—our small surgery, mostly matters of first aid, and then the horses; the horses are important to us. Should we see the surgery now?" It was more an order than a question. The two rose with Parker, and Paul got up and followed them.

The surgery was a small room at the very end of the left wing of the house. Though the corridor they went down had no windows, Paul thought they were headed in the direction of the fenced enclosure he had seen earlier from his room. As they entered the surgery, Paul was a little surprised to see the contents of his trunk placed neatly on wooden tables along the wall. In the center of the small room was a steel surgical table with a large adjustable light over it. Glass cabinets with a few sterile packs and some instruments on their shelves stood against another wall. There were two deep porcelain basins for scrubbing up and cleaning things. The room had no windows, but there was a metal door in the rear of it. Paul suspected that it led into the garden that he imagined was on the other side. It was a small room, and it felt a little crowded with the four of them in it.

After Paul had opened up the three wooden cases that looked like silver chests and had unwrapped the four instrument folds on the table, the questions and examinations began. Parker translated for the doctor, and the other man, though he showed some mild interest, stood somewhat to the side and did not participate in the talk. Though the doctor was interested in most of the instruments, and Parker, though he seemed knowledgeable to a certain extent about their use, was more concerned with quality, the conversation focused for the most part on size. The doctor handled the smallest curved kelly clamps, was most interested in examining the miniature retractors, and took a good deal of time with questions about the thinnest sutures, the 4–0 silk and gut with the atraumatic needles attached to them. Though Pfeffer did not deal in anesthetics at all, Paul had some reasonable knowledge of them, and he was able to answer most of the doctor's questions about dosage and its relation to body weight.

A considerable amount of time went by. Paul could see that the doctor was intent upon having many of the instruments and sutures, and when they finished talking they had agreed upon a long and extensive list. There was a little difficulty when the doctor insisted that he keep the samples themselves, that the placing of an order was impossible. But Parker spoke sharply to him in Spanish and then translated his insistence into reasoned English. The amount of the order was so large that Paul, rather than lose it, agreed to the doctor's request. When they'd finished, the doctor was jubilant; he went to a corner cabinet and brought out a bottle of mescal. His toast was long and totally incomprehensible to Paul, but he raised his glass and smiled and nodded as if he understood, and they all drank. The Mexican with the tight suit drank with them, but his participation seemed perfunctory. It was four o'clock by the time they left the surgery, and Parker insisted that Paul stay the night.

"We'll have dinner at eight. The house and the pool are yours until then. I'm sorry that I can't spend more time with you. I've some business; you understand."

Paul had not seen the pool and wondered briefly about where it might be, but he was tired from the long session in the surgery and said he would like to rest, if that was okay, to go to his room until dinner. Parker, with the doctor trailing, took him to his room and left him at the door. The doctor seemed to want to linger, as if he had more questions, but Parker took him firmly by the arm and led him away and down the stairs.

Paul lay on the bed in his room. The soft lights of the afternoon sun filtered through the curtains. Though he was tired, he did not sleep. The fact of having come to Bisbee after fifteen years away from it and Bisbee itself held his mind awake. Naco was pretty much the same as he had remembered it, its poverty and its dust, and though he had never been this side of Naco, and though the elegance of this house seemed oddly placed here in the wasted desert, the weather of Mexico and the enigma of its people were familiar to him and left him only troubled in the way he always had been when he came down here in his past. But Bisbee had changed dramatically. What had been a thriving copper mining town in his youth was now a half-empty retirement town for the elderly who could not afford a better place. When he'd come through the town, slowly, on old Route 80, he'd seen them on the sidewalks with canes and some even with walkers. He had seen no one who looked to be under forty, and there were no children at all. There had seemed to be little in the way of buildings that had not been there fifteen years before, and the old places, the ones he remembered, had not been kept up; paint was peeling off them, and the yards that had been well planted and kept up had gone mostly to weeds.

Still, it was not the youth of his high school years, but this later time that had brought him here that he was thinking about. To pass through the changed place of one's youth, then through the town where he had first been with a woman, then to find himself, selling surgical instruments in an elegant house in the desert moved him to a kind of numb depression, and for some reason he was thinking about Taunton.

The windows that lined both sides of the rectangle of the old ward were wide open on that perfect morning in San Diego ten years ago, and their cotton curtains blew both in and outward, at times a gentle gust lifting the whole line on one side up to flutter and ride into the room four feet or more. Occasionally they brushed against the arms of the men in the beds, who did not seem to mind at all, who were awake or sleeping, some with thermometers in their mouths. The men's eyes were black and blue in various shades, and their noses were white, bandaged with adhesive tape and splints: septectomies and rhinoplasties. In the solarium, at the end of the ward and beyond the nurse's station where Nasty Jack and the rest were, the coughing was subdued this early morning, only occasionaly wet rumbles and deep breathing.

Paul had had the duty here (his first Navy medical duty) for only a week, but because he had been assigned the care of Nasty Jack, and because the duty was night duty and he was alone and in charge of the whole ward, when Taunton came on the day shift the morning before, Paul felt like a veteran as he showed him around before the other corpsmen arrived. Taunton must have been seventeen, but he looked like twelve; he was bewildered and afraid, and his way of handling this was to be subdued and deferential and formal. The second morning he arrived early, at six, a full hour before it was time to come in, and after he had changed into his white smock and combed his hair he said he would be back, and he had gone out the door at the end of the solarium and sat on the bench in the garden among the flowers. Paul could see him sitting there through the windows as he made his rounds of TPRs. Then the woman came.

It was clear that she was much older than Taunton, old enough to be his mother. And she probably was his mother, and as Paul constructed it as he watched them, she was passing through; she was here out of some difficulty, divorce or death; she had little time, and the way Taunton rose when he saw her and her quick embrace and the way she pressed on his shoulder to get him to sit down with her and the way she leaned forward insistently and began to talk to him, all suggested to Paul that the meeting was important to them beyond its necessary briefness. She was telling him things; her hands stayed in her lap, but her body moved at the shoulders and her head moved forward as she spoke, and Taunton, though still, looked continually into her face. And then, after a while, the curtains still rising between Paul and the couple to throw a veil over their conversation at times, she suddenly paused and her body relaxed in its place and Taunton's body relaxed with it.

And that was the circumstance of the memory that Paul could not forget or deal with or approach with any degree of understanding. It was really an image memory, and this is the way it always came back to him at certain times. There was nothing in it to give him trouble, but what did give him trouble was the fact of its coming back to him and that he could never understand what it was in his current life, what particulars, that caused the image of Taunton and his mother or his possible mother to rise up in him, to become real again, and to make him sad. It was the way, after the insistent and time-forced talking, that the two of them relaxed back into themselves. His view of them or their view of themselves or the future or past that their discourse was about all fell away, quickly and comfortably. What had been talked about was somehow finished and settled and they had time, and their relaxation was both that and an entrance into that time.

They sat and looked at each other for a very long time. Then Taunton lifted his arms and stretched and began to slowly gesture. His hand pointed out the flowers they were sitting among; he glanced over and pointed at the white curtains blowing in the windows. He saw Paul watching them, and then he touched the woman on the shoulder, and she turned to look. And then they both looked at Paul through the window. And then they smiled at him, raised their arms up in the soft breeze and waved at him.

The dinner was simple but very well prepared: steak, boiled potatoes and crisp green salad. There were only three of them at the table; the tall Mexican with the thin mustache was the third. The doctor was absent. Parker had little to say, and it struck Paul that the other was there to provide him with conversation. They talked mostly about film. The Mexican was very well versed in Latin American cinema, something that Paul knew almost nothing about, and he held forth on everything from political implications to style and what he called "filmic technique" to *machismo* and its effects on the treatment of sexuality.

Parker spoke only when it would have been inappropriate for him to remain silent, but the Mexican was very suave, and the discomfort that Parker's reticence might have caused did not materialize. Even so, the fact of the meal's ending was more pleasant than the meal itself, and Paul was glad to be able to retire early, thanking them and telling them that he would have to leave before nine in the morning to make an appointment in Douglas. When he reached his room and sat on the edge of the double bed, he found he was indeed quite tired. It was only ten o'clock, but the time in the surgery and the slight unpleasantness of the evening meal had both had an edge of tension in them. And then too, he thought, there was Bisbee, Naco and those old remembrances. He was alone now, and as tension left him, so did his strength. He rose heavily, undressed and went to the bathroom and washed. Then he turned the light off and got into bed, and in a few minutes he was asleep.

He was awakened by a sound he could not immediately identify, a kind of faint but sharp cracking or clicking, in what seemed the distance beyond the closed windows. He was a little disoriented, but the room was moonlit and he quickly knew where he was. He reached to the table beside the bed and checked his watch; it was two A.M. He rose to his elbows, listened and heard nothing, but when he slipped back he heard it again, a kind of snap that now seemed to come from what he thought was the area beyond what he remembered was the garden. He got up and went to the window and looked out.

There were seven of them. They were walking on a path that must have started to the right of his window, below him in the house itself. He could see the crushed stone of the path gleam in the moonlight; it ran out and beside the edge of the garden, then bent slightly to the right and ended at the windowless, modern building he had seen earlier. A door in the side of the building was standing open, and bright light came from it and flooded the moonlit stone where the path ended. He could see into the door a little. The room beyond seemed large; there were loops of what looked like thick cable on the floor, and he saw what he thought was a large movie camera standing on a sturdy tripod, the points of its legs among the cable. He could not see the source of the light, but he could tell that it came from somewhere deep in the room.

Parker walked alongside the path, in the dirt, supporting one of the women. She, like the other, wore a bathrobe, and she was stumbling a little. Parker held her arm at the biceps, and he seemed to shake her slightly from time to time as he righted her, as if he were trying to wake her. The second woman walked with the three men. Two of them were in bathrobes also. They were dark, probably Mexicans, but the women both had blond hair and from this distance seemed light complected. The third man was the one Paul had eaten lunch with, the Mexican with the ill-fitting suit. He, like Parker, walked beside the stone path. He was a little behind the others, and he seemed watchful as he brought up the rear.

The woman with the two men in bathrobes was active, moving her arms, bumping often against them, touching their shoulders, once even sliding her hand over the buttocks of one of them. The doctor, Gabriel, was there also. At times he was walking beside Parker, shaking his hands and speaking intently to him; at times he fell back to the men and the other woman, urging them to keep up. Paul saw him shake his head, throw up his arms in frustration, saw Parker turn his head and speak to him. The line was jagged and faltering, but it eventually reached the door. Parker assisted the woman in and the others followed. The doctor was the last to enter, and he pulled the heavy door slowly shut behind him, gradually narrowing and cutting off the light.

Then Paul heard the odd sound again. It struck him that it had not stopped but that the attention he had given to the progress of Parker and the others had cut it from his awareness. The window was closed, and he had heard none of their talk, but he had been able to see both the urgency and tension in it. It was gone now, and the sound drew his attention. He unhooked the frame lock, lifted the window to the top sill, and leaned slightly out. The moon was full and he could see most of the circular wrought-iron enclosure clearly; an edge was blocked by a window bay to his left, but the whole of the small stable at the end was visible.

A man stood in the center of the fenced enclosure. He was wearing jodhpurs, an embroidered Mexican shirt with billowing sleeves and a cowboy hat. The click had come from the small bullwhip he held in his hand. As Paul watched him, he flicked back the handle, curling the tail of the whip like a fly-rod line in the air behind him. Then he moved his hand quickly and slightly forward, and the tail moved back, rolling upon itself out in the air in front of him. When it reached the end of its roll, Paul heard the click again. Then the length of the whip fell to the ground, and Paul saw the two small animals, moving close together, as they passed out of sight where the bay window blocked off his vision. When he looked back to the man with the whip, his eyes continued on to the small stable, and he saw the other man, sitting cross-legged on top of the flat roof. He was hunched down, but he was distinct in the moonlight, and Paul could see the oblong device in his hands and something long, thin and silver, almost needlelike, extending from it. He saw the man look down at the device, push at it, and then he heard the whip snap again. When he looked back, the animals entered his field of vision.

They were trotting side by side. They were very close to the fence, and he could not see them clearly through the embellished ironwork. They were only slightly larger than small dogs, but their movements were not doglike; they were statelier, more formal, and they trotted rather than ran. It was only after they had reached the far side of the circle, where he could see them without the fence intervening, that he saw they were horses.

His head jerked back, hitting the top of the window frame; the sound was loud to him, and he ducked inside and moved away, fearing the men would hear and see him. He waited a few moments and then edged back until he could see the man on the roof. The man was intent on the object he held and was not looking up at the window. When Paul leaned out again, he saw that the horses had stopped running; they were standing side by side close to the man with the whip. The larger of the two dipped its head and shook it, and its yellow mane rippled in the moonlight. There was something about their heads; something protruded from the sides of them. Paul made the connection to the man on the roof and realized that they were headphones, and just then the man snapped the whip over the heads of the horses, the larger of the two stiffened, and Paul saw the man on the roof as he poked at his oblong instrument.

The larger of the two horses moved slowly away from the other then, and Paul could see it more distinctly. It was obvious that it was the male; something aggressive about the way it moved made him think it was a stallion. Its yellow, full tail was long, almost touching the ground, and there were ribbons of red and blue fabric of some sort woven loosely into it. Its body was thoroughly brushed out, no matted or gnarled fragments of hair, and its mane was loose and flowing and clipped even and straight where it fell, parted, to each side of its crest. It was naked but for the headphones that, given its ordered beauty and careful grooming, seemed a strange violation of its formality and strength. Its hooves glimmered in the moonlight in a way that did not seem natural or appropriate, seemed almost theatrical, but was nonetheless lovely. Its partner, the female, dipped her head and pawed at the earth, kicking up motes of dust as the male stepped, almost prancing, slowly to the end of the enclosure near the stable where Paul saw a large straw basket on the ground. As the little horse pranced, its haunches rolled and its tail bobbed, fluttering the ribbons. When it got to the basket it lowered its head and reached in and withdrew something, and when it turned back, its head high, Paul saw it held the stem of a rose in its mouth, the blood-red blossom so large that it obscured half of its cheek and eye. It pranced back; the whip snapped again, and when it reached the place where the tip of the whip rested it lowered its muzzle and gently laid the rose on the ground. It turned then and looked up at the man with the whip, who nodded, and then it returned to the side of the other horse. Then it was the female's turn and the difficulties began.

The man snapped his whip, and his partner, this time lifting and pointing the aerial of his device down at the horse from his place on the roof, poked at his buttons. She moved out from the male and stood alone between him and the man. She was no more than a foot high at the shoulders. Four hands, thought Paul, dizzied a bit at the ridiculousness in the conventional measurement. Less aggressive in her stance, almost feline, she kicked again at the earth, but her head remained still, tilted up, looking at the face of the man with the whip. She too had fabric laced in her tail, but it was shorter and slightly less full, her mane not parted but lying to the side of her crest, combed out down to the withers, and the earphones looked even more ludicrous and wrong than they did on the male. She seemed withdrawn; slightly fatalistic was the way Paul would have described the way she stood, the tilt of her head as she looked at the man.

Again the whip snapped, the buttons were pushed, and she started off, walking and not prancing like the male had, in the direction of the basket. The man's head turned to follow her, and when she got halfway there she stopped, kicked at the earth again, and then raised her head and turned back around and looked at him. This time the whip came not as a cue but a threat, the tip biting into the dust no more than a yard from where the horse stood. She bucked slightly, her forelegs rising a few inches into the air, and when she came back down on her hooves she stood still, taut and slightly vibrating. The whip snapped again, this time closer to her, and when it bit in she wheeled and loped off toward the iron fence, running so close to it that her body might have touched against it, went halfway around, then cut from it and moved up close beside the other horse again, this time right up against him, a little back, and pressed her head into his neck and shoulder. The man with the whip raised his free hand in a gesture of frustration, then turned toward the man with the machine and snapped his fingers. Paul thought he could see the man throw some switch or turn a dial and push other buttons. When he looked back, the horse was standing off by herself. She threw her forelegs up in an awkward gesture, trying to hit at the phones, but she could not reach them. She shuddered and shook her head violently; then she began to turn in tight circles. She would spin in place, then run off a few feet and spin again. Twice she misjudged her distance from the iron fence, and when she came out of her spin running she struck her head against it. When she saw the male and tried to get to its side the whip would come down between them and she would wheel away.

Finally the man with the whip gestured to the one on the roof without looking at him. The horse was running along the fence, hitting its head against the iron; then it slowed to a limp. When it pulled up, it staggered slightly then fell against the fence, its rear legs buckling; it finished on its knees, its forelegs stiff, its head hanging. The male moved to it and stood against it, between it and the man.

Paul was sweating profusely. He looked and saw the drops falling from his brow to his hands where they gripped the sill. When he looked back up, he saw the man moving toward the two horses. He had dropped his whip, and when he got to them, he reached down and took hold of the male and lifted it. Gripping it under his arm, he unbuckled the headphones; then he lowered the horse to its hooves and pushed on its buttocks, sending it away. He was rougher with the female. He grabbed her with one hand by the skin at her withers and tore the phones free. Then he threw her away from him. She broke down when she landed, rolled in the dust, her legs kicking feebly in the air, then struggled to her feet and staggered to the iron fence again and leaned against it. The male watched her, waiting.

Paul saw the man return to his whip and pick it up. With the earphones in his other hand, he gestured with a nod to the man on the roof. The man climbed down, out of Paul's sight on the other side of the building. The man with the phones and whip entered the stable. When Paul could see them again, they were headed around the rear of the garden in the direction of the modern windowless building. They carried nothing now, and they leaned toward each other, talking. In the enclosure, the two horses stood close together against the fence.

There was nothing to think of or figure or plan, and Paul could not even imagine doing any of those things. He came back from the sill and closed the window carefully. He was shaking, and it took him some time to get the buttons of his shirt fastened. When he was dressed, he went to the bathroom and gathered his few toilet articles. As he reached the door, he realized that he had forgotten his watch on the bedside table and went back for it. It was three-fifteen. He returned to the door, opened it carefully and stepped out into the hallway. He didn't know where his car was, but he was fairly certain about the direction. He had noticed a spur running from the circular drive off to the left wing of the house, and he thought it would be there. He descended and headed down the long hallway in the direction of the surgery at the end of the wing. The house seemed empty; he could hear nothing, and when he got to the door of the surgery it was not locked. The room was dimly lit by a small fluorescent night-light in one of the glass cabinets, and he could see well enough to get to the back door. He pushed the dead bolt and slowly opened it. It opened onto the garden, and he saw that though there were a few high growths in it, it was mostly rose bushes and the growths were too spare to provide much protection, so he moved quickly to his left in the direction of the fenced enclosure, pressing against what remained of the building until he reached its far end. He saw his car, the Lincoln beside it, in a crushed-stone parking area a few yards from the building's edge. He headed for it, but before he got there he pulled up, turned off at an angle, and moved to the fenced enclosure. The building cast a shadow in the moonlight, and he felt somewhat protected when he got to that part of the enclosure he had been unable to see from his room. He gripped two of the bars, put his face close to the fence and looked in.

The horses were still standing where he had last seen them; he could hear what sounded like a soft mewing coming from them. He was close to them, not more than twenty yards away, but they were in the same shadow he was in, and their palomino yellow looked dun colored. The male's muzzle was moving slightly, rubbing against the muzzle and face of the female, whose head he could not see clearly behind the male's. Then the male paused and snuffled, his head moving up and scenting. Paul could see the kid-glove nostrils opening and closing. Then the male's eyes found him at the fence, and they stood and stared at each other; the female moved forward slightly, bringing her head into full view beside the male's, and she too stared at him.

Paul had a sense that the staring could go on for a long time; he didn't feel he had a long time, but now that he was here and they were engaged in some way, he knew he had to do something. He had no idea what that something might be, but he knew that he could not simply turn and walk away, and so he stood there.

Their eyes were crystalline and clear. The night was silent; he could hear no birds, and there was no breeze stirring in the garden. He could see, dimly, the modern building beyond, but he could not see the place where the door was; there was no light seeping around the frame. He turned to look at his car, but he did not release his grip on the fence, and when he looked back he saw that the horses still stared at him. He had to do something. But it was they who did it, and he never knew if he had given some sign or not, done a thing that he was unaware that he was doing, something that moved them, starting the process.

The male moved away from the female, walking oddly backward, and when his head reached her haunches he nudged her forward, away from the fence slightly. She staggered out from it, and then she paused and did what Paul had seen cats and young colts do. She stiffened her forelegs and stretched her back and loins, dipping her belly and bowing her spine. When she came back to her stance she shook herself, her mane and tail bouncing, and gave a brief high-pitched and quiet whinny. The male nudged her again, and both of them began to trot toward the place where Paul stood with his face pressed between the bars. But they did not stop when they reached him; they followed the curve of the fence, picking up speed, changing from a trot to a canter. The male was on the outside and a little to the rear of the female. He was watching her motion as her stiffness left her. He held back a little as she attained some grace and power again and moved into a slow gallop. They looked like horses on a miniature carousel as they passed Paul and went around the fence. After three turns, they were beginning to glisten as they came to a light lather. Then, on the far side of the circle, they turned off from the fence, slowing as they moved to the ground at its center, where they pulled up and stood, wet and breathing deep and effortlessly, shaking their heads and bodies, looking again to the place where Paul was.

He was getting nervous as he realized how much time was passing. The moon and the sky and the shadows were not changing; it was still dark over at the modern building, and there were still no birds. And yet he knew he must have been standing there for too long. He thought he had done what he could do, though he had done nothing. She seemed okay now. Their running and now their standing, free of the fence as support, showed him this. Maybe it was done to show him. He pulled his face back from the fence and released his grip on the bars and began to try to turn toward his car. As he stepped back he saw that they were not finished yet.

The male came at him first. He kicked at the earth twice, dipped his head and seemed to tighten and gather himself. Then he ran at the fence, and when he was six feet from it he leapt up into the air. He got as far as the iron crosspiece below the spikes near the top. One of his hooves thudded against it; then he fell back. He hit the ground on his hooves, struggled to stand, but fell over and rolled and came to his legs. He tried it two more times, but each time he came up short. Then it was the female's turn. She was smaller and lighter; her muscles were smoother, but she looked proportionately stronger. She got a little higher than he had on her first jump, and when she landed and came to her stance she paused and looked up for a long time at the top of the fence. Though he was back a little now and half turned, he could see her clearly through the bars. She seemed to be looking at the fence with great intensity. He thought her eyes were on the black, gleaming spear points at the tip. Her head was cocked slightly to the side, and her mouth was slightly turned up at the corners, almost as if she were smiling, her nostrils opening and closing rhythmically as she breathed. When she turned she was already half running, and as she picked up speed he could see that she was coming in from the side this time, like a high jumper approaching at an angle, her eyes fixed on the bar. When she gathered and went into her jump, he lost her for a moment in the iron matrix, and when she appeared again she was free in the air over the spears. Her body seemed fixed and poised there. Her lips were drawn back, and he could see the small ivory blocks of her teeth, the dark cave of her nostril, the dome of her eye. Her blond face was like lacquered wood. Her legs were stiff and extended, her head rising from the smoothe curve of her arched crest and back. Her tail completed the arc, and even the blue and red ribbons in it seemed to stand still in the air. And at the center of the lovely curve of her spine, just touching it, was the round and white full moon, a globe from a circus act. He moved and reached up for her, and as he did so he saw her pupil contract. She fell down from the moon then, and before he reached her she was impaled on the spike.

Her scream was high-pitched, long and ethereal, and though it was not loud it cut through him as he lurched back. She didn't kick out, but he could see her flesh under her yellow skin squirming. The head of the spike had gone into her belly, and when she sagged, the arch from her head to her tail turning convex, she was like filigree on the fence. He moved quickly forward again to her, reached up and took her legs in his hands near her body and lifted her. There was a slight sucking sound as she came off the spike, and when she cleared it the spike was wet and there was some flooding from her wound down onto it. He got her down and under his right arm and put his right hand under her belly on the wound and pressed into it. She bucked slightly; her head jerked, hitting against his chest; her eyes were frantic and wild when they looked up at him. He gripped her more tightly, pulling her head into him with his free hand. Then he moved off, as quickly as he could, and headed for his car. He heard a whinny and a snort behind him.

Chapter 3

When he got to the car the door was open, but he suddenly realized that he did not have the keys. Whoever had parked the car had them, or Parker had them. She was seeping into his hand; he could feel her juices flowing between his fingers, sticky and warm. He stood in the open door of the car for only a moment, and then he made his decision. He squatted, still holding her against him in the crook of his arm, and fished under the front seat until his fingers hit the metal kit. He pulled it out, pushed the door closed, and then headed around the car and the Lincoln in the direction of the front of the house. When he got to the fountain and the circular drive he saw that the windows of the house were dark and he could hear no sound. Moving into a slow trot, he headed up the driveway he had come down the day before. It was darker now; the moon had moved into a high cloud cover, but he felt too exposed on the naked road and after he had gone no more than a few hundred yards, had passed the hill where the road turned, he moved into the low brush to his right and stopped. She was still seeping. His wrist hurt from the force needed to press his hand into her to apply direct pressure, and he dropped to his knees and laid her down on the ground. The wound gurgled as her position changed, but she lay still beside him, breathing deeply. He opened the metal kit and took out a thick wad of gauze-covered cotton and an Ace bandage. He pressed the cotton to the wound and it stuck there; then he wrapped the bandage tightly around her. When he got up he was a little stiff and he staggered slightly. Then, with the case in his hand, the horse back in the crook of his arm, he set off up the road, keeping to the dark at the shoulder.

It was six in the morning by the time they got to the shack. The sky had been growing lighter for over a half hour, and though he was exhausted and moving slowly he was aware enough to be feeling very nervous as the light came on. They were out of the low hills and totally exposed on the road in the desert. He had seen no one yet, but he was sure that it couldn't be long before he came upon someone or someone came upon them. If it was someone from the house, that would be one thing; surely it couldn't be long before they found both of them missing and put things together. But he was almost as concerned that it might be someone else, some rancher or farm worker. What in the world could he say to them; what sense could any of this make? Then he saw the edge of the shed roof off to his right, about a hundred yards from the road, in a small, shallow arroyo. It must be a rancher's shed he thought, one of those used for the storage of animal feed, for range cattle probably. He turned and headed for it. He felt he should be hesitant, should go slow and check it out before he got too close to it. But he was too tired to care, and when he reached the back of it he went around its side and unlatched the door without hesitation. When he saw the inside he felt sure that the place was not in daily use. There was a scattering of loose hay in one corner and a smaller pile of ripe alfalfa in another, but there were no bales and he could see no implements. Without checking further, he went in and took the little horse to the pile of alfalfa and put her down on it. Her eyes were a little glassy, her coat sweaty and her mane matted. He peered down at her, and then he felt his lids falling. He had to stagger back to catch himself from dropping, and he turned from her and moved to the pile of hay and sank down on it. He watched her shallow but regular breathing from his place in the corner across from her as he quickly drifted off into sleep.

When he woke up it was very hot, the sun was high and it was ten o'clock. He looked over and saw that she was still where he had put her and that her breathing was less frequent and shallower. He knew he couldn't wait, and he got up stiffly and began to search through his pockets. There was a handkerchief in the rear pocket of his pants and a larger, monogrammed one in the breast pocket of his suit jacket. He hung the jacket on a nail and spread the handkerchiefs out over its yoke. He was not really fully awake, and he had to shake his head to clear it. He wished he had some water, cold water to splash his face with. The thought of it made him realize how parched he was. He licked his lips, but his tongue held little moisture. What in the fuck am I doing here? he thought, but then he looked over at her again, saw the way her barrel shuddered as it rose and fell, and forgot the question.

He got the metal case and took it to the small wooden table that sat under a window against the wall. He thought it odd that there should be a table in the place, but when he saw the way the surface was full of nail holes he figured it had some special use. There was plenty of light in the shack, and he only had to pull the table a few feet from the wall to get it slightly shaded from the direct sun coming through the dirty window.

Then he took his shirt off and carefully ripped the sleeves out of it and separated them lengthwise down the seams. When he had prepared the contents of the case, he went over to her and lifted her gently and brought her over to the table. She made no motion, gave no recognition of the movement and seemed close to coma. He rested her on her back, her hooves in the air, her legs splayed. He took his shoes off and wedged them in on either side of her to keep her in position. Her head rested on a line back from her shoulders, her neck totally visible to her throat latch; her tail lay fanned out behind her, its strands and those of the ribbons in it still on the nail-pocked wood. Her hooves glimmered, and he had an urge to examine them, but he knew he had no time. The wound was halfway between her vagina and her elbows, in mid-abdomen. It had ripped slightly, was about four inches long, and a loop of intestine was protruding slightly from it. He stood over her for a moment, looking down at the strange and vulnerable vision of her, and then he set to work.

He got the two handkerchiefs and the ripped shirt sleeves and placed them on the inside of the open lid of the case in the table's corner. He took one of the sleeves and wrapped it around his forehead as a sweatband, tying it in the back; the other he ripped in half crossways and fumbled to tie a piece around each forearm above the wrist, tucking the tails in under the fabric. Then he took the two handkerchiefs and spread them out on the table beside her. There were a couple of sterile packs in the case, and he took out one of them and opened it. He held it on the outside, taking care not to touch its inside surfaces, and when he had it open on the palms of his hands he dropped it on the handkerchiefs. It gave him almost a square foot of sterile cloth area. All the instruments and syringes in the case were contained in clean paper packets, and after he had taken the small bottle of Xylocaine out and stood it on the bare wood of the table, he ripped open a syringe and needle, some hemostats, a pair of Metzenbaum scissors, and a scalpel and blade, letting them each slide from their packets to the sterile square of fabric. Next he ripped a package of gloves open, dropping them and their small packet of powder onto the instruments. He was already sweating profusely, but the wristbands were catching the moisture. After he had opened a sterile pack containing two absorbent cloths, he turned away from her and drenched his hands in alcohol from a small bottle and dried them with a cloth. When he was finished he threw the cloth to the side.

He had forgotten to clean the edges of the wound. Gall rose in his throat, but he held it down, and using a large sterile clamp as pliers and a smaller one to hold the remaining cloth, he turned again to the side and poured the alcohol from the clamp-held bottle over the cloth. The bottle bounced and clattered when he threw it and the clamp across the room; she stirred a little, but she was beyond waking, and she quickly settled back into her coma. Being careful not to touch the wound or the loop of bowel, he washed her belly with the drenched cloth, flooding the alcohol down her sides away from the wound itself. The fluid darkened her short blond hair for only a moment before it evaporated. Then he ripped the powder packet, sprinkled his hands, and holding only the turned-up cuffs, pulled the rubber gloves on, pushing between the fingers to snug them up. He heard a sound in the distance, and he paused with his gloved hands in the air and turned away from her toward one of the dirty windows. The sound did not get closer, and in a moment it began to fade. He thought it was a motor of some kind. When he turned back and saw her, saw the wound and bowel and the instruments, he was shocked by the madness and by the newness of what he was about to do.

He had assisted at surgery in the Navy and he had scrubbed up and demonstrated the use of new instruments in his time with Pfeffer, but he had never been alone like this, had never had to make choices beyond the mechanical. What if he killed her; what if she woke and struggled while he was working, while he had her bowels out of her body? Would he have to kill her intentionally, cut her throat with the scalpel? She was beautiful the way she lay there, vulnerable and open to him, to his care and responsibility. Her hooves glimmered in the air, and now he saw for the first time that the glimmer was that of jewels. He leaned over and looked closely at the hoof nearest him. There were large diamonds set in the side of it, some moonstones he thought, opals, and at least two rubies. At first they seemed at random, but then he thought he could discern some pattern. He thought he could see the shapes of letters or possible symbols, but he wasn't sure of them. There was *something*, that was sure, but whether the jewels formed the positive or the negative space, setting off some message on the surface of the yellow hoof itself or were themselves the message, he could not tell. He caught himself as he reached out to turn the hoof to get a better look at it. He had almost touched it with his sterile glove, and he pulled back quickly, shaking a little, and looked again at the wound. He saw the bowel loop pulsing, pushing a little farther out of the hole with each shallow breath, and he knew he could not linger, couldn't put it off any longer.

Holding the loop of bowel to one side then the other, he used the Xylocaine to anesthetize the edges of the wound. He filled the syringe a second time and set it aside in case he found she needed more. Then he insinuated his fingers inside her and caught and carefully brought forth more of the bowel. He found some flakes of rust and a little black paint a few inches down, and he picked them off with a hemostat. After he had explored two feet of intestinal loop, arranging them below the wound in a pile on her belly as he proceeded, he was satisfied, and he worked them back into the hole. They were slippery and hard to hold and he was afraid to grip them too firmly and it took him some time to get them back inside her. The wound itself was fairly clean, only a few jagged edges, and these he clipped off with the Metz, clamping and tying off the bleeders that developed with thin gut. The hardest part was the peritoneum; he had no retractors and no help and bowel kept pushing up in the way, the muscle sheath kept closing in on his fingers. But in time he managed to get the atraumatic sutures in. He had to keep turning his head away to shake sweat from his lids. His headband was soaked with sweat now, but he could do nothing about it.

Very little muscle had been ripped; he could see what he thought was bruising and some other marks, but the rest looked all right. The deep fascia sewing went quicker and easier than he had thought it might and the upper layer gave him no difficulty. The subcutaneous tissue was easy. He could see the sticky fluids had already begun to heal there, and the fat was easily malleable and she had little of it; soon he found himself closing her skin. As he worked his way out, the tension lessened, the small intense space in which he had worked seemed to open out, and he became increasingly more aware of her whole body and even the spaces around it: the open metal box, the dirty floor, and his ridiculous shoes propping her up. The shoes were dark cordovan, with leather heels and soles; they went with his tan suit, summer weight, and as he looked at them he thought that he had never belonged in them, certainly he did not belong in them here, but they had been oddly functional, had served their purpose, and though they looked pathetic with their scuffs and dust, he figured they would serve him for a while more; they were better than nothing at all.

Then he put in the last skin stitch and was finished. He had some collodion, and he used that instead of a bandage, thinking it would seal the suture line and the stitches well enough, and that she would be less likely to mess with it than with a bandage. He lifted her and took her to the alfalfa pile, spread the remaining sterile pack under her and laid her down on it. Then he got his suit coat and covered her. It was almost dark now in the shadows where he laid her down; the sun had slipped past the dirty window, and he thought it must be well past noon, probably even later. But he did not check his watch. He went to a far corner of the room and slumped into it. The floor and wall boards were hard, and he remembered the scattering of hay and struggled to his feet again and went to it. Falling off, he was aware of his arms, bare to the shoulders, and how that didn't feel right at all.

When he awakened it was night, and the moon was high and bright again and illuminated, though dimly, the interior of the shed. He saw a movement where she lay, then he saw her head come up in the moonlight and look back at him. He fancied he could see her eyes, and he got to his feet and went over to her. When he got beside her, she dropped her head, exhaled and snorted softly, and he reached down and ran his hand over her poll and forehead, stroking her, feeling her damp ears. He thought she might have some fever, but he wasn't sure. He knew he'd have to watch her closely for infection. She pressed her head into his hand.

By ten o'clock they were back out into the night again. The road was dirt now, had widened into two lanes and was straight and flat. They moved in the desert brush, a hundred yards from it, mostly in a straight line, but bending to avoid the dark shapes of low growth, mesquite and barrel cactus. He had attached the metal kit to his side, running his belt through its handle, and it pulled at his pants and hit against his hip as he moved. He had managed to get her to nibble at bits of alfalfa from the pile before they'd left, and he could smell a hint of it on her breath. He had eaten and drunk nothing in a full day now, and it was getting to him, and he stumbled from time to time in his growing weakness. When they came to the ridge of a low rise he saw the lights of Naco in the distance and he pulled up for a moment. The lights were dim and flickering, but there was a place closest to them where they were constant and brighter. The Casa Blanca he thought, a place to go. He pressed her tighter in the crook of his arm as he started down from the ridge. A breeze came up and lifted his coat-tail out behind him. He was a dark figure with a small horse held under his arm and like a silhouette cutout as he moved off with her in the moonlight toward the Casa Blanca.

Chapter 4

The Casa Blanca was set off a little from the edge of the town of Naco and set off by its size, materials and design as well. Beyond it, after a row of seedy bordellos down the dirt street from it, the desert began, and after a few dimly lit low houses and shacks there was nothing. It was made of white stone and white painted cement, and its second story rose well above the town's low buildings and sported an open half-moon balcony with low thick pillars and a stone railing. The prostitutes would stand on the balcony in colorful clothing when it was time for the soldiers to come in from the fort, and even the cars that headed for the cheaper bordellos down the street would slow some as they passed, the occupants either wishing they had the money (which really wasn't much) or fearing the elegance of the place, somehow feeling it was above their station. Oddly, the soldiers who did come to the Casa Blanca were usually the cruder, more foolish and ignorant ones, the ones with little self-awareness, some money, and no sense of occasion or place. Sometimes new men at the fort would stop, drawn by the classiness, but upon seeing the behavior of their fellow soldiers there they would not stay long.

Beyond the balcony, through large glass doors, was the small ballroom. There was a half-moon bar to the left; it had a thick glass counter and its base was white stone. The dance floor was hard wood, and there were small tables around it. To the back of the ballroom were offices, and below on the ground floor were the rooms. The style of the prostitutes came from *Vogue* and *Woman's Day,* and through a strange mixture they carried it off. This style was a tradition that began with the construction of the place itself, fifteen years before, and the force of the physical class of the Casa Blanca kept it going. What kept the place itself going and in good repair and well staffed was not the fort or the town boys from Bisbee, but the wealthier Mexicans who owned *ranchos* close to the town. They would rent the whole place at times, to entertain guests and business associates, and they did this enough to keep the money flowing. Out of boredom, perhaps, the prostitutes liked these occasional weekends and anticipated them. The soldiers who came, though loud and ribald, were seldom funny and their demands were totally conventional, quick and childish.

Fifteen years before, Paul had been here even before the opening. The Casa Blanca had then been a small white house on the other side of town. There was a woman he loved there, a girl really, and he had come down with high-school friends a couple of times. They would go to the place, which had a small yard in front with a low picket fence around it, and they would stand in the yard and talk with the few prostitutes who came out to get some air and talk with them. They were all virgins, and they would only talk and laugh shyly and then leave. The prostitutes were dressed simply then, in loose, flowered cotton dresses, and their hair was straight; they seemed innocent, but even the youngest ones, and the one he loved especially, though no more than sixteen, were really wise.

The first time they went there she was demure and only eyed him occasionally, though enough that he would catch it, and didn't come over and talk to him as the bolder ones did. The second time, when they went into the living room of the house and laughed and fidgeted, she sat on the arm of the couch and joined in the awkward talking but addressed nothing particular to him. She did smile at him and he smiled back and their eyes met for a moment. The next time they were in the yard. It was a starry night, and though she was not close to him he could read the mouthing of her words when he looked at her. He thought she was saying "Come here," and when he looked away nervously and then looked back, she mouthed the words again: "Come here." He walked over to her then, and she put her hands on his shoulders and, not touching against him with her body, put her mouth to his ear. He could feel the touch of her hair, lightly on his cheek and her warm breath as she spoke. "Come here," she said, and that was all she said, and when her face withdrew and came back to where he could see her and she could see him she smiled at him and nodded. That was when he fell in love with her, and he left immediately.

After two weeks away, during which he felt (and he knew how foolish it was to feel so) that she was thinking about him and missing him, he thought he was ready, and in a few days he knew he was, and he managed to get only one of his friends to go with him, a Mexican friend, Alejandro, and they drove down to the place. When they got there there was no one in the yard, but they could see lights and hear talk and laughter from the house. He thought it might be soldiers, and he was upset and quickly disappointed. But then the door opened, and a line of prostitutes came out. They were carrying suitcases and cardboard boxes, laughing and talking. He saw the one he loved lugging a large box, and as he passed through the gate and went to help her she and the others greeted them warmly, chattering and pointing to their car. There was only one car in the drive in front of theirs, and there were ten women, and he and Alejandro quickly got it that the women were going somewhere and that they welcomed a lift. He helped the one he loved with her box, got her in the front seat between him and Alejandro with her box on her lap; it was so large it hit the roof of the car. A fat prostitute got on his lap at the door, holding her suitcase out the window. They got four in the back, the ones on the outside also holding their cases out the windows, and once they'd negotiated the drive and got the other carload of women in front of them so they could follow they started off.

The one he loved was pressed tight against him, thigh to thigh, and he was excited, but his agitation was overpowered by the women's loud talk and laughter, which grew more animated when they came in sight of the new Casa Blanca. They could see it for a long distance before they reached it. It looked large and pristine and elegantly empty; its lights were blazing, and as they looked at its curve of balcony they saw three men in tuxedos—the bartender with a white towel over his arm and two waiters with trays in their hands—come out from inside. The bartender saw them first and took his towel and waved it. When they got there, the women piled out of the cars, picked their suitcases up from the ground where they had dropped them before opening the doors, adjusted their clothing, and headed for the door below and to the left of the curved stone stairway that led up to the balcony, and laughed and jostled their way through it. Some were so excited that they didn't even thank them for the ride. But some did, the one he loved among them, and these urged them to go up the stone stairway and inside, where they could have a drink and wait for them and see them in their new dresses. When they had all gone in, he and Alejandro considered their offer briefly, but they were embarrassed at the way they were dressed and by the tuxedos they had seen and by the clean new grandeur of the place and they decided to go back across the border; maybe they'd come back some other time. They didn't even think of stopping at one of the other brothels. They were stunned by the new Casa Blanca.

Two weeks later he came back. He put cologne on, and a jacket and tie. Alejandro could not come, and though he did not want to go alone he feared he was on the edge of losing her completely, and he knew he could not wait or he might never go. Somewhere inside him he knew he could not let that happen.

At first he did not recognize her; she no longer looked sixteen. He was seated at the bar, sipping a Cuba libre, keeping his eyes on the mirror. There was a small number of people in the place, a few soldiers, some *gringos* that he took to be civilians, and a number of young Mexicans. The band was playing slow tunes, and a few couples were dancing. The bartender wore a white shirt, as did the waiters, and the customers, except for a few of the soldiers, all wore jackets, and some wore ties as well. The prostitutes moved among the tables; some sat drinking with the men and some danced, both with men and with each other. He was not sure he recognized any of the women. They all had their hair done up or laced with ribbons, and they wore a great variety of dresses, both brightly colored and elegantly subdued. They were all in stockings and heels.

He felt her beside him, some light touch of fabric on his hand, before she spoke to him and he saw her.

"Joo come here," she whispered, as he turned to her.

She wore subtle makeup on her eyes, rose-dusted lids, and her lips matched. She was taller in her heels, and when he looked to where her hand rested over his on the bar he could see the way her nails were painted, rosy too, with her half-moon cuticles outlined. Her dress was rose and white, tight cinctured at the waist, with billowing sleeves; silver braclets were at her wrists. As she moved against him he could feel the firmness of her body under the thin fabric. Her hair was done in loose curls that reached her shoulders, and her earrings were made of connected parts so they could click faintly and ring. Her nose was straight and turned up slightly at the end; her lips were full and when she smiled he could see the slight gap between her front teeth, and the tip of her tongue.

"Joo come here?" she said, more definitely than before, and she reached up and touched him briefly on the cheek.

"Buy me drink?"

She said it plaintively and almost apologetically, and he got it that she didn't really want it but that it was the thing to do. She motioned to the bartender and he brought her a glass of faintly rose-colored liquid. She sat down and tilted her head to the side, her hair falling down lovely, almost touching the glass top of the bar, and smiled again.

"Dance?" he said, and without any movement or change of expression, her head still tilted, still looking at him, she said, "Jess."

47

They danced slowly. He was not good at it and was careful and a little stiff. But she was good, and she was able to make it sufficiently graceful for them. When they turned, and at what were good times, she pushed against him briefly but not lasciviously, and she really didn't kiss him on the neck, but brushed her hair and her lips against it when their motion made it right. He held her somewhat awkwardly at the waist, but after a while he opened his hand there, letting his fingers touch the rise of her hip. When the number was finished, they went to a table away from the dance floor, somewhat to the side of the room, and a waiter brought them fresh drinks without their having to ask for them. He talked to her, trying to find a way of conversation, about the move and about the beauty of this new place. He wanted to talk about the change in her, but he couldn't bring himself to do so. She looked at him and nodded, understanding a bit of what he said, but not much, just understanding the tone, the discomfort she could see in his face and the awkward urgency in his inflection. The place was not too crowded, and many of the men in it, the Mexicans especially, seemed to be here to drink, talk and look around. Though some of the soldiers went out with some of the women, an equal number didn't stay long. There wasn't that much business, and she listened to Paul talk, and they danced again. He held her a little tighter, and when they returned to the table and he fumbled to talk again he held her hand and didn't look away from her as much, searching for proper words. When he began to run out of words and there were more silences between them, she squeezed his hand, running a rose nail along his index finger, leaned closer to him and, gesturing slightly with her hand in the direction of the rear of the ballroom, whispered across the table, "Come here." They rose then and went hand in hand to the back of the room and down the dark staircase to where the rooms were.

What he remembered most vividly was what happened after they had gotten into bed and pulled the covers up. She had kept the room dark, leaving only the small bedside lamp lit. He remembered the lamp as one of those cheap Old West ones, with a tan shade with the shapes of brands on it and a stem that was a small horse with forelegs elevated in the air. He could have watched her take off her clothing, had pleasure in seeing the way she did it and how her body was gradually revealed to him, but it was dark enough that he didn't have to see, and he was concerned enough with the way he took off his own clothes, thinking that she might be watching him, not to watch her. He only saw the curve of her small breasts and the roundness of her moving buttocks as she slipped under the covers and he got in beside her. She shivered, and whispered as she moved close to him, *"Hace frío,"* and when she touched his shoulder and felt how cold his skin was she clicked her tongue, pulled back and rolled away from him and reached for a button on the wall beside the bed. She turned back to him then, cooing and rubbing against him. Even though his skin was cold he rose quickly to her and reached to kiss her, but she pulled back again and brought her hand out from under the covers and put her finger in the air, gesturing for him to wait. Then there was movement and noise outside the room and a knock on the door. "¡Pase!," she said, and the door opened and three Mexican men entered, the last one in flicking the light switch, flooding the room.

They stood at the foot of the bed for a moment, looking at Paul and smiling. Then she spoke to them rapidly in Spanish in words that Paul could not understand at all. The three turned, two of them standing back a little and watching as the older one dropped to his haunches and began to fiddle with the small space heater at the foot of the bed. It took him a good five minutes to figure the switches and the pilot, and there was plenty of talk, laughter and argument among the three. Both of them rose on their elbows to watch, and after a while the man got up and turned and smiled, and even in the lighted room they could see the high flames and hear the hiss of the gas.

He didn't make love to her; she made love to him. And though she was gentle and helpful, very open and warm, he could remember little but a kind of mechanical movement of their bodies that had seemed odd in the presence of their growing warmth and wetness, and when they were finished he was more relieved than satisfied. But if she knew this, she didn't act as if she did, and she laughed and helped him dress when she had dressed herself, and she even sat with him and had a drink afterward, and when he left she stood on the balcony and waved to him with her hankie. He could see through the rear view mirrow that she was still waving when he turned the corner two blocks away and headed for the border.

He never returned. He did go to the cheaper brothels down the street.

The women were wild there, or at least acted as if they were. They sat on his lap, bit his earlobe, and had pictures taken with him; they danced alone and shook their bodies in front of him to hot Mexican music. They exposed their breasts and let their skirts ride to the tops of their stockings when they looked at him, their red lips sneering. But sex with them was very quick, as if they had somewhere to go, and they kept their pelvises flat against the mattress and did not rise and open up. After a while he stopped going there, and though he was not content with the teasing of the high school girls he started to go out with after that and felt wiser than they were and was able to see their flirtatious kisses as the childish things they were, he felt that these were the circumstances he should be in, that he had wrongly jumped ahead somehow, and he accepted them. He saw that this was no ideal, but everyone else was doing it as well, and he could talk about it, lie about it with his friends. He knew, really, that he could never go back. He thought of her, never once wishing that things had been otherwise between them. She would always be the first one, and he knew that he would remember her better than if she had been a high school girl.

Even then he was aware that he loved memory better than his daily life. He could not have put it into words, but he knew it nonetheless. As time passed, he began to consider the possibilities of her life. He knew it couldn't be or have been very good; still, to imagine and think of it gave richer texture to his memory of her. Not that he could have taken her away and saved and redeemed her, but that as time went by she would think and speak about him. She would laugh with others, but he thought sweetly, about his awkward virginity, and in doing so she would remember her own. The memory that remained strongest in his mind was of when she had put her hands on his shoulders in the yard of the old Casa Blanca. Her breath was against his ear and she was saying, softly, in a whisper, "Come here."

Chapter 5

He saw the lights dim while he was still beside the desert roadway, moving among the shapes of cactus and brush. There were other lights now, low and fairly close, that he saw to be the few scattered houses at the end of town. The place had been a beacon for him for miles, and the lights had been so bright that when they dimmed a section of the sky seemed to go out. He pulled up, catching himself at the edge of panic, but then the lights leveled off; no longer a glare, they remained as a strong intensity that could still guide him. He hitched her up gently, pulling her more firmly against him, and set out again.

It was not long before he came to the first outbuilding, another feed-storage shed. It was a good distance from the house it seemed to belong to, and though there was no electricity in it the moonlight was bright enough and he was able to find a pile of gunny sacks in a corner. He took one, and when he had skirted the house and found a shallow and dry arroyo between it and the next, the last house he would pass before he entered Naco proper and got to his destination, he stopped and eased her into the sack, folding the mouth back so that her head could protrude as he carried her. Then he moved to the road itself, and standing as upright as he could manage and walking slowly, he headed for the town's edge and the Casa Blanca. His suit was sweat-stained and dirty; his ridiculous shoes were severely scuffed. He reached up with his free hand and adjusted his tie as best he could. The medical kit that hung from his belt seemed a foolish encumbrance, but he could not think of removing it. When he got to the high stone side of the Casa Blanca he folded the mouth of the sack over, covering her head.

He moved to the front of the building and found that there were only a few cars parked in the dirt under the balcony. In fifteen years the stone had worn, and there were a few cracks visible, but the façade and the balcony above him were freshly painted and the wide stone stairway also seemed in good repair. As he headed up, holding the banister, his exhaustion came in upon him and he had to pause before he reached the top. He rested for a moment and then continued, and when he reached the balcony he didn't pause but moved through the open doors and stopped when he was just inside of them, the sack held tight under his arm. He saw at a glance that there were not many people in the place, men sitting at a few tables, a small cluster of men in uniform in a corner. Those who were facing the doorway glanced up, and some turned in their seats to look at him. The click of playing cards at a table near the door stopped. When the bartender saw him, he lifted a small section of the bar and came out toward him, his hands raised and his head shaking.

"No, *señor*. No, no, is closed."

Paul managed to get his wallet out of his back pocket.

"*Por favor, mucho dinero aquí,*" he said.

The bartender slowed when he saw the fan of bills that Paul's hand fingered from the fold of the wallet.

"I just need a little drink, a little wash . . . *agua?*"

One of the card players laughed and spoke briskly in Spanish. Paul looked and saw that there were four women at the table, each holding a fan of cards. Beyond them, and further back in the room, he saw another woman, alone at a table near the empty stage. The bartender looked over at the woman who had spoken, then turned and shrugged.

"Hokay, hokay. Come in, *hombre.*"

He took Paul over to a table a good distance from the occupied ones and motioned for him to sit down. When he was seated, he looked around at the place before putting the gunny sack on the floor at his feet. Some of the soldiers were looking at him, and three who sat together at one of the tables were poking each other, laughing, putting their heads together and nodding over at him. The Mexican men in the place paid him little attention, but most of the prostitutes were curious. Nothing seemed particularly threatening, and he relaxed some and loosened his belt and removed the medical kit and then settled back into the chair. He had given no order, but the bartender brought him a bottle of beer and a glass and another glass with water in it. One of the prostitutes, the one he had glimpsed at the table alone, moved over and sat in the chair across from him. She had brought her own drink and she sat silently, sipping it and looking at him, smiling, and looked around to the other tables from time to time.

The place seemed pretty much the same as it had been fifteen years before. The tables were different, and the kick below the bar stools was worn, but outside of that it was the same. The prostitutes were the same too, but as he looked around the room, appraising them and the situation and what he might expect from the soldiers and other patrons, he began to realize that there were changes and that they were in him. Even in his exhaustion, this moved him. It had been fifteen years since he had walked out of this place, a place that then had not been for him so much a reality as the fulfillment of an image of reality that had been gathered from magazine ads and movies and other fake grounds. What could not be faked, what hadn't been, was the actual sex itself, and all at once he saw the way in which he had been cheated. She had been fine, and she had tried hard, and in a way he thought what he had missed was not the occasion of his own loss of virginity but the possibility of hers. He had manufactured one for her. He had, beyond all reason, made her out to be in the same innocence that he had been in. And she *had* been innocent, though not in the way he had constructed her, but in a better way. He had been her first virgin. And even if that wasn't literally true, it was true enough. The first time is a different time for everyone, in anything, and after that it becomes similar, it gets turned into common procedures and into memory. And he had faked his memory in this and had cheated himself. But what was worse and was a true shame was that he had never once really had her, not in the way she had been, not as she really was.

Now he saw the bright and disheveled dresses the women wore, the way their makeup was a little behind the current fashion, their hairdos taken from magazines a few years old. They seemed to be dressed and waiting for something slightly in the past, as if now was too cold, too hard and mechanical and could not make room for romance. Maybe he would walk into the place, as out of the same magazine, would choose the one who wished for him and would take her away. He felt that this explanation of what he felt was a little fuzzy, was not it exactly, but his head and body were fuzzy. He had come a long way in a few hours. And yet he thought he was pretty close to the truth of it, some truth about himself. It had to do with memory. He drank from the glass of water and felt a deep discomfort in his stomach. His foot pushed into the gunny sack on the floor. He needed to be sure that she was there, needed her to bring him back from rumination on what he'd lost, something that had been twice lost. When his foot touched her she moved slightly, just enough so he knew she was still alive. Then he came back to where he was and looked at the woman sitting at the table across from him.

At first he thought he was seeing things, something evoked from the place and his dwelling in memory. She was the right age, he thought, and the way she smiled at him was the same as that image he carried with him, that came up to him more often than he had always thought was appropriate. He could have given some time to musing on the fact of her sitting there and why she seemed to be some other one, but before he could begin to do so, she spoke to him.

"You've come back," she said. "You've come here."

And before he could even think of what to say, he answered her. "Yes. I've come back."

<hr>

She had him sit on the worn couch in the dimly lit parlor. She got a clean white towel and a smaller colored one, spread the white one over the cushion beside him and rolled the other into a kind of pillow. The little horse rested on the towel, a fold of it covering her lower body; her head was propped up on the makeshift pillow, her matted yellow tail with the twists of ribbon in it sticking out and hanging in a dirty mass over the couch side. When she had first seen the horse, when he had taken it out of the sack, she had been shocked, had sucked her breath in, backed up, and fallen into one of the easy chairs. But she had recovered quickly.

"I have seen this horse in movies," she had said. "This is trouble."

He had only nodded, and she had gone quickly to get the towels. They had left the new Casa Blanca and gone to the old one, where she lived. It had looked the same as he had remembered it from the outside, though the fence was now broken in places and slats were missing. Inside there was less furniture, and a few tasteful prints were on the walls. He wondered why and how she lived here, when she had lost most traces of her accent and gotten so much English, and he had begun to ask her these things. But she had hushed him and left the room, and in a moment he heard the water running as she filled the tub. He figured he would ask her later. Somehow he knew there would be a later, though

54

he had no idea what it would contain. As the water ran, he settled back in the couch.

It was the first time in almost two days that he did not need to be attentive. He was exhausted, and it was only the gnaw of hunger in his stomach that kept him from falling asleep. He looked over at where the little horse lay; her breath came easily, regular movements of her belly as it rose and fell, a whisper of sound from her nostrils. She looked okay, but he could see the patch of matted hair, the edge of the collodion-sealed incision, and he knew he would have to tend to her, inspect and redress her before long. As he watched, she opened her eyes and looked at him; then she closed them again and moved her head slightly on the rolled towel.

Soon she came back into the room, barefoot now, and walking lightly. She had taken her clothing off and scrubbed the makeup from her face. Her cheeks were flushed from the rubbing she had given them. She wore a flowered wrap. Her hair was brushed out. "Come," she said, and helped him to his feet, guiding him through the doorway and into the hall that led to the bathroom.

In the bathroom there was a small padded chair, and she made him sit in it. Then she got down on her knees and took his shoes and socks off. His feet were filthy, but he was too tired to feel any embarrassment about her seeing them. She got him to his feet again and helped him get his jacket off and loosened his belt and pulled his pants down. Then she lifted each leg, holding it by the ankle, and pulled his pants aside. She stood up and unbuttoned his shirt, her mouth making a little O when she saw that his sleeves were ripped away at the shoulders. When his shirt was open, she ran her fingers through the tangled hair on his chest, down over his belly and hooked her fingers in the band of his undershorts. She pulled them down until they fell at his feet and he could step out of them without her help. Even in his exhaustion, her place before him on her knees and her actions moved him and he came up in erection. She looked down and chuckled. Then she looked up at him, smiling, and shook her finger.

"Joo want something?"

He smiled back down at her, and she reached and took his penis firmly in her hand and pulled at it. Still holding it firmly she led him to the side of the tub, supporting him on her shoulder as he stepped in and lowered himself into the water. The water was hot, but not too hot, and it enveloped him in warmth. When he was settled, his head against the porcelain, she sprinkled some grains of fragrance, a rose scent, into the water, reached in over his crotch and stirred it with her hand. Then she smiled and left the room.

He could hear the click and light clatter of dishes in another room, and soon he could smell something cooking. Before long she came back carrying a tray. When she knelt at the tub side, he saw the plate of scrambled eggs, ham and toast, and the glass of hot milk with yellow butter floating and melting on its surface. She fed him slowly, with small forkfuls of eggs and small pieces of ham, and she tore the toast into small pieces and put them in his mouth. Between bites, she put the glass to his lips so that he could sip at the warm milk. When he was finished, she got up and put the empty tray on the floor by the chair. Then she came back to the tub and stood beside it. She loosened the belt of her robe, then let it slip from her shoulders to the floor. Her breasts were small and hung down a little and he thought he could see some light rose powder around her nipples. As she leaned over him to get into the tub, her breasts moved away from her body, hanging down, and he thought he remembered them that way.

The tub was large and freestanding and she was thin and not too big. There was room for both of them. She sat facing him at the other end, smiling, and then she began to wash him. She took each of his feet in her hands. He had to bend his knees and lift his legs out of the water for her to get to them. She washed them with a sponge and a bar of soap, scrubbing between his toes. She rubbed at the calluses with a small piece of pumice stone, and with a nail file she cleaned the dirt from under his nails. Then she washed his legs with a soapy cloth. To reach to his crotch she had to get to her knees, and she fell back once, splashing water from the tub and laughing lightly. As she washed his scrotum with the cloth, wiping thoroughly between his legs, he wondered if she had done this for any other man. He didn't think so; her actions were not practiced, but playful and exploratory. Still, she was a professional, and maybe she was acting. She was not awkward, but her expression changed in unpracticed ways. At times she was serious, at others her mouth formed that O he was becoming accustomed to seeing, and she seemed to be covering what was new ground for her. He was aware that her actions in the water cleaned herself as well as him. He didn't want to think of the juices running from her, those she had accumulated from other men that night, the ones she had given herself to for money. But he could not help but think of them. Still, it didn't seem to make much difference. She was up on her knees, washing his underarms and his chest. She leaned forward and kissed his nipples, lingering, and he felt the old moral story come real. The groin's solution was not the solution, not to anything; it was the awareness and the care, the attention to the details that were at once the private details of the body, of his body and of hers, but were also the general details, the touch of the flesh in some concord. And the concord was of place only, this place, and though she might bring others' fluids and remnants with her, and he might do the same, the others did not come with them. It was just the two of them, just that and a slight touch of memory of innocence and the loss of it and the sense that this regained it somehow, corrected what had been thwarted, for him at least; he wasn't sure about her.

She washed his face, touching his lids beforehand to close his eyes against the sting of the soap. She rubbed the cloth carefully in the creases beside his nostrils and she made little circles with it, cleaning his ears. Then she shampooed his hair vigorously, telling him with a voice one might reserve for little boys to keep his mouth closed and hold his breath when she pushed his head down under the water to rinse it. She dunked him three times, shampooed and dunked him again. Then, while he was lying back and resting from the cleaning, she washed herself. When this was done, the water was thick with dirty suds, most of which came from him. She helped him from the tub then, sat him on the chair and dried him.

When she was finished she led him from the bathroom to another room, the bedroom, and helped him into the bed. The coverlet and sheets had been turned back. Halfway in, he said, "Wait," and with a towel around him he went to the living room and got the horse. He brought her in and placed her on the towel at the foot of the bed. He felt he should look her over now, but he didn't think he could make it and he got into the bed. He was almost asleep in moments, but he felt her naked body against him as she herself got in. She tucked herself against his back. He felt her suck a piece of flesh at his shoulder into her mouth and hold it there.

His mind drifted to thoughts of the little horse, then into the past, to San Diego and Nasty Jack. She held him firm and still in her mouth for a while, and even before she let him go he was asleep.

Chapter 6

Jack's breathing had a way of steadying in the night into a shallow wet rhythm. Never deep and seldom punctuated by deep sucking, because it gave him chest pain and wakened him, it was as if his threshold were a gauge that kept the rhythm between pain and its ending. The cloth screens around his bed in the solarium, isolating him from the others, were white but looked faintly yellow in the wash of the dim night-light in the ceiling at the center of the room. Paul would have to enter to check him. He slept sitting up, his knees open, his frog body bent forward, his amazing head hanging as if he were inspecting his crotch. He would lift and turn his head slightly when Paul entered, and they would pause there, two jaundiced figures in the dimness.

Jack couldn't see him; his eyes, from too much time spent in this pain-relieving position, were swollen shut, his cheeks, full of fluid, pushing up and almost covering his sockets. Paul would speak softly, "Hey, Jack," to let him know who he was, and then he would touch his arm, make sure that he was dry, and would urge him to lie back, to get him to begin to drain.

The magazines his wife brought daily were scattered on the chair and floor and some were even at the foot of the bed. He could not talk anymore, but he would get agitated if anyone tried to remove them. Paul learned through questions that Jack answered with headshakes and awkward nods that he planned to read every one of them once the swelling went down. When Paul would return later, Jack would be sitting up again, rocking a little in fitful sleep.

When the ward was touched by any kind of breeze, it would lift and mix the sick green of the Air-wick with the scent of cancer rot from what remained of the meat of Jack's throat and lower face. Even in the dim light Paul could see the bare bone of his lower jaw and below it the flesh of the blood rubies hanging down. The front of Jack's sleeping smock was stained nightly with blood and bits of colored flesh from the ruby pustules that were always ripe. Above the tortured gore, Jack's nose had almost disappeared; it had pushed back and up into his almost indistinguishable face, and his nostrils looked out like dark eyes. His chin and neck were like a hunk of raw flesh that had been torn from the belly of some large animal. Paul knew they had a relationship and that Jack tried to follow instructions, to do the thing that would open his eyes again, but he couldn't make it. In the daytime he was ignored by everyone, left to lie in his own excrement, and their relationship had begun on Paul's first night of duty on the ward. Gagging, and blinded by his tears, Paul had cleaned him, set him as right as possible, and Jack had raised his arm, extending it for a handshake, and Paul had taken it.

When Paul went back out into the world in the morning, everything was bright and hard-edged, the colors of buildings and flowers and trees seemed artificial and fake, and very quickly he came to find some real terms with Jack. It was as if he descended into a kind of purer reality with him, a place where there were no choices or options, and where every gesture and move had significance. It was the reading of the magazines that mattered and nothing else. And so he got the restraints and put them on, and he talked to Jack for long times in the night. At first the restraints were loose; they would only serve to wake Jack when he sat up in his sleep to ease the pain. Then, in a few days, Paul tightened them some and, in a while, even more, and Jack began to overcome the swelling.

Paul started to come around in the daytime to check him; the other corpsmen looked at him strangely. He would sit inside the screened enclosure, at the side of the bed, would talk softly about various articles in the magazines that sounded as if they might be of interest. Sometimes he would read a sentence or two aloud, stopping always when they started to get interesting or dramatic. Jack would manage what now looked like the hint of a smile, and they would both make sounds indicating they knew that the other understood the game.

It all happened at once. He went to see Jack one evening when his shift began, and there he was, sitting up and waiting with a face again. It was not a completely distinguishable face, but it had eyes and nose and there was a white towel wrapped around the place where the neck would have been, the ruby gore covered, and though Paul could see the bare bone of the lower jaw and a little shredded flesh around the towel's edge, it was a real face, that of a fifty-year-old man, and what was left of its mouth was grinning. Jack motioned for Paul to sit in the chair beside the bed, and Paul, grinning too, did it. Then Jack picked up a magazine, and with almost prissy care he found a place in it, held it up in the air in front of him, shook it out, and began to read. His voice was hardly understandable; it came in spurts as he raised belching air from his lungs and into his wasted throat, past the place where his larynx had been and the tracheotomy tube was now inserted. The story was about a woman who had freed herself from shame.

When he had finished, he lowered the magazine to his lap, breathed wet and deeply, and looked over at Paul. The belching and the slurring in his voice and the long pauses he had needed to get back strength enough to go on had made the story hard to get without careful attention to every sound. At times Paul could only understand a sentence when Jack had gotten to the end of it, and he would have to go back over it quickly in his mind, and by then Jack would be into another sentence, and Paul would have to hurry to catch up. The story did not unfold as something read; it was more like hearing something made up as Jack went along, but really it was more like something he was remembering, falteringly from the past. His mouth would move, searching or perhaps rehearsing, and then he would stop and swallow as if his mouth and tongue had found the structure and the matrix of the words he wanted to say, but not the words themselves. And the matrix would go down into his chest, and when he belched and the language rose and emerged, it was as if the matrix found and ordered and stuck to the words deep in him as thought, it was as if his voice was not his, but was brought up from another voice, the voice of memory deep in him, and the voice echoed softly in the air as if issuing from a long-ago closed-off cave. He looked at Paul, and though his face was not capable of expression in any familiar or recognizable way, Paul thought he saw a kind of freedom in it, a kind of relief after profound release, and Jack managed what was clearly a smile, and he spoke softly and more distinctly than before.

"That's the story," he said. And Paul got up slowly and leaned over and reached for him and took his head carefully and pressed it against his chest. Jack gave in to the gesture gracefully, and when Paul held him he kissed him on the top of his head, his lips pressing among his thin strands of sweaty hair, touching his scalp, and when he released him and they separated and were able to see each other again, there was no hint of embarrassment between them. Paul patted Jack's arm and winked at him.

"That was one hell of a story," he said. "Hey, I'll see you later." And he went out and pulled the cloth screen closed behind him.

The next evening, when Paul came to work, the screen was gone, the bed fresh and tightly made up with clean sheets and sharp mitered corners, and Jack was gone.

"Well, we're rid of Jack anyway," the corpsman from the previous shift said when he saw Paul looking at the empty bed, and then he quickly walked away when he saw Jack's wife coming from the nurse's station. She was a small woman, simply dressed, and though probably no more than mid-forty she looked older; her face was heavily lined and it looked a little dirty, and her eyes were watery, but her pupils were sharp and clear.

"Jack's gone," she said. "And I want to thank you. He . . . "

"I understand," Paul said. "Jack was all right."

"He wanted me to give you this magazine."

Paul took it from her, held it awkwardly along his leg and then said, "I'm sorry."

"It's okay," she said. "Really, it's about time. It was . . . well, you know . . . hard for both of us . . . his face, and . . . "

"It's better this way," Paul said, hurrying to keep her from breaking down. She caught herself, turning from it, and looked at him.

"Well, goodbye then," she said. And she walked away.

Later, when he looked through the magazine, he discovered that the story Jack had told was not there. There was a story; it was called "The Woman who Escaped from Shame," but the setting was somewhere else and the shame the woman had escaped from, though it had to do with loss of family wealth and with some personal family difficulty, was no more than a social shame at bottom, a shame that came from having to take a job like a common person. And this story had a happy ending that solved everything. The shamed woman married a wealthy and well-positioned customer whom she met in the shop where she was forced to work, and the marriage elevated her again to where she belonged. The story was a circle. The magazine was one Paul had never heard of. Though in English, it looked imported from a foreign place. And the story itself was fragmented and written in an unfamiliar way. Paul read the story through again, searching it for some clue, but he found none, and when he was finished he left the magazine on the chair beside Jack's empty bed. When he came back to work for his night shift, to relieve Taunton, the bed and the chair and the magazine were gone, and the beds of the other men in the solarium had been rearranged. He thought of the story and the magazine in the time that he was married to Lisa, but not often, and when that was over, though he thought of Jack on occasion, he seldom thought of either story at all . . .

＝＝

It is the dream of each adolescent girl to have him come to her dressed in garments that are not familiar but have a source that she awakens to in known resemblances. On a horse or deck, emerging from below decks at a docking, entering the dusty village square in magical, clean shoes, in the club car of a train, at a sports event or even on a mountain trail, he is dressed in just that way, and he sees her and remains a little moody and silent about it initially.

She can do nothing but give in. She is not coy, a little manipulative as she has been with boys, and this is her appeal, and the first thing she has to thank him for, to love him for, is that he does not take her up on it to begin with, but only looks at her, not at her body but directly in her eyes. It is always at a distance, in a crowd, across a river, in a waiting room, on a curved bridge, under a family picnic canopy in rain where they have gathered and he is some visitor or other, a friend of an uncle, godfather of her brother, a business acquaintance of someone, from another place, a skilled sportsman, a flyer, a lieutenant, a not-yet-renowned doctor, never an attendant, a dancer, a woodwind musician, a spendthrift or bargainer, occasionally a boxer or a poet, not a singer, not secretive but secret, usually rich, never ostentatious, firmly gracious and controlled.

And she can do nothing but give in, and he looks directly in her eyes, and then he turns to her father and they engage in conversation. Will he stay? He won't stay. He is only passing through, an hour, maybe two, and then not to dream about exactly, but to remember the way he changed things, the flavor of the day, her posture, the various attitudes of family and friends. Will he stay? They are talking, and her usually stern father is laughing, his eyes have brightened, and he invites and urges him graciously. He will stay the night at least.

The night. She is in her room, can hear her parents' muffled breathing beyond the wall; her father has a smile on his face, dreaming. But *he* is not dreaming. He is sitting at the window looking out: a beautiful night, a full moon and a light breeze. He is in his bathrobe, chin on his knuckles; he is not thinking of her but of the future, some dealings there that don't trouble him. They are worked out and he is sure of them. But there is something that troubles him, that keeps him up. It could be a kind of pleasure in his life or in the graciousness of these people, some mild stimulation. He has no people of his own; he is a loner. He doesn't know what it is that troubles him, if only slightly, enough to keep him up. It is she. She is not sleeping either, but she is not troubled. In the morning he decides to stay on for a while.

The first thing is a rose. He says he found it broken at the stem and only casually picked it up. And now he carries it, dwarfed in his large hand, and comes upon her sitting in the garden and says, well, take this, a rose for a rose, and smiles into her lowered lids; her dress is turned back just below her knee; her hem is showing. He passed it across the stitches to her open palm in her lap. Her lids are dusted a light rose.

And for her there was always music in the background; it got her started. And when the frames came, it faded, and the narratives were silent. It was all in gesture and idea, his leaning toward her on a blanket under willows at the river, touching her with his life story. And the details of the story were unimportant; it was the confidence and his relaxed hand on his knee and the giving into her as vessel and her own modest posture under the flimsiness of cotton and crinoline, her simple dress, her woman's makeup, her strap sandals, hair up in a bun with one shell comb, absolutely no jewelry, a finger beginning to feel naked, fancy

63

of the ring as a kind of signature of possession, of ownership; there's a leash attached to it, a filament that he holds only to guide her. And away they go into the vague glorious, but away from the concrete: away from Mother, from the dishes, from her father, from the smell of fresh, raw chicken, from the drunkenness and sweat of men, from sternness even in snoring, from the ache of the forced smile of the hostess, from the stretched and tortured pelvis, from the betrayal of the dead husband, from ointment for entry, from memorized activities, dead dreams, and the smoking of cigars.

And what do adolescent boys dream of? She is unsure, but figures it is jerky, measured in anxiety and vivid only in flashes, and she doesn't really care. It is her daughter she constructs the dream for, convinced the ones she has are similar. Her second husband's sternness is abstraction and a kind of weakness. He would keep them both in the kitchen. He often calls her by her daughter's name, confusing their positions constantly. If her daughter dreams of anything, it is the dead husband her mother tells her of. And then one day he *does* come, and she and her dying mother grow estranged.

Once he has her, and from the beginning, he chases other women. Her mother knows of this; she has her sources, but she doesn't tell her: the dream materializes in his handsome figure, enigmatic gestures, and his empty past, and he becomes a substitute for dreaming, which is all the mother had, and as the dream is fractured in reality for her, her daughter takes it up. They get married, and her mother dies, secretive and disillusioned.

They were sitting on the porch. Her father had a halter in his hand. Her husband stood at the railing, smoking his pipe. The two men were talking, laughing. She was alone and unattended when she gave it up. Her daughter was half risen from her chair, her mouth in an O. The men turned their heads in fake surprise and resignation. A dull bell on the halter. Her brother was at the door: "She's gone."

And he was chasing other women and catching them. One had a barrette in her hair, a body like a bag of melons, buttocks like a valentine. She, on the other hand, had small breasts; her hips were relatively straight. She had a long neck, though, and she thought her eyes were good. She had made a catalogue, feeling shame as she did it, as his spirit withdrew from her in their third month. Another one, older but unmarried, was found dead and violated and cast off in the woods, and it was this one that got her interest up and a vague suspicion. There was talk and fear in the village and on the surrounding farms, fear among women, mostly curiosity among the men.

He hadn't come on a horse, but in a wagon, a six-seater, and with other men. His arrival was brusque, dust rising in her father's courtyard when he drove in. There had been drinking and laughing well into the night, cigar smoke thick in the air, and before it got too late and her mother took her in, he caught her eyes and held them and she demurred. She had stayed away, troubled and excited, but without imaginings. She thought she wanted something, anticipated something, but she had no idea what it might be. And the next morning he caught her eye again and decided to stay. He courted her, and she could do nothing but give in. They sat at the river. He brought her a flower in the garden. He took her riding in the wagon. In the evenings they walked in the woods, talking, hearing the distant laughter of his cronies. He seemed to tell her everything about his feelings. In a while her eyes stopped lowering. She wore modest clothing and rosy makeup. Her scent was always flowerlike, and his was tobacco. He touched her hand fleetingly and in a while held it. He lifted her and held her firmly. He bought land and horses. Before she knew it, the courting was over and they were married. She pressed her bouquet. Her brother caught her garter and everybody laughed. The wedding cake had been too sweet. Her father had got a little drunk and stayed with the men. She couldn't remember the presence of her mother or her wedding night. She thought he had been gentle, but it had hurt. She had wanted more of it, but he had only held her, she thought perfunctorily, and then had gone to sleep. He taught her very little, though she had wanted to learn. He had brushed his teeth, and she had missed the tobacco. There was a certain distance in him that she felt as shame.

The men were overly solicitous. The women stopped meeting her eyes and became subdued and silent when she approached. She noticed what she thought was a certain smoldering rage in her brothers. Her father was chummy with her husband. She was in the kitchen, in her mother's place, and her father seemed more relaxed with the arrangement. Her husband built their house without consulting her. She cooked for his cronies, including her father. Weeks turned into months. Her older brother left, suddenly, and the young one drew apart. The men ate ravenously, and only when they were done did she and her little brother eat alone. Winter came, and she covered up her body with layers.

It was snowing. The fence posts were capped, and she could see the drifts against the barn in the moonlight. There was a full moon, and the ruts from wagon wheels and footprints were dark grooves and spots in the snow at the barn door. She went, bent against the flakes hitting her lids, to the second-story loft door, where the barn cut into the hillside. There was smoke coming from the chimney, and she wondered about it. Seeing them, when she got in, she felt totally estranged from the men, but not from the woman. It was a kind of age estrangement; they were like boys. She was above them in the hay in the loft, warmed by the bricks of the chimney beside her. She could see over the loft's lip, see most everything, and hear it all.

The horses were standing in their stalls, their eyes wide, their heads turned and watching. They stomped occasionally, bobbing their heads and throwing them to the side. The men surrounded her. They had her on her back on a low bench, her arms over her head and tethered to the bench legs with rope. One of the men was between her legs and in her, and another knelt beside the bench, touching and squeezing her breasts awkwardly. There were ten of them in all, and some stood well back from the bench, talking and laughing and pointing. One man stood over her, bending his head and looking, curious like a little boy, and her father and her husband sat in chairs a few feet away. She was not fighting. There were cuts along her legs, bruises on her hips and face, and her hair was gnarled and wet. If she had worn makeup it was gone now, and there was dirt on her cheeks. She made no sound, and her expression was one of spent horror and a little curiosity; her eyes seemed earnest and moved constantly, always away: to the horses, above the heads of the men, to the large closed door.

She felt things had been going on for a long time, felt that a kind of boredom had set in now and that the men's talk and laughter was a little forced, was getting awkward and needed something new. Then she saw her husband rise from his chair, her father follow him. Her father had a shirt on, with long tails, and he wore his boots. The shirt covered his nakedness, but then she saw him rise up between the tails and saw her husband drop his pants and kick free of them. He grabbed the hips of the man who was in the woman and pulled him back. The men laughed and hooted, and her husband moved between the woman's legs, thrust her hips wide and entered her. Her head rolled from side to side, and then she saw her father straddle the bench, his hips and thick buttocks obscuring the woman's head and face. She could see the wet strands of the woman's hair beside her father's thigh. The men laughed, and the horses snuffled and kicked in their stalls.

To make the plans was itself a kind of escape. She could dictate her own behavior, and the realm in which she was dictating was one in which her experience had before been spontaneous, controlled only by the will of others, the ones who brought her the shame: her mother, father and her husband. Her approach was to dress even more simply than before, more modest and virginal. This was easy, because she still felt like a virgin; she felt untouched at the core and equated that with virginity. But she wore jewelry: a thin, gold ankle bracelet, a rose ring on her index finger, a gold choker just thick enough to suggest a collar. She painted her nails a faint rose, and her makeup was all rose and a little fleshy, like the tight pink buds of new roses at the edge of their opening. She wore her hair tight and slightly oiled, and above her ears, and she touched her lobes with rose oil. Her dress was loose and simple, but she tucked it in tight at the waist and picked fabrics that would cling slightly. It all worked, and it brought him back to her, but she bided her time and kept the lights off and avoided opening fully to him, but pulled him in with her planned innocence. It was a real innocence when it came to sex, but she had knowledge of another kind, a knowing that he did not have. She waited, and in the waiting gradually discovered techniques, began to understand what it was that could move him, things that he didn't know of in himself until she found them out for him. And in the course of things, she was giving him time also, but even though she was closed off to him and he could not reach her, she was able to discover that were she to open up to him it would make no difference. He was naive; he had no technique; he was insensitive, like a child; he was a fool. And she gradually began to discover that it was not technique that she had discovered and he lacked, but that it was a deeper connection, a kind of wisdom. It was not about the way bodies worked but about the way emotions worked and how they were connected to the body and were not sensations. She began to discover a certain exquisite skillfulness, an almost frightening one, and began to realize it as a great power. She led him on with it, knowing it had application beyond him. He began to give up everything for the sake of her. He stopped work on the house. Her father grew angry, jealous and distant from both of them. She prepared her little brother for his leaving. She got the knife ready.

Spring came. The tight buds started from the roses. They found the woman in a washout in the forest. The men gathered, subdued, in the yard. They bowed and were solicitous to her. She went now without covering in her simple dress. She never teased him, but she had a way with him. He wanted her often, and he thought he had her and that there was more to come, and once she gave in a little to him, fueling his expectations for a few moments on a moonlit night.

"No, leave the light on," she whispered as he reached for it. He stopped, his arm extended toward the candle, and turned back to her, a smile of expectation on his face. She tossed the covers back, and he smiled, and when she turned and climbed upon him, he grinned. His face was alive in the candle, and the moonlight washed across her cheeks and breast, and as her body and her mouth moved and curled, his grin faded and his eyes opened wider. He had been thrilled by her new posture; it was about as far as his imagination could go with her. But now she was doing things that he had not imagined, things he didn't know existed, that were somehow inside of him, that would have been impossible as fantasy even had he been able to imagine them as action. They were not action, but in it, and he wasn't even sure of them as they occurred. What he was sure of was that he couldn't bear to look at her above him, couldn't stand the way her face burned his eyes for long. He had to look away, roll his head to the side, in order to look back. And once, when he did look back, he saw her arms above her head, weaving; then he saw the way the moonlight shone on the blade. Now she was grinning, or grimacing, or intensely concentrating. And when his chin tucked in and his head lurched up, he saw the leather handle standing in his chest. He was curious, vaguely regretful, and then he was dead. She pulled the knife free with both hands, and then she reached down with it and severed what remained of their connection.

There were relatives in another town, distant ones, and she sent her little brother to them. Her father thought she was pregnant and was in a rush to get her married. She loosened up the waist of her simple dress and did not disabuse him. He mourned her husband, but only his jovial company; he'd been the catalyst, and her father and the cronies didn't know quite how to have fun without him. She waited until they buried him and gave up their search for the murderer. Then she left the dishes in the sink, her father's dirty clothing where it was. She took only a horse and a few garments and she didn't say goodbye.

Her makeup thickened on her lids as time went by, but it was always rosy and carefully applied. It took her a year to find her place in the distant town that she went to, but when she found it she was sure of it and felt she was happy. She started out in households, but there was only kitchen work and the awkward groping of husbands, and she wasn't paid enough to live well. Then she went to the streets, where she could earn something with her skills, but that was dangerous and uncertain. Finally she came to the house, the one the priest called "the house of shame," and she settled down. She had turned to the priest briefly, only halfheartedly expecting something different, and she found it took only a slight nudging when she tested him to get him. He was like the rest, dumbstruck and unaware, only slightly less foolish and less virginal. *She* was the virgin, pure and untouched and untouchable, and she found that there was not one of them could reach her. There might have been. She vaguely knew that, but she knew that the time for it had passed her by, and she was altogether in herself now and didn't need it. The men who came to her at the house of shame needed it, but they didn't know they did. They thought they came there for other reasons entirely. But *she* knew it, knew how to tap into it, and she had a way of leaving them both fulfilled and expectant; they were frustrated, and they kept coming back to get it, and she was very popular.

In the evenings she would sit on the stone terrace at a large table with the others, her friends, all the strong, robust women. Their gestures, in their loose sleeves and low bodices, were free and open and expansive. Their bracelets would clack sharply in the twilight. They talked of clothing and books, of herbs and spices, of geography and of fine music. They talked a lot and loudly and with assurance, and they listened intently to each other. They drank strong black coffee, and when they ate they ate very little. They were extremely fit. They seemed to know everything that was practical, and they were exact in detail. Of the impractical, they knew it too, and they spoke in bright and useful ways about it. It was only when the birds stopped singing, the shadows lengthened and the first stars were visible at day's end that they fell silent, the chorus of their voices diminishing in number until the last note of coda had faded. They would sit still then, their breath deep and regular, until they heard the sound of the first motors in the distance. Then their eyes would grow bright and as cold as steel, and they would adjust their clothing and set their faces and go inside.

Chapter 7

P aul woke gradually, the last notes of Jack's story dissolving into sleep as he came away from it. Then he started; there were voices beyond the door. He rose on his elbows, looking down to where the horse slept at the foot of the bed, and listened intently. When he heard the light laughter in the talking, he relaxed and slipped back to the pillow. In a few minutes, Mary Grace came in with a cup of coffee. She sat on the edge of the bed.

"Did we wake you? It was my friend, Esperanza; she was curious."

He sipped at the rich dark brew, and she watched him do it.

"I thought at first that it might be them, that they'd come for me."

Her mouth was an O again, as she touched him lightly on the arm.

"We could start for Chihuahua," she said. "Then maybe Monterrey."

"Somewhere," he said. "We can't stay here."

They ate breakfast, eggs again, but this time with chorizos, and more coffee. Then he gave her a list of what he needed and some money. She waved the money off, but he pressed it on her. Later, when she returned, she helped him clear the kitchen table and clean it. She watched as he brought the horse in and put her on a clean pillowcase on the tabletop. He peeled as much of the collodion off as he could manage, being careful not to tear the stitches free. There was no infection that he could see, and he cleaned the incision carefully with water and a little soap, then dried it and swabbed it with fresh collodion. Though he wasn't at all sure about dosage, he figured as best he could, and gave her a shot of penicillin, inserting the needle in her thigh where he suspected the best muscle tissue was. She flinched only a little when he put the needle in, but she did flinch, and he took that as a good sign. Maybe she was still at the edge of coma, but she seemed to be coming back a little from it. He lifted one of her lids and watched her pupil contract slowly as the light entered. That was good, too. Mary Grace asked if she could brush her out a little while he dressed. Maybe it would help her spirit. He thought it might, and he smiled and said to go ahead. When he came back from the bathroom, washed and shaved and dressed in the thin jeans and blue sport shirt she had picked up for him, she was finished. The horse still lay on the table. She had removed the blue and red ribbons laced in her tail and cast them aside. Then she had brushed her out. The horse's tail was silky and fanned out behind her; her mane was parted, and the short hair along her back was free of gnarls. She looked much better, better than he had expected she would.

He wanted to look more closely at her, to check her body over and get a better look at the jewels set in her hooves, but he knew he had no time and that he would have to wait until later. While Mary Grace was packing up, he took the horse's temperature rectally, realizing as he did so that he had no sense of how to read what it meant. It was 101.6°. He got a bowl and a washcloth and tried to get some water into her. She wasn't able to drink, but her thick pink tongue came out and took the drops that he squeezed onto it. As he worked, he tried to think about what was happening and what might happen. The whole thing was still like a dream to him, but he was rested and feeling better and beginning to wake up from it a little. He had had no chance or energy to talk to Mary Grace yet. So far it had all been care, touched with an odd wonder, and nothing but the immediate expectations of the next step. But what would he do now about Pfeffer Instruments, his job, about his apartment in San Diego, about the rented car he'd left behind? And why in the world didn't he just take the horse to the local authorities in Naco, or sneak her across the border and turn her in there?

By the time he had the horse ready, Mary Grace was packed. She went to the front door and opened it and looked around. He moved up behind her, holding the horse in his arms, and he saw the Oldsmobile she had rented in town.

"What about the house?" he said.

"Esperanza will watch after it," she answered. "It's okay. She's my friend."

She went out to the car first, opened the trunk and put the suitcase in. Then she opened the back door and motioned to him. He went out quickly and put the horse on the seat and covered it with the pillow case. Then they got in, and she backed the car out of the driveway and headed for the road to Cananea. While they were passing back through Naco and out the other side, they did not speak. He sat low in the seat, and she was careful to avoid ruts in the dirt streets and to drive slowly. When the houses thinned out and the road broadened into the narrow paved highway, she picked up speed, bringing the speedometer to forty. They were silent for another ten minutes, and then he asked her to pull over. They switched places, and he began to drive. When they were moving again, and all around them were low, rolling hills with brush and some green and a few trees and only an occasional house set back from the roadway, she told him about the movies, one in particular in some detail.

———

Chico brought the first one over on a slow day in the spring about two years ago. Parker and the two others (I don't know their names) didn't come with Chico but arrived a little later in that black car of theirs. Chico always brought the movies; it was his job for them I think, and he took them at least as far as Monterrey, I've been told. I don't know how he got them across the border, but he must have had a way, or someone else had a way. It can't be that Northern Mexico provided enough business for them. I doubt, now that I think of it, that Chico had much to do with that; he's slick, but not all that smart. I think that Parker and the other two and the rest at Parker's *rancho* didn't want to deal for themselves in Mexico. I suspect they thought it was too risky and not worth the risk. That's why they used Chico. At least I think this is the way it all was.

There's a room downstairs at the Casa Blanca. It's a kind of theater, a few couches and a projector behind a glass panel and a white wall. Really, it's a nice and comfortable room, and we sometimes sit there and talk when there isn't too much business; we use it as a lounge. Those who want to see movies, mostly the soldiers, pay a little when things aren't busy. When things are very busy, we take them down there while they're waiting. It keeps them from being impatient. The films are straight pornography, the kinds the soldiers like: American men, like them, sometimes even in uniform, and Mexican women. At times, Chico has slipped in odder ones, ones with ropes and masks, but the soldiers don't like them, and most of the women hate them, fearing that the soldiers might get ideas. Really, these soldiers don't have much in the way of ideas about such things; they're very limited, but you can never tell. We've had a few bad things happen over the years since I've been there. Oh, *Dios*, has it been fifteen years?

The movie Chico brought that day was of better quality than any he had brought before. I mean the technique was better, better lighting and sharper images. There were two couples, two young and well-built men and two women; the women had their hair bleached, to look like *gringas*, I suppose. They did what couples do in movies of that sort.

And the room itself was nicely done. Somebody involved had some taste: the furniture was well designed, and the rugs were woven tightly and dyed with good earth tones. The women wore expensive underwear and sipped wine from good crystal when they weren't busy.

In this first one the horses were there as observers. They both wore halters with what looked like velvet ropes running from them to rings in the wall. The larger one, the male, stood very stiff and still. He had backed up against the wall so that his velvet rope was slack, and the female, who was tethered close to him, pressed against him, her head a little behind his, pushing into and nuzzling his neck. They didn't move much, but we could see their heads and eyes move when the people moved, changing positions. They were brushed out and their tails and manes were well combed and woven loosely with colored ribbons. At times, when the people's movements gave us sight of them, we could see the way their hooves glimmered and sparkled. Their eyes were just a little wild, and there were places where it seemed the film had been cut, times when the horses seemed to be beginning to get agitated when voices rose and movement quickened. The film was a silent one, but we could read the nature of sound from the people's movements and gestures. Though the camera moved from time to time, zeroing in on parts and members, when it pulled back it always included the horses in its view; mostly, still, they reappeared as background to the action. Even in this first seeing, they were beautiful and odd and somehow awesome. The ribbons and the velvet ropes and the gleaming hooves were like the women's underwear; the feel of both was of humiliation, but there was a stronger sense of it with the horses. The women seemed to belong there, dressed that way and doing what they were doing. At least they seemed to have had some choice about it. The horses did not.

When the movie was over and the wall turned white again, I and the other women just sat looking at each other. There was some brief, uncertain, laughter, but it took a while for anyone to talk. Finally, my friend Esperanza said, *"¿Es sexy, no?"* and some of the others nodded and smiled. I didn't think it was sexy, or at least I could not give that particular word to it, and I kept still. Parker stood by the door of the room, and the two others asked us questions about the movie. They wanted to know how we felt about it, what we thought the soldiers would think about it, what kinds of men (and women) we had run across would like it. Their questions were skillfully put, interjected into conversation, and they had a way of flattering us so that we felt like authorities of some kind, and most of the women talked freely after a while.

I managed to say a few things so that my silence wouldn't stand out. It was hard for me, because there was something about the movie that I couldn't accept, something about the horses' presence that was both right and wrong. I had seen many kinds of movies and many kinds of real things, very extreme things, but this one was something outside all of that; it was altogether different. I could not place it, and whether or not I liked or did not like the movie, whether I could name the kind of person who would like it, seemed too simple and beside the point. I could not find a comfortable place for it, anywhere in my experience, and that I did not like at all. It was of course the horses, their size and their presence and their containment on the screen. After a while, questioning began to become useless; the women got tied up in stories and reminiscences, and Parker and the two Mexicans left. When they were gone, Chico rewound the film, packed it up and took it away.

Every few months Chico brought another movie over to the Casa Blanca. All of them had the horses in them, and after we had watched them, the two Mexicans asked questions. Parker never said a word, though from time to time he would come over and whisper something in the ear of one of the others. In time the questions were more probing, had more to do with the women's likes and dislikes, and near the end of the showings, that doctor, Gabriel, came with Parker and the other two. His questions were fewer and more hesitant and, I guess, more clinical. It was just a few months ago that they brought the last one to show us. I don't think I can explain my response to it. I can only tell you how the movie went.

There were six horses running in the wash at the edge of a mountain river. Two were Morgans and the rest were palominos. Behind them, in the shallows of the river's fast center, large white objects jutted up; they looked huge, and only where the water flensed and sprayed out from them were they rounded; their forward edges were almost sharp, rectangular. Behind the river was a meadow, and behind that were rounded hills running up to where bare rock, cathedral-like, stood against the sky in the distance. The manes and tails of the horses blew in the air and the spray from the running river. Three of the horses were stallions, the others smaller mares. The horses pulled up, gathered in a group, and shook themselves. Two of the mares dipped their necks, lowered their heads and drank from the river water. A pair, both palominos, stood and nuzzled each other. The group gave the impression that they were on a kind of outing, a vacation from all care. They stood together, shaking and frisking and drinking water, and then they walked off, as if exploring, together along the river's edge.

It was then that the camera moved slowly back and the horses and the river began to fade from focus. When they were almost gone, wine-colored drapes came in from either side of the screen and closed them off completely. Music started, a small group, possibly a quartet. There was a flute and I think a harp and strings. And the camera continued back until we could see the heads of four people and the two little horses off to the side. They, like us, had been watching the movie within a movie. It was the same room as always, but the furniture and appointments had been changed. Now the furniture was all Spanish, or what some call Mediterranean: dark, heavy wooden chairs and a couch upholstered in rose and wine velvet, a thick wine rug on the floor, many large pillows, and tapestries hanging from the walls to the side of the draped screen. In front of the drapes, and between them and the area where the four people sat with their backs to us, was a low stage, a place that was slightly elevated and apart, and it was here that the two small horses stood.

They were not tethered this time, nor did they wear halters. Their tails and manes were no longer loosely laced with ribbons, but were tightly braded with fabric that matched the room's colors: wine and rose braided into the tails half way down, where it stopped and the yellow remaining fanned out like strawbrooms. Their manes were constructed of tight individual braids, with more fabric and small beads connected at the end of each braid. At times the music had instruments that clicked, as if we were hearing the beads hit against each other. The horses' yellow hooves were, as before, inset with those clear and colored jewels, but they seemed brighter and larger this time, set off against the tightness of the braiding. Even the hair at their fetlocks was braided, the beads resting near the coronets above their hooves. They seemed dressed for some aggressive action, and their bodies looked taut and tense. The female pressed against the body of the male, but not as closely as before, and she was not looking at him this time, but out at the four people and occasionally to her left, at a place off-camera. A long, snakelike tube lay on the stage at their hooves, its end invisible, its length cut off at the frame's edge, and to their left as we faced them, and also on the stage, was a large straw basket.

Then the people were moving, and our eyes pulled back to watch them. The two women, no longer blond but dark brunettes now, wore Spanish dresses; one wore a tiara and the other had her hair pulled tight around her face, twisted into a single thick braid that hung down the center of her back. The men wore high, tight Spanish pants, shoes with tapered heels, and flowing shirts, one white and one rose colored. They moved to the women, and the women moved to lounge against cushions and receive the men's fondling.

Then they began to remove some of their clothes and to really get started, and the camera did what was usual in such movies, moving from ecstatic faces to body parts and contortions. The music rose and fell as the four adjusted themselves, changed partners, became now a group of three with one watching, now a tangle of all four. The horses watched as we watched, and when movements in the foreground went on too long, or between engagements there; our eyes would go to the horses, who remained of interest though doing nothing but standing. At one point, while one of the men mounted one of the women in a conventional manner and the other two sat back in chairs looking on, there was a thin flash of movement behind them from the little elevated stage and what I knew later was a whip came up in the air.

Then the male horse moved from the side of the female and went to the straw basket; his head dipped down and came up holding a rose. He held it in his jaws by the stem. It was a long stem, and as he moved down from the stage he held his head high and pranced in order to keep the flower at the end of the stem free and elevated. He moved to the woman, who was on her back, and when he got to her he lowered his head and she lifted hers slightly and took the rose stem from his mouth with her teeth. She was the one with her hair pulled back tight, and now she held the rose in her teeth like a Spanish dancer, her head moving to the rhythm that her partner above her provided.

It was not so much the bringing of the rose itself, though that was a startling enough event, as the fact of the horse's entrance into the passionate stage that he had been elevated and apart from that had power to move and change our sense of what we were watching. I think that we were supposed to see the animal nature of what was going on with the people, and at the same time were to see something that was highly ritualized and somehow significant beyond the physical.

It did not work. The horse stayed down when he came down; he moved around the two on the carpet and he allowed himself to be touched and petted by the two sitting in the chairs, but he remained aloof, his head constantly turning to where his partner stood on the small stage in the background where, consequently, our heads also turned, always away from any power of engagement that his moving among the people might have accomplished. The placing of the rose in the woman's teeth had made its impact, but it began nothing that was comparable in power. But then something did happen that was very powerful, but I think its power was not the intended one.

The female horse was shaking slightly on the platform; she looked somehow naked, even in her trappings, alone and vulnerable. And as we watched her, the scene went out of focus and when it returned we were again looking at the film of the horses that had begun the movie. Again the horses moved in the edge of the river. This happened for a few moments only, and when the scene faded and then came back up again on the room and the stage, it was only the two horses that were in the frame.

The male had mounted the female from behind and was engaged in penetrating her. It was clear he was searching for entrance, but her braided tail fell to the side of her quarter facing us, and we could not see the specifics of his prodding. His forelegs were up in the air at her withers, his jeweled hooves dancing and hitting against her neck and chest. His head bobbed and his thighs rolled and shifted as he frantically moved to enter her. He would take small stumbling steps behind her, his hooves pawing, the beads laced at his fetlocks bouncing, trying to move closer. He nipped her neck, and she arched her head up and back, bowing her whole body so that her croup lifted on her stiff rear legs as she opened and presented herself to him. Then he was in her, and the muscles at the base of her braided tail contorted, curling her tail almost into a ball of hair that hooked away from her rump, the broom end of it quivering on the matrix of muscles over her left rear thigh. We could see the dark thickness of his penis then, as it slipped in, withdrew slightly, and moved in again. Her head moved even farther back, almost standing straight up in the air now, and he extended his neck and banged his own head into the side of hers, nipping at her cheek, nuzzling hard into her. She pranced her rear legs open until they were separated a good foot and a half, and she pushed back at him with her rump, shifting her hooves to gain better purchase, to support him on her and allow him deep into her at the same time. Then he gathered his forelegs around her like pincers, his hooves pressing deep into the skin at her chest, and began moving into her in earnest.

As we watched this magnificent sight, the camera slowly began to pull back from its tight shot of the horses linked together, and the figures of the four humans slowly began to enter the field. The first two were the man and woman sitting in the chairs that were facing us, the chairs flanking the vision of the horses behind them. The two, half naked and touching themselves, were smiling lasciviously, looking at something in the immediate foreground that the camera had not as yet pulled back enough to make visible. Then it began to become visible. It was the two others on the rug, and the angle of the shot was such that, above them, in the background, the two horses remained in our sight.

The woman was on her hands and knees, and the man was pumping into her from behind. They both wore horse's heads, papier-mâché masks that covered their heads completely and were affixed somehow at their collar bones. He was standing in a kind of crouch, his legs and feet forward of her hips. Their hands and feet were shod in artificial hooves that looked as if they had been formed from leather. Around the man's waist there was a thin cord, and tied at the back of it was a horse's tail that hung down, splitting his buttocks. She had a tail also, but hers was made to look as if it had stood up completely and then fallen back to fan out over her naked back. The tails were long and flowing and looked like real hair. The woman reached her horse's head back and twisted it to the side, trying to see behind her. The man lowered his, contorting his body so that he could touch the end of his muzzle against her shoulder. His hooved hands hit lightly against her buttocks as he pumped into her. She pawed her hooved hands on the rug.

And we did watch them; it was impossible not to do so. They filled half the screen, and their movements, though awkward and forced, were startling and exciting. We had not expected them. Still, very soon we tired of them, and the two horses, who it was clear now were meant to appear as a kind of background, as an echo only, drew our attention away from the man and woman, pulling our eyes above and behind them to where the horses were moving, naturally toward climax.

The male was stroking longer and deeper and then, really unlike the way of humans, he pushed deeply into her and remained there, his hooves gripping her tighter, his head pressing down and into her crest, holding on. She began to move then. She contracted the muscles in her buttocks and then loosened them, pushing back into him, then contracted them again. Then the contractions began to take over her whole body. Her head moved from side to side with the rhythm. Her eyes were open and glassy; his were closed. Her whole body was concentrated into a force that held and released him, that pulled him and sucked at him. And then he was quivering, and as we watched, his rear legs rose slowly off the floor and hooked around her own at the gaskins until she was supporting his whole body on and in her.

She was smaller than he was, but she was a dynamo under him, and he was riding her, and as if she were exulting in this power to hold and support, to possess him completely, her head stopped moving and her eyes focused, and she turned her head to see where he was on and in her and then she pumped vigorously back at him. His head came up from her crest then, and he extended his body upward until he was standing stiff legged, his front hooves set at either side of her withers, standing on her back. His eyes opened, his pupils dilated and his nostrils flared. Then his whole body was shaking. His tail stood straight up in the air behind him like a flame, and he came into her, vibrant, flooding, total, and impossible to understand.

The humans had faked the same coming at the same time, or if they had not faked it and it had been real it would have made no difference to us. In comparison, what they did was nothing, at least not for us. They had only been an annoyance to us, a kind of visual haze in the way. And even now, as the four moved to come together in some way again, we watched the horses, watched the male's forelegs buckle, his whole body collapse upon her, watched her brace in her power to support him.

Then in a few moments the female lowered herself to her knees, moved ahead slightly, and he slipped out of her and from her, sliding off her back and falling the few inches to the floor of the platform of the stage. She buckled her forelegs also then, turning a little; then she nuzzled him where his nostrils slowly flared and closed, and his tongue tip lolled out of his half-open mouth. He licked her, and she moved lower, herself nuzzling and licking at a place in his groin that was not visible to us from where we were. Then, for a while, they both moved, lying on the stage and shifting themselves lazily in small increments of motion, nuzzling, sucking in pieces of flesh, licking, pressing, breathing into each other.

═══

The horse had raised her head slightly to a position where Paul could see her in the rear-view mirror. Her eyes were hazy, but she seemed alert. He could see her following the lopping phone wires that ran along the road, or perhaps she was watching the changing cloud patterns that were in the sky. Before they reached Cananea, they pulled over to the side and took her out. She was stiff on her legs and wobbly, but she was able to stand. She even took a few tentative steps before she stopped and looked up at them. They laughed together, because her look was as if she were asking for approval for her ability to move without help. She nuzzled in the spare ground in the sand at the roadside. They got her some alfalfa they had brought with them, and though she did not eat much of it, she did eat some, and they were heartened at the sight of her slow chewing and chomping gracefully at it. Then they got her back in the car, put her between them on the front seat, where she lay like a large cat. She kept her head up, watching the dials and reflections from the dashboard. Only when they were entering the outskirts of Cananea did they cover her with the towel to keep her out of sight.

They spent the night in Cananea, and Paul made phone calls, one to his landlord in San Diego, one to Pfeffer. It was their plan to head for Hermosillo in the morning and then cut over the mountains in the direction of Chihuahua. After they had put the horse down at the foot of the bed with them, Paul turned off the lights and got in beside Mary Grace. He was tired, and though he wanted her and reached for her and kissed her, he felt himself begin to slip to the edge of sleep even as he did so. She could tell it, or at least he thought she could. They turned away from each other, settling on their backs beside each other, their arms touching. There were lights flickering from the road, points and washes on the wall and ceiling. She began to talk then, very softly, to begin to tell the story of what had happened in the years since he had first met her. He heard only the very beginning of it. He was asleep in a few moments, and when she knew it she stopped.

PART II

SOUTH

Chapter 8

P aul woke in the night, feeling the body of the horse shift at his feet, and remembered the rose that the male had carried, both in the iron enclosure and in the movie that Mary Grace had described. Then, before he drifted off again, he remembered another rose, something he had seen years before on the six o'clock news.

A woman was standing at the edge of the rocky crest of an oval quarry more than a hundred feet above the dark, still water somewhere in Southern California, near Hollywood; it was twilight, and the woman was the mother of a boy of sixteen who had jumped from the crest a few days before. The quarry, though posted, was a place to swim and the boy had jumped on a dare. When he hit the water he made no splash but slipped into the depths and never came to the surface. The authorities had been diving and dragging for three days, but they could not find the boy's body. There were boats on the water, men in them with grappling hooks, and there were other men standing at the rocky brink. High up around the crest there were still some spectators.

The woman stood at the place where the boy had jumped. The camera was at a distance, and only her form was visible; her expression or the subtler meanings of her gestures could not be understood. She stood still for a while, then she reached her hand out to toss something. When it hit the water, a searchlight found it out; it was a rose, still with some petals left from its fall. It rested on the flat surface where it landed. The boy knew nothing about roses; it was probable that he could not even distinguish them from other related flowers. The only things the mother knew about rituals were what she had gathered from looking at women's magazines and what her friends and neighbors, those who knew nothing about them either, had told her. One neighbor had been to Hawaii, where she had thrown a lei in the water from the cruise ship at the end of her vacation.

What the mother had wanted to do was to jump herself, to plunge in where her son had gone, to die or to go down and find him, alive and well, in some recess among deep rock, a kind of cave with air in it, where he was trapped. But she threw a rose. It was a memorial. And though it had no specific source in ritual at all, she thought it must have, because she had seen people in dramas do similar things and when she saw them she was moved.

Though Paul was wiser than the woman was, or at least he thought he had more information, he had gotten choked up when he saw her throw down the flower. He was living in Portland then, working the north coast for Pfeffer. It was his first assignment. Lisa, the virgin he had married upon leaving the Navy, was living with him then. He had met her in Chicago, after high school and Bisbee, and she had waited through his Navy years for him, and now they were in a new place, starting their life together. Their marriage was consummated, though pristinely, and she was still like a virgin to him. He felt he had few cares, but he did not look to the future in other than a vague way, kind of drifted through the present, and his real life, the one that moved him, was in his past as it always had been. Though he now lived with her, it was the frustrating times when she had thwarted his advances that he saw in her; only that aroused him, and when they made love the music and the roses were not present for him, and he had to put her in their past, where she was unreachable, in order to find the thing in him that might be love for her, desire for her. None of this worked, and from the beginning she began her slow drift away from him and her desiring of other men.

One evening, after they had seen a business associate of Paul's off at the airport and were on their way out of the terminal, passing the various numbered waiting areas for departing and arriving flights, the following thing happened.

They were passing a waiting area that seemed empty, though Paul had a peripheral sense that there was someone there even before he heard the sound. It was a sharp sound, a crack of some kind, and when he turned to the sound he saw the two figures sitting beside and facing each other on plastic seats. The mother was young, possibly in her late twenties; the child beside her was the kind that then had been called mongoloid. Given the vision of the child's face as Paul turned and caught sight of his expression, the name seemed right, as if the term were one of racial identity.

She had slapped him, had pulled her hand back beside her other hand; they were both in the air in front of her breast in a gesture that made it look as if she was holding some large glass bowl that the lighting made invisible. She was looking through the bowl at his face. On it was a look of utter wonder, one that seemed almost awesome because of the nature of his face. His forehead was large and protruding; his jowls were fat and hung slightly. His thin lips formed an O. He was on the brink of weeping, and this was puckering his face, exaggerating the depth of his lines and creases. He looked primitive and old, innocent and wise at the same time. The expression of wonder was stronger than the remnant of fear that remained from his brief anticipation of the slap as it came. He was as fixed as those painted figures are, the ones who see hell and are held in the painting at the moment before they drop into it. And his eyes were on her, sharply focused, ready to fracture, the wonder in them purely accusatory. And the mother was forced to cover her face with her hands.

They passed them, and Paul found that he was weeping. He had not wept in public at any time that he could remember. Lisa did not see it, but others whom they passed did, glancing at him, then turning away in embarrassment. He pulled himself together in a moment, but the vision of the mother and child stayed with him. It had been immediate and not remembered. Unlike the past, it could not be manipulated when it happened. Later he did manipulate it, gave it a history that qualified it, placed it: Somebody important had left on the flight; the mother's frustration was precipitated by this leaving; it had less to do with the child than with the passing of this other; after she wept she took the child up in her arms and soothed him. But all these qualifications could not remove the picture from him. What was foremost there was the power of the violated trust. Though the mother had not asked for this child, he had arrived and she had taken him on; she was culpable. The slap had been intended to shock him away from her, to transform him into the child that she wanted. But its real effect had been to awaken him for a moment, to show him that his trust was not and could not be absolute. There were boundaries, and though he slipped back into the oblivion of himself, the realization would not really leave him. It would come up at times, and he would always, for the rest of his life, be uncertain. And even before they drove out of the parking lot, Paul knew that his marriage had ended; it would all be his closing off and her wandering from now on until it came to a formal stop.

He was quick to move up in Pfeffer. He was the best instrument man they had, and he was charming and articulate about technical things. He could scrub up with surgeons and talk to them in ways that he had learned as a surgical technician in the Navy. He treated them with military respect, as if they were officers; he urged them into a masculine realm that stood against the organizational power of the nurses. His area quickly broadened, and within a year he was traveling around the country; they were using him to crack the more difficult markets. He was away a lot, but Lisa did not seem to mind.

——

To sleep and then to wake from sleep. To come back to oneself disoriented at first, waking in motel rooms, places that are at first uncertain, and sometimes to have to rise and pull the drapes back, to see the outside, the car and the landscape, in order to remember: this is Colorado, Arizona, Mexico, Texas. And sometimes to not come back completely, so that the whole day is lost and forgotten, the paces gone through and only the book containing the orders as a record of having been somewhere. At times to wake fully and located, but only rarely, and then to see the fog of the previous day by contrast, but not to weep for it. Some mornings like a gathering of forces, some like a slow entrance into a new world or some promise of one. To wake always in a different place, beside a different or changed woman, or that vacancy that was the image of one in the dream that is lost upon waking to her absence, to the sight of the odd new light, the unfamiliar color of the drapes filtering it. To not know the state, city, or directions. To rise up and walk out with a clear head into the parking lot and what passes for the present. To forget the past, have it leave like the dream before waking, and to get up into that parcel of new time in Chihuahua, remembering almost nothing of the passage through Hermosillo, her figure in the driver's seat or beside him, the horse like their child on the seat between them, the adobe and the dust and the poverty. Then slowing in the ruts in the fractured road and climbing. Donkey carts and vague figures through the dusty glass, laboring into the foothills and then into mountains. Sleeping in the enclosure, itself enclosed in the cuts of the roadway bending, almost a pathway, material of residue of villages, of outpost, uniforms, music, the smell of resin, and only the image of three children at the roadside, filthy and waving, as a clarity, and how they stopped and for some reason showed the children the horse, and how the horse stood and then moved slowly among them, their tentative touches and the smiles of innocence. And to turn over, realizing that the rehearsal was only to allow for the space of waking; the lines of a play that is now over, and to write the first gesture of the new one on the artery among the bones and ligaments at her thin wrist.

"Good morning, Mary Grace."

"Good morning, Pablo."

The horse up and around already, sniffing the room's objects and stretching.

"How many days has it been now?"

"It's Saturday. Tonight we go see Johnny," She said, "and tomorrow . . . "

"Torreón?"

"No. Around it; it's too big."

"And then Monterrey."

"Sí, and then maybe Corpus."

They brought food into the room, breakfast and lunch, and around two o'clock, when there were no cars in front of the other rooms and before new ones came for the next night, they snuck the horse out and drove away from the edge of the city and let her out so she could move around a little. They found a small arroyo a short distance from the road where there was a gathering of yucca in full bloom; the place was barren except for the yucca, but they were lovely and gave it a lush life; the little horse seemed alert, and though she moved slowly and was careful, she had her legs firmly under her now, and her testing steps seemed more aware of her condition in the past than a state of weakness in the present, and they were cheered by her quick recovery. He thought it must be six days now, but he wasn't exactly sure.

When they got back to the room it was close to five o'clock. She was still a little frisky, and they played gently with her, and after that they made love, naked and exposed to her on the bed. When she saw them beginning, she wheeled and left the room, but after a while she came tentatively out of the bathroom where she had gone and stood at the foot of the bed and watched them. Their actions were strong, but not violent, and she seemed comfortable in their presence. From time to time one of them would be in a position where they could see her watching, and they met her eyes.

For him, the lovemaking was a strange and difficult thing. He felt he needed to be outside of it, to be able to look into it, but he could not find a way to do so. This was the first time since that first time fifteen years ago, and there was something he wanted from it, something he felt should be monumental. But it was lazy and natural; it was not really passionate, and it seemed to require nothing in the way of skill. He could not tell where she was in it, and he knew that this was because he didn't know where he was exactly. It didn't frighten him, but he felt that if he thought enough about it it would do just that. Catching the eyes of the horse was difficult too, but it seemed to be a needful thing, something necessary and almost moral. He thought for a time that he was beginning to find a way into it, but then it was over. And when it was finished the horse came up on the bed with them, and the three of them lay in a heap there, drifting in and out of sleep.

When Paul and Mary Grace awakened, the room was dark; the sun was gone, and only the lights from the parking lot and the road beyond it lit the room enough so that they could see. They got carefully out of the bed, easing so that they would not wake the little horse, and after they had bathed together and dressed, they put food and water out for her and left the shower curtain open so that she could get into the bathtub if she had need. When they were ready to go, Paul went back and stroked her gently, feeling that she should see them going and not awaken to their absence without preparation. She lifted her head up from where it lay, and before Paul closed the door behind them he saw that she had dropped it to the pillow again and was settling into sleep.

The place was called Club El Monte, and although the rise it sat on was no more than a small hill it was a mountain away from the rutted dirt streets and the ramshackle board houses they had passed to get there. The final road had emptied into a small dirt plaza, surrounded by a square of dilapidated structures, small houses, most with broken windows and corrugated roofs, in the doorways of which red and green lights, bare bulbs, glowed dimly. There was noise and scratchy music coming from the shacks, some women dressed in cheap, provocative clothing stood in doorways, and men, Mexican and mostly drunk and staggering, moved from one place to another, going in or stopping to talk with the women, some of whom were urgent, some disdainful; others were friendly, a little drunk also, and lounged against the buildings talking and laughing with the men who approached them. Above the plaza, to the left as they came into it, were the bright lights of Club El Monte, and Mary Grace pointed and said "there," and Paul bounced the car slowly through the plaza, out of it, and onto the winding drive that went up the hill.

There was a small parking lot directly in front of the place, about thirty cars in it, a few of which were taxis, some dark, others with drivers in them, smoking and listening to radios quietly. There were no windows in the front wall of the place; the only opening was a large, thick wooden door that had two wrought-iron carriage lights flanking it. There were numerous spots poking from the flat roof of the building, some lighting the wall, some bathing the parking lot and the drive. The place was quite large, the wall rising a full two stories, and on the lower half of the wall, as high as a man could reach, were a variety of posters. Some advertised boxing and wrestling matches, some the appearance of various musical groups; others were political, the faces of stern politicians. Hung at both sides of the door, and covering other posters, were two large ones, without illustration, that said simply and in large block letters, *¡Especial Esta Noche: Johnny Hotnuts!* They left the car and went to the door, and Mary Grace knocked heavily on it. It opened slightly, and a very large, tough looking man stuck his head out.

"*¿Sí?*" he said, looked them over briefly, then said "Hokay" and opened the door wider. They had to touch against him as they slipped by.

The place was dark and full of smoke and noise, and it took Paul a few moments to see and get oriented. There was a spotlight following a group of gaudily dressed mariachis who were moving among tables that were very close to each other, a good number of them, perhaps forty, in a half-circle around a small dance floor with a stage behind it. The stage was dark and empty, and the dark shapes that began to materialize at the tables were drinking and talking, facing away from the stage, watching the mariachis or the bartenders.

The space behind the bar was brightly lit, and the bartenders had very theatrical ways with their drink-making, tossing glasses and catching them, holding bottles high in the air so that streams of liquid poured from them glittered in the lights. They were dressed in sparkling white jackets and black bow ties. More men and women sat along the bar, and Paul began to see that most of them were Mexican and that not all the women, perhaps no more than half of them, were prostitutes. He counted only two people who looked like they might be gringos at the bar and he didn't see any at the tables. The atmosphere in the place was festive and expectant, and though a few men at the bar turned to look at them when they entered, there was no aggressiveness in the looks and Paul felt at ease in the place. A waiter came over to them, looked at Paul, and said, "Table for two?"

"*Sí*, yes," Paul answered.

"Joo have come to see Johnny?"

"*Sí*," said Mary Grace.

He took them to a good table, one that had been vacated by a man and a woman that Paul saw were headed toward a door at the end of the bar. The table was only slightly to the side of the stage, and there was only one row of tables between it and the dance floor. As they sat down, Paul heard music coming from another source, and when he turned he saw the flashing lights of a jukebox in a corner. The music was some popular song, a singer like a young Frank Sinatra, very romantic, low key and moody. The waiter came with their drinks, and he lifted his to Mary Grace and then sipped at it. When he had replaced it on the table, he said to her, "Why Johnny? Tell me again." He couldn't hear everything she said over the sound of the music and laughter and talking, but he pieced it together with what she had told him on the way over.

"Johnny is one tough Mexican, Paul. He's been around for a long time, and he's managed to stay free of *politicos* and gangsters too. There's stories that in the beginning, when he was just coming up, they wanted a piece of him and one of the men they sent out got killed. Then for a number of years he worked only the small places; they kind of forgot about him. It was enough for them that they could get him by keeping him out of the better clubs.

"But he was good, and he got a kind of following, and people started to want him, to demand him, in the big places. I think they got it then that they just better leave him alone and take what they could get from drinks and the gate, let him appear where he was in demand. And that got to be everywhere.

"He may be rich now; I'm not sure, but I know that money is just not a big thing with him. He quit playing the grand places a few years ago, and now he doesn't appear often, and when he does it's in smaller places like this, and not for tourists, but for his own people.

"I met him at the Casa Blanca two years ago. He came in for one night, and we had a good crowd. It was a week night and most of the customers were Mexican, but there were a few soldiers there too. The soldier I was with was drunk and yelled a lot during the show. That didn't seem to bother Johnny, but when the soldier got rough with me at the table, Johnny came right down off the stage and started to pull him off me. The soldier was big, and Johnny, you'll see, isn't. But he was tenacious, and with the help of the waiters he got the soldier out of the place.

"After the show, Johnny came over to me and introduced himself and asked me to come and have a bite with him. We went to a nice quiet place and had a late dinner, and we had a good talk. When he took me back to my house, he walked me up to the door, and the next night the girls at the Casa Blanca were a little in awe of me and told me that I was lucky to be favored by Johnny. They thought I'd fucked with him, but I didn't.

"Johnny knows what's going on. He'll know about the horse and Parker and his men if anyone does. He'll help us out. I'm counting on it."

As she was finishing she had to lean even closer to him to be heard. The sound of musicians tuning up behind the curtain on the stage was mixed for a few moments with the man on the jukebox singing "Bye, Bye, Blackbird." Then the jukebox was shut off, and lights came up brightly on the stage. There was a rush of laughter and yelling when the curtains opened to reveal a quintet of musicians dressed in rumpled tuxedos. They began to play immediately, a kind of overture of soulful Mexican ballads, while people at the bar turned toward the stage, some leaving it to grab what remained of spaces at the tables. The bartenders toned down their antics, moved more slowly, being careful not to make noise with ice or bottles, and the lights behind the bar dimmed. When everyone was settled in, the first violin, who was also the conductor, waved his bow, and the quintet moved rather abruptly into "Johnny Be Good," the old Chuck Berry tune. After a few bars, four women moved onto the stage from the wings, two from either side.

They were dressed in black stockings and garters and pointed-toe high heels with black patent-leather bows on their toes. They wore very short skirts that came only to their crotches, where they were covered with G-strings that sparkled with sequins. Their midriffs were bare, and each wore a kind of loose white halter, the tails tied in a knot above their navels. They were heavily and carefully made up, but their hair was loose, laced with colored ribbons, and bouncing in all directions as they did a modified chorus-line twist, moving sideways, arms linked, until each pair met at center stage and they commenced their high kicking.

There were catcalls and grunts and animal-like snorts from the audience. The women heard them and grinned and kicked higher. Then they broke off into pairs again, took the hands of their partners, leaned back until their heads were almost upside down, and spun in a circle, small stepping with their toes almost touching each other. When they had finished this move, they fell into line again, this time facing away from the audience, and with legs stiff and spread they leaned over from the waist until they could look back at the audience between their legs, their hair hanging down to the floor, the bright moons of their bare buttocks above their upturned faces. This gesture drew great whoops and yells, and men from the audience stood up and grabbed their crotches and threw rich guttural calls to the women. Paul could see the women grinning in response, but it took him a moment to notice that they had actually dropped the corners of their mouths down to get the grins to appear on their reversed faces. Then they rose up, still facing away from the audience, still stiff-legged. Each of them raised her left arm straight up in the air, extended an index finger. The fingers came together and lowered slightly, pointing at the conductor. The conductor in turn pointed with his bow at the drummer, and as the drummer began a very quiet roll, the woman turned their heads over their shoulders so that the audience could see their faces. They brought their arms down in unison, moving their fingers to their lips, indicating that everyone should quiet down. As the yells and calls grew more infrequent and then stopped altogether, the drum roll came up gradually, and then the conductor spoke loudly and clearly, savoring each word.

"*Señoras y Señores* . . . Ladies an' Gentelmens . . . *Putas y Gringos* . . . Johnnneeeeeey Hotnuts!"

The drum roll increased abruptly as he finished, drowning out the cheers from the audience. The four women moved their fingers from their lips and extended their arms out again, this time gesturing to the wings at the left, and stepping back slowly from center stage. A spot suddenly lit the curtains at the end of the stage. The roll continued for a few moments. All eyes were fixed where the spot lit up the vacancy. And then Johnny Hotnuts came out.

He must have started his entrance a good distance back in the wings, because he appeared not running or walking, but sliding. It was as if he were on some invisible conveyor belt. His slide was regular and constant and it took him a good twenty-five feet, all the way out to center stage. As he moved, he held a stationary posture, his right hand audaciously on his hip, his left arm elevated and bent at the elbow, the hand palm up and open, as if he were carrying something, a tray of drinks or a large ball of some kind, or was posing for approval.

He wore zoot-suit pants, tightly pegged at the ankles, and he slid on bright black patent-leather shoes. He was small and very slim, and the pants hung in the crotch almost to his knees, not in exaggeration of his masculine equipment but in diminution of what might be there. A long gold chain looped down from his belt and back up to where it disappeared in his pocket. His white, baggy-sleeved shirt was open to the waist, and his thin chest was hung with chains and emblems. Below the loops of metal, a deep curving scar ran down from beside his navel, disappearing at his belt. Like a thin white snake sewn beneath his skin, it seemed to pulse when the spot hit it. His face was a moon face, his hair so greased and slicked back that it looked like wet metal. He wore a thin pencil-line mustache and had a gold front tooth. And he was fixed and sliding, and the audience, during his slide, did not yell out but seemed as one body to be taking in breath in preparation for an outburst. He stopped sliding very slowly, and when he did stop he had a microphone in his extended hand. Someone had moved from the side of the stage and put it there, but it seemed to just appear. The vision of him had drawn all eyes, and nobody saw the figure move out to hand it to him. When he stopped, he didn't move or change expression for a moment; there was enough time for the joke of the microphone's appearance to be realized. *That* was what his hand was out for from the beginning. Everyone seemed to get it all at once, and a great roar went up from the audience.

Then he brought the microphone to his mouth, but the audience was now applauding, and he moved it away and began a deep bow. When he was half bent over, one of the women stepped forward and gave him a swift kick in the rump. There was a drum shot, and he straightened abruptly with a shocked look on his face. He wheeled around amid yells and laughter from the audience and stalked up to the four women, who were now huddled together, and each shook her head vigorously as he accused her. They were all taller than he was, even taller in their heels, and he looked ludicrous as he pointed and shook his finger at each of them, his head back as he looked up into their faces.

Finally he gave it up and shrugged and turned back to the audience, and all the women threw him the finger behind his back and two gave him the raspberry. He jerked his head around quickly, but they were demure again. Shrugging and shaking his head, he turned around again to face the audience.

The performance was not easy for Paul to understand. The sight gags at first seemed clear enough; the women would gesture both lewdly and derisively behind Johnny, and when he would catch them at it he would chase them around the stage, sliding and mincing. He never caught them, and most of the time he could not be sure who the culprit was and he would shrug and turn and appeal to the audience. Each of the women got a turn to do a number, an awkward but lewd dance, and a strip. When they stripped they took everything off, and for Paul the strips moved from a kind of pornography to a pure natural dancing. They even took their shoes off, and one of them removed her makeup and the ribbons from her hair, dancing wildly and sweetly at center stage. While the women did their dances, Johnny looked on with a quizzical expression, but he did not gesture as he might have, stealing their time from them.

Paul soon discovered that the sight gags were not all visual. Johnny kept up a constant repartee with the audience in Spanish and with the women as well, and what he said seemed to have as much to do with the humor as did the visual pratfalls and other movements. Paul knew he was missing half of what was there; he could feel it in the attunement of the audience and their pleasure in participating with Johnny. Mary Grace tried to translate for him, but things moved too quickly, and often she, like the others, couldn't contain her laughter and get what was said into English. There was a moment in the show where he thought Johnny Hotnuts saw him, or saw Mary Grace. He wasn't sure which. It was just a flicker that looked like recognition, a slight slippage in the rhythm of the performance, possible eye contact, but it was gone before Paul was sure of it.

There was no intermission; Johnny seemed to be able to get enough rest while the girls danced, and while the last one was doing her turn, Paul let his attention drift a little, his eyes move around the room. Every face that he saw was filled with pleasure and a kind of glee, but he thought he could see an edge of anticipation in them as well, and he could not figure the source of it. He turned his head a little, so he could see back to where the bartenders were, and as he glimpsed them leaning against the bar, no longer at work, he felt Mary Grace's hand on his arm, and he turned back to the stage.

The girl had finished her dance, and she and the others were moving off the stage to a soft drum roll, applause and a friendly wave from Johnny. As the applause died down, Johnny moved to the edge of the stage, and Paul could hear a few whispers rippled through the room: *Ah, el cuento. Anécdota. Cuento de hadas.*

He bent closer to Mary Grace and asked, "What are they saying?"

"They say, 'the story, the tale,' " she answered. She touched his arm. "Wait. I'll translate it for you."

When Johnny got to the front of the stage, he raised his hand, indicating that he had forgotten something. Then he turned and gestured to the wings where he had originally entered, snapped his fingers, and the spot appeared again.

"*Aquí, aquí; aquí mismo,*" he whispered, and two men came out from the wings, one carrying a high stool and some object wrapped in fabric under his arm. The other had a small table. The spot followed them, and when they got to where Johnny was, they put the table down and the stool beside it, and Johnny indicated that the object should be placed on the table. When it was there he fussed with it, walking around the table, moving it slightly, then stepping back and looking at the whole set up when he had it the way he wanted it. He looked toward the bar then, raising his hand to his forehead and shielding his eyes from the light, and called out.

"*Por* Johnny, *agua; agua fresca, por favor.*"

While the waiter was bringing a pitcher and a glass, Johnny shook the hands of the two men and gestured to the audience. They applauded briefly. Then he poured a glass of water and drank it down. It was so quiet now that Paul could hear the water splash in the pitcher, thought he could hear Johnny swallowing. There were a few muffled coughs from the audience, but there was no other sound.

Things had changed, and Johnny no longer looked comic or ridiculous; he didn't exactly look serious, but his whole act now seemed no more than a preparation for what was to come. There was a feeling of tight fellowship in the room, a sense of community that Paul felt apart from. It was not only the language. There was more to it than that. He turned to Mary Grace, wanting and expecting some contact. She sensed his looking and put her hand on his arm to keep him from speaking. She was watching the stage intently, and when Paul looked back there, Johnny was perched on the stool, at the very front of the stage, looking out at the audience. He ran his tongue over his lips and began to speak. His voice was high-pitched and at times keening. At times he got down from the stool and went to various places at the edge of the stage to address a point to particular people or small groups in the audience. Mary Grace let his first few sentences go by, and then, with her eyes fixed on Johnny and moving with him when he moved, she began to translate. Her voice was soft, and at times it was difficult for Paul to hear her. At times he would have to fill in what he thought sentences must contain only after she had reached the end of them. He could not see her lips move, and he quickly gave up trying and watched Johnny with the others. It was almost as if he were a strange ventriloquist, his words coming in melodious Spanish, then changing somehow in the air and coming back again as a transformed echo, faintly, close to Paul's side.

"*Una gran tristeza hoy día es que nuestra sociedad no tiene sitio para sus hijos. Esto lo notamos en el vacío de sus rostros, en la falta de curiosidad. Tienen rostros como los de los comerciantes y de los políticos, como los de los carteles que están afuera, pero sin el olvido que puede venir con el tiempo.* . . . A great sadness today is that our society has no place for its children. We see it in the vacancy in their faces, the absence of inquisitiveness. Theirs are like the faces of businessmen and those of politicians, like the ones on the posters outside this place, but without the forgetfulness that can come with age.

"And with the old it is pretty much the same. They too are disenfranchised, but in a different way; they are cast out from a place where there is no room for them. They are thought foolish, their attentions of no use in the busy world.

"But Johnny speaks of the children only now; there is want for it, need for it, and what he speaks of is a condition that is correctable. But he has no hope for it, being a realist when it comes to ideas. And the problem he speaks of is one of ideas, that there are too many of them, that they are not grounded, and that from this comes talk in the air, nothing but rhetoric.

"And who will teach them to look at the desert flowers, the configuration of wind-blown sand, the weave of fabric, the details to the rear of the picture, be it moving or still, the mountain sides, cuts of arroyos and deeper cuts, all the textures of the world. The learning used to be natural, now the teaching has to be an art. This was always a problem, a responsibility of parents, but it is worse than it ever has been these days."

He reached over from where he sat, filled another glass with water from the pitcher and took a long drink from it. Then he took out a handkerchief, shook it out and wiped his brow. He put his hands on his knees, leaned slightly forward, scanned the audience and began again.

"There was a man once in the past who had plenty of money, two young children and a good wife. He was a *mestizo*, but he had the kind of bearing *criollos* like to carry and the features to go with it. He was a doctor of sorts who ministered to the illnesses and injuries of the people, and he also had some skill in what we would call today botany. His interest was in crops and the uses of various substances to make them better. His wife was gentle and passive and had no real control over his children, and since he was rich, the children had no real need to work and thereby enter into the world. Even young, they realized that they had expectations coming from their father's wealth, and they spent their time in learning how to play, knowing that when they became adults the play would not really change much, but would be taken seriously, and they would have nothing to do but enjoy themselves. The man wanted them to come to a time when they had nothing to do but enjoy themselves, but he knew that if they got there without learning they would have nothing to enjoy, would be bored and unhappy.

"The man had been working with farm animals, work horses and cattle. A malaise had set in, over the years; the animals had been sluggish, and he thought that the reason had to do with nutrition. He was studying one mare in particular. He had kept it grazing in a place where he had treated the soil with a chemical concoction that he had devised. He'd had successes with the substance, and the place where he grazed her was one where growth was lower than elsewhere, but extremely green and hardy. He had managed to get her pregnant, and though the malaise had not left her, he had expectations from her foal. She was very heavy and very close to her time, and he locked her away, keeping her from the eyes of his neighbors, and waited; he set out his own bed in her stall, and spent as much time as he could there.

"One night he awakened to the sound of her moaning, and he got up and went to her. She was lying on her side, her belly like a gigantic melon. She was breathing heavily, and he knew she was ready, so he sat beside her and waited. Her breathing was regular and deep and she kept at it for a long time; listening to it he nodded off, and only came awake when he heard her loud snorting. He got up quickly and went behind her and saw the small head of her foal protruding from her. It was on its way out, and he grabbed the towels and the rubber syringe he had ready and watched it. It came quickly, and when it popped out behind her a tremendous flood of fluid came following it, washing over the foal and up to his ankles before it spilled under the boards of the stall and into the one beside it. When he looked up, he saw that her belly had completely deflated. She gave a deep sigh and fell back, exhausted.

"The thing that he noticed about the foal when he cleaned it and sucked the juice from its airway with the syringe was its size. It was extremely small, just the size of a cat, and yet it was well formed, and even as a newborn seemed very strong. When he had it right, he left it with its mother and went into the house to sleep.

"The horse grew quickly in the next few weeks, but it did not grow large. It came up from cat size to the size of a small dog, and when it got there it had lost its gangliness and looked completely mature. It reached only to a place below the man's knee, and it stopped growing when it got there, a small, strong, perfectly formed palomino. For six months he did not reveal it to anyone, and then he brought his wife out and showed it to her, and then one day he took it to show to his children.

"The children were playing, making some sort of adult-like party in the yard to the rear of his dwelling, and when he got there and called to them they were intent on some social graces and did not look up.

" 'Children, see what I have here,' he called out, and then they did look up, and when they saw the small horse walking beside him, they got up from their chairs and rushed over and reached to touch the horse tentatively, with mouths open, in obvious delight and awe. When they got over the initial shock of it, which only took a few minutes, they wanted to appropriate it, to take it into their play, but the father would not let them do so, and took it away, to their disappointment, and locked it in the barn.

"The next day, and from then for as long as possible, he used the horse to teach his children about the details of life around them. The horse was naturally inquisitive. It was of a size that could enter the children's life easily, but it was independent, not like a dog or a cat. Before long they were following it, watching the way it learned of its surroundings, from barn to house, through the stone-fenced enclosed land that was the man's domain. And through its comings and goings, which was not like their play at all, they started to note the configurations of flowers, cactus and other growths, the way of the weather with them, what wind did, the working of root systems, the force and passage of small streams, and all the many details of the life they had been living in and around but had not noted before.

"And they learned of anatomy and physiology through the horse, as well. Their father would give them lessons at the end of each day. He, they and the horse would stand and sit in the barn. He would give lessons on the horse itself, noting sometimes, with a stick as a pointer, how muscles bunched and worked and moved, how those of the horse were related to those in their own bodies. He showed them pupil dilation and contraction and its relation to light. He explained sex, copulation, gestation and birth. And before the children were aware of the idea of it and what it meant to them, they had quit their games, quit generalizing to words with capital letters that had no basis in their experience and were therefore vacant, and started to come up with real, tentative, conclusions, the ones that had health and were drawn from the details of the real world. They began to stand more erect, they lost their baby fat, their eyes found proper focus and cleared the milkiness that had been a characteristic of them before the horse came. Most important, to them in the future, though they did not know it, and to their father in the present since he did, was that they ceased planning for the image and external trappings of the adult life that had formerly drawn them; nor did they mull over their short pasts. They were in the present, where children should be, and they were happy there.

"The father remained busy with his work with crops, and he managed to reserve as much time as he could to continue with his experiments on the plot of land that he had treated. The mother of the little horse had recuperated, and was now ready again, and he made an arrangement with a neighbor to settle her with a strong palomino stallion that the neighbor possessed. The settling occurred. Soon the mare was pregnant again, and as before she was delivered of a small horse, this time, as the father had wished, a male. The children were delighted, even though in a brief time the new little horse had drawn the female away from them. She became distant, running with her mate. But the children had learned enough so that they could accept the reasons for it. In time the father set out to fulfill his expectations with the horses; he managed to mate them, and again he took up residence in the barn and waited. He watched as the small mare filled out to a normal size, but he became quickly alarmed as she continued to grow, her belly becoming terrifically distended.

"It is hard for Johnny to describe what followed, because the story has it that the distension became quickly bizarre and almost like a comic-book. Her belly grew to eight times the size of the rest of her body. It was grotesque as it stretched and expanded, coming to a size that was so large that her legs had to stretch out, in front and in back, and rest upon it. It was like a gigantic ball that she rested against or sat upon. It was as if she was stuck to the moon. Then one night as the father watched her she burst, gushing her fluid, and her foal, a long-legged colt that at birth was four times her size, rolled out and staggered to its hooves. The man buried the tortured wreck of her; the male palomino jumped the wall that night, and in the morning the father consoled his children the best he could."

Paul was straining to catch the last sentence of the whispered translation. He could not be sure he had heard correctly and when her words trailed off and no more came from the stage in Spanish, he turned his head that way.

Johnny Hotnuts was standing at the front of the stage now, a little to the left of where they sat; he was leaning forward slightly, his hands raised in front of him, extending in a gesture as if he were measuring the diameter of a huge ball. His shirt was wet with sweat and stuck to his chest in places, and there were beads of sweat on his glistening forehead. He dropped his hands, turned and walked quickly to the table. Paul saw that in addition to the covered object there was now a kind of easel standing to the side of the table. The easel too was covered with cloth. When Johnny got to the table, he took the edge of each cloth, one in each hand and pulled them quickly away with a flourish; then he stepped back to the side, the cloths hanging in his hands, and stood still, looking out at the audience.

There was a communal intake of breath in the room. Paul had an urge to rise and go to the stage. He almost did rise up, could feel his thighs push him, but Mary Grace's hand on his arm kept him where he was long enough for him to see that the horse was not real. It was a replica. It was not even a stuffed horse, but it was so well constructed that it looked like one. Only the constant, glassy light reflecting from its stone eyes kept it from being alive. It stood in the center of the table, a palomino, jewels set in its hooves, its mane and tail tightly braided and laced with strings of jewels. Only the locks at its poll were free, the yellow hair allowed to fan out. It wore no halter, but its sides and flanks were dressed with markings, some painted, others burned in brands. They looked like figures of some kind, or embellished letters, and Paul remembered the way the jewels in the horse's hoof had seemed to form some pattern when he'd looked at it, before he'd closed her wound. It seemed so long ago, and though he leaned forward and squinted the figures were too small to make out from this distance.

And the stance of the horse model was in some way familiar too. Its left foreleg was slightly raised in the air, bent at the knee, but it was not in mid-stride. The raised leg and the jeweled hoof was a kind of gesture, almost a pointing, emblematic. Its head was slightly elevated also. It seemed ready and poised for some action, and at the same time it seemed static, elegantly aggressive and austere. It belonged as a statue in a temple, or on a frieze, in an altar; it did not belong here.

Behind it was a rendering of it, slightly stylized, on a white sheet on the easel. The rendering was an outline in black ink. There were various lines pointing to various places on its body and at the end of them, in the white space around the horse, were brief captions written in Spanish.

Paul could feel the whole audience leaning forward to read them. He reached for Mary Grace's hand, but she pulled it away, and he looked back and tried to decipher. The legends were brief, and in them were words written in italics, some had exclamation points and others quotation marks. He could make out nothing beyond that. Then he saw Johnny drop the two cloths to the floor and step forward. He turned his head and looked for a long time at the horse and the rendering. Then he turned back to the audience and cleared his throat. He had their attention quickly, and holding them, he went to the table and poured and drank another glass of water, wiping his mouth with a ridiculously large checked handkerchief that he pulled from his rear pants pocket. The handkerchief was the size of a large pillowcase, and when he had wiped his mouth, he put his face into it, blotting the sweat from his brow and cheeks, thereby making the size of the handkerchief serviceable, moving it from any context of comedy. He folded it carefully, put it back in his pocket, stepped forward a little further, and resumed his story.

"Now the darkness begins, and we will wish many things. We will wish that the man had not been so arrogant, had not thought to game with nature; we will wish the wall had been higher; we'll wish the children well, wish humanity were different from what it is.

"Only a few saw the male horse running before the man captured him and hid him away again. But a few were enough. The word spread quickly, and in two days a delegation was at the man's house demanding knowledge. He gave it to them, understanding their insistence and their power. He brought the little horse out, and though some were frightened at the sight of it, most were curious, and there were those who were thinking about uses for it. He tried to tell them it had been an anomaly, but there were those who wandered and found the patch of miniature and hearty growth, made the connection, and insisted, out of a greed for something that they could not articulate, that the patch be opened for the public good. The man did not tell them about the birth of the colt or the death of the other little horse. He knew it would make no difference. That he had kept this thing from them made everything that he could now say suspect, and the story was so bizarre that he knew they would not possibly believe it. He made secret plans to leave. But that night robbers came. They killed him and his wife, searched for the children but could not find them, and took the horse away.

"What happened in the next hundred or two hundred years is not certain. Nor is the story I have just related anything but a tale of beginnings. In it the children of the man, the sister and brother, escaped, went elsewhere, had two children between them, a boy and a girl, and these in turn bore children. The family, as it extended, took in worthy outsiders, grew but remained relatively closed. One of the things that closed them was this story that was handed down, becoming sacred in time.

"In the town that the man's children escaped from, there was a long period of darkness, vague and violent adjustments, fundamental change. There are many stories and fragments of stories about that, and this is only one coherent version of what might have happened.

"They had no use for the little horse, but they could not help but value it. It was unique, and all they could figure to do against the time when they could find some use for it was to remove its uniqueness, make more little horses, and thereby gain at least something in quantity. So they grazed their horses on the plot of rich growth, and more small horses were born, but when they mated the horses most of them did not bear others but suffered the same grotesque death I have told you about. Only one in twenty bore another small horse. And these rare horses were valued in households, initially because of the way children took to them. But in a while adults became nervous about children who had associated with the horses. They seemed too centered and immediate, had no ambition in the way the adults conceived of it, and appeared wiser than they should be. So the horses were taken away from the children, became useless again, and this ongoing uselessness in the face of a thing that people recognize as magnificent is what caused religion to grow up around the horses.

"It began with prayers and ritual actions over the bodies of little pregnant mares, behavior to ensure the birth of a small horse and avoid the catastrophe of the coming of a larger one. And when larger ones came, which was most of the time, rituals grew up around that event also. The foals were kept in captivity, treated as pariahs, and when they grew up they were killed in blood sacrifice. And this butchery caused a diminution of the herd as a whole. Too much time was spent in attending to the little horses, to the neglect of the large ones, and this and drought and communal frenzy brought bad times. The population of small horses did not increase. It was not that adults grew old and died so much as that little horses escaped, simply walked away and were not seen again.

"I cannot say how the iconography of the chart here grew and developed, but it would seem that it stands as evidence of turmoil, decadence and the factional development of mysterious cults of the horse. There seems to be no core religion from which the rest splintered off; it would seem that no use for the horses was ever discovered, nothing that could be a lesson to live by. Only greed and a passion without clear material object seems to emerge in the factions in common. The society in which the first horse was born is lost to us. It can be figured to have been near here, but it could have been elsewhere as well. Occasional little horses are seen, but always by little children, and what little children say they have seen is not taken for much account, and so only a few take their existence seriously; the rest see them as childishly mythic, harmless dreams and fantasies. But Johnny's story is not about the present, and he does not wish to play speculative games with you. You'll imagine too, if you know about Johnny, that his story is nothing but a story, maybe, and that it is told to entertain you, to give you pleasure; what can I know about little horses, about these?"

With that, Johnny Hotnuts turned to the chart on the easel, and as he turned he extracted a telescopic pointer from his pocket, pulled at the tip to extend it and began to read the brief legends. He would read one and then turn the pointer to the place where the line went on the horse's body. His voice would change as the contents of the legend changed. At times he was derisive, at others he would chuckle lightly; sometimes he spoke in a voice of wonder. Paul understood none of what he said, but he heard the variety in the tone, and as he watched Johnny and the pointer and heard his voice, the richness of the iconography came alive for him. Tension grew in the room; there was some foot-shuffling, some discomfort as Johnny spoke. Somehow it was as if what he was doing, his tone changes, were inappropriate, even blasphemous. As if he noticed the feel in the air, when he finished reading the legends and put his pointer away and turned back to the audience he smiled in a knowing way.

"Well, now, I can see that you are bothered by the way I read these things. Johnny can see that. I didn't think my story had any message, nothing to learn from, that it was entertainment. I don't know. There may be some believers here that I am unaware of. I think maybe *all* of you are one up on me; you must know more than I do about this thing. Let me leave the little horses to you then. Hey! And let's get on with the show!"

Johnny waved his arms at the wings, and the two men rushed out and took the table and easel away. Then he bent down and picked up the two cloths from the floor, and when he was standing again he held them like veils in his extended fingers, smiled and winked, and bowed deeply to the audience. The applause started in the back of the room, at the bar, and then it came forward and got louder. When it reached the front of the room and Paul and Mary Grace were clapping, it was joined by yells and hoots, and soon everyone had risen. Johnny came up from his bow and began a little dance, his small feet mincing in place, his arms moving the veils, turning them in little circles in the air. Then, with a glance over his shoulder he cued the quintet and it swooped quickly into a loping waltz tempo. Johnny raised his eyebrows, swiveled his hips and the audience let out a laugh. Then, as the four dancing girls came back out on the stage, applause rose again, and when Johnny bowed and received a quick kick in his behind, the audience took its seats and settled back into the ribald and foolish antics of Johnny Hotnuts' extravagant sexual review.

Chapter 9

I t was late and they were traveling the rough roads that led away from Club El Monte. The shacks along the rutted street were now darkened, the doors closed, the various colored lights invisible. The street was empty of other cars, and there were no people anywhere in sight. Mary Grace was pressed close against him, and he could see her bare knee, bluish where the dim dash lights washed it. Johnny was small against the door, almost blocked out by Mary Grace, and in the back seat was the model of the horse, the easel and the large artist's pad containing the rendering.

"*Por allí,*" Johnny said.

"Turn left over there," Mary Grace told him, and he pulled into a smooth blacktop road that wound into some low foothills for a few blocks. They came to a street where Mary Grace motioned for him to turn in and they stopped in front of a large and impressive house that was fronted by a rich, formal garden.

"This is the house of Abelardo García. Johnny stays here when he's in Chihuahua," Mary Grace whispered to him as they got out of the car.

The house seemed to grow in size as they moved up the long flight of stone steps from the street. Paul could see wings disappearing into tall trees, openings into courtyards.

"An important person?" he whispered.

"Yes. More or less," she said.

When they got to a small, two-story structure rising at the end of one of the wings and tucked among trees, they stopped at a dark door and waited while Johnny got out the key. Paul was holding the horse model under his arm; it seemed strangely still to him, unyielding. Mary Grace held the artist's pad, and Johnny had leaned the easel against the building.

When they got inside, Johnny showed them to a small solarium, a room with a quarry tile floor, windows looking out on a small lush garden, various planters hanging from a high-beamed ceiling, and three comfortable velvet couches around a glass topped coffee table. He excused himself and left them. They sat silently and waited. Paul wanted to speak; he had many questions, but he could not select the one he wanted to ask first and she only smiled at him and then pointed out things in the room for him to look at without speaking. He saw the lovely earth-toned rug hung on a wall, two Mayan smiling dogs on small tables flanking one of the couches, painted wood masks of some kind.

When Johnny returned he wore a clean shirt, his face was rosy and freshly washed, and his mustache was gone. He carried a large copper tray in his hand; it had pewter handles and was a perfect circle, and on it were three cut-crystal snifters, a bottle of fine tequila and one of brandy. To the side was a small stone dish with wedges of lemon in it and a stone saltcellar with a small silver spoon. He placed the tray on the glass table and sat down on the couch across from them. He was so small, his feet barely reached the floor. He pulled them up and gathered his legs on the cushion.

"¿Por favor?" He motioned to Paul and the tray. "Johnny is very cansado." He smiled briefly, and his gold tooth glimmered.

Paul leaned forward and poured tequila for himself and Mary Grace; Johnny accepted a brandy. When they were settled in with their drinks, Johnny began to talk softly to Mary Grace.

Paul listened, but they spoke rapidly, and he could make nothing out of it. At first their talk was light. They laughed quietly. There seemed to be bits of old reminiscences in what they said. Paul could not think they could be finding enough to say about the time at the Casa Blanca when Mary Grace had said she had spent an evening with Johnny. After a while, the talk turned serious. Johnny did most of the talking, and Mary Grace injected questions and brief comments from time to time. They bent more toward each other, closing him out slightly, and Johnny came to recognize this in time and raised his hand as Mary Grace was speaking, indicating that she should stop.

"My friend, please excuse me; she will explain it to you later. Please feel free to explore the place. There are many interesting things here. We will be finished before too long."

Though Paul had thought that Johnny must speak a little English, his words still came as a slight shock. They were without any trace of accent and came with ease. But with the shock he also felt relief; it was hard to sit with them and yet be excluded in this way.

"Right. Thank you," he said, and he rose from the couch and left the room. When he looked back he saw they were again engaged, speaking intently and leaning toward each other.

The house of Abelardo García, if this small section of it was at all representative, was the house of a very rich man indeed. In the room to the front of the solarium, he found three small but very choice paintings, hung side by side on a wall almost hidden by a potted fern: a Tamayo, an Orozco and a small, very primitive piece by an artist whose name he did not recognize. There were many Mesoamerican artifacts, and they were not shards, but small animals and pottery pieces. On the wall of the stairway that led to the second story, and also inconspicuously placed, were six small smiling faces, clay Mayan masks. What impressed Paul the most were the many rugs and tapestries, mostly contemporary, but some old. All were tightly woven and colored with subtle vegetable dyes. He paused in front of one piece in particular for a long time. It was a small rug, a ritual mat of some sort. On it were various crude, stylized figures, men, horses and other animals, and though indecipherable to him, it was clear they depicted some story. He could see there were twelve panels, four in each row, and that they were meant to be read in sequence. In the beginning the men had the animals as subjects; then the animals were worshipped in some way. And in the last four, the men were gone and the animals were involved in some kind of social intercourse. He thought of Johnny's story when he looked at it, and he thought of himself in possession of the little horse.

He could see her waiting in the room for him, small and incongruous in the dim light he had left burning. He wanted to get back to her, not to dispose of her, but in some way to begin more intentionally to dispose of their situation together, do something that would give him understanding and power in it. Since he had found Mary Grace again, the direction of things had been hers, and although at first he welcomed her taking over, the pace had become too leisurely and ambiguous, and he now wanted a more dynamic focus. He heard her step below him on the stair before he heard her voice.

"Paul, we're finished; it's time to go."

When he descended he saw that Johnny was waiting there with her. She had a roll of paper under her arm, and Johnny had a brandy snifter in his hand. As Paul reached the bottom step, Johnny extended his hand, smiling.

"Many thanks for bringing Mary Grace, and thanks too for coming to Johnny's show," he said.

They shook hands. Johnny squeezed his tightly and held it.

"Good luck," he said.

They drove back in silence. When they entered the car, Paul immediately asked her what she and Johnny had talked about. But she said they had to drive carefully. It was dark, and the lighting here was not good on the streets, and she would tell him everything when they got back. It was indeed dark, and the route back was circuitous. Mary Grace knew the way, and she gave him directions. He drove slowly and with care, and it took them almost a half hour to get back to the room.

After Paul had wakened and checked the horse, who he suspected had slept at the foot of the bed where they had left her the whole time they were gone, he went to the bathroom, to the shower. There was a small puddle of yellow urine in the tub, and he knew when he saw it that she had at least gotten up once. He washed it out, undressed and showered, and when he came out Mary Grace was in her robe. She smiled at him, and came over and kissed him lightly on the cheek. Then she went to the dresser and came back with the roll of paper she had left Johnny's with.

"Here. I've translated. I'll shower while you read it."

He heard her slip from her robe. A brief vision of her small breasts came to him and he smiled, then he heard the water rushing in the shower stall, and he took the roll of paper and sat against the pillows propped up on the bed and unrolled it. It was a thick piece of artist's drawing paper, and on it was a tracing of the little horse that Johnny had lectured on with his pointer in that strange and uncomfortable interlude in his show. The legends and the straight lines running from them to places on the horse's body were there as well, but now the writing was mostly in English. It was obvious that she had translated quickly, including notes when she wasn't sure. He couldn't tell about the question marks, if they were hers or part of Johnny's original. Turning the paper and studying it, he read the legends and noted each of their reference points with care. A few of the legends were clear and direct statements, but most were not; some he almost laughed at; others bothered him in ways he did not quite understand. At times he was moved, thrust into his past somehow, by words that seemed strangely familiar. When the shower stopped, he was wakened to the absence of its sound and realized he had been lost in time, in the details of what he had been studying, and had no idea of how long she had been gone. He reached to the bedside table and checked his watch. It was two in the morning, and as he came back to time he felt the weight of tiredness flood in upon him. He dropped an end of the paper, letting it roll back into itself, let his arms fall on the spread and moved his legs to get comfortable. His foot touched the little horse where she lay below him, and he moved it, not wanting to wake her. She herself moved a little, touched in her sleep, then settled back in. The next thing he knew he awakened in the dark room as Mary Grace touched him.

"You fell asleep, Pablo," she whispered. "Come on, let's take your clothes off."

He did not realize what she meant at first. He had showered, and he would not have any clothing on. But when he looked down at his body in the darkened room, he saw that he was fully dressed. He did not remember dressing again, and then he remembered that she had bought him a bathrobe and slippers before they had left Naco. He couldn't remember if, in the nights since Hermosillo, he had worn them, could not really remember those nights clearly at all.

"It's still a trouble, Pablo; you still think they might be coming any minute. It's okay. We'll be safer soon."

He let her do most of it, enjoying it, and in his enjoyment he was aroused slightly and came awake almost fully again. She pulled his socks off, loosened his belt, and when he raised his hips she slipped his pants down. Then she did the same with his underwear. He laughed a little at the fact that he had put them on as well. He sat up so she could get his shirt off, and they both laughed when the collar caught on his chin. He let his hand fall on places on her body, sneaking up under her nightgown as she bent over him, and they laughed at this as well.

When he was naked she got him under the covers and stood up in the faint light that came through the drapes from the outside. She smiled at him, a corner of her mouth twisting up, and then she lifted her nightgown over her head. He could see her nipples, dark spots on her breasts. She saw him looking at them and wiggled a little. Then she slipped between the sheets and moved against him.

"You're tired, Paul," she said. "Aren't you?"

"Yes," he said. "But I want to hear about Johnny, what he said."

"Yes, okay," she said, and reached for his penis and ran her fingertips over it. It began to harden.

"First let me do something for you; it'll be good for you. Then I'll tell you what we talked about."

He relaxed and spread his legs a little, and she chuckled at his quick response. Then she pulled the covers down and got out of the bed and went to the other side, where she knelt on the floor. He turned slightly, opening his legs wider, lifted the right one and moved it to the other side of her head. Now she was between his legs, and her laugh came from deep in her chest, and she began.

His expectations brought him fully awake in their promise of her mechanical skill and the fact that he had gotten to know her, felt a kind of full possession of her, and would now experience them. She had been his first ideal sweetheart, the one that is never risen to, his first full frustration of adolescence, and he had, appropriately, failed her then. He thought now that the failure had as much to do with her own innocence then as it had to do with his. She had been young and had known only crude soldiers. But now it was fifteen years later. He had had some women, had at times felt proficient with them, and she had had God knows how many men. Even as he felt her first breath in his crotch, he realized that he had risen through curiosity and a kind of oncoming possession of her that would subject her, but not to his will. It had been *her* idea, spoken of as a kind of curative of some kind: it would be good for him. But he wanted this to be more than that, wanted it to be the first real time, that corrective to the one fifteen years ago, and he began to recoil slightly: that it should be this way and not more conventional like before. He thought briefly about the time a few nights ago, how it had gotten by him before he could place it as a monument; he had not had time to ready himself for it. What he remembered more vividly was the bath she had given him. It was that he wanted to feel as preparatory to this. He felt himself locked up in his mind, and for a long moment feared that he would be unable to get free of this and of measuring, of "experiencing" what she was about to do to him, for him, and would miss what it could be because he would be counting it and not having it. But very quickly she took the fear from him.

He was in her mouth, and the silk of her wet tongue was touching him as it made garbled words, not in Spanish but English, moving him as food would be moved, in that urgency to speak with a full mouth, to answer a pressed question across a table. The words were coming and clicking and he raised his head to see her, her eyes smiling, creases at their corners, then opening into dark moons as she took his testicles, each between thumb and index finger, as if delicate grapes tested for ripeness, her lips opening into an oval larger than he was and reaching for more of him, her neck extending as she swallowed all of him, her pupils rising slightly as she went down, still talking, so their eyes were together. Her lips locked at his base; then her head moved back, her mouth distorting along the length of him, the language becoming clearer, the syntax more ordered, snatches of the words' warble and click, somehow in rich and half-coherent dialogue: moove, sweet, my, lick, -ing, cup, cum, yu, suck, bit, luv, here, taste, now?, dear, give, delicious, throat, Paul, rib, soon, me, -art, silk, juice, bite?, -ther, meal, dawn, brr-, food, o, slick, gee, pearl, tong, and then the garbling into tender sounds only as she swallowed again, slowly, over and over.

He could see her breasts, small and vulnerable in the air when she moved back, her throat contractions and her wrists, the film of her black hair, an earring, the way her eyebrows moved in expression, her nostrils flaring, a drop of pearl saliva, her creased brow, rose shadow at her expanding and receding cheek. And there was nothing of experience at all, nothing learned, no wisdom or generalized behavior, no men or women, nothing in his head through which he watched her. What there was was his slow expansion, her talking, the enjoyment in her face, his realization of his own smile, and the whiteness of his penis appearing and disappearing. Then he heard the two words come together, and it was as if she had her hands on his shoulders, lightly, her mouth against his ear: *come here.*

He rose to his elbows, reached down and touched her cheek. It pushed against his fingertips as she took him in again, holding him this time, her tongue moving, her lips caressing him, her eyes in his eyes. In the corner of his vision he could see the shadow of the little horse's head between their two heads. It seemed to be looking down at her, still and serious. She saw it, and her eyes crinkled again; then they expanded, the pupils dilating as he began to flood into her. His legs vibrated and he took the sheet in his fists. His whole body was shaking, but he kept his eyes on her. She was shaking too, but she watched his face. She was passive now. Only her lips moved, holding him, and her throat as she swallowed. After a long while, she delicately released him and slowly crawled up his body from the floor, licking his stomach and chest as she came. She stopped at each nipple and at the cups of his clavicles, and when she reached his mouth her tongue entered it deeply and he tasted himself.

It was minutes later when she rose from beside him and went to the bathroom. He heard the water running and in a few moments she was back. He was now fully awake, but no longer pushed to alertness through intensity. His mind was clear, but his body was relaxed. He didn't want to move at all, but he found that there was no effort needed for him to move his hand to cover hers when she lay down again beside him.

They were on their backs, and he felt his eyes fill up, and then felt the lines of wetness run from the corners of his eyes and down his cheeks. He wept with no effort and without any desire to hold back. His breathing remained regular, and he did not think she noticed, nor did he feel it important to speak of it to her. There was nothing really he felt he could say. And she didn't seem to need for him to say anything; at least she gave no sign. He held her hand, and in a while she turned to him and kissed his cheek. He held her for a moment, touching her hair and face, and then they lay back again. He pressed his legs against hers and in a while he nudged her foot with his own. She laughed lightly and squeezed his hand, and then he spoke.

"What about Johnny's scar?" he said. "Do you know anything about that? It looked pretty brutal."

"It's not as bad as it looked under the lights," she said. "It's a very old scar. From a long time ago. Nothing of concern now."

"So what did he say? Did you learn anything?"

"Johnny knows of Parker," she said. "He's had some dealings with him over the years. Not much and never personal or in person, always at third- or fourth-hand. It was mostly old business having to do with bookings and in some cases, quite a few years ago and before the horses, setting up showcases for movies, getting them around to people in position, those who might have influence that could affect distribution.

"Johnny says that there are only a few movies with the horses in them and that Parker and his people have business with them in Mexico and that his move with them is South, and North into the U.S. too. The horse ones are only going big in Mexico City and only as a few in a group of thirty or more that are odd and what is called kinky. They are very finely made and shown mostly privately, to small groups for large amounts of money. Johnny has heard about something going on in the U.S., in Hollywood he thinks, but only snatches of veiled rumor.

"Because of all this, Johnny doesn't trust that Parker would be after the horse we have solely because of the movies. He doesn't need to make those specific ones; he has gotten rich and is getting richer through all the others. So there must be some other reason. And he is after the horse; that's for sure. Already the word is out. Johnny picked it up the day we left Naco. Johnny does not trust Parker or that we can in any way be sure of him, sure of what he will do. We could give the horse up to Parker, find a way of doing that, but even then you've been to his *rancho,* seen what goes on there. You're a gringo, and Johnny thinks that Parker would not now trust that your going there was innocent. He might be suspicious and not let it end like that. Johnny is not sure what he has to lose by letting you go with the information, but he wouldn't like to see us take the risk. Parker is a suspicious man, Johnny says. Anyway, we don't have to give the horse up just yet. I know you don't want to do that. Neither do I. We have some time, a little room for decision.

"Now Johnny thinks that Parker will have a pretty good line on us by this time. He will know about the car. I have a green card, and he will have checked with people he has at the border. They keep a list of any of us who cross, so he will know that we are probably still in Mexico and heading South. Johnny thinks that the best bet is for him to have someone take the car down and over to Monterrey and turn it in there. Parker will keep someone checking in Naco to see if and when the car is turned back in. Maybe he will have a way of knowing that you spent time in Corpus Christi years ago and would head there as a way out of the country. Johnny thinks this might work to throw them off, for a while at least. In the meantime we can fly down to Mexico City.

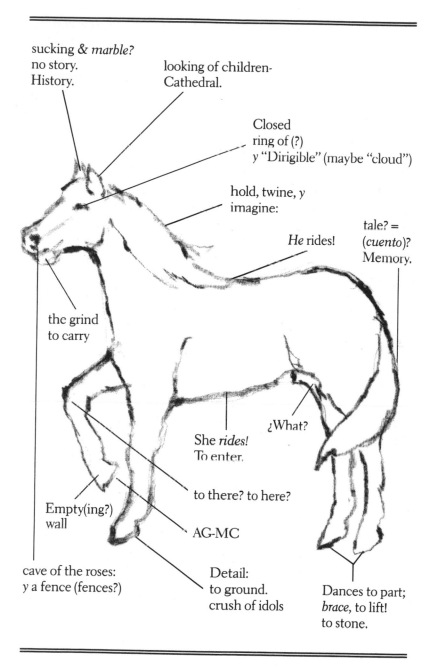

sucking & *marble?*
no story.
History.

looking of children-
Cathedral.

Closed
ring of (?)
y "Dirigible" (maybe "cloud")

hold, twine, *y*
imagine:

He rides!

tale? =
(*cuento*)?
Memory.

the grind
to carry

¿What?

She *rides!*
To enter.

Empty(ing?)
wall

to there? to here?

AG-MC

cave of the roses:
y a fence (fences?)

Detail:
to ground.
crush of idols

Dances to part;
brace, to lift!
to stone.

"I agree with Johnny, and I told him it was okay to go ahead. He'll get you a visa and a passport tomorrow. We'll have to fly down separated, and I'll have to find a way of taking the horse. They won't let you in that far with an animal without a lot of checking, and we can't have that. In Mexico we can stay lost long enough for Johnny to try to find out what is going on. Mexico City is big, and Johnny has many friends there; he'll put us in touch with someone. He will get word to us how things stand when he's had time to check. Paul, this is getting deep and complex now. We could just drive out of town and let her go; we could go to Mexico City without her. Do you want to do that?"

He *did* want to do that. He wanted to get free before he got more involved. He had a sense that soon there would be no possibility of quitting. They could go to Mexico City together, and soon they could get back into the States and he could live with her and resume his life with Pfeffer. He had money in the bank there. Their life would be comfortable. They could go on vacations, buy nice things to put around them. Maybe they could even have children. He wondered if she was capable of bearing children. Everything would be relaxed, fairly predictable, pleasant.

"No," he said.

"Hokay, Pablo. I'm glad you feel that way. Mexico will be fine. You'll see. And we can trust Johnny. He's wise, and he knows what's going on and he'll find out more. Johnny is my brother."

Chapter 10

The man came early in the morning to take the passport photo. Mary Grace was up and around, but Paul was still sleeping. She woke Paul, put the horse in the bathroom, and let the man in. He was rushed, and when Paul had only his shirt and tie on, he indicated that that was enough, centered him in front of one of the walls and took his pictures. He spoke briefly to Mary Grace in Spanish, and when he was gone she told Paul he'd said he'd be back in two hours; the plane left in three, at ten o'clock.

When they were showered and dressed, they prepared the horse. There was not much they could do. Mary Grace and Johnny had talked it over the night before and had opted more for diversion and boldness than for disguise. She braided the horse's tail tightly and then bent the braid as far back as she could get it and bandaged it halfway up with adhesive tape that the photographer had brought them. He had brought a paper bag with this and other things in it. Then she waxed what remained of the tail hair, getting it as tight as possible so that it looked something like a freshly snipped one. She waxed the mane and fetlocks also, pressing the hair into the body so that the mane was hardly visible. The hooves were the hardest part, and the toes and nails she painted on them with fingernail polish were not too convincing. But when she was finished they at least did not look like horse's hooves, though they didn't look much like dog's feet either. They didn't figure that there was anything they could do for the head.

When they were finished, they stood back and looked at her where she stood on the carpet. Her head was hanging and she looked forlorn, but she looked comic as well, and they grinned at her and at each other, trying hard to keep from laughing. On the way to the airport, Mary Grace painted her lips and eyes with bright colors and put the large flamboyant hat the photographer had brought back with the passport square on her head. He had brought her a dress also, very loud with renderings of flamingoes on it. At the departure entrance, Paul helped her out and got the large metal dog carrier from the trunk. She held the horse in her arms. It now had a rhinestone collar with a short leash attached to it. Mary Grace called out loudly to a redcap. He didn't even glance at the horse, but took the carrier and the suitcase that sat beside it, put them on his cart and led the way into the departure lobby.

Paul took the car to another entrance, the only other one, a hundred or so yards away. The photographer was waiting, leaning against a taxi, and when Paul pulled up he came over. When Paul had taken his suitcase from the trunk, the man nodded to him, smiling slightly, and got in the car and took it away. The suitcase had only a few things in it, some clothes Johnny had provided, some toilet articles and a couple of pieces of cheap Chihuahua pottery. Paul got back to the terminal in time to see Mary Grace at a counter where animals were checked in. She still held the horse in her arms, but as he watched from across the room he saw her ease it into the door of the metal carrier. An attendant put it on a cart beside four other carriers and a man came and wheeled the cart away. Paul went to the check-in counter and got his seat assignment. Then he returned to where he had been standing and waited. When the call came, they lined up, still apart, and when they were on the plane and seated, he could see Mary Grace's hat about six rows ahead over her seat back. As he watched, she reached up and took it off. Soon the announcements came, the plane taxied away from the loading ramp, and in a few minutes they were in the air. There would be nothing to do now for a while. The plane was prop driven, and it would take close to three hours to get to Mexico City. He had a window seat, and he looked down and watched the ground recede. Soon he could see the perimeters of the city and the bare land and hills and mountains opening up beyond it, and soon even the land lost its character, becoming only color, tan and light brown. As he watched, it darkened and began to lose focus. They then rose beyond the misty edge and entered the cloud bank proper, and it was gone.

He remembered his time in the Navy in San Diego as a kind of cluster of fragmented images permanently jettisoned from the narrative matrix in which they had occurred. In some way shuffled in his mind, each image came to prominence; they appeared in no order, unless it was the one provided by the circumstances in which they were remembered. There were the photo booths downtown, where high school girls gathered and would sit on the lap of a sailor for a quarter or kiss him for a dollar, the picture then sent home to civilian friends to show them what it was like to be in the Navy. You could get your hair cut down there, each bit of cologne, each clipping of stray hair an extra charge, and there were lockers where you could store your uniform and go out in civilian clothes to be recognized as Navy anyway by your shoes. There had been Balboa Park, the Shakespeare theater, and the trails through eucalyptus, places to eat sandwiches and drink beer, the smell of the zoo, alive and ripe, drifting in on shore breezes.

In the solarium where he had tended Jack and watched him come alive and then die, there was the sound of suction machines, worked-up belches, and the whispered talk of visitors. After the men had their larynxes removed, they began with messages on pads of paper, frustrated scribbles, attempted jokes that wouldn't take in the absence of voice inflection and verbal timing. Then they were taught to belch, to bring up air and form a kind of talk in it, mouths and cheeks moving and half of the words lost, the others muffled sound in a cave. Some of them managed sentences before they died. And he at times found himself waking from dreams in which he could not speak out and would come to himself with his mouth working in the way he had seen their mouths work, trying to bring up air, to say things that needed to be said. In the morgue, his first medical duty early in his tour, he had at first mistaken the pools of blood inside the elbows and knees, the post-mortem lividity, for bruises and had written them down on the chart under marks and scars, to be laughed at by residents before they corrected them. He was awakened there, when on the graveyard shift, to file the bodies of the ones who died in the night. And there was ice cream eaten from sterile basins, the sending of new men to central supply for a package of Fallopian tubes, the naive practical jokes of young corpsmen frightened by sickness and death and trying to find ways of handling it. *He* had handled it, was fascinated by it, and only at times did he recognize the depth of his depression.

When he looked out the plane window, the sky was clear and there was nothing but clouds below them, fantastic, thick and billowy. He could not see Mary Grace's head a few rows up, but he could see the edge of her flamboyant hat on the rack over her seat. He had never been to Mexico City, had no real picture of it in his mind, and yet it was another new thing, and even given the circumstances he was in he looked forward to newness now, each movement in the narrative that was not of his own making and therefore open and in no way claustrophobic to him.

He had been transferred to Corpus after two years, to a small command. He was very good with patients, especially the dying. He had ways to put them at ease, and this got around. He was good in surgery too, was conscientious and was better than the surgeons were at dealing with nurses and patients. The transfer was easy to get. In Corpus, a young doctor had put him in touch with Pfeffer, introduced him to a salesman who came there. By the time he was discharged he had the job.

In Corpus it was lying on the beach on Padre Island on the Gulf, thinking about San Diego, thinking about Lisa, who had kept writing and who had gone to secretarial school in Chicago and then to a job in Tucson; she was waiting for him. He was not thinking much about the place he was in, not thinking much about the future at all. It was in Corpus that he started to drink heavily, glasses of whiskey without ice or water, with a twist of lemon. Though at times he thought about Bisbee and high school and Naco, he seldom got back beyond that to his childhood, and only when his days got short did he begin to study Pfeffer's instrument catalogues and other corporate literature. He went back to Chicago to see his mother when he got out, but didn't stay long. He had a week, and he spent most of his time driving around in his mother's car, passing vaguely familiar streets, trying to find houses, stores and other places where he had spent time. He found some; others had been torn down; some were in circumstances that had changed so drastically that they and the feelings he vaguely wished to get from them were irretrievable. He walked sidewalks in the centers of the old towns, but he did not come upon a single person he recognized. He tried to remember childhood friends, their faces and gestures and what they might be like were he to meet them, and in doing this he came to recognize that he had had no friends in his childhood, that the faces were vague to him because he never had looked into them in the first place; he had not known them at all. He had been nine when they left for Bisbee, and he had left nothing behind him.

The streets of the old town, the small octagonal centers with wasted World War Two shrines in tiny untended parks, the changed and absent stores and houses, these were west of Chicago in the old suburbs where he had lived, alone, with his parents. His father was dead now, his mother into a new life there, one that was indifferent to him. He had no relatives; like his parents, he was an only child. And since then his mother had died too, and when he returned from Portland for her funeral there was nothing left for him at all.

Moving his head from the window, he looked down at the floor between his feet. He imagined the little horse down there, in her cage in the cargo hold. Maybe she was sleeping, maybe standing, looking around, alert. He was riding on air on her presence. He had come from one circumstance and he was going into another. He knew he could not release her and would not, at least for a long time. When he lifted his eyes, he saw the corner of the hat again. He would hold on to her also. He would give up neither of them without a fight.

———

And so they came to Mexico City, and if there was anything remarkable about their time there, given the volatile circumstances they came from, it was that nothing remarkable happened, at least for the first two months. Getting out of the airport proved as easy as leaving Chihuahua had been, and they reached their hotel, a small place off the Reforma, up by the Zona Rosa near the foot of Chapultepec, without incident. They sat in the back seat of the taxi, the metal animal container between them, and Mary Grace pointed out sights in the Zocalo and other places as they passed them. The air was warm, but there was a stiff breeze blowing, and the city was relatively free of smoke and pollution. Even the traffic was thin as they drove into the city. When they got to the desk, Mary Grace picked up the key and suggested that Paul go to their room while she checked for messages. There was one, a brief note from Johnny: *Wait one day.*

They unpacked a change of clothing, and after they had showered and dressed they went shopping. In the Zona Rosa they found shops where they got clothes for Paul. He had little cash with him, and rather than use his credit cards, Mary Grace paid for them. On the way back they bought some soda and bottled water and they found some rolled oats in a natural food shop. When they got back to the room, they fed the horse and then pulled the curtains across the window and rested. In a while they dressed again and went down to the hotel restaurant and ate. They took a brief walk in the evening, and when they returned they were both tired and after Paul had checked the horse's incision and they watched her walk around the room, exploring it, they went to bed. It was only ten o'clock by then but they slipped quickly into sleep.

The next morning there was another message waiting for them at the desk. Brief as the first had been, it stated only a appointment. They were to be at the Art Museum in Chapultepec that afternoon. They decided to spend most of the day in the room, but it was hard to stay there. They decided to go out, but not together, to spell each other.

Paul went first, walking the mile or so up the wide Reforma to the mouth of Chapultepec; he thought that he would find the museum, get the lay of the land, but when he entered the park he decided against it. He returned, walking the other side of the boulevard, stopping occasionally to browse in shops that caught his interest. When he got back, Mary Grace was itchy and ready to go. She was out an hour or more, and Paul spent the time of her absence urging the horse to move around the room. The room was too small for her to get any speed up, but Paul played with her a little, giving her at least a little stimulation. He checked her eyes, finding that they were clear, and he felt her, trying to get some sense of her temperature. She seemed warm, but he was not at all sure how to gauge what this meant in an animal of her kind and size. She was still weak, but she didn't seem feverish, and he thought that she had escaped infection. He wanted to wash her down, but he wasn't sure that he should do so; she was a little matted and there was some dirt and gnarls in her mane and tail, and he wished he had a decent brush and comb. He looked closely at her hooves, handling them in a way that he had not done before, and counted the jewels set in their walls. Even though he moved them and looked with care, he could discern no pattern that he could understand. Mostly the jewels were set deeply in, enough so that a palm passed over the hoof cleared them, but some protruded slightly, and he thought these might be working themselves loose as the wall of the hooves grew a little. He didn't know if hoof walls grew at all; he thought that there were parts of the hoof that did, but even of this he was unsure. He thought he'd better get a book about horses, and found himself laughing at the idea. As if any book could really tell him about her. He remembered the arrows that pointed to the hooves on Johnny's chart, but the messages at the arrow's ends had been enigmatic. Each hoof was different; there were differences in number, pattern and kinds of stones. Her left front hoof seemed the most promising. It was the most gem laden, and it was the elevated one in the chart. He looked at it with care, but in the end he could get it to yield nothing. He gave it up after a while, pushed her rump and got her walking again.

When Mary Grace came back, she brought some good cheese, crackers, and a quart bottle of beer. They ate a little, and then they left for the museum; they put the DO NOT DISTURB sign on the doorknob as they went out.

Chapultepec was not crowded; still, there were enough people walking the paths and visiting the various buildings so that Paul did not feel conspicuous. There were groups of school children in lines behind teachers, and there were a few tourists groups with guides leading them around. When they got to the art museum they lingered outside for only a moment. They had no good idea what was expected of them or what they should expect, but they knew they had to do something so they paid and went in. They stayed close together, moving from painting to painting, even tried to talk to one another about what they admired.

Paul saw the man before Mary Grace did. He was small, dressed in suit and tie, and he was standing at the railing that lined the broad stone staircase to the lower level. Paul nudged Mary Grace, and as she turned they both saw the man look at them. He nodded almost imperceptibly, and then he took the magazine he held in his hand and placed it deliberately on the stone bench at the rail beside him. He walked away then, moving to the far side of the room, to a place where he could see the bench.

Paul took Mary Grace's arm, and they went to the bench and sat down. They could not see the man now, and after they had sat for a few moments, Paul picked up the magazine and they rose and moved to another painting. When they were in a position where the place the man had been was visible to them, they saw that he was gone. They waited until they had left the museum, had made their way two blocks beyond it, before they found a bench to sit on, and checked the magazine. There was a note inside it, an address printed in a small, careful hand. When they had returned to the hotel, Mary Grace got a map from the desk, and when they were back in their room she located the place. It was a good thirty to forty miles from the city proper, in an area that looked hilly and rural, near a lake. They decided not to take a taxi from the hotel, but to pack up and carry their things the few blocks to the Reforma and catch one there. The city seemed full of taxis, and they thought any one of them would be hard to trace. It was five o'clock now, the rush hour, and there was plenty of traffic. It took them over a half hour to get free of the city itself.

A few miles beyond the outskirts, after they had passed the working-class suburbs and the makeshift rubble homes of destitute squatters who had come to crack the wealth of the city if only to gain some portion that would keep families alive and together, the road began its gradual twist and rise, moving beyond the dry lake basin in which Mexico City sat. The growth remained little more than scrub, but it thickened, and after a while there were taller trees and they could not see far ahead. They passed by farms in narrow valleys, a few meager towns, but when the road bent gradually to the right and climbed a little higher, they found themselves in an almost pure wilderness, high half-desert country, some cactus and scrub but mostly pine, aspen and oak.

They drove for another half hour, and when they reached what felt to them like a high plateau, the taxi slowed, its motor quit laboring, and they were in high growth on a dirt road that twisted severely. The driver was looking, but it was Mary Grace who saw the road sign, no more than a wooden cross with a word painted on it. She tapped the driver on the shoulder, leaned forward and pointed. He came almost to a stop, then turned sharply to the right. Now they were in a narrow, rutted lane. Paul could see that gravel, some of it fresh, had been spread in the deeper tire ditches. There were several bumps, but they did not bottom out, and in a few hundred yards of twists and turns they came to a small clearing where the road ended.

They put the animal container on the ground; its wire mesh was tight, protecting its interior from any clear sight from the outside, and though the horse moved and made sounds and the driver glanced at the container, they were sure he guessed nothing. He got their suitcases out of the trunk. Mary Grace paid him, and he worked the taxi around and moved off slowly, back down the rutted lane. They watched him go out of sight, and then they turned and looked around. At the end of the clearing was a path. It went straight for a few yards, and where it turned to the left they could see that it rose quickly and that there were sections of railroad ties set in and held by stakes that served as steps. They moved to the path and started up it, Mary Grace in front with one of the suitcases. It went on for only a short distance, perhaps fifty yards, but it was steep and they went slowly. Mary Grace was well above him when she reached the end of it and stopped. He saw her put her suitcase down beside her and stand and look, and in a few moments and after a few more steps he was beside her.

They were standing on an outcropping of rock. Below them was the lake, flat as a piece of glass. They could see the other side, but only barely, a few roofs tucked among trees, very small at this distance and only noticeable as the evening sun lit them. To the left, the rock rose up a little, and they could only see a few feet. The house was to the right, slightly below them, only fifty or so yards away. It was large and stucco white and had a red tile roof. From where they were, they were looking down into its patio and the deck that hung out a little over the lake's beach. There was a short wooden stairway leading from the front of the deck down to the beach, and a small sailboat and a rowboat had been pulled up on the sand near it. A wing of the house, on the far side of the patio, bent toward the lake, and they could see its line of sliding glass doors, entrance to the patio, opaque in the soft wash of late afternoon light. At their feet was a path leading down to a small porch at the side of the house. There was a door there, and as they looked at it it opened and a large woman with a bandanna around her forehead came out, followed by an old man in brown work clothes. She called out to them, hurrying along the path, the man behind her.

"¡Buenas tardes, buenas tardes! ¡Bienvenidos!"

Mary Grace answered her, and she and Paul followed them back to the house, the man lugging the two suitcases and Paul carrying the animal container. Inside the door was a small alcove and beyond it they could see half of the large living room. The windows at the far end of it were visible, and through them the lake gleamed like smoked glass now, as the sun lowered.

"Bienvenidos a la casa de Abelardo García," the woman said as they gathered close together in the alcove, and then she gestured toward the living room, and they followed her into it and to the back, where there was a hanging staircase that they ascended to an airy balcony, off which there were three doors. She led them to one, and they entered a large bedroom with a set of glass doors at the end of it, beyond which was a small patio set into the side of the hill that ran up from the water to the rear of the house. Paul stood to the side, still holding the animal container, and the old man put the suitcases down. Mary Grace and the

127

woman spoke briskly for a while, and then the woman smiled at Paul and nodded and she and the old man left the room, closing the door behind them.

They saw the couple only occasionally during the next two months, mostly in the mornings when they rose early. The woman would bring in groceries, and at times they would hear her moving in the kitchen as early as six o'clock. Once a week she cleaned the house, and on those days Paul and Mary Grace would stay away, exploring the lake edge in the rowboat or on foot, sometimes walking trails up in the hills to either side of the house. They would often take a picnic lunch, and at times they would come upon the old man working at a planter or pruning a tree. When he was aware of their presence he would quit whatever it was he was doing and retire, leaving them alone. The woman was friendly but never overbearing, and she took her lead in conversation from Mary Grace and listened carefully to the few Spanish words that Paul was able to address to her, answering him slowly and carefully, always with a smile.

The time went by slowly, and though it did not hesitate there was never that sense of quickening when days seem over before they are begun or are lost in anticipation of the next or in some furious activity that rushes them. They talked a lot, letting their conversations go where they wished to wander, not pushing them but staying with them until they moved to another place or until they moved and the change of place or landscape altered them. Sitting in cushioned outdoor chairs on the bricks of the patio, among flowers or on the weathered pine of the deck before them, above the beach and lake, drinking tonic at times or Campari, or when there was a chill in the air and a breeze, sitting inside and watching flowers, deck and lake through windows, they would see the flicker of lights go on at spots on the other side, see the flickers reflected on the lake's mirror halfway across.

And at midday they would walk the beach, would swim sometimes. The little horse would stand at the water's edge, her hooves beneath the surface, watching them. There was almost never a ripple on the lake, and the water below the surface was still and clear, and they would dive and see each other as if suspended in amber, and when they surfaced they would see the horse, standing and waiting where they had left her.

The horse led them along the beach, and it was she who found the little coves and the caves back in under the rock overhang. She took them into the caves, and it was she who raised her head so that when they looked where she looked they found veins of minerals in the rock, opalescent, some narrow and perfectly defined lines of copper, others that looked like onyx and gold. They studied the lovely patterns, the way seeping water wet the rock in different places, the miniature alluvial fans where the sand gathered at the walls. And it was she too who took them off the hilly trails, led them into hidden byways where wild flowers grew and once took them to a vine-covered arbor where they had to stoop to pass inside, where they found the remnants of a child's hideaway: broken, makeshift little chairs and table, a wooden spoon, and bits of bleached adult clothing, weather-worn beyond certain recognition.

The horse was filling out, losing the edge of thinness she had taken on after her surgery. The old man left small bales of hay in a shed to the side of the house, and they fed her only bits of it, but often, and she was eating well. There were brushes in the shed as well, and Paul brushed her in the morning and Mary Grace did the same in the late afternoon. Her tail fell, long, silken and thick, like its own alluvial fan, over her golden haunches, and when she moved it swayed. Her mane, parted down the middle now, fell in yellow waves along her neck. Her eyes were perfectly clear, and she held her head up; she was alert, and the glove leather of her tan nostrils opened and closed easily when she breathed. Her wide hooves had lightened perceptibly in color into a rich creamy yellow, and the occasional flash of the jewels in them was no longer prominent against their new luster. She was losing some of the jewels; her increased activity and what Paul took to be some growing within the hoof wall pushed them out. They would protrude and sparkle singly for a day or two, and then Paul would look for them, and they'd be gone. Only the slight concavity that had been their setting remained as evidence of their going. And then that too would disappear, heal over, and Paul and Mary Grace would note it with pleasure. She was growing stronger and healthier, and the jewels going was not a loss but a kind of clock measuring their gain, hers and theirs: she was getting better, and they were getting to know each other. It wasn't long before it was time to take the stitches out, and when he did she suffered their removal with no evident pain. The incision was completely healed, and only a faint white line remained.

She sat with them in the evenings, would climb up into a leather easy chair. Her tail hung almost to the floor, fanned out, and the gentle downy slope of her barrel and flank displayed itself. She held her head high, and she watched them as they talked, moving slightly to the source of the words, her nostrils opening slightly, and sometimes Mary Grace would sit on the arm of her chair and caress her neck and scratch her.

And the evenings passed. They were long, languorous, and relaxed. They would eat simple desserts in the living room, cheese and fruit occasionally, and when it got late they would drink brandy or warm milk with nutmeg. Mary Grace told him her memories of their first meeting and their brief affair. He had been her first virgin, in a way, though not her last, but he had been the way she thought a virgin should be, passionate, quick, but with an air of gratefulness that softened both the passion and the quickness, a little fumbling and awkward, but careful, wondering in the details but a little abstracted because of the awareness of the occasion. Her own virginity, she said, had been torn from her, though the act itself was gentle enough. The man had been a little drunk, and he was in her and then through with her before she had been able to experience even the beginning of it. And even the pain was over too quickly, and she did not really remember much about it at all. She imagined she must have hurt the next day, but she wasn't even sure about that. She remembered Paul, she said, because he had made her feel both wise and vulnerable at the same time. She remembered the responsibility she felt with him. She wanted to make his first time the way it should be, as her first time should have been, not necessarily good, but at least memorable, a touchstone in his memory, or at least a remembered ritual of change.

He told her that much she had accomplished, that he had thought of her often. She said she did not want to make too much of this first-time business, though; it was just that for her it was the beginning of something, a kind of knowing, that went beyond it almost to now. He wasn't sure what she meant exactly, how this fit into what she had told him of her life so far, which was close to nothing. He realized that he had asked her very little about her life so far, surely less than was appropriate, and that he had told her very little about his own as well. And then he realized that he really didn't want to know or tell and that the past, his as well as hers, was not the point at all. At least he didn't think it was. Still, he thought that they should say something, say some things about it. He told her this. She said, "Come here," almost whispered it, and they laughed lightly and smiled at each other, and then went up to bed.

═══

The horse ran in the shallows at the lake's edge, her hooves kicking up a spray that at times would envelope her whole body. She would kick her legs at times, dip her head and throw up jets of water. Sometimes she would veer into the lake and swim out a good fifty yards, only her head visible on the surface. At first this frightened them, but they soon saw that she had her bearings. She would pause in the water and her head would rotate, and she would swim back again, and when she walked out of the lake and got up on the sand she would shake herself like a wet dog, and then she would run off down the beach. They took to letting her out alone after a while, and sometimes in the dusk they would watch her from the living-room windows, see her run by in the water at the lake's edge. She did not stay out long, and in a few minutes they would see her standing on the patio, at the glass doors, looking in at them. They'd let her in, would sometimes wipe her down with a dry towel, and then she would go to her chair and settle in for the evening.

Abelardo García's house was a beautiful and comfortable place to spend time. Its appointments were not unlike the ones Paul had made note of when they'd paused that evening after Johnny's show in Chihuahua. Here the artifacts too were more than shards, and the house had lovely hangings on its walls. Paul wondered some about the place, about García and Johnny's tie to him. He spoke to Mary Grace about this, and she said she would ask Loíza, the housekeeper, But Loíza had no answer, and Mary Grace seemed to have no real interest in the matter. Paul could find no evidence of the house being lived in. Everything seemed new and unused, and in time it was as if the place were their own, their own first home.

Johnny called twice in the first month of their stay. He and Mary Grace talked for a long time, intensely, in Spanish. Paul understood nothing of what was said, but he could hear the urgent passing of information in her tone, slightly muffled from the alcove where the phone was. After the calls, they would wait until the evening and she would relate the news. There wasn't much either time, at least none that altered their situation.

Parker and his men had indeed been around for a while, but though the word was still out for the little horse, those who knew of it no longer seemed pressed to get what they could by finding it. There was still much talk; the subject came up frequently, but it was now often a story told over drinks. There had to be some people still searching, of course, and this was not to be ignored, but Johnny thought that they should hold tight where they were, try not to worry, to let things fall out as they might in time. His second call, as Mary Grace reported it, reaffirmed this advice. He had heard nothing new.

One morning Mary Grace set to work early in the kitchen. He was awakened by the sounds of her clattering below, and when he was dressed he and the horse went downstairs to see what was going on. The counter beside which she was washing vegetables—small cherry tomatoes, scallions and peppers—was full of good things. There were three kinds of cheeses wrapped in foil, two bottles of white wine, bunches of grapes, a couple of tins of paté, and various packages of thin crackers. Beside this was the cooler, and a loaf of crusty bread, a jar into which butter had been spooned, and various small cakes. When he went into the living room he saw that the beach umbrella and canvas bag with the blankets and towels in it were ready at the glass doors. He came back into the kitchen smiling.

"I guess it's a picnic today?" he said.

"Sí, Pablo; load the boat, will you?"

"Hokay," he said, and he went up to the bedroom and got his hat and changed into shorts and then came back down and took the umbrella and the bag and put them in the boat. There were a couple of folding beach chairs under the deck, and he loaded them in also. The horse followed him, staying almost at heel, touching her muzzle from time to time against his knee. When he was finished Mary Grace was ready, and he lugged the heavy metal cooler down to the beach and put it in the prow.

It was eight-thirty when they rowed out and away from shore. The sun was already bright and there was just the edge of a breeze, not even enough to stir the mane of the horse where she stood, like a still figurehead in the prow, but enough to keep them from sweating. They headed down the beach, Paul rowing and Mary Grace watching the shoreline. When they were a good half mile from the house, Mary Grace called out. He turned and saw her pointing, and then he worked the boat in toward the shore. As the prow scraped on the sand, the horse leapt out, landing with a splash in the shallows, trotted up on the beach and shook herself briefly and then took off at a gallop. She ran a good hundred yards, but before she went out of sight where the shore turned, she pulled up and turned around to look back at them. They laughed, and Mary Grace clapped her hands together loudly and the horse sprinted back toward them.

Paul and Mary Grace got out, and Paul pulled the prow of the boat up on the sand, throwing the anchor into the shallows at their feet. Then he unloaded their gear and food. Mary Grace got the blankets out and spread them on the sand, back and slightly under the overhang of rock above them, still in the sun. Paul set up the folding chairs. The place was a small inlet where the beach went under the rock overhang. At the very back was a cave. The horse went into it when she returned from her run, but by the time they were set up she was back out again, standing and watching them. To the left they could see for quite a distance, but to the right, in the direction of the house, they could only see down the beach for a short way. They were at a place where the shoreline turned and the rock on that side jutted out slightly, a huge boulder protruding almost into the lake itself. Back where they had set up, the breeze, what little there was, was completely cut off, and only when they moved to the lake edge could they feel its touch on their faces.

They put the cooler behind, in the shade at the mouth of the cave, and then they adjusted the blanket a little, pulling the ends out. They moved their chairs slightly, getting them where they wanted, and then they sat down. Their movements had been quick and efficient, and when they were finished only the horse was still moving. She had been watching them, moving herself into positions where she could be close to them and see, but far enough so as not to be in the way. Now she circled to the beach side of their blankets and chairs and stood between them and the lake and looked at them. She dipped and threw her head back, and it was as if they had finished their work too efficiently, had rushed time a little, and ought to have more to do. They laughed at the anticipation they saw in the horse's face and head movements, and they turned in their chairs and looked at each other.

They rose and took their clothes off slowly, watching each other do it. Neither of them wore underwear, and when she stretched to pull her jersey over her head he saw the half moon curves of the bottoms of her elevated breasts and the line of black hair running down from her navel. She dropped her jersey on the blanket, watching where it fell, and as she brought her eyes back up to look at him, she took her breasts, one cupped in each palm, and lifted them. He could see the rose polish on the nails of her index fingers where they touched the flesh under her nipples. She looked down at them, and when she did this he could see the faint rose color of dust on her lids.

When her head came back up, she was smiling a twisted smile, and her eyes stopped at his stomach, the smile opening and the tip of her tongue touching her upper lip as he unzipped his shorts and let them fall to the sand and stepped out of them. He felt himself hang free in the air as his legs parted.

They moved across the blanket toward each other, and though his eyes were intent on watching her face, imagining himself in her eyes, anticipating being in her mouth, he caught the slight sparkle in the corner of his eye and glanced fleetingly for the source of it. He thought he saw a brief pinpoint of light, a sudden flash on the other side of the lake; it flickered twice, and then it was gone. He caught the slightly quizzical expression on the horse's face below the place where the light had blinked and very close to him, and then he moved his eyes back to Mary Grace's body, bringing them up across her hip and the dark curled bush at her crotch, to her small navel, her breasts and her face again.

Then they were on each other on the blanket and in the sand; they were in each other, his mouth in hair and musk, his tongue in her dark ring. He felt her nails scrape his testicles, raking them, her lips at his rim, penetration, and then the coolness, the wash as he left the sun and entered her, her words in their private language not heard but touched into him, alive in his brain. And then real talk and turning and other entrances. And at one point she lowered herself down upon him, and before he disappeared into her he saw the little horse standing behind her, framed in the arch made by her spread legs. The flat mirror of the lake was beyond it. The horse looked like a statue enshrined. Her eyes were constant and knowing. She did not look accusatory, but she looked distantly wise and judgmental. There was nothing of idea in her. She was a detail, and yet somehow beyond that; in a frieze possibly. She did not move a muscle. Ever her open nostrils were fixed in place. He thought she had the power of marble, the resolve of hard yellow hickory. Her presence seemed to keep him where he was, as if he and not she were the witness, in the exquisite details, the only place where he now thought was life.

And there were other days passed in similar ways, some on the beach, others in various places in the house. But there was never anticipation of them such that its urgency blocked out the day they were in, one in which there was no physical contact, but reading, talking and exploring. And sometimes the best part was after hours of touching. They began to construct a history of themselves at this place. They would sit in the living room in the evenings and recall things, a day on the beach, a hike on some particular evening when late sun had made the flowers seem to swell, each detail of a particular event in each others arms. They held soft bites of each other's flesh in their mouths and told tales to each other in them, remembrances of what things had felt like to them hours before. They trailed off in their separate pasts at times, but never more than briefly; they were too full of the present, and only what they shared seemed truly meaningful. Each came to know of the other's past in snatches and disconnected bits. Paul learned of her country sources, somewhere further south, of a period of study at the university in Tucson, fragments of a rape, a dead mother, and another brother. She learned about Lisa, his divorce, travels with Pfeffer, Illinois, Corpus Christi and alcohol. They each constructed the narratives from such pieces, but both knew that the stories they made of them were only tales, and as such not to be trusted. If there is such a thing as a true past, and if it is needed to really know a person, they really did not know each other at all. They knew this, but they neither trusted the construct nor the necessity of one. They had their days, or their days had them, and this was enough for them.

One afternoon, Paul came upon Mary Grace on the deck sketching. She had found charcoal and paper in the desk in the library; she told him she had sketched some as a child, and thought she would give it a try again. She was making studies of the little horse. It was posing for her, standing still a few feet from the railing. Once she began she didn't want to stop. She would sketch flowers in a planter, the rock formations along the beach, the house itself. But in all the sketches the little horse appeared. The drawings were good, if simple, but she said she could not seem to get the horse right, couldn't capture her. After a while, she gave it up, but not before Paul tried to help her. He began to comb the horse more carefully in the mornings, began to clean its ears and teeth, to scrape bits of dirt and growth remnants from its hooves. Its activities on the beach and in the woods had knocked most of the remaining jewels free from their settings, and there were now only two opals, five diamonds, a moonstone, and a couple he could not identify. He thought that the better he could get the horse, the more cleaned up and elegant, the better chance at the right drawing for Mary Grace.

While he was cleaning the sole of one of her hooves, using not just the stiff brush, but a knife, he scraped some dead pigment away and discovered the slot. He was on the patio. Mary Grace was in the kitchen, and without telling her he took the horse into the shed where the bales of hay were kept. It took him only a short time to get the cups out, to discover the diamonds. He poured them out on the wooden bench in the shed in a small gleaming pyramid. He ran his finger through them, looked at a few carefully, then put them back in their cups and locked the cups back into the hooves. He knew that this was an answer to a lot of things, a suggested answer to others. Though it had nothing to do with why they had taken the horse and kept it, it surely accounted for why they were pursued. He hadn't counted the stones, but the little pyramid had risen inches on the table's surface. He thought the diamonds were very valuable. The trickiness of the hiding places in the horse's hooves was something he could not figure.

He hurried back to the house to tell Mary Grace about the diamonds, but when he got there he did not tell her. He wasn't sure why, but he felt that it had something to do with what now seemed a delicate balance, something precious that he might lose if he told her. It would change things somehow, and he didn't want change. He knew he would have to tell her before long. To hide it from her would itself be change, but he decided to wait a little, for a few hours at least. When he got to the kitchen, the horse trailing behind him, he came up behind her, slipped his hands under her arms, and cupped her breasts in his hands and kissed her neck. She laughed lightly.

"So early, Pablo?"

===

And there were times in which they had gotten beyond lust, both the frantic and energetic kind and the kind they arrived at lazily after hours of sun and talk, in the late evenings after a light dinner and a little drink. She would twist her smile or she would get herself where he could see her while he was watching the horse or lake, and the touch of both these actions would be ripe with casualness that, while not always practiced, was knowing. She knew things, and it was close to the beginning that he gave up any tactics of mastery. He knew nothing comparable, not a thing as rich, jaded or touching, and he gave in quickly and became a follower. And then he was as quickly connected again as her skill carried him to new levels of passion in which he discovered his own powers. They were powers of immediacy, and like the powers of good dancers, of the ones who are led in dancing, they were attuned to the here and now, to nuance that was specific in her. It took him a while to know that she was not being touched in the way he was, but thoughtfully, almost historically, touched into revision and not what he wanted to think was love.

Soon enough he was past passion's novelty and new thrill, and while he surely knew that sex was the proper avenue, the only right one for reaching and undoing her, he became aware that they were not really getting there at all, but that the sealed circle in her was only receding and tightening; he was getting under her skin, and that was closer, but the place he needed to get to had tightened beyond elasticity and remained apart. He thought of it as undoing her, using the word in a literal kind of way: untying her, releasing her from bondage, helping her to get loose. But he recognized his dip into egocentricity and ignorance; what did he know about it, who was another kind of virgin?

It was the horse, finally, who helped them, not once but often. It was she, in her attention to details and in her humor and in her very presence, who helped to the temporary breaking and entrance. It closed again, always, but the entrance was real, and for him that gave her a promise she could not have been aware of before it happened.

He had his head between her legs, his cheek resting against her thigh, his ear hearing a deep artery within her. She was leaning back in the couch cushions, her arms leisurely thrown out, and he was sitting on the floor below her. He could look up into her, her damp hair, the rise of her belly beyond it, her wet and flattened breasts, and then her neck and her tilted chin, her head slightly to the side; breathing deeply, looking out the glass windows beyond the chair where the horse sat. She turned and lifted her head up and looked down at him, her lips and cheeks glistening with his sweat and fluids, her eyes shining and focused, and he knew his own face and mouth were glistening too; he could feel the faint touch of one of her black hairs along his nose and cheek; it had caught between his teeth and been plucked out, and he could see the beads of fresh sweat on her shoulders.

Her face was beautiful and relaxed and giving, but he could still see evidence of the thing that could not be broken into at the corners of her eyes. She smiled, but the tightness and the edge of distant care remained there; he turned his head slightly and sucked in a piece of her soft flesh and she warbled very quietly, and when he looked back it was still there. She was above him, still in possession of herself wrongly, and though he did not value loss of control or sex or moisture or even intimacy at that moment, he was drawn to sadness by her inability to come through him and escape, even for a moment. He was quickly angry and frustrated, but he did not let her see it, and to hide it from her he called out softly and with mock urgency and command, "I'm thirsty; bring me water!"

He heard a sound, and when he looked up at her, her head turned again and he knew she heard it too. She was watching something he could not see. Then he saw the horse coming. It had a glass in its mouth, a tall glass. It had taken the whole rim in its mouth, and its neck was bowed, its head pointing directly at the floor so that the glass would stand upright below its muzzle. It was prancing slightly, keeping the water in the glass still. And though its head was down, its eyes were open and elevated and looking at them when it came into his view; its head, then the glass, appearing over the smooth curve of her thigh. Its lips curled back from the circle of the rim, making a larger circle as Mary Grace reached out for the glass, and when she took it from the horse's mouth the horse stepped back, then brought its head up, neighed softly and looked at her and at him.

He looked up at Mary Grace. She had raised the glass up in the lamp light at arm's length, and he could see the pearly saliva circle shine around its rim. She brought it down then and brought it to her glistening face and lips and drank deeply; then she reached it down to Paul. It was still half full, and when he drank from it he could taste her and the horse and himself in the cool water. He looked back up at Mary Grace and he somehow knew in the way she looked at him that she had tasted the same thing. Something broke then in the corners of her eyes, her pupils dilated and he felt that he was looking deeper than he had before. Then he saw the tears at the corners of her eyes and felt his own on his cheeks. They looked into each other's faces for a long moment, and then they both turned and looked at the horse.

The horse's eyes were wide open, her pupils also slightly dilated. Her head was very still, and the tears fell, spaced out in the air, clear small globes in the lamplight; there were dozens of them. He knew that Mary Grace's mouth was in that O, though he was gazing at the weeping horse and could not see her. In a while the tears stopped falling, and the horse moved back a step, then paused again. Then it moved its head, up and down, slowly nodding. Paul came up then slowly from the floor, moved over Mary Grace's shining body, and entered her anew.

——

"It's only a name given to the way a person can behave. It sounds like psoriasis, and it too is an itch that can't be scratched away. It's when a man can't get enough of sex, simply can't get enough, and is never satisfied. I think you got it, Paul."

"Don't make me laugh."

Sitting in the living room again, drinking tea in the evening after dinner, little cookies on the glass table, the little horse lounging in her leather chair.

"Well, you act like it sometimes." She smiles her crooked smile, arm on the couch back, twists her body in a lovely way, her legs along the cushion.

"Well, really, it's not funny. There was a man in our neighborhood when I was growing up," she says. "He had it. It was a small place, and everybody knew almost everything about everybody else. He did it with his wife all the time. He would come home at lunch. He only had an hour, and it was a long way, and we would see him almost run into the house to get it. People on the job and his neighbors, who included almost everyone in the town, laughed at him behind his back, and there were dark stories that he even did it with his children, a young boy and girl. Nobody laughed openly at the children. Everybody felt sorry for them because of what they thought he did to them. They were worn looking even though they were eight and ten, and they were quiet and didn't talk much about anything. Out of ignorance, we were cruel I think because we didn't see how frantic the man really was, how frustrated. We couldn't see how he worked to keep it private, to not go after other women, or other men. He did go away sometimes, to other towns. When he came back he seemed calmer, but this would only last a day and then he would have those creases in his forehead again, those quick, disjointed movements.

"What I want to tell you, though, is not about him. Both he and his wife had been born of mixed marriages, one parent Mexican and one gringo, and the children were more American-looking than they were Mexican. He killed himself when the children were just teenagers, shot himself in the head with a pistol one morning. People were eating breakfast when they heard the bang. Afterward, it got out from one of the policemen who was talkative that when they found him he was in a room at the back of the house.

"In the room was a miniature wood-and-cardboard village he had been working on. He must have been at it for a long time, years maybe. It filled the whole room. There were houses and public buildings, roads with real dirt in them, even carefully carved figures of people and animals, small horses and cattle, little cats and dogs. Everything aimed at scale, but the man had not been a good craftsman, and the place was strange, a kind of dream landscape, because the scale was slightly off. The people were too big to get inside the houses, and the houses were too tall and narrow, the streets too wide. He had done good with the horses and cattle, but the cats and dogs were as big as they were and looked like beasts from a much earlier time.

"I don't know. They say it looked as frustrated as he did, and so he killed himself when he saw he could not escape himself by constructing it. I don't really know. But it's the boy, his son, that I want to tell you about.

"After the father died, the mother tried hard to keep the family together, but she couldn't manage it. She had to send her daughter off to live with her sister. There was some rumor that the real reason had to do with the boy's behavior, that he was fooling around with his sister, but this could just as well have been some spillover rumor, something to fill the lack of things to talk about when the father was gone. At any rate, it soon became clear that the boy was like his father; he had it too, and even the older, experienced women who liked it that they could have it from him were not enough for him. He couldn't get enough, and there was talk he was doing it with animals as well as women and as many of the girls his own age as he could get. He was nervous, quick to anger, delinquent, and on his way downhill.

"Then something happened. I don't know why it happened. Some said he was sleeping with his mother, that she did it as the only way to soothe him, and that this was the cause of it. He simply stopped himself. He didn't get any less nervous or less wild-eyed, but he got very involved in things, things that brought him money. He started to make book, and even while he was still only fifteen he had a hand in the organization of horse races in the neighboring town. He did other public things: prize-fighting and wrestling when it got going strong. He seemed to like the violence, and so he promoted them and made money at it. The older women quit trying to get him after a while. The rumors were replaced by other kinds of rumors. It was said he was getting involved in things that had to do with sex, but that he himself was now sexless. Before he was seventeen his face hardened into a kind of mask. I don't know what happened after that. That was about the time I left, and when I came back in the beginning for visits I didn't notice him around and there was no talk. So I don't know what became of him. I think what happened is just that he put his energies elsewhere. There's a name for that, too. I don't know why it happened; all the rumored explanations of it were too simple as far as I'm concerned. I think that unlike his father he found a place where he could put his passion, his drive, a place where he could get the pressure released. That's not odd, I guess. What is odd though is that he shut his own sexuality off completely and got involved in a darker sexuality, in another way. How it turned out dirty for him I can't say, but I suspect that the need was to just drive it into the ground, to force it through the dirt into oblivion, to keep trying to get rid of it. It seems right that it was his mother who turned him out.

Everyone saw him as better off than he had been, but even at seventeen his eyes were a little vacant. I remember that when he was chasing after women his eyes were clear and sharp."

=====

The days went on without another call from Johnny. One day the time seemed right to him and he told her about the diamonds. He took the horse into the bedroom, removed the cups and showed her the stones. She was hurt that he had kept it from her, but the hurt was appropriate, and they talked about it. Contrary to his fears, it did not change things for either of them. He told her about his fears and how he had tried to protect what they had by not telling her. She understood, and in a way they both were glad for the test, and felt both reassurance and greater confidence in each other because of it.

The little horse took them down the beach as if they were children. They, on the other hand, felt like the parents of a precocious child. The horse found more caves, passages through the rock formations that went by circuitous routes to the cliffs above the beach. She led them to the discovery of patches of wild berries. She taught them, through her example, how to be alert and satisfied, how to sit in a place for a long time when there seemed nothing to be interested in and then to discover interest. They would take their chairs down to the beach and look out on the surface of the still lake. When they sat there long enough, they would discover the way the colors altered as the sun moved. Their evenings on the deck and patio and in the living room became longer, more punctuated by spaces of silence that they were comfortable in. He remained passionate, she receptive and, in her way, almost passionate too, and they made love whenever they felt like it, in a great variety of ways and places.

There was a dull knowing in them that each felt at various times, about Parker, the little horse, the diamonds, but Mary Grace had great confidence in Johnny, and Paul trusted her perception of him, and in time the knowing got to them more seldom, and it grew almost imperceptible. He found he had to work now to think of her as a prostitute, to bring up imaginings of all those men, to feel the anxiety and pain that made him just another sexual customer. After a while he quit working to think of it. He knew he had been testing his feelings hard and that the test was now over. He felt he knew her now as well as he knew anyone or ever had. What he didn't know was that the sex was getting good for her, not the pleasure of her control or her new love for him, but the sex itself. And he couldn't know, though she told him, that this was a totally new thing for her and was of extreme importance in the way it went beyond itself into something basic and of person and integrity and of the very self. She said she felt like the perfect virgin, the way that ought to be. First you figure how everything works and then when you've got it down pat, it all comes together at thirty-two. What a world if everyone was trained that way, what an explosion, no, a slow tapping of deep pleasure, in and of the self. She laughed when she said this, making a joke of it, but underneath it she was dead serious.

And the little horse grew even stronger and more beautiful. They found themselves watching her hardening muscles move, the way she held her tail, the clear pools of her eyes. And they found when they looked in mirrors that their eyes were as clear as hers, their pupils sharply focused, their brows flat and relaxed. When they sat in the living room in the evenings, the moonlight washing off the lake and through the glass, they felt that they had nothing at all to gain.

———

They came at them on a particularly lovely evening. They were quick, and though there was some fumbling awkwardness because they were not fully sure of the interior of the living room they gave them no time at all to recognize their loss. The sun was sinking, its light refracted by low cloud cover at the horizon across the lake; the total surface of the flat water they could see from where they sat, the horse in her chair, Paul in another and Mary Grace unwound on the couch, had turned rose red. There was no breeze, and all the flowers in the planters on the patio were as still as paintings, and all of them, their stems, leaves and petals, were dusted a light rose color, as if a kind of glaze or thin wash had been applied to the canvas. It was as if there were no glass in the windows. They had the plush comfort of the inside and the delicate exhilaration of the outside at the same time. Even the filament ends of the little horse's mane and tail were touched with rose, and he could see a rose blush on her cheek and the edge of her brow. They lifted their amber

143

brandy, and when they sipped and looked into the snifters they could see faint rose water in the pool.

He saw her head rise quickly and smoothly from where it rested on her hooves; her ears were erect and pricked, and he could see her face elongate slightly, her lips pull back, and the dome of her right eye swell. She was staring into the patio, listening, and her head slowly cocked to the side slightly. Her tail twitched at its roots. Then she turned her head back over her shoulder to look behind him. He saw her eyes expand, her pupils contract, and the skin at her forehead ripple slightly, and as her mouth opened he heard them coming from the alcove.

They were on him from behind as he was beginning to rise. He caught a glimpse of one of them, then saw Parker coming around the end of the couch. Mary Grace was turning. Then he smelled the chloroform. A hand had gripped his shoulder as he was rising. He was not far enough up to push against it. He went with it, throwing himself back as hard as he could, flinging his arms out. The back of his right hand caught one of them in the face. There was a yell and a stumbling, and he was able to turn to the right enough to jerk free of the hand that had his shoulder. As he turned, he saw Gabriel at the glass table. He had a rifle and he was pointing it at the chair where the horse was. Paul couldn't see the horse, but he heard the dull thump as Gabriel fired. Hands groped at him as he jerked around in the chair and caught a glimpse of the horse rising, the dart embedded in the cushion of the chair's back. He got his left arm free, saw hair over his shoulder, and reached for it. When he got it, he pulled it, ramming the face down into the bone of his shoulder. He heard her yell out, "Paul!" She seemed to try to yell again, but her voice was muffled.

"Get the fucking horse!" It was Parker. A forearm locked around his throat, and a hand came down with something in it. The smell of chloroform again, and he twisted his head and sunk his teeth into the pad below the thumb. The hand ripped back. Another yell. He saw Gabriel cross in front of him, heading for the couch, heard someone move away behind him. They had him then, one locked on each arm, his arms pulled back to the sides and behind the chair.

"Get the pad." The voice was soft and controlled and very close to his right ear. The grip on his left arm altered, and then he saw the wadding out of the corner of his eye. It came in from the side and covered his nose and mouth. He tried to hold his breath, but he had none to hold, and he had to suck it in. His head was held as if in a vise and he could only see in front of him. He saw the doctor pass, heard stumbling to his left. Then he heard the horse's scream.

It was high-pitched, almost ethereal, and it went on for a long time. It was not a scream of fear. It had the power of a train's whistle blown in the echo chamber of a station. His wrists moved involuntarily; he wanted to cover his ears against it.

"¡Jesus mil veces!" somebody yelled, but the words were swallowed in the scream.

"Get her! Dino! Get her!"

And then he saw her. He was almost out. He had to work hard to keep his eyes open. The flowers on the patio were slipping, the rose wash growing brighter, more brilliant, causing them to recede behind it. And even in his mind's growing dullness he knew that it was incredible that she came from behind him. He heard the scream approaching, growing even louder. He forced his scalp back, trying to lift his brows, keep his eyes open. And then she entered the side of his vision. She was in the air, at a level with his head, and just in front of him. He saw her forelegs extended, hooves together as if in a dive, the reach of her neck, her head at the end and parallel to it, her mane floating free of her crest. When she hit the floor in front of him, she was half way between the chair and the windows. He saw her rear legs extended behind her, saw them come down so that her rear hooves landed directly behind her front hooves on the floor. Her tail opened like a fan when she landed. Then he saw the muscles in her quarters bunch and gather, her gaskins tense. Her head came down, her muzzle pointing at the floor, and when she leapt forward her forelegs were limp-wristed, her hooves hanging down from her knees, and the fan of her tail closed into a thick rope.

For a moment it seemed as if there truly were no glass in the doors, that she would hit the patio at the end of her leap and in two more would make the deck and then the beach. Then the glass door in front of him turned opaque. He saw Gabriel and another man come into his vision from either side. Their hands were extended before them; they were leaning ahead in mid-stride, reaching out for her. There was a loud cracking sound as her forehead struck the glass, and as Gabriel and the other pulled up, their arms moved back in front of their faces. Her body slipped through the shattering as if it were liquid. His eyes were beginning to swim, he was losing focus, but he thought he saw the knife edges of the hole she was in closing on her haunches as they passed through it, the points combing her tail. Then she was gone. What he heard was a tinkling at a great distance. It was in a rose haze. He thought it was the slow shattering of some delicate glass flower.

Chapter 11

He was awake, but he could not get his head up. He was on a couch of some sort; it felt like leather against his cheek. It was dark, but there was some light, a dim bluish color, and when he moved his eyes he could see the edge of a raised platform, thick cables on the floor, the legs of a tripod. In a while he found he could turn his head, could even lift it slightly. There was something across his chest and his legs were bound somehow at the ankles. The room was square, white cinder block; it had perforated panels on its dropped ceiling. Along one wall was a kind of stage setting, an overstuffed chair and a small Victorian table. There was a painting, hanging on a fake wall behind it, a lurid piece, horses running in surf tinted to look like flames. The chair faced the platform, and by turning his head slightly he could see that the platform was covered with pillows, various fabrics, paisleys and brushed cottons. Behind the platform, at the other side of the room, was a heavy wooden device, vertical four by-fours and a crosspiece of the same dimensions. There was a thick canvas sling hanging down from it, and at the side of one of the vertical beams was a handle, some kind of crank. The whole structure was painted; vines and flowers in various colors twisted around the wood. At its base, the structure rested on large rubber wheels. His neck began to hurt him and he lowered his head again.

When he woke up he smelled something and he heard a heavy wheezing. There were people talking now, and as he reached for the words the lights suddenly came on. He lifted his head slightly and saw

146

someone coming toward him. It was Gabriel. When he leaned over him, he could see the pudgy face, sweat in the mustache, and could smell bay rum.

"You're awake? Good," he said, and then his face turned away. "Rudy. Give me a hand."

They took the strap from his chest and lifted him and carried him to the chair. When they had him in it, they took other straps, and after they had removed his shirt they tightened one around his chest under his arms and another around his stomach; then they put his shirt back on. He could feel Gabriel's sharp fingernails as he tucked the shirt in at his waist, and when they were done he saw him coming at him with a wet cloth and a comb. Gabriel washed his face and then, standing between his legs and bending over, he worked the comb carefully through his hair, using his free hand to fluff and arrange it. He could see the others in the room through the doctor's movements, and he could now see the dark shape of the animal he had smelled and heard standing off in a corner, dipping its head down and eating something from the floor. He thought it was a pony or a small mule, a donkey maybe; its ears seemed long enough for that. He heard a scraping, and when he looked back in front of him to the platform he saw that they were moving it, four of them, one at each corner, lifting it and carrying it away. On the other side of where it had been there were two women. They were dressed in robes. One had her legs crossed, her robe open, and he could see thin straps at her thighs, the edges of dark stockings, and some tightly fitted outfit rising to her naked breasts. He thought her breasts had makeup on them, a blue that enlarged her aureoles. The outfit, nipped in at the waist, had vertical ribs, feathers where it fanned out brushing her breasts. Both of the women were sitting in high-backed wooden chairs facing him. He caught the look of one of them, a peroxided blond, and though her eyes seemed close to vacant, she smiled. He could see bits of lipstick on her teeth. He looked at the other one. Her hair was darker, but there were remnants of blond at the tips. She saw him looking and raised her arm and extended it and pointed her finger at him; he heard the faint click of the heavy rings at her wrist. Then he heard another sound, and he turned his head. It was the tripod he had seen earlier. It held a large movie camera, and someone behind it altered its position. When he heard the voice he knew it was Parker.

"Ollie. You and Flaco get the rack ready. And fix the lighting. Gabriel. Is he okay? Does he need more?"

The doctor came back to him again. He lifted his hand up to his face, and Paul flinched and withdrew from it.

"It's okay," he said softly, and then he brought his hand up again, lifted one of Paul's lids, bent over and looked in. He took a pencil light from somewhere and shone it in his eye, then moved it away.

"He's coming back too much; I'll give him more."

"Yeah. Well, *see* to it. We're almost ready."

He used a tourniquet, injecting him in the vein in the crook of his left elbow. It came on with a rush, and he felt he was standing up and falling backward. His head hit the chair back and his stomach rolled, but he was able to bring his head forward and focus without much difficulty. It was now as if he could see, even though he was not looking. There was no effort in his gaze at all. They had moved the rack to where the platform had been. He could see the two women on the other side of it, looking at him through the beams.

"Bring her in."

He heard the camera whir and saw that Parker had it pointed at him through the structure of vine and flower painted beams. It stayed on him for a while, and then it swung slowly to the back of the room. His eyes followed where it went, and out of a dark corner he heard the shush of the wheels and saw the contraption she was in come into the light, saw the four men, one at each corner, their heads covered with various masks, pushing it. One of the masks was a horse's head; the others looked vaguely like cats or tigers. The light caught the metal edges of the table and the superstructure of poles and rods. It was a conventional stirrup table, the kind used in gynecological examination. He had seen many of them, had stood between the elevated, draped legs passing instruments. But there were no drapes this time, nothing to isolate the place of the operation from the patient, to hide the sexuality of her position.

Her legs hung in the stirrup slings. There were leather cuffs around her wrists and ankles, thick thongs attached to them and running to the table's undercarriage. She had some play, but not much. Her head rolled in a half-drugged stupor. He tried to call out to her, but all that came out of him was a whisper. His throat was as dry as cotton, and his brain couldn't get the words set in his mouth. When they had the table in front of the rack, the camera following their movements, they stepped back together in a parody of a ritual gesture, turned their animal heads inward at their corners and bowed deeply. Then they moved out of the camera frame, and went to get the animal.

Paul could see the camera lens move over her body, then recede to where the two women sat watching, then zero in again on him. Somewhere he recognized that their set up was makeshift, that they needed more than one camera and that they had needed more rehearsal time. He wanted to grimace or look bored, to stick his tongue out or say something. He needed some behavior that would change what they were doing, that would do something to ruin it. But he could manage nothing, was dimly aware that whatever he might have managed would make no difference. They could edit it out, take what they wanted. He was only able to get his eyes moved from the lens itself, to rest them on Mary Grace. He could see her eyes. He caught them as her head rolled; they were half open, and he could not tell if she could see or recognize him. Then they narrowed slightly, and he thought he saw a glimmer and the beginning of a slight smile, but her head rolled to the other side again, and he lost her. He moved his eyes to the left slightly and saw the twisted grins on the faces of the two women among the beams. They had taken their robes off, and he could see their spiked heels, the feathered outfits that encased their torsos, the ribbons laced in their hair, thick metal rings at their biceps. They should have looked provocative, but they looked wasted; even the brightness of their makeup, their red lips and lids, only set off the chalkiness of their faces, their pocked cheeks. They seemed dressed for some ritual; both had vague animal shapes painted on their foreheads. But there was no philosophy behind them, nothing to push their images into lust or shame. Then he heard the vague scuffling, the dull thud of hooves, and when he managed to turn his head, he saw them bringing the donkey in.

He had heard of donkey shows being performed in Tijuana. He might even have read something about them somewhere. But he had never seen one. In his imagination they had been scenes of utter but faked violence, tableau-like. The image of the crowd, dark men with cigars in some kind of arena theater, was always the clearest part: their yells, their inability to stay in their seats, their drinking and their leers.

The woman was always the marvel and not the donkey; she was special in that she could take him in, was one in a million and had to act out the rape. The men in the audience knew this, and the whole image had a kind of communal cast to it. Violence seemed ready to break out in the audience at any time, but if it did it would have to do with a poor show, with unconvincing acting and not with the burgeoning bestiality that the enactment could provoke. Always, in the image, the figure of the animal was vague.

It took them some time to get the donkey into the sling, elevated and trussed up. They walked him between the upright members of the rack, two on each side of him, as if they were loading him into some sort of starting gate. But when they got him there and were working to get the sling fixed under his chest, he reared slightly, balking, lowered his rump and moved back. His head had been between her legs and close to her while they worked on him. He might have caught the scent, something sexual but wrong, and his head came up twisting, hitting against one of the upright timbers as he reared and snorted. Even though he lurched back, he seemed sluggish, as if he were in some way ill or recovering from some illness. He staggered and his snort was wet and should have been stronger.

They tried twice with no success. Then Parker waved his hand sharply at them from his place behind the camera, and while one of them held the donkey by its bridle the other three moved the rack back a few feet. Then they blindfolded the donkey and tried again. This time they made it, and Paul could see him slowly rise up, the barrel of his chest swell and broaden, his forelegs reach out and test the air like a blind man searching for a wall. One of them turned the crank then, the ropes creaking as they tightened under his weight. When they had him up, the slings secured and the broad leather collar that held his neck and looked like some warrior's protective chest shield in place, the one with the horse-head mask climbed up the structure and took the blindfold off. Paul could see the donkey's eyes blink in the light, his head jerk from side to side, testing the trussing, his hooves paw tentatively at the air. They wheeled the rack slowly forward then, and when they had it up as far as was necessary, Paul could see the weight of him hanging over her, his broad thighs between her own. He bent his long head over and looked down at her, his ears stiff and pricked, and when he saw her he jerked his head up and seemed to try to lift himself back from her, as if he feared he would fall and crush her.

Paul could see that she was looking up at the donkey. Her legs spread, swaying in the stirrups, opening to get away from the touch of his rough hair. Then, as if she knew they wanted this opening and acceptance, she let her legs close slightly, and her knees touched the bulk of his thighs. He flinched a little at the touch, pawing heavy thuds on the floor, and tried to move back again. One of the women left her chair and moved back and behind him, a little to the side, and reached between his legs. His haunches froze in place, his hair bristling, and he tried to get his head around enough to see what she was doing.

Paul could see his eyes opening wider. His hands dug into the fabric of the chair's arms. He wanted to lurch, to fight the bonds, but he knew they had the camera on him and that they wanted this too, to get it on the film, to construct later in the editing some romantic story, the culmination of a past that had brought them here, the lover and the beloved victim, the degraded and the voyeur. He tried to hold tight, to imagine the nature of the passion that might be in his expression and to change it, to give them as little as he could. He wanted to believe that she was doing the same, but the enormity of what was going to happen kept pushing the drugs away. His stomach kept twisting, knocking the air out of him, and he could not hold the rational view of things that he needed.

The woman was moving her hand between the donkey's legs. He could not see all of it, but he saw the animal's flanks quivering, its legs slowly spreading as it lifted its hooves and stepped delicately to each side. Its tail rose up and twisted, its buttocks jerked lower. Then he saw two of the men in their cat masks. They had their shoulders against the rack's uprights and they were easing it forward. The other woman rose and came around the stirrup table at Mary Grace's head. She was leering, her body turned so that the camera could catch it, and she came to Paul's chair, touched his knee and lowered herself to the floor. He looked down as she reached for him and began to do what the other was doing to the donkey. He knew his face was twisted again, but he could not fight it. He looked away from her hand and back at the donkey and Mary Grace. She was holding the metal sides of the table now, her head pressed back, looking up at the donkey. He could see the hardened, almost sculptural line of her profile; it was placid and certain, and he could see the cold edge of her staring eyes, her gaze constant and focused. Her arms were flexed and rigid along the shining metal rails of the table, and the edge of her belly that he could see over them, though it moved with her breathing, was shield-like and inviolable. Even her breasts glistened like oiled steel.

She was in a position known as passive, the oldest of positions. She had taken so many men that way, and he thought that taken, held, possessed, controlled and even ruled were good words for it. He tried to think of others, of the exact one, but even the ones he had began to crumble in the drugs as he did so. His head wavered, his lids drooping, and when he jerked awake again he saw the whole of her, the power of the fixed vessel that she was, the integrity of the container that needed no filling but that formed and defined whatever it was that entered it. He knew very clearly for a moment that if he had truly touched her he had done something almost impossible.

And then she was moving, the resolve of her was rising to the surface and moving her invulnerable sheath. He could see the wires of her sweat-matted hair shifting, turning to a stony rose color under the lights. They came to rest in thin lines, carved furrows in her cheek, cut in from temple to chin. He saw the hard, flat sheen on her protruding forehead, the dry granite of her nose and lips, the smooth column of her neck, the inverted stone bowls of her breasts, her belly like a larger bowl. Then he saw the way the donkey had frozen in place above her like a massive statue, saw its head rotate slightly and become fixed also, its eyes like large marble balls looking down at her.

And Paul looked down at her also. Her hips were larger; her whole girdle had expanded and hardened and now flared out, massive, mature, and somehow earthbound below the thick cylinder of her waist. The donkey hung above her, his head fixed, his legs set askew in the air, the girth of his chest poised. And she was poised also, and under the lights that now isolated them from everything he was sure of her, sure that she had turned literally to stone, that she was more than below the stone; she was of and in it.

Then the drugs pushed him again, his eyes swam, and he felt for a moment that he was standing at a great distance, was on the side of a hill looking down at the ruins of an ancient city. There was a small oval

courtyard surrounded by an iron fence, and in the middle of the courtyard was this statue: an elegant animal poised over the body of a stone
woman. She was larger than he was, a giant of a woman. Her body was
open and ready for him, but her head was turned to the side. She had
stone rings set in her ears, a hooked nose, and though her eyes were
vacant and had no pupils, her look was piercing, and permanent, and
in no way accusatory. It said, "Look at this; this is the way it is." And
he knew, even at his distance, that he would have to deal with the look,
though it asked nothing of him.

Then the stone was moving; he thought he could hear the slabs
grinding. Her head was turning, rotating away from the donkey. She was
looking at him now, but her look said nothing. Then the columns of her
bent arms rose together and her legs opened. He could see her toes
hardening, her stone thighs tighten and flex. Then he saw the hard fist
of her left hand in the air, a tight capital at the end of her forearm, fixed
in a gesture of complete closure and containment. Beside it her right
hand had risen; it was open and rigid, the palm set at a right angle to
her wrist. It was austere, but welcoming and submissive: it said, "Come
here." He looked briefly at the place of the donkey's entrance. He felt
himself hardening and his stomach rolled again. Then he brought his
eyes up to the donkey's chest, his extended neck and his huge head,
above everything, in the air.

The head was like some disconnected cartoon figure, and if it hadn't
been for the eyes, Paul felt somewhere that the look of it might have
gotten him free again. Its lips were pulled back from its buck teeth. Its
muzzle above its mouth was rippled, its brow furrowed, and its long ears
stood up straight, a little splayed. The donkey was moving its head from
side to side, as if he were looking for something, trying to pick something
out, something familiar that could locate him. He started his screaming
at the same time as she started hers, and his mouth opened and closed,
his lips curling and his nostrils flaring. Her screams, under the huffing
guttural honking of the donkey's, were almost songlike, as even as the
constant tones from a stone whistle or wind out of marble; they were
relieving, getting air and tension out, cathartic, almost relaxing. They
were controlled, and he could hear the power of her in them. But the
donkey's were frustrated, unsettled and arhythmic. Paul thought he was
screaming too, like the donkey, but he was not sure. He had no way of

connecting to it, and he knew that if he was he had no way of stopping it.

The eyes in the twisted, massive head were huge now, half glazed and turned up slightly, the head's movements hypnotic, a constant rolling from side to side. The screams continued, and somewhere in the middle of them he found a place where he could withdraw again, move back a fraction. He could see the huge brown head in the air above her, the strings of saliva now running from the donkey's mouth, the moons of the tortured eyes looking skyward.

And in his place he knew that the donkey too was being brutalized. He knew that Mary Grace was handling it, was in control of it. She had a circumstance of specific dimensions to deal with. He moved his eyes, now swimming in the drugs, to where she was. He could see the fist and the open palm still stationary in the air, could see the shine on her fixed knees. She was looking up at the donkey again now, her eyes wide open and unblinking. He could not see her pupils, and there was no expression in her profile at all. Her lips were even and set. Not a hair was moving, not a drop of sweat. She was aglow with sweat, but her body was like oiled onyx. She had all the power and control. The animal had nothing but the pain. Paul knew that he, like the donkey, was hard and stiff, that they had the camera on him and the woman down between his legs, but this would be in the background of the film, and the things he wanted to be in, to be in a position to work to change them, were in the foreground beyond his reach. Still, he had edges in his mind, and though they were fuzzy and he kept losing them in the drugs, he had more than the donkey had.

The muscles in the donkey's neck bulged and spasmed, his chest swelled and pumped against the riggings, his head rolled to the side and his scream continued honking. He was among beasts. He was lost and alone with them, and he was the perfect virgin, violated. He was doing a thing he should do, part of his days and ways, but he was wrongly alone with it. Paul saw his legs reach out in the air, then bow inward in a gesture of clasping. He did this again and again, until it became like a kind of ritual. It was as if he would do what was appropriate for him to do and if he kept doing it her body would finally be there for him to hold onto, she would be below him, her tail and sharp spine, her braced haunches for support. At the end of each attempt at grasping, his legs kicked away, pawing the air, then locked back in, trying again, searching to clasp her. Near the end there was only pumping and despairing wheezing and a long whistling from deep inside him, as if even the scream had given up.

Paul could hear Mary Grace working, breathing, moving now, getting through it. But when he looked down at her he saw that she was still fixed in her postures, stonelike, impenetrable and whole. The donkey managed to fart loudly then, and when Paul looked up he saw him throwing his head, sending his saliva strings out at them. But they were beyond his reach, and these two weak gestures of outrage failed.

He looked through the flower-painted beams of the rack, around the moving bodies, and saw Parker. He was standing beside the whirring camera now and watching. His face was cold and placid, the hint of his unforced smile almost friendly. He was leaning comfortably against the tripod, his legs crossed at the ankles. Paul was coming, and he could see in the edge of his vision that the donkey's haunches were vibrating, that he was coming too. In the middle of the end of it, his eyes on Parker, he knew that he would have to kill him. He would do it for Mary Grace and for himself. He felt his hand tightening around the handle of a broad-bladed knife. He would pierce him deeply and cut his heart in half. It was something he would do. He did not know quite where he was now, but he knew the difficulty he was in was grave. Still, he had no doubt about it. He would kill him. And he would do it with a knife. That way he would be close to him when he did it; it would be intimate, and he would be sure of it. This resolve and the small and distant release that was his orgasm let him begin to drop back from the edge. He tried to return, to push another time against his bonds, to break away and go to her, free her and hold her, but he could not manage it. The vague blue of the lights was swelling up, becoming rose again. He felt he had her cheek in his hand, her face tucked against his neck. Both the donkey and the little horse were watching them, standing guard over them as they drifted into sleep.

PART III

NORTH

Chapter 12

We were heading south. I was in the front seat at the door, and Morales had the back seat to himself, his feet up, and his head propped on pillows in the corner. Marv drove slow and carefully, but picked it up a little when the road straightened some. We were in hilly country, close to the western coast, with the Golfo, beyond Sierra San Pedro Mártir, better than fifty miles to our left. Marv leaned forward over the wheel a little. I could see some tensing in his arms. He was watching the desert browns and the way the hills got greener in the eastern distance.

"I didn't know Mexico could be like this," he said.

"This isn't Mexico, only a thin finger of Califas. *Bandidos* used to come here from the mainland, a hideout. Some lived here. Maybe there are still some around here."

"Yeah? Christ, I hope we don't run across any."

"We could go down to La Paz, and then a little farther is all. We'd be across from Los Mochis, between it and Mazatlán; directly across from Eldorado; that's Mexico." His voice was labored, dry, and had a creak in it. He had never fully come back, never lost that hollowness in his face. His eyes were milky again, the chalk was under his skin. And now his voice was in trouble.

The women had said they'd meet us in La Púa, or at least Connie had.

Verta said she'd be back as well, but I doubted it. I knew Feli wouldn't come. She had that look in her face at the bus station. There was a certain formality in our goodbye.

In the morning after our meal at the fine restaurant, Morales seemed pretty strong, and we had eaten breakfast in the motel patio, under an umbrella in the sun. Marv was a little strange at the table, and there was some private talk among the women while we ate. After a while it came out, from Marv actually. He told us Connie had to get back to settle things. She wasn't going to work there anymore, but she had to quit in person, to straighten some things out. It was clear that Verta didn't want to go yet, not with Morales still the way he was. She kept looking at him, checking him out. She seemed distressed, and it seemed to me that she knew that if she went back now that would be it. Connie was bright and reassuring, and Marv, though down about their going, had no doubt that she would return. Feli stayed out of the talk, and when I caught her eye she looked away.

"But why leave here and go to some other place?" Marv said.

"La Púa," Connie answered. "It will be better there," is all she said. And Marv accepted this, trusting her.

The mountains came in a little over us as the road cut closer to them, and then it would move away some, and the sun seemed brighter. It began as a good road, fairly new, but then in a hundred miles or so it got rougher and Marv had to slow down again. He was still leaning forward at the wheel, seemed to want to push to get there even though he was moving deeper into Mexico, farther away from Connie.

"What about Sally?" I said. "What about the car, your buddies back home?"

"That's later," he said. He didn't turn his head, but kept his eyes fixed on the road.

We stopped for lunch. We had brought food and water with us and we found a small oasis with some trees and rock. When we got Morales out and down in the sand against a rock he looked worn and tired in the shadows under the trees.

"Are you all right?" I said.

"I think so," he said. "I'm tired."

"Do you want not to talk?" Marv said. He reached and helped Morales adjust his pillow against the rock.

"No, that's all right. It doesn't seem to make any difference."

"Well, at least there's a fucking lake in it finally," Marv tried to laugh, but it was hollow.

"Right," I said.

"I wonder why the fuck I drowned that colt," Marv said. "I really wish I knew."

"Some things are always hard to figure, like you and Connie." Morales smiled.

"Yeah. Well, *es muy simpática, y la voy conociendo más mejor en español. Es muy lista. No debe estar en ese lugar.*"

"That's pretty damn *good!*" Morales said. "That's three good sentences. Only *más mejor* is wrong, and *la voy conociendo* is way beyond where you should be. She's a good teacher. Or you're a good *estudiante.*"

"It's the teacher," Marv smiled.

"Do you think Verta will come back?" I said, and Morales looked at me and didn't smile.

"I'm sorry," I said.

"Connie will bring her," Marv said with complete conviction.

"Feli won't," I said, and neither of them spoke.

I knew she wouldn't come back, and I really didn't think the others would. I had no trust in Marv's perception at all, but I wasn't sure how Morales saw it, and I remained a little bit unsure. The bus for Tijuana had left in the late afternoon, and though Connie had hugged and kissed Marv with much enthusiasm, she was the first to jump on and find good seats for them. Feli had followed her, and it was Verta who lingered, touching Morales' shoulder and dabbing at his forehead with her handkerchief. He sat on a bench outside the terminal, and she bent over him and fussed with him, touching his hair, squatting and looking into his face. It was only when the bus was ready to leave that she moved away, looking back and waving in a resigned way that I took to be a final goodbye. She got a window seat, and as the bus pulled out I saw her staring at him through the glass. She was not weeping, but she wore an expression of deep concern touched with an edge of resignation. Connie and Feli were already engaged in conversation, and though Connie looked back just before the bus started up, Marv was already moving toward the terminal doors and did not see her.

We got to La Púa in the late afternoon of the second day. We had made good distance on the first, close to four hundred miles, and we had stopped late in the night and left again early in the morning. La Púa had few places to stay and the ones that we might have chosen were full, and it was suggested that we drive on a little to Loreto, a larger town a few more miles south. Loreto was much smaller than Ensenada, a lovely town with what looked like a few good shops and restaurants. We drove through it, but we agreed that we liked the even smaller La Púa better, and we returned to it, and when we got there we headed a few miles north again, on a secondary road that ran along the Gulf. We found a quiet little place, just a few attached rooms, a small restaurant, and a narrow beach set in a gentle dip of cove. When we got out of the car, Marv pointed to land out in the Gulf no more than a mile or so offshore.

"Is that Mexico?" he said.

"Oh, hell no," Morales answered, leaning on my shoulder for support. "That's just an island. Mexico's a hundred miles across."

We were on the coast again, but this time it was not the Pacific. The Gulf was calmer than the ocean had been off Ensenada; it was almost flat in the late afternoon sun. The next morning we were told the island was Coronados.

Morales had slept for the last four hours of the trip, and once he had bathed and changed he seemed a little better. There was an outside place to eat, a platform close to the bay, without any railings to block the view. We had abalone in a kind of stew, the muscles pounded soft and tender, and a bottle of rough wine. There were even fewer people in the place than had been in the one in Ensenada, and only a few people shared the restaurant with us. One older couple, who looked like seasoned tourists, and a few Mexican couples. When our meal was over, the sun was sinking deeper, it was almost dusk, and we opted against drink and for coffee. The sun was behind us, and the water seemed bluish as the line of light receded. We could see a few lights coming on, faint flickers down the shore line, and we thought we could pick some out on Isla Coronados.

Morales was in good spirits and told us things about the Baja. He said it was a different culture, really, from Mexico. He talked a little, though still vaguely, about home and his father. Marv watched him, nodding at what he said, and asked some questions. The night came on gradually, but there were people at the small bar now, music was playing faintly, and we felt no need to rush. I think we were all a little tired from the travel, but the light Gulf breeze was a pleasure, and we lingered.

There was a point at which Marv seemed ready to urge Morales to continue with the story, and I saw this and moved my hand to his arm to stop him. Morales was looking out at the Baja. Shadows filled the hollows in his cheeks, flattening his profile. He was still and silent, and he seemed to need that. We stayed a while longer, each quiet and lost in thought near the end, and only when the coffee was stone cold in our cups did we rise and go to our rooms and beds.

—

"We're getting there," Marv said.

But had he meant some common destination in a larger sense, we were not getting there, the three of us each bent on his own design or the lack of one. We had only the most recent times in common and the hint of that larger, naval past which was only a toy world for moderns; visits to ancient gunboats confirmed it, as did the silence in which we stood before pictorial representations. That was in San Diego, a tour of the mothball fleet in the harbor. Sailors between wars we were, and thus not sailors at all; our only ship's duty had been on the S.S. *Neversail:* the real and despairing name for ships bolted to the docks in boot camp. And so the past was a matter of watertight compartments, each sealed against the sea's entrance and each set off from the others for safety's sake, whether the rush be of ocean, lake or small pond. And so the compartments turned in on themselves in no linked order: card players in one, in another sailors gazing at old photographs, and in the stern of this one, which, given some optical trick in wash at the gunnels, seemed to be constantly trying to keep up with me, the huddled and receding figure of Morales wrapped and hooded in his blanket.

Oh, we *were* getting there; I could see it in the hollow stare in his eyes, some brief flicker where he looked beyond me, where I imagined Marv knelt in the prow, hand raised to brow and sighting like a figure head at the on coming island toward which I rowed, my back to it and counting on his navigation. Morales smiled dimly as his hood cast a shadow over his nose and mouth, and Marv called out again.

"Keep it straight. We're getting there."

We finally got to a hospital in Loreto. It had been a week since we'd left the women at the bus station in Ensenada, five days since we had settled in north of La Púa. In the second day there, Marv had started to try to reach Connie. He called numerous times and when he wasn't calling he was working with Spanish-language books he found in town, or getting Morales, when he was up to it, to check his vocabulary, syntax and accent. We'd sit together after dinner or lunch, and being excluded by the language, I'd sometimes drive to the town, finding what I could of interest. Then, on our fourth day in La Púa Marv reached her and relaxed a little, and we both turned with more careful attention to Morales.

"She says there's been a lot of working-out to do. Verta's had trouble settling things up. *Se da por supuesto.* I get that. But she'll get back to me soon. I gave her the number."

"Speak in English, Marv," I said.

"That's pretty good," Morales said, "the way you stuck that sentence in there." He said it in a whisper; though it was midday and the beach was sunny, he said it in a voice of a kind usually reserved for quiet midnight reflection.

"Look, man," I said. "You're really not getting any better."

"That's right," Marv said. "Let's get to the fucking doctor."

We had to wait in the small out-patient clinic of the hospital for quite a while. There was not much business, but the nurses and doctors, of whom there were many, seemed unconcerned about our presence, and it was only when Marv went to the desk and passed a few words with a nurse in Spanish that we finally got some attention. The doctor who looked Morales over was young and didn't seem to be comfortable in what he was doing. He had a casual, superior manner that was clearly a defense against inexperience, and it was only after he had done the usual things and then directed us to admissions that his manner changed. Marv said a few words to him, again in Spanish, and Morales stiffened his voice a little.

"He's asking him what the fuck is going on. Does he have any idea at all of what might be wrong. What's his provisional diagnosis. Why admit him." We stood around Morales where he sat, and Marv translated for me.

"He doesn't know shit," Marv whispered. "He says some tests."

When it was clear that we weren't having any of it and were leaving, the doctor's eyes flashed a little, I think in concern as well as anger, and in the end he seemed almost desperate. He pressed a large bottle of pills on me as we got to the door.

"*Vitaminas,*" he said.

When we got back, Morales was exhausted, and when we got to his room we helped him into the bed. It was late afternoon, and he said he thought he could sleep until dinner maybe. We were getting ready to leave him alone, when he spoke.

"Would you call my father?" he said.

"Christ, man, it's not that bad, is it? It can't be *that* bad," Marv said.

"No, no, it's not that it's so bad. It's just that he might be worried I've been so long."

"Oh. Well, sure," Marv said. "Does he speak English?"

"I didn't know your father was alive," I said.

"No. He has no English."

"How about your sister and brother?" I said.

"They can't be reached," he said.

"I'll do it," Marv said. "How do I do it?"

There were no phones in the rooms; there was only one, and that was in the office, and while Morales was sleeping Marv called his father. Morales wrote down some things to say, and Marv rehearsed them with him before he went to the office to call. Morales was going to wait until Marv called and came back, but while I sat with him he drifted off, and I left the room and went to find Marv. I didn't know why Morales didn't wait until the next day, when he was rested, and call himself. He seemed strong enough for that. But though Morales was clearer to me, to both of us I think, at bottom he was still opaque, and part of the knowledge our friendship had brought us was that there was a part of him that was sealed beyond any entrance. As I got to know him better this got even clearer, and so I gave up trying to figure about his father then.

"What'd he say?" I said. "Did you reach him?"

"Yeah. He didn't say much really, not much that I could get anyway. An odd sort of accent. He heard me out. He seemed to understand. Talked slow, you know, but only a few words, and I'm not sure I got them all. I'm sure he got the message. I wish Connie would get here."

We sat on the veranda, in woven straw chairs with small tables beside them. Marv's last statement was as wistful as I had ever heard him speak. He looked away from me when he said it, and I found I had reached out and touched his arm to reassure him. I thought it was false reassurance. As the days passed, there seemed to be no chance that she would come back. But I was wrong.

"What do you make of this sickness that Morales has?" I said. I wanted to pull him away from Connie for a while before I had to speak of her.

"I don't know what the fuck to make of it at all. I've been through all the medical stuff I know. I'm sure you have too, man. There just aren't any symptoms. Just the way he looks, and that temperature in the beginning. But that's gone now. Nothing seems to hurt him. Shit, I don't know. Do you think Connie will come back?"

It was the first time he had expressed any doubt at all, and though I'd been waiting to bring up Kansas, his home and friends, to get him back on what I thought was his right track, I knew that I could not do it then. I think in a strange way I feared that if I did not reassure him about Connie he too would get sick. I could almost see the edges of a physical stress not unlike that in Morales' face come across Marv's as he asked the question, and I think I felt some kind of fear for my own health as well as I answered him with care, recognizing how fragile he was and how important my answer would be in the situation.

"Of course she'll come back. Didn't she explain it? She wouldn't fuck you over that way. She just needs to get it all right and settled behind her. Give her a little time, man."

"You're right," he said. "I guess it's just that I miss her. She's all right, you know? I really like her."

"I know," I said, and smiled. "It's not all that hard to tell."

Marv laughed and came around a little. It was good to see the creases leave his forehead, to see his muscles tighten again.

They came back the following afternoon. They called in the evening from Rosarita and said they would catch a bus out in the morning. Morales was rested and a little stronger, and he even left his jacket behind and came with us to the bus station. Connie was the first one off, and though she lowered her eyes a little shyly, when she saw Marv she couldn't hide her grin, and when he hugged her and then picked her up and held her almost at arm's length in the air and looked at her she laughed vibrantly. And when he lowered her they danced in a circle for a few moments, touching each other and kissing. Verta came off the bus behind her and made straight for Morales. She was gaily dressed and made up, but the severity of concern in her face and eyes, that grew even more severe when she saw what state he was in, muted the bright-colored clothing she wore. She sat beside him on the bench at the station, touching him here and there, speaking softly and secretively to him. Feli was, of course, not with them. I had known this from the beginning, and yet seeing the intensity of the two couples' meeting hurt me a little. It was not her absence as much as their exclusionary involvement that I think touched me. The circle of the three sailors would soon be breaking up. I knew it was almost time.

———

"We're getting there," Marv said, and "there" was a small extended finger of Isla Coronados a little way offshore. It was two days after their arrival, and things were settling into something again. It was Morales himself who suggested a little picnic trip, and though Verta expressed her concern she could see that Morales was set on it, and she did not press it. She and Connie would go shopping. Connie had things to buy, important things, she said, and winked at Marv, who laughed and kissed her cheek when we left to get the boat.

I was rowing, and Marv was at my back in the prow, and I faced Morales, who was gazing over my shoulder to where Marv was, and beyond him to the island.

"A little to the left," Marv said. "There's a little beach."

We got the boat into the shallows, and Marv jumped out and pulled us up onto the sand. After we had unloaded the ice chest and the bags of food, Morales climbed out of the stern and stood in the water up to his calves and looked around. He had dropped his blanket in the boat as he climbed out. He was thinner, it seemed to me, than he had been when we left San Diego, but his hair was clean and Verta had shaved him, and in his shorts and loose shirt he looked better than he had in days. It was good to see him free of the blanket that seemed to shrink him. The trip over did not seem to have taken that much out of him, and he walked between the two of us as we moved from the beach to the slightly higher ground and looked for a place to set up.

It was not a lovely island, but where we were it was empty, and the Baja and what Gulf we could see on each side from high ground was indeed lovely. The water between the island and the land was dead calm, and there was only a slight tide ripple on the Gulf side. It was clear, but the sun was mellow and not too hot.

We found a place with a few low and scrawny trees, some ground and a few large rocks and boulders. There were some scraps of paper there, and the remnants of a long-dead fire, but there were no cans or bottles, and the ground was not recently tramped down; weather had cleaned the place sufficiently, and it seemed fresh and all our own. We were not hungry yet, but we were thirsty, and we drank beer and then went back to the small inlet where the boat was beached and had a leisurely swim. Afterward, Marv searched the island for shells and stones to bring back for Connie, and Morales and I took in a little sun, drying our naked bodies in it. By ten we were dressed and hungry, and we opened the bags of food and spread the newspaper we'd brought along for a tablecloth over a big rock with a relatively flat top. Marv and I sat on other rocks, and Morales sat on the ground against a larger one, using his rolled-up jacket for a pillow. He was shaded from the sun, and his face seemed to suck up the shadows he was in. He didn't look as good as he had when we landed, his nose was beginning to protrude again, but his voice was stronger than it had been the day before, and I took it that the shadows were tricking me and that he was indeed in better shape than he appeared. Still, I knew it was relative, and I could not conjure up the figure of the Morales I had known at the tissue bank in San Diego for comparison.

"What a glorious fucking day and place this is!" Marv said when he returned from his exploring. It was funny to hear him use the word "glorious"; I doubted he would have found a use for it in Kansas.

"That's *glorioso* or *espléndido,*" Morales said.

"That's what I meant," Marv said. "A real pisser." We laughed, and Morales shook his head.

"*Vas a ser un mexicano sin darte cuenta.*"

"What's that?" I said.

"He says I'm almost a Mexican," Marv laughed.

"What about your father, Morales?" I said. "I don't know why I thought he wasn't living."

"He's all right," Morales said.

"It's the story," Marv said. "It makes him seem too old, that it's a different time. You know, history."

"It is," Morales said.

"What does that mean? You mean the story or your father or what?" Marv said.

"Go on," I said.

We ate our sandwiches and sipped at fresh beers. The sun was directly over us now, or almost there, and Morales had put a hat on to keep it off his head, a straw hat that we had gotten in town. He didn't seem at all tired now, but seemed comfortable leaning against his rock.

"I don't know what in the fuck that really means about your father, or whatever," Marv said.

"Go on, Morales," I said.

"It's like when you drowned that colt," he said. "If your father came here out of that story you told about it, what would *he* be?"

"That's right; that's got it," I said.

"That hasn't got shit," Marv said. "You're talking shit again, you guys."

We laughed, and this time it was Marv who shook his head. He spoke two long, oddly guttural sentences in Spanish, and that got Morales laughing and shaking his own head again.

"What did he say?" I said.

"Oh, nothing," Morales said. "It's the *way* he said it. He's too much."

"When my father found I'd drowned the colt, he didn't beat me. He had always been stern, and he did punish me, took away my privileges or something like that. We were never close, but we did have a very strong kind of comfortable family connection, I guess you'd call it. I was sure I could count on it and know where I stood with him. That, in a way I guess, *did* make us close, whatever close means. But when I drowned the colt, he changed, and the distance from him that had been our closeness became only distance. He just couldn't be sure about me anymore. I think if I could sit down with him and tell him the whole story, just go over how I saw the mare die, how I then took the colt down and drowned it in the pond, even what *he* did and how he acted when he found out, I could change it just enough to change him back to how he was before it happened, how he was toward me."

"Where would *you* be then?" I said.

"Fucked if *I* know," Marv said, and Morales choked on a mouthful of beer and coughed and sputtered.

"Doesn't answer much, does it?" he said, once he had gotten control of himself again.

"Is your father still alive?" I said.

"He isn't, no. He died a few years ago. I'm not even sure what it was that got him. I was already in the Navy. Just a call and a funeral. And that was all."

Morales had his head down, the hat covering his face entirely. He seemed to be thinking; he was very still, and for a moment I thought he might be sleeping or not feeling well. But then his head came up again, and he looked at Marv and smiled gently. "Lakes and colts and ponds and fathers," he said.

"Exactly," I said. "Go on, Morales."

Chapter 13

He could see their eyes, one set to the right and above the other, a little off in the distance in the darkness. They didn't move or blink. He moved his hand to the side of her face, but it was his own he touched, and when he moved it down to find her, to reach the rise of her hip where she was tucked against him, it was only his thigh that he found; the spoon his body made was empty. He squinted without raising his head and found that the eyes were only reflections, points on the metal beam that began to come into focus. He rolled over to find the source of the light but was immediately taken with his stiffness; his calves cramped and tightened and he had to stop in his turn when he was on his back. He could see nothing above him, and then he could see the surface of the pocked concrete. He felt a distant sharp bite in his groin, and he reached his hand to it. Wiry strands of his pubic hair were stuck to his leg. They were brittle with some dried substance.

He picked it away, and the bite was gone. When he could turn he saw the outline, a pencil-thin rectangle of light. He let his head fall back to some rough surface. It felt like a blanket, like the kind he had been issued in the Navy. Where was she? Could she still be alive? He was sure she would be. And as he knew this, the image of her below the donkey began to come back to him and with it some sense of time and location.

She would be alive; he had seen her handle things. Even the sound of her screaming now came back to him as something that had some hope for him in it. It had worked for her in its way. He knew she would be alive. But he needed to get to her, to get her out of here, and coming fully awake in these thoughts he began to reach around for his clothing, but he could feel nothing but his own naked skin and the rough surface of the blanket. He rolled to his side again and pushed himself to a sitting position on what he felt now was a bed of some sort.

He was shaky, weaving a little where he sat, but he managed to right himself. He shook his head, feeling the last edges of the drugs still with him, just a slight touch of them, and he moved his bare feet, searching for his shoes. Nothing. Then he stood up on the concrete floor. He could see more clearly now. He was in a basement room. It was windowless, but the light lines at the door let enough in so that he could see to the four walls. The place was completely empty. There was only himself and the bed, a cheap folding cot; there were no clothes. As he moved to where the door was, he found he could feel the stiffness in his legs, a pain in his stomach and a burning at both wrists where they had bound him, but the cramps were gone, and by the time he had crossed the room he found he was steady on his feet.

He reached to the edge of the light and moved his fingers along it looking for a knob or handle. Finding nothing, he moved to the other edge and did the same thing. When his hand was above his shoulder, he felt the tube of a hinge and knew that if there were a handle it would have to be on the other side. He went back, and almost at his knee he felt a little cup in the metal door. He put his left hand flat on the wall to the side of the light crack and with his right he pulled slowly back. The door was heavy, but it was not locked and it moved open a little without a sound. When he had it open a foot, he was able to put his head out through the space and look around.

The first thing he saw was a staggered series of long four by fours, beams standing vertically a few feet from him. When he looked up he saw the bottom of the deck they supported. Their ends were imbedded in dark soil, and where they ended the soil lightened, becoming sand. There was a slight sloping down, and no more than twenty feet from the point of the deck was the lake. He looked to his left and right and saw that on both sides of the deck the ground sloped up abruptly; near the top of the slopes there was some ground cover and beyond it the dark shapes of trees. He paused and listened, but he could hear nothing, not even night birds. There was no breeze at all, and when he looked back at the lake he could see that it was perfectly still at the edge.

Could he go up the slope to the house and find her? They had taken his clothes; he was naked and he did not think he could handle things in this state. If he could handle them at all. Still, it had been easy so far, too easy. The door had been open. He knew that it had to make sense. Someone would be watching. Maybe they wanted him to get out, but why take his clothes? Did they think he would try to escape without her? He couldn't figure it, but then he figured one thing. They did not as yet have the horse. If they had it there would be nothing left for them to get, no reason to let him escape. Maybe they thought he would lead them to the horse, would go around the lake to find her, and that they could not lose him if he were naked. It seemed crazy, but he could find no other explanation. He looked out through the wooden beams at the lake. It was the full moon that had provided the pencil lines of light. He could not see it from where he was under the deck, but he could see the lighted surface of the water, the way it turned silver after a few hundred yards. Whatever they might figure they won't figure this, he thought, and he moved from the doorway out to the edge of the deck. For a moment he thought he would get on his knees and crawl to the water, but the thought of himself seen moving in this posture like some naked and subject animal revolted him. He pulled his shoulders back then, and standing fully erect walked down and into the edge of the lake.

The water was cool, but not cold, and when he was in it to his waist he stopped for a moment and looked out across the still surface. He could see a light, just a flicker in the distance slightly to his left. The house, he thought; from this angle the light seemed almost on the surface and extremely far away. Then he turned around and looked up at the deck. There was a dim light, a night-light he thought, in the living room beyond the glass doors at the back of it. Then he thought he saw something, a dark place at the deck's railing. It was perfectly still, and he thought it must be a chair or a table. And there was something beside it, a tube standing on thin legs. A telescope, he thought. That was the flicker of light he had seen while he was making love to Mary Grace on the beach. They had been watching them, had watched them, probably, for weeks. Then he saw the curl of smoke in the moonlight. The hair came up on his arms. He stood very still, staring, trying to penetrate the position of the figure. Finally he gave it up; there was no movement, only the curls of smoke rising. Whoever it is, he must be facing away from me, he thought. Or she must be. He turned quietly and slowly in the water, and when he was facing away from the house he lowered himself in up to his neck. Then he took a breath and sank. When he was a tight ball under the surface, he pushed off, diving along the slowly sloping bottom, pulling sand through his hands. In a few feet the bottom dropped off quicker and he left it, scissoring his legs and sweeping his arms in a wide breast stroke. When he knew he had little breath left he came slowly to the surface, easing up so that only his head rose out. Then he started a slow side stroke, keeping his body under the water. Soon he felt he was far enough from the house and he rolled slightly and moved into a crawl.

He used the flicker of light as a beacon, catching it from time to time when he rolled his head from the water to take air, keeping it to his left. At first he could see the curve of the shoreline to his sides, but before long he was far enough out so that it moved into the distance and was gone. As the water ran over his body, he felt his groin become clean. At first he could smell the rancidness of his right armpit as he stroked out, but that was washed clean in a while too. He felt stronger for a time, but very soon he felt that he was stroking too quickly and he slowed down, loosing his rhythm a little, and began to glide between strokes. The lake was light and it sparkled around him. He could see where it flattened and turned silver ahead of him, but the place where it turned did not get closer. Soon he began to pause, to tread water and rest. And when he had been swimming for a long time and was resting, he rotated in the water and looked back at the shore behind him. It was very close to him, much closer than he had imagined it would be, and he felt his strength leave him in a rush and the energy it was taking to keep treading, keep himself above the surface, leaving him as well.

The swimming seemed easier than the treading, but when he began to stroke again his arms were heavier than they had been. Then his legs cramped, and he had to stop again, to do most of the treading with his arms. He could still see the light in the distance, but it had gotten no closer, and though he fought to keep the thought away, he realized that he might not make it. Maybe he should go back, but when he looked behind him he could see that that was a long way too now; the house seemed to sink into the lake a little, the deck seemed no more than matchsticks. He turned again and began to swim.

He began to count his strokes. He would take five and then would glide until he almost stopped. The first two were to get him going, the following three to make some headway. He kept loosing count. He tried to think of Mary Grace, but it was little help; his mind was getting exhausted too, and only the strongest recent images of her would come to him, and those he didn't want. He thought of Parker, could see him dimly standing beside the camera, that smile on his face, his body loose and relaxed. The image helped him a little. It was getting harder to tread when he had to stop and rest. It was hard to get his head up far enough to check the light, and when he did manage to find it he thought he had drifted from his course, and thought when he continued he tried to make the proper alterations his body found it hard to be sure it was doing so. Twice he had to pull up coughing, his mouth and nose running with water. Treading, he had to lean his head back to keep his mouth and nose above the surface. His breathing was becoming wet; he could hear the gurgling in his ears. He paused and rolled on his back, trying to float. He could get and keep the position for only a very short time, then his legs would sink, and he would be upright again, having to fight with heavy arms to keep his head up. Once he tried sinking; he took the deepest breath he could. It raised him slightly and then he began to sink under. He let his limbs hang loose, resting them. He caught himself on the edge of sleep, sinking deeper, and when he fought to the surface he found that it was a long way up, that he had sunk deeper than he'd intended. He couldn't hold his breath long enough. He sucked water into his lungs before he reached air, and when he came out into it he was vomiting and coughing.

It took him a long time and about all the effort he thought he had to get himself settled again, to get his breath and a part of his mind back. He had to bob, go under and come up again, over and over, taking in breaths and then holding them. When his eyes cleared and his breathing became almost steady, he managed to turn himself in a circle. He was at the very center of the lake now, his head bathed in moonlight. He lifted it and saw the moon over him. He figured that now the closest direction to solid ground was straight down, and he thought that it was probably time for him to go there. For no reason other than that he was breathing, was still alive and had his head above water, he revolved in a circle again. He saw the shape of the house in the distance, then a far and woody shore. Then he saw the flicker of the light; it went out of his vision to the left as his head turned. The image of himself screwing himself into the water came to him. His mouth was now full of water and it was beginning to leak into his nose. When his eyes were resting on the flat surface and he was getting ready to breathe the water in and go under, he saw something.

At first he thought that it was something in his eye or something, a bit of grass or a bubble or a twig, a few inches from his eyes on the glassy surface. Then he saw the delicate V of the ripples moving out and away from it, and he knew that it was something moving toward him and that it was not as close as it had first seemed to be. He had forgotten that he was holding his breath, waiting before he gave in. He dropped his head back; his nostrils cleared the surface and he blew air out on the water and sucked fresh air in again. When he brought his head back, his eyes were half submerged. The point was now an odd double image of a V; there were four vectors moving from the point that was moving toward him. His mind was leaving him, going to some dark corridor of attention, and then he went under.

He felt that he was trying to sink, but that he could not get his head completely under. It was as if he were hooked up in something. He could feel a tugging, almost a pain. He wanted to reach up and disentagle himself,but he could not make his mind find and lift his arms. Then he felt that he was rising up again. There was a kicking, and in a moment he knew that he was moving his legs. His head cleared the surface and the thing he had been hung up in, that was pulling at his hair, was gone. He managed to rotate his head, to search for the source of the pulling and holding, and there she was, her head no more than inches away from his own. He felt her breath on his eyes, saw her nostrils expand, and then he was sinking again. As his mouth went under, he saw her muzzle reaching out. She took his nose in her teeth and bit it. His head jerked back from her; the bite had hurt him, and he began to come out of delirium, to cross back from the edge. Her head moved on the surface of the water; he could feel a slight turbulence against his chest, and then she came in at him from the side, nipped at his ear sharply, then released it and took a mouth full of his hair, jerking her head back, yanking at it.

"Ouch!" he said, and the sound of his voice was very loud in the silence, but he knew that it was he who had said the word, that he was almost completely back. He was treading the water, could keep his mouth and nose above it now. He had some control of his arms and legs. Her head was circling his own, causing a gentle maelstrom; she was watching him, staying very close to him, hitting her muzzle against his head at times.

"All right," he whispered. "I'm all right now," and he managed to bring an arm out of the water and touch her ear. Then she moved off a little from him, went out about ten yards and stopped and turned, waiting. He kicked, and managed to bring himself half horizontal to the surface, to work back into an abbreviated side stroke again.

The two heads moved slowly on the surface of the water. The horse's head was smaller and quicker, and it would move off at a good pace, then stop and look back. At times it would return slightly, and sometimes it came all the way back and moved in a circle around the other head, moving in sometimes, even nudging the head, rooting under the chin. His stroke became hypnotic, automatic, and it edged him into sleep. But her rooting at him kept waking him up. She was irritating, and he felt anger, but he had no energy to drop his stroke and push her away. It went on like this, and he had no idea how long it went on. He would see her in front of him, the V spreading out behind her, and then he would feel her nip and push, and then see her head move out from beside his own, get ahead of him again. And he kept following. He really had no will at all; there was only her will, the irritation of her insistence. And he kept sinking, and she kept pulling him up by the hair, bringing his head to the surface. And finally when he sank he hit something with his feet, and he had enough energy to push off of it a little, to stroke out yet again. And then he could stand, the water a little below his neck.

When he made it to the shallows she was already standing there at his feet, puffing slightly. His legs buckled and he went to his knees in the sand. She moved up against him and pressed her head into his stomach. He fell slowly, turning and putting his hands out to catch himself. Then he was on his back, stretched out, his feet still in the water, looking up at the moon. There were no stars and only a wisp of clouds moved as a faint breeze came up. He could feel the water rippling against his toes. He lifted his head up quickly, thinking he had fallen asleep. She was there, only a foot away from him, standing in the sand and watching him. In a while he was able to sit up. He looked down the beach but they must have been beyond some turn because he could not see the lights of the house. She stood there. She looked almost dry now, her yellow hair soft in the moonlight. When she saw him looking at her, she lifted her forelegs off the sand and rose up slightly and turned and moved a few yards back. He turned, and when he saw behind him where she was he could see the darkness of the rock cliff rising. She stopped and waited, came back a few feet, then moved off again.

Then he was on his feet, a little unsteady, but able to follow her. The breeze touched his body, but it was warm and drying and he felt no chill. Even his hair was drying now, beginning to wave. When they got close to the rock wall, she moved along it to the right. Then she made a turn into it and disappeared. In a moment he saw her head a few feet away from him, protruding like a carving from solid rock and staring at him. When he got to her he saw the crevice. It came only to his waist, was a slit there and formed an inverted V as it opened at his feet. He had to get down on his knees to enter. When she saw him drop, she turned and went deeper in. He followed on hands and knees, and after a few feet the sand in the slit ended and he reached up above him, touching the rock sides of the slit, and slowly rose to his feet. His head touched the top of the opening, and he bent his knees slightly and went on. The passage turned, and then opened and heightened and he could stand fully erect. In a few more feet it opened considerably into a half lighted cave. He looked up and could see edges of the sky through thin openings above him. Something moved there, brush growing on the flat above, pushed a little by the breeze. The cave was small. Where she stood, on the other side of it from him, he could see some dark places on the ground. He crossed and found a mossy area. It looked large enough, and when he dropped back to his knees and ran his hand over it he found it soft and dry. Then he let himself slip to his side.

She stood and watched him as he adjusted his body, altered the position of his legs and turned his head to find a good, comfortable place for it. His eyes were closing as he saw her move toward him. Then he felt her drop and come into his lap facing him. He could feel the gossamer of her tail touch against his legs. He opened them slightly and it slipped between his thighs, her haunches settling, warm on his groin. Her head came up. He felt her breath, her nostrils against his chest. Their stomachs were together, and he could feel her take a deep breath, shift a little and settle in. His own breathing steadied also. She moved her haunches slightly. Her tail touched against his buttocks, and then she pressed herself deeper against him, taking a piece of skin on his breast gently between her teeth. He managed to bring his hand up, to move and then rest it on her neck. She snuffled and then she growled softly, and in a few moments they were asleep.

=====

The trip north was like a dream of transformation. At least it was dreamlike in the way the immediate past kept crumbling in the memory, becoming like the distant past as soon as it was over. They would find themselves in some place, in some circumstance; they would solve it or it would be solved for them. Then they would sleep, and when they awakened the previous day would be gone from them, and they would get on to the next one. He wasn't sure how long it all took. He had begun to lose track of time even at the house. The only measure he had was his fluctuating thoughts about Mary Grace, his anxiety and rationalizations, and his trust. He wasn't sure what it was he trusted in or how he could find a way to trust at all, but he knew he could not question it too deeply; it was what kept him going, at least in part, and he knew he needed it. Parker also kept him going and he held to that image of him beside the camera.

When he woke up in the morning, she was still tucked in against him. Her eyes opened when he moved and looked down at her. The cave was lighted from above; the moss under his body was cool, but when he reached out and touched bits of it beside him it was warm. They untangled themselves from each other and both rose stiffly, stretching and moving their limbs. When he felt loose enough, he headed for the crevice that had led them into the place, but when he looked back for her he saw that she had moved to the other side of the cave and was not following.

"Okay," he said aloud, "you're the boss," and he went back to where she was. There was another opening. She went into it and he followed her. After a few feet they came out into a larger cave, this one open to the beach at the mouth. The cave was in a small indentation in the coast, the rock wall moving almost to the water on either side. They went down to the water, each stepping immediately into the lake edge. He got to where he could submerge himself and went under, rubbing his body with his hands. She rolled in the shallows and then moved back to the sand and shook herself. He went out a little farther and after only a little hesitation drank the lake water. Then they both stood in the air, letting themselves dry in the early sun.

He had little idea of what to do, but he knew what not to do. He couldn't head down the coast to the house; they would be watching for her, and now they would be watching for him too. They surely would know he was gone by now and having lost him temporarily would watch the house with care, and would be watching other houses close by as well. He couldn't go to any houses then, nor did he think he could stay long in the woods surrounding the lake. Naked as he was, they would surely figure that he would stay in whatever cover was available.

He could go up to the road, to any one of them that he could find, and just stop the first car that came along. That would begin to end things. But he figured that Parker would know, and he would be right, that he wouldn't do that. He hadn't turned her over in the beginning, and he wouldn't do it now. The only answer he could think of was movement. He needed to get some distance away quickly. He had no knowledge of the country, how long he could expect to have cover. But he knew which way north was, and when the sun had dried them he started along the beach, and when he saw a place where the rock seemed climbable he started up it. She was behind him now, following, and in minutes they had reached the cliff.

They stayed in the brush and trees along the first dirt road they found that seemed to lead in the right direction, and in what he guessed must have been three hours or more they came to the wooded edge of a narrow valley. The going had been rough, and he couldn't be at all sure of the time or the distance they had covered. They were in thickly wooded hill country for most of the time. He had gone slowly, and still he had cut and bruised himself. There were spots of blood on his ankles and legs, and he knew his feet were in very bad shape. They crossed a few dirt roads and a few trails, but in time there were no more roads, the growth had gotten steeper and thicker, and he figured they must have been getting away from where people were.

When they reached the edge of the thicker growth and looked down the hilly slope into the valley, he could see the patchwork of a few farms. He didn't hesitate long, but stepped out of the treeline and worked his way down the sloping brush hill that led to the brown and occasional green of the valley floor. When he got there, there was no more protection, no more trees, and what brush there was came only to his knees. There was no one about, but when he lifted his hands to his brow and sighted, he thought he saw some figures, people moving slowly off in the distance at the edge of the closest farmhouse he could make out. His stomach rolled and he could feel himself blushing in his nakedness. He knew that he had to go to them.

The adults, two women he could see now, were facing away from them, working in the soil as they approached. There were two children with them. Paul and the horse were close now, and he saw the children stop moving. He thought they must have seen them, and he reached down and picked the little horse up and held her in front of him at his waist so that her body covered his groin. He took a deep breath and continued to move toward the women and children. The women stopped working; they had turned too, and the children were leaving them and running toward him. As they got closer, he could see that they were a boy and a girl, maybe five and six years old, and when they were twenty yards away they stopped running and stood and stared as he approached them. They could now see that he had nothing on, and they didn't know what to make of it, but when he got closer they could see the horse too, and their eyes opened wide and broad smiles came to their faces. The women were beside them then. One seemed the mother and the other her daughter, a woman of twenty-five or so. When he was close enough for them to hear him, he spoke the only thing he could think to say.

"*Por favor, señoras.* Can you help me?" They hesitated, then bent toward each other and spoke very quickly in Spanish. There were little clicks in their talk, small intakes of breath between sentences. He could hear the children's excited voices as they stood against them and looked up at them. The mother looked down at the children, then shrugged and came forward. When she was a few feet away, she spoke. He could not understand a word she said, and in a moment she understood this. She moved closer, her eyes on the horse held at his crotch, and removed the shawl that she was wearing. It was worn and a little rough, but it was large, and he maneuvered to let the horse down to the ground and get the shawl around his waist.

They took him to a room in the back of the small farmhouse; it was clearly the master bedroom. The furniture, even the bed, was hand-made, but carefully so; the room was extremely neat, the bed made and the dresser and small table covered with doilies. There were pictures of Christ and the Virgin on the walls, ones that had been cut from magazines, glued to pieces of wood and framed with polished wood. Above the frame holding the picture of Christ and tucked in behind it were a couple of palm fronds. He had left the horse with the children in the small fenced-in yard before the house. The woman brought him cloth-ing, a rough shirt, some worn and baggy underdrawers and a pair of overalls. She brought him shoes too, but he could not get his feet into them. As he tried, he felt the cuts and scrapes on the sides of his ankles and on his soles. His feet were swollen, and as he noticed their condition they began to hurt him. There were many places on his body that hurt when he had the clothing on and it chafed against him. When he was dressed he went out, but he could find no one in the living room. Then he heard the children laughing, and he went to the front door and stepped out on the porch. The older woman was sitting in an old rocker; the other was nowhere in sight. In the yard the children were playing with the horse. The woman began to rise from her chair when she saw him, but he motioned for her to stay there, bowing slightly; she smiled when she saw him in her husband's clothes and barefoot and she settled back and watched him as he went to the edge of the porch and sat down.

The boy and the girl were sitting in the dirt. The horse moved around them, sneaking in at times to nudge them, then frisking away. At times she would move up to one of them and stand there, accepting their awkward petting. It seemed that they had already taken the little horse into the natural course of things; she was no longer a wonder to them. A mangy dog came around the edge of the house at one point. When it saw the horse, it stopped, stared a moment, and began to snarl. The horse heard it, turned and walked deliberately toward it and then stopped, bunched her chest muscles and snorted. The dog turned and went back around the house and out of sight.

In a few minutes he saw the woman coming back across the field in front of the house. There was a large man beside her. She was pointing, and Paul thought that she was directing his gaze not to him but to the yard and the little horse and the children. The man stopped and leaned forward a little; then he threw his hands up from his sides and continued on. When he reached the fence, Paul could see that he was around sixty, and worn-looking. He was dressed in overalls that were the twin of the pair Paul was wearing. His eyes were on the horse, and after looking at it a while he nodded in a gesture of confirmation. Then he looked up at the porch to where Paul was sitting. A wisp of a smile crossed his face when he saw the clothing. He extended his hand when he got to the porch. Paul stood and took it. It was almost twice as large as his own.

Paul spent the remainder of the day resting. The woman brought him coffee and bread, and after he had napped and awakened, he ate lunch with her and the children. He noted that she was quite a bit younger than her husband, perhaps only forty. The children were quite young for a couple their age. The farmer had gone back to the fields. The woman freed the children from their little chores, and they played with the horse in the yard. In the afternoon, Paul, the children and the horse took naps. Paul slept in the farmer's bed. By late afternoon he was beginning to feel some strength again, at least the aches in his body were deeper now, the superficial cuts and scrapes only a slight annoyance, and he felt he could think clearly.

He needed to reach Johnny. There was no phone in the house, so he couldn't begin to try just yet; still, that seemed the only thing he could do, and he thought later he could talk with the farmer, who had English, and find out what was possible. He also knew that he was too close to where they'd held him. He could be as close as a few miles, and even though he felt safe where he was now, he did not trust his feelings. He slept again and was awakened by a light touch on his shoulder. When he turned he saw that it was the boy who had touched him and then stepped back a little from the bed. He smiled at him, and then backed out of the room. When he had dressed and was ready, he went to the kitchen. He had managed to get the shoes on, and thought they were tight he could tell that the swelling had gone down a little.

The table was set; the farmer and the children were there, and they all ate together, beans and tortillas and small bits of meat stew that was rationed carefully. There was little talk at the table. The farmer had some things to say about his work that day. He mixed Spanish with some English, translating some of the talk for Paul, keeping him from feeling isolated. Paul picked up enough to know that the children had some things to say about the horse. Their father listened, but he did not pursue their conversation.

When the meal ended, the mother ushered the children away and the farmer got two pipes and a can of rough tobacco from a shelf in the room and suggested to Paul that they go out on the porch and smoke. When they were settled in chairs Paul thought it was time for him to speak, to find out what he could about the possibility of reaching Johnny, of finding a phone, of learning something about a possible passage north. It was a clear night, with a light breeze; the moon, though beginning to wane, was still close to full and it lit the yard beyond the porch. They could see a good distance beyond the yard into the fields. Before Paul could begin his questions, the farmer spoke.

"We don't have many horses around here. They're expensive and not near as sturdy as *burros*, and if we did have some they would be an indulgence, something for children to ride around on. It isn't only the size of the little horse that fascinated my children. The fact of having a horse around at all was something that gave them pleasure as well. To be able to play with one, to pretend that it was their own. There's another reason too, and I want to show you something after a while. I've known about the little horses, but this is the first time I've seen one walking around.

"Some believe that the little horses came from Oaxaca, others think it was Taxco, and there are those who'd like to place them somewhere in the Yucatan. The Yucatan always sounds good: the ruins, the Indians, the myths, all that business. I'm one of those who believes that they came from a greater distance, from the North, and later, about the turn of the century. You understand now that I'm talking as much about the stories as the horses. You've got to interchange them as you listen; I don't know anybody who ever saw one. To be blunt about it, I think it was a North American who brought them down here, as a wonder, but as a pollution too. But there are a lot of stories, a lot of ideas about their origin, and mine is just one of them. Who can really know? One thing is sure, though. All the stories have blood in them; greed always rises up, people get killed, families are broken apart, innocent families sometimes."

The farmer leaned forward in his chair, reached out and knocked the bowl of his pipe against the porch edge. Dead ash and a few flickers of live coal drifted to the ground. When he leaned back, Paul saw a small instrument in his hand and he watched him carefully ream the bowl, take some tobacco from the can and tamp it in. Paul knew he was not finished yet, that what he had said so far was really a kind of prologue. He would tell a story soon, and it would have the flavor of something remembered, or once memorized, or heard somewhere. It would not be in his own speech exactly, but more formal than that. His preparing to tell it, the things he had said so far and the careful cleaning and loading of the pipe, was a familiar thing. Johnny had done similar things at Club El Monte. Paul thought that Mary Grace, before she had told him about the movies and the man who shot himself, had done them too. The farmer lit his pipe then with a wooden match and leaned back and began.

"Around the turn of the century, or maybe a little later, a man came from a place up north to settle somewhere down here in Mexico. He had some education, and he was alone, and it was not long before he found a woman to marry. She was a woman of mixed parentage; her father had been a gringo, possibly a cowboy working down here, and her mother was Mexican. There was some evidence that the man was mixed too, at least the story has it that he was dark and that he spoke good Spanish. It was easy to see how they matched up. They had two children, a girl and a boy, and then the woman died. The man couldn't handle the two children alone, so he kept the boy with him and managed to get the girl placed with a relative of his dead wife. It was while he was living alone with the boy that he started to get involved in things that finally resulted in the coming of the little horses. That part of the story is not too different in any version of the story that I have heard. It has to do with the development of crops that horses ate and, well, you know, in a while there were little horses.

"The man chased around for a while. The story has it that he went with a lot of women. Then he found a woman he liked a lot and he married her. Her husband had died, leaving her with two children, a boy and a girl, and when he married her, he brought his son with him. The rest of the story has to do with a lot of trouble between the children, with some brutality on the part of the stepfather, and a falling out between husband and wife. When things were going strong with the little horses, the son and the stepson, who were a little older now, became pitted against each other, and the daughter became a pull between them. Rumors had it that there was a variety of sex going on in the family. Sometimes there is killing, sometimes fire."

The man finished his story abruptly, and when he was done he sat for a while, puffing on his pipe, the smoke rising into the night in thin curls. Paul sat in the other chair, trying to put the pieces together. There was Johnny's story and the one Mary Grace had told and now this one. They were only stories, and yet they were all connected. He felt foolish thinking about them, taking them seriously. Still, one thing was real. There was the little horse, and he had her, and he knew he could not bear to consider letting her go. Whether or not he thought of the stories in a serious way, he knew that *he* was serious, and that he still had a way to go. In a while the farmer rose from his chair and turned to him.

"Come with me; I want to show you something."

He led him off the porch and around the side of the house to a small barn. When he got the large swinging doors open, the moonlight bathed the dirt at the entrance and Paul could see his darkening figure as he went in and took an oil lantern from a nail on one of the walls. When the lantern was lit there was enough light to see the whole of the inside: two stalls with *burros* in them, their heads hanging sleepily, some crude equipment, and ropes and harnesses. In the corner there was a rough wooden table with some object covered with a large piece of cloth on it. The farmer went to the table and motioned for Paul to follow him; when he got there he hung the lantern on another nail beside the table.

He looked at Paul for a long time, and then removed the cloth from the hidden object.

The skeleton was only half there, and where there were bones missing, great care had been taken to wire in substitutes. One of the rear legs was made of pieces of wood, something that looked like ebony, highly polished and almost an exact replica of the other. A few ribs looked like ivory, but on closer inspection Paul could see that they were some sort of polished stone. Where the teeth were missing more of the stone replaced them, and the small skull looked completely whole, the even sutures in the bone standing out in perfect lines. Where the hooves had been, cuffs of tin had been used to approximate their size and shape. There was a tail made of lightly woven straw hanging down behind the hip bones, and more straw had been used to lace a mane along the spine. But for the shape of the head, the little horse might have been a dog, but the skull was clearly that of a horse, and its tilt gave it expression, something altogether beyond the grave.

"I found it in the shale down by the river a few miles from here. My wife and children have seen it; that's part of the reason for the children's fascination with your little horse. You're the only one I've shown it to. I've had it for about two years; I've been working on it."

"I can see that," Paul said.

"Look over here." He lifted the mane behind the skull, and Paul saw the area that had been reconstructed. There were faint lines where stone had been fitted into a hole.

"I figured at first that he had been hit with something, a club maybe. Then inside, at the base of the jaw, I found this." He opened a small cigar box on the table and took something out of it and placed it in Paul's hand. It was a bit of metal.

"It's a bullet," the man said. "I thought at first that it was a club of some sort, that the horse had died a long time ago, but it was shot, and that bit of shot is not something old; I'd place it at no more than twenty years ago. And it could have been much later than that. I found this, too."

He took another object out of the cigar box, and Paul recognized it immediately. Though it was rusted, it was clearly one of the cups that he had found locked into the hooves of the little horse.

"I think this cup went into the horse's hoof. It seems shaped for that.

But maybe it was something more recent, something having to do with greed, something illegal; I don't know. But your horse; have you looked at the hooves?"

"I have, I . . . "

"Wait!" the man said. He had turned his head toward the door. Paul thought he had heard something. He reached out and touched Paul's arm, then moved quickly to the door. When he got there he was framed in what remained of the moonlight. Paul could see his profile as he turned toward the house. He looked stricken.

"*¡Dios!*" he said, and then he moved out of the frame quickly, heading in the direction of the house. Before he got to the doorway, Paul smelled the smoke. Then he came to the door and saw the man running toward the house. The smoke was lifting in a seeping cloud over the roof. There were flames spewing from the windows, and as he saw the man reach the porch and enter the flames at the door, he saw the whole roof come alive with fire, and as the flames rose it began to slowly sink. Then he saw the horse coming out of the window beside the door. It was in the flames for a moment, then it was free in the air. It cleared the porch and landed on the ground running.

"Here!" he yelled, and the horse bent into a gallop and came toward him.

He reached for whatever he could grab at the side of the door. He felt a length of rope and something else that he had to rip free. By the time the horse got to him, he had moved out and begun to turn. He saw the roof fall in and a huge billow of smoke rise over the house and then more flames. He could feel the heat on his face. He thought he saw figures to the side of the house in the smoke, but he did not pause to be certain. When he finished his turn away from the house, he was running. He could see the horse in front of him in full gallop. When he reached the edge of the first cultivated field he stumbled and had to fight to keep from falling. Then he was running again. He could see her in the moonlight, vaguely, far out in front of him. He ran as fast as he could, keeping his eyes on her; he knew he could not catch her, but he was determined to keep her in sight.

Chapter 14

He had clothing and shoes that almost fit him, and he had the gunnysack he had pulled from the wall and the length of thin rope he used to thread through it to make a sling. He kept to the edges of farmland, in hill country and away from roads. The weather was good, mild at night with enough moon left to see by. It rained twice, but only briefly, and he found places where he could hang and dry his clothing afterward. And he found things to eat, berries and vegetables he could get to without much risk at the edges of fields. She foraged on her own when he rested, and water was not a problem. He moved by day when it seemed reasonable, when he was in thick wilderness, but most of his movement was by night.

In the beginning he fell often, tripping over roots and stones, and once he thought he had hurt himself badly, but in the morning he found he only had deep bruises on his calves and buttocks. He cut himself, but no infection seemed to develop. After a while he got better at night travel, better at judging by moonlight. Each morning he checked his bearings by the sun. Four times he came upon people; twice they were adults, but he saw them soon enough to get the little horse in the bag. The children, once a boy and a girl and another time a boy alone, saw the horse, and he let them approach her and play a little with her before he moved on. He didn't think it was a problem.

He counted four nights of travel, but after that he lost count. In the beginning it was tough; he was sore and his legs and shoulders hurt him and he didn't have much wind, but sooner than he would have thought he started to feel better. He didn't relax. Each choice of directions and movement demanded some thought, but thought and decision started to come quicker, became more decisive, and after a while he began to see and appreciate some skill in himself that he did not know he had. He thought he was making good time. At least he was getting away from something. But he knew that to get back he could not keep going this way. The distance was ridiculous, maybe a thousand miles. He decided to give it two more nights of walking. Then he would have to do something.

He could not believe they had not all died in the fire. Someone could have made it out through the back of the house, but he did not think so; it had happened too quickly. He wondered what they would think when they found the skeleton in the barn, the bullet and the rusted cup; he hoped it would throw them off a little, make them think. He thought of the farmer and his family, tried hard to bring their faces up so he could mourn them in a proper and specific way, but he found it hard; it had all been so quick, and he had only had an hour or so of clarity while with them. All that he could really feel was a responsibility; having the horse and keeping her had been the cause. It had been the cause of the thing before as well. He did not want to think about that, about Mary Grace, what was happening to her now, if she was still alive. What was at the center of his thoughts, at a still center, was Parker, that image that kept him going.

The little horse remained calm and certain, but not oblivious to the terms of what was going on. She was alert. When she roamed away from him, he could see that she kept herself hidden and watchful. He felt himself in tune with her. When they slept, her sleep was not fitful, but it was shallow, and when they rose from sleep she was ready to go immediately, her eyes clear and her ears perked. Once he removed the cups from her hooves and checked the diamonds over with some care. He knew nothing of gems, but he thought he could see they were not finely cut. They were too large, he thought, for setting, and he figured them to be rough-cut, in a state for transport and possible sale, to be cut further later. They looked very good to him, without any flaws that he could see.

In two more nights he came in sight of the lights of a town, and he did what he had been doing and made his way around it. He continued on for a few more miles and then came upon another group of lights, much smaller than the first. He was in the foothills above them, and he decided that it was time to make some move. He thought it best to do it in the daytime, so he camped in sight of the village lights. In the early morning he found a stream and stripped and washed his clothes and dried them on rocks in the rising sun. Then when he was dressed again and as neat as he could get himself, he put the little horse in the gunnysack and made his way down out of the foothills and moved toward the village.

The place was composed of two streets that intersected at a square in which there was a small church with a bell tower. There were some alleys running from the main drags, but they were narrow, no more than footpaths, and down them he could see low plywood shacks, with tarpaper and tin tacked to them. The main streets were dirt, and the one he entered had wood sidewalks. There were a couple of buildings that looked old and important to the town; one was a bar, adobe and tiled, with arched windows and open, carved doors. As he passed it he could see the saw dust on the floor inside and two men seated at the bar drinking what he thought was coffee. Across from it, and down a little toward the square, was a place that looked like a public building of some kind. There were four or five signs extending at the door. The street was almost empty. He figured it was close to ten o'clock, and he couldn't understand why. He moved from the dirt of the street to the boardwalk; there were two men sitting on a bench on the other side, old men, smoking and talking. But there was no one else, no children or women. There were two battered pickup trucks, parked behind each other, in front of the public building. As he neared the square he heard laughter and talking and saw some children run across the square in the direction of the sound. He hitched the gunnysack up on his shoulder and touched the body of the little horse through it. He heard her muted snuffle through the fabric and felt her move. Then he came to the corner where the boardwalk ended and there were wooden steps leading down into the dirt of the square itself.

There was a fountain in front of the church, and he could see the crowd gathered around something happening on the other side of it. As he watched, a few more children and some women and men joined the crowd. One of the men lifted a young girl so that she could see over the heads in front. Then he heard a general shushing in the crowd and everyone went silent and there was only one voice speaking mildly and a number of distant clicks. He moved around the fountain to the back of the gathering. No one noticed him, or if they did they took no interest. He could see over the heads in front of him, but not too well, and he moved to the side where he had a better view.

There were two boys, a girl and a man sitting on the stone ledge of the fountain. The boys were close to the same age, around ten, and the girl was a little younger than that. She was sitting on the man's lap, a boy on either side of him. The man had a hat on, a fedora, and he was

dressed in a suit that was a little too small for him. The boy on his left
was small and wiry and dark. He was smiling and seemed to relish what
was going on. He sat close beside the man, almost touching him, but
he seemed self-contained, alone in his pleasure. The other boy leaned
in a little against the man, his body back a slightly, almost hiding behind
the man's shoulder. He was smiling too, but his smile was forced and
somewhat twisted, almost like a snarl. The man, obviously the father,
held the girl around the waist, and though she was not moving, her
gesture suggested that she was held against her will. Her face was turned
slightly, watching the boy on her left. She and the man holding her were
not smiling. The man looked straight ahead. It ought to be the mother
there, Paul thought, and then he heard someone speaking.

"*Eso sí, eso sí. Ahora no se muevan; quietos.*"

There was a click, and when he looked back from the fountain, he
saw the tripod with the large box camera on it and the man rise up from
his squat.

"Another. *Otra más. Pablito, acércate un poco. Bueno.* That's it."

The boy came out from behind the father's shoulder a little. The
father turned his head, smiling for the first time.

"*Está bien, m'ijito,* my little honey buns. *Sonríe para la cámara. Smile
para este caballero tan simpático!*" The father's voice was smooth and
purring, oily almost, and the boy, lighter than the other in complexion,
blushed and smiled his sneering smile up at the father. Then there was
another click.

"Okay. *Muy bueno. Ahora alguien más.* Somebody else now."

The father moved his arm away and the girl jumped down from his
lap. She moved to the darker boy and grabbed his hand and pulled him
down from the ledge and they ran off together. When the father got
down, he lifted the other boy up, higher than was necessary, and put
him on his feet, tousled his hair and squeezed his arm. Then he reached
down and swatted him lightly on the buttocks, and the boy moved off,
looking back at the man, the camera and the photographer sullenly.

Then another group, this time six children and a man and a woman,
went and climbed up on the ledge, and the photographer moved from
behind the camera and went to them and began to arrange them where
he wanted. He was tall and lean, dressed casually in khaki pants and a
loose checked sports shirt. He wore low boots and his sleeves were rolled

almost to the elbows. When he turned, Paul saw that he was a gringo, light complected, his skin freshly sunburned, his hair almost a tan color, with bits of gray in it, and curly. He had a thick mustache and a broad forehead. He was squinting a little in the sun.

Paul reached to the mouth of the gunnysack to make sure that it was open sufficiently and stayed where he was. People left and others came and joined the small crowd. Some looked at him, and some even spoke. He understood nothing of what was said, but he took the brief talk to be pleasantries, and he nodded and smiled. That seemed to work, and no one looked too oddly at him. Once a man in uniform stood beside him. He was sure it was a local policeman of some sort. But the man only looked at him blankly, watched the photographing for a while and then moved away. Paul was getting tired of standing, and he worried about the state of the horse in the bag. But he could feel her steady breathing through the rough fabric; she seemed all right, and he thought this was really the best place for him and that the photographer was his best bet. The man was efficient, and he spoke gently and kindly to the people, even joked at times with the audience.

Paul couldn't quite figure what it was he was after in the pictures, but he could tell he was after very specific things. He took great care in arranging those he was photographing, and the expressions he seemed to be capturing were interesting if unconventional. He took a lot of time with each group. After what seemed about an hour of standing, Paul thought he'd better move away. To stay too long might itself be conspicuous, more conspicuous even than being alone. He walked to the side of the square where there were some benches. They were on the same side as the crowd, and he could still watch. All the benches were empty, and he picked one at the end and sat down, putting the sack on the seat beside him. He wished he had something to read, something for his hands to work with, anything to make him look occupied. He picked up the gunnysack and put it on his lap and opened its mouth. He looked down into it and saw her staring up at him unblinking. Then he reached in as if he were adjusting something and touched her muzzle and the side of her face. Then he took what time he could in closing the bag up and adjusting it on the seat.

He felt a presence beside him, and when he turned he saw the little girl and the boy from the photographic session standing there. They were both smiling, the boy bolder than the girl, but it was she who reached out and poked her finger into the side of the sack, then quickly withdrew it and winked at him. He winked back and smiled. Neither of them spoke. He had nothing to give them, and there was nothing he could say to them, but he welcomed their presence and he did not want them to leave. He smiled again at the girl and then at the boy, and he reached out and patted the sack and winked again. They giggled; the girl spoke with a lilting voice to the boy, who nodded his agreement to what she said. They stood there for a long time, and then there were some voices and movement from the fountain. The three of them looked over at it. The crowd was breaking up, and as it dispersed they could see the photographer carefully placing his camera in its leather case. Then he was folding his tripod. The children nodded to Paul, bowed a little and ran off. The photographer, his camera case hung from his shoulder and his tripod under his arm, was moving across the square now, and as Paul turned to watch him he could see he was headed toward an automobile, a fairly new Ford that was parked in front of what looked like a small restaurant on the street that intersected the one Paul had come down. He got up from the bench and took his sack and moved off after him.

The car's trunk was open, the man bent down over it adjusting his equipment when Paul reached him. He had tried to plan what to say, to figure something convincing and appropriate while watching the photo-taking, but he had come up with nothing. When he reached the man, he simply stood there, a little to the side, and waited. The man was intent on the contents of the trunk and did not see him. But then he did see him or was aware of his presence at least, and he rose from the trunk and turned and smiled and spoke briskly in Spanish. Paul grinned at him and lifted his shoulders.

"Oh, you're a gringo," the man said, a little laughter in his eyes. He looked him over, noting the gunnysack, the worn overalls.

"Is there something I can do for you?"

"Yes. Right; I'm from San Diego, I . . . "

"Well, how about a little lunch," the man interrupted.

"I don't have any money," Paul said.

"Hey, come on. It'll be good to talk a little English. It's been a month for me."

They went into the restaurant. It was really a bar that served food, and when they were seated and had ordered they began to talk. The photographer talked first, giving Paul time to get himself and his story together, and when the food came, beans and tortillas and some coarse meat, he waited for Paul to eat, telling him more about himself as he nibbled at his food. Paul was not that hungry, but the taste of cooked food was something he realized how much he had missed as he tasted it, and though he tried to go slowly he found himself wolfing down what was before him.

Ronny was from California. He told him very early on that he was a homosexual, that though he had done landscapes and some collage experimental stuff, most of his recent work had been portraits and those, up until the time he came down for this trip, photography of homosexual men, formal shots mostly, nothing sexually provocative. For some reason he wasn't exactly sure of, these portraits had gotten him interested in family things. He wanted group shots now. At times he wanted fathers, at others mothers. He had been at it down here for two months, and one of the things that kept him interested was that he didn't really know why he chose fathers in certain families and mothers in others. He knew why he had come down here, though. It was the children, their special faces, their relationships between each other and with their parents. It was very different down here, and though he did not understand it yet, he knew that he could see it clearly. He figured he would have some ideas about what it was before too long. He was working, he thought, on a book of some sort, a book of photographs. He had no idea of the length or name or real theme of it. But he did know that it would have something to do with families. He was just about done now. He had taken hundreds of pictures, and he was sure that a fair percentage of them were good. He would find out in the darkroom when he got back.

He talked on, and he was facile in his talking, and Paul could see that he was giving him a chance before he had to talk, some chance to get to a point where he could explain himself and do it with some ease and lack of embarrassment. After a while, when Paul had not spoken a word other than those necessary to keep Ronny's talk going, Ronny slowed down a bit. There were more pauses between sentences, and finally it seemed he had nothing else to say for a while, had begun to repeat himself, and this was clearly distasteful to both of them.

"Look," Paul said. "It's been a long story, and really I can't tell it to you, at least not yet. I'm in a little trouble though, and I need to get North. I can pay you, but not just yet. But it sure as hell would be a help to me if you could give me a lift. Where are you headed next?"

"Shit, I don't need any money, man; sure you can have a lift. I've got a little more to do here this afternoon, and then I'm heading to Durango. I've got some friends there. Maybe a couple of days, and then up through Sonora and back to L.A., and, hey, you don't have to tell me anything."

"Where are we?"

"This town you mean? We're just outside a ways from El Jazmin. You mean you don't know where you are?"

"That's part of the story. I left near Mexico City close to a week ago on foot."

"Christ! That must be some story. We're sixty or more miles from there."

Paul waited in the square while Ronny finished taking pictures. By one o'clock he was finished, and when he had packed the car trunk, they left the town and headed North. The roads were narrow but not bad, and they made fairly good time. Ronny told him more about his photography and Paul told him about his job with Pfeffer, the Navy, and some about his high school years in Bisbee. Everything he said made these things seem historic, in a way as if they belonged to another life entirely. Ronny said he had come out in college, had lost all family connection in the bargain, and had immersed himself in photography to get through school. It was only after he graduated that he made some connections through a studio where he had taken some work, had met a group of men who had been a help to him, a network of friends who looked out for each other. He had lived with one of the men for two years. It was good times, but now he was alone, and he liked the freedom of it. He had been making good money doing free-lance fashion work. He had made enough to take six months off, to work on the family series. The little horse was in the sack on the back seat of the car, and Paul knew that soon he would have to take her out; it could not be good for her to stay there so long, and she had not eaten since morning. He figured he would have to show her to Ronny soon. He didn't want to do it, but he was feeling better about it. He had, he thought, a pretty good sense of Ronny; he was okay. He liked him, and he thought he could trust him, knew he would have to.

They made it to Aguascalientes before nightfall, and Ronny found a motel with a vacancy sign. When they got to the room, Paul saw that there was only a double bed in it. Ronny saw him look and said he was sorry and that he hoped Paul didn't mind, but that was all they had.

"Mind? This is the first bed I've seen in over a week."

Paul left the horse in the sack on a chair in the room, pressing her before he went out to help Ronny unload his equipment from the trunk. Along with the tripod and camera case were two other cases full of exposed film and a large suitcase. When they had everything in, Paul knew that he could not wait any longer, and he asked Ronny to sit down on the bed, that he needed to talk to him. He himself sat in the chair beside the rough wooden table. The place was really not a motel but a row of wooden buildings, small bedrooms and baths; it had probably been a hunting or fishing lodge at one time.

"Look, I think the best way to explain this, or at least to start to, is to show you something. I think this is going to shock you, but really there's nothing to worry about; it's just that I didn't want to spring it on you without any preparation."

He got up from his chair and crossed to the one with the sack on it. He lifted the sack up, put it on the floor, and opened the mouth. The sack swelled as the little horse got to her feet inside of it, and then she walked out into the room. Her eyes were sharp and clear, and her muzzle was high, sniffing. She was a little stiff on her legs, and she shook her tail to get it to fall out. She looked up at Paul and pulled her upper lip back and whinnied softly; then she looked at the bed, where Ronny was sitting. He had been slumped a little, but when he saw her he jerked upright, his hands rising from his knees, his eyes widening.

"Christ! I've seen that horse before! In a movie, but there were two of them!" It was Paul's eyes that widened then, and with his hands behind him he groped for the chair arm, staggered back a little and fell into the seat.

Chapter 15

I t had been in Los Angeles, about a year ago, maybe more, at a private showing. A friend had told him it was something he might find of interest. Not a friend really, but an acquaintance of a friend, someone who he remembered had spoken Spanish. He remembered he hadn't liked him much; he seemed to have an edge of cruelty in his bearing, but they had spoken Spanish together, and that was a gain for him because he was already thinking about his trip down here and needed the practice. They had gone to a house in Eagle Rock, on the Pasadena side of L.A., a large old place, a little in the hills, with a good-sized piece of land around it. There were a lot of people there, only a few of whom he had seen before, mostly in and around the bar scene. There had been a party, a rather elegant and subdued one, he remembered, with soft chamber music as background and very good booze and fresh shrimp and other things to eat. There were drugs, too, but that was handled discreetly. The talk had been casual and light, and there had been very little carrying on and nothing loud. He thought that some of the people were straight, but he was not sure about that now. He couldn't remember specifics about the party too well. He thought there had been some unsavory types there, but maybe he was wrong about that. He was sure he remembered that there was a lot of money present though; it was not just the clothing, but the jewelry, and most of all the behavior.

The movie was shown around midnight. They were ushered into a screening room, not a makeshift one, but a real one, with theater seats and enclosed projection booth and a full-size screen. There was even a curtain hanging in front of it, and he thought an automatic device to pull it open. He remembered that when the lights went down there was a whirring as the curtains parted.

The image came into focus slowly. It was that of a small man walking down a beach. He was dressed in baggy pants and a loose white shirt opened to the waist, and his hair was greased down flat on his head, shining in the sun. He made quick little mincing steps, and though the shot was at some distance from him, his occasional winks and nods at the camera could be seen. Then a structure came into the foreground from the side. It was a kind of wooden deck with a row of steps leading up to it from the beach. The little man moved from the beach and came up the steps, the camera following his movements, and when he reached the deck itself he was among beach chairs, air mattresses and gliders with people on and in them. Most were men, young men, though he thought he remembered that there were at least three women, and he was sure he remembered two of the women; they were heavily painted, dressed only in black underwear and large summer hats. The men were standing and lounging against each other, some were sitting on the laps of others, kissing. They were variously dressed, some shirtless and muscular, and there were at least two couples who were totally naked, fucking each other on air mattresses and, he thought, a pair going at it on one of the gliders. They were all very sun-tanned, and he couldn't remember seeing bathing-suit lines on any of them.

The little man moved among them, pointing and smiling at the camera, doing little imitative bumps and grinds. He had a thin, pencil-line mustache, and he would twitch it in funny ways as he moved around and among the couples. At times he would sneak up and goose one of the men, and there would be gestures of humor and laughter. Ronny remembered that the movie at first was silent, but when the camera moved in on one of the engaged couples—a muscular man kneeling behind a thinner one and pumping into him—and held the image, music came up and within it the sounds of the lunges and groans and then the voices of others. The camera held on the couple for a while, then it pulled back so that the whole deck was visible again, and every-one on it was engaged in some kind of heated sexual activity. Everyone but the two painted women; they were sitting in chairs alone, their legs crossed, and were smirking and sometimes laughing at what they saw. He remembered that it was about then that he started to feel uncomfort-able with what he was seeing. The two women, because they were not involved in the activity, were oddly focal, and though he was enjoying watching the sex the men were participating in, he found he had to keep looking at the women, and their looks and laughter were derisive, de-meaning what they saw. The feeling he had that he didn't like was that the movie had a point, and that the point seemed to be homophobic, ugly and cheap. He didn't know if others in the room felt the way he did at that time, but he thought he remembered that there was very little comment from the audience, and no urging or laughter at all. He remembered a smell of tobacco; people had lit up cigars. They were strong and offensive, and he had thought it odd to be smelling them in this gathering. Things continued, and then almost at the time that he recognized his absence from the situation the little man entered the frame again, this time with the horses.

He remembered that the progress came in slowly from the right side, from a kind of patio that was behind the deck. The woman came in first. She was dressed as a kind of innocent maiden, in a long white dress with a white lace veil. She might have been a bride. He thought he remembered that the bodice of her dress was open and that the edges of her small breasts were visible. She carried baskets of flowers, roses, the wicker handles of the baskets hanging from her wrists. Her arms were extended slightly, as if she were offering the flowers. Maybe she was some sort of sacrificial victim heading for some idol or some bacchanale that she would be forced to enter, where she would be deflowered. Her steps were processional and very slow, and he remembered that her eyes and cheeks were dusted a light rose color and that her lipstick was of the same hue. Not quite a maiden, bride, or whore, her movements and her gestures were emblematic, but ambiguous; she looked ahead and up slightly and not at the sweating men who were engaged with each other in various postures. As she moved in from the side of the frame and the train of her dress came into view as it slid across the wood of the deck, the two horses entered behind her. They were not tethered together, but each had a set of reins running from a harness to a place that was still off-camera. The reins might have been leather and the harnesses too, but whatever they were they were covered with rhinestones and colored bits of metal. The horses like the woman in front of them were moving slowly, their reins taut, holding them back a little, pulling their heads up so that their forelegs moved in a kind of prancing. The horse nearest the camera was smaller than the other, probably the female, and she pressed in against the larger one, staying a little back, so that both of their heads were visible. Both had ribbons in their tails and manes, and all of their hooves sparkled. There were things set into the hooves, kinds of jewels possibly, and their palomino bodies looked smooth and freshly brushed.

There was a new kind of tentative laughter in the audience and some body movement. He thought he remembered voices that were steady, explaining things to others, but mostly the atmosphere was becoming a little unsettled; people had risen from their seats and some were milling around. There were a few loud voices, and the smell of cigars grew stronger. There was no clear handle yet, no real integration of this new and startling event into the erotica that had preceded it. He thought the little man with the baggy pants was something they could find a way to understand, but the woman and the horses were another thing altogether. The sight of them, their slow movement, but most of all their potential, was a new issue, and he remembered feeling a general anticipation in the room, one that he shared. It was not a titillating anticipation, but a need for some sort of resolution, a resolution that would explain things and put them at ease again. He thought now, looking back at it, that what did happen was really totally unsatisfactory, but was accepted as sufficient because the need to do so was so great. Anything might have done it, even the vaguest of turns.

The woman moved slowly among the naked and half-clothed bodies, the engaged and the casual, her baskets held out before her, and the horses followed in her train. Then the little man came into the frame holding the reins out with limp wrists at his chest. He was strutting slightly, but when he came into full view he stopped doing that and started to slide his feet over the deck, to seem to float as on some conveyor belt behind the horses and the woman. He was dressed as he had been dressed before, but Ronny remembered that from this angle he could see the loop of a gold chain running in a deep curve from his belt loop to his pocket. They moved in tandem to an open place near the deck's railing, and there they stopped. They were so situated now that they were flanked by the two painted woman in their chairs. They were in the background, and before them were the sunstruck bodies. More were engaged now, possibly all of them, and Ronny thought that the action had passed the point of newness and titillation, had moved over the brink into that need for variety that follows the first, almost insouciant need. The bodies were not consumed now, but half occupied, minds in the way making choices. Rhythms were smoother and slower, dances were minuets and not twists.

The woman stepped back against the railing, but she did not lean against it; her posture was still poised and formal. The little man smiled toward the camera and took his reins and hung them delicately over the railing. The two women flanking them grinned, glancing derisively at the glistening bodies. And the little horses pressed against each other, and when the man reached down and unhooked the reins from their halters they did not move away. Then he tapped each of them, with two fingers smartly on their haunches and the smaller of the two looked back at him and the other stepped forward to one of the baskets, dipped his head into it and came up with a rose in his teeth. The little man tried again to get the smaller horse to move, and this time she did, but she did not go to a basket but moved up against the other horse and, walking very close to him, went with him as he took and deposited the rose beside a pair on one of the air-mattresses. She followed him as he went back and got another rose and took it to another place. At times he would put the roses beside people, but at others he would drop them delicately on top of some body, and once he even held a stem out in his mouth to be taken into the mouth of a kneeling man, to be held in his teeth like a Spanish dancer.

There was some light applause that rose from the audience, some oohs and aahs, and some definite release of tension. It was as if the delivering of the roses solved everything, linking the progress and the horses to the sexuality of the movie, and though Ronny remembered that there was nothing at all erotic about the roses or the way the horses delivered them, he felt in the audience an acceptance that there was, a pretending, a needed belief.

There was little else to tell. The movie had no real ending, just a slow fade out and a rise of music in the middle of much ongoing activity.

"And this has to be the horse, the demure one, or one very much like it. I don't know what to do with this, man. Jesus, can I take her picture?"

"The lake, what was the lake like? Did the little man have a scar?"

"Well, I remember it was empty. It could be seen behind the deck and the action as a kind of horizon, a neutral backdrop to the action. I think it was quite large, almost oval. It was as flat as a piece of glass. What kind of scar?"

"On his stomach. A long one; vertical."

"His shirt was open on the beach, and it was open all the way when he had the reins. He wore some neck jewelry I think. He was dark and wiry, thin but hard. No, there was nothing like that. Nothing at all that I remember."

The little horse came up to Ronny's knee and nudged him. He jerked away for a moment in reflex, but then he relaxed again, realizing his foolishness and knowing that he had nothing to fear. She moved in again and touched his leg with her muzzle and rubbed it against his leg briefly. Then she walked over to Paul and climbed up on his chair and settled into his lap.

"Jesus! I don't believe this."

"Believe it. It's happening, and there's a lot more of it, too."

Ronny went to a restaurant and brought back food for them. The best they could do for the horse was a large salad, and though she had not eaten that day, she ate carefully and slowly, searching among the lettuce for carrots and other things she liked. They both watched her as they ate. When they were finished, Paul leaned back in his chair, his exhaustion coming in upon him. He felt stiff and he ached, and though he was full he felt a little woozy, as if he had not eaten for a long time. Ronny had some brandy in the car and he got it and gave Paul a good shot of it. They drank together, watching the horse as she moved around the room. The brandy revived Paul, and rather than wait until morning he told Ronny the story of the little horse and of Mary Grace and Johnny and Parker. As he told it, he realized how strange it was and he also realized that he was not sure of all of it, not even of those parts he had been involved in. He kept feeling he was missing things, leaving them out, forgetting them. His narrative was jerky, and he was not sure of the time of things. His stay in the house with Mary Grace came and went in a sentence, and though he reached back for it, to get more of the leisurely flavor of it, he knew as he tried that he could not do so, and he moved on.

Ronny listened attentively, nodding at times, but he did not speak, asked no questions and had no comments. Paul might have thought that the rehearsal of the story would make it in some way rational, even explain some of the things in it. But it did not do so at all. When he was finished, was sticking in more details that he had forgotten, he realized that if anything he was more uncertain about it than he had been before. Ronny's behavior didn't help this at all. His nods were not gestures of understanding, but urges that pushed Paul forward, to points of understanding. And these never really came; they were nowhere in the story at all. But he did not tell Ronny about his resolve to kill Parker.

It was a private resolve, but it was more than that; it was a kind of node in him, part of him now, a little packet of energy that he knew kept him going, wherever it was that he was going, and he could not release it and still be sure of staying on track.

When Paul was finished, Ronny asked a few questions, but they were about details. He did not ask Paul why he didn't give up the horse, and Paul took the absence of the question as some evidence of a ground of understanding between them.

Later, after they had finished their brandy and had talked about what other things were possible to be talked about after the story was ended, Ronny saw how drawn Paul's face was, how little he had left, and he suggested that they get to bed. It was nine o'clock. Paul thought he should take a shower; he knew he needed the cleansing and the feel of the hot water, but he didn't think he could manage it. He was standing beside the bed. Ronny was in the bathroom, and the little horse was standing next to one of the chairs looking at him. He slipped the strap of the coveralls from his shoulders and let them and the baggy under-drawers fall to the floor; then he sat down naked on the edge of the bed and took his shoes off. While he was bending over to get the laces, he heard Ronny behind him a moment before he spoke.

"Christ, man! You're torn apart."

"Am I? I don't know, I . . . "

He felt Ronny's fingers lightly on the bones at his shoulder, and then he was sitting on the bed beside him. He was in his underwear and socks, and Paul could see the darkness of his lower arms and the tan line at his neck, below which was his white chest, his head like a bronze sculpture above his shoulders.

"Hey, come on; we're going to the bathroom. I'll fix you up."

He stood and helped Paul to his feet. He was unsteady. Sitting on the bed had brought his body close to a posture of needed sleep, and Ronny waited for him to get his footing before he helped him to the bathroom. When they got there and Paul saw himself in the large mirror over the sink, he was shocked awake a little by the sight. There were deep scratches and a few scab-encrusted cuts on his chest and belly and some running on his thighs. One long cut ran from his stomach, through the pad at his waist and to his groin. He couldn't imagine when he had gotten it, but he could see that it had needed stitches, and when it healed there would be a broad scar there, almost an inch wide. Ronny saw him looking at himself, at the cuts and deep bruises and the crusts of dirt.

"Your back is even worse, and you've got a mean-looking gouge in your ass."

Paul reached behind him and felt it, the hump of contusion and the jagged edge of the torn flesh. He couldn't feel any pain at first, but when he pressed it harder he did feel some, very deep and aching. His mind moved back over the days, but all he could remember was his acute attention to the outside world. He could see places with great clarity, hills, farms, smooth rocks where he had made his bed and eaten, specific movements of the little horse ahead of him. He thought he could remember the time he had fallen; that was early on, but he couldn't be sure of it. He thought it was something in his leg that he had injured then, his calf maybe. He tried to flex his calves, but he couldn't be sure that he was doing it when he tried. He looked down at his feet, and he could see the raw flesh and the new calluses and the way his toes were twisted. He remembered a distant, ongoing frail pain at the ends of his body and along his spine. He opened his toes and flexed his ankles and feet tentatively. The toes unfolded a little, and he felt the pain in them.

"Look, you have to have a hot shower. I'm going to get in there with you, to make sure you don't fall. It's going to hurt a little. Maybe more than that. Okay?"

"Okay," he said, and Ronny helped him closer to the shower stall, and with his other hand reached in and turned on and adjusted the water temperature and the spray.

"Reach in and feel it," he said. And Paul put his hand under the spray. It was hot, but not too hot, and he nodded that it was fine.

As he was getting him under the stream, Ronny flipped the lid from a small square case that was sitting on the counter beside the sink and got a tube of shampoo and a bar of good soap in a plastic container out of it. He pulled a washcloth from the towel rack and dropped it beside them. He had one leg in the stall as he eased Paul under the stream of water, and when he had him there, his head bent and the spray forming a flimsy umbrella over him, he stepped out, still holding Paul by the elbow, and pulled his underwear and socks off. Then he got into the shower with him. He soaped the washcloth and his hands and then, hanging the washcloth over his shoulder, ran his soapy hands carefully over Paul's shoulders and back. The water stung a little and the soap a little more, and Paul could see down into the drain, the streams of dirt mixed with threads of blood and bits of scab washing away. Then Ronny was using the washcloth gently, going over places that needed it, scrubbing lightly. He pressed his hands against Paul's back, moving him forward a little in the stall, and then he was on his knees, running the bar of soap over and between his buttocks, cleaning them, using the cloth again to work at the hump and gouge. The cloth hurt him and he bucked slightly and heard Ronny's muffled voice in the water at his hip.

"Sorry, got to get it clean."

And then he was washing his lower legs, and Paul held to the sides of the stall, lifting each foot as Ronny ran the cloth and his fingers between his toes, around his ankles and scrubbed harder at the bottoms of his feet. Then he rose.

"Turn around," he said, and Paul turned and faced him. They were inches apart, both blinking in the water, and Ronny put his hand up and placed it on top of Paul's head, urging him to bend, and he did so and through the spray he could see the wet hair at the other man's crotch and the whiteness of his penis. He felt something cold on his scalp, and then could feel a tingling as the suds came up, a few dirty ones falling to his stomach and Ronny's groin. And then there was a rush of dirty water running down his chest. Ronny rinsed him and then drenched him with more cool shampoo, running his fingertips briskly through his hair. The second rinsing was less dark, only gray, and after a third wash the water was clear and the suds white. Then he soaped his chest and stomach, again using his hands and the cloth, and then he got down on his knees again and washed Paul's thighs. When the cloth slid into the crevices at his groin, he could feel a tingling that was not caused by the soap, and looking down he saw his penis begin to extend and rise. Ronny didn't look up, but he spoke again in the water below him.

"That's all right, man. It's only natural."

Paul was too gratefully soothed and too tired and too well cared for to feel his embarrassment rise into anything significant. He only felt a little warmer, that he was flushing a little in the water. And as if he knew this and really in the most appropriate way possible, Ronny didn't linger at all but took his soapy hands and the soapy cloth and washed Paul's extended penis and his testicles. He washed them thoroughly, gently, but efficiently. Paul felt and saw his fingers and continued to harden. Ronny finished, and then he held his hands in front of Paul's groin, using them as a kind of tilted wall that deflected the shower spray, washing the dirt and suds off, and Paul's penis began to sink in the flensing.

"See," Ronny said. "We're just about done."

He got up again and faced him, and then he started slightly, glancing quickly at his feet. Then he was laughing. The little horse was in the shower with them. Paul felt her bumping against his shins and knees, and when he looked down and saw her matted and wet body, her head raised and looking at him through the spray, he laughed too. He moved back to the wall of the shower, and Ronny got down again and scraped and scrubbed with the bar and his hands, washing the little horse. She arched her back like a cat as he scrubbed her spine, and she curled and spread her tail, presenting it so that he could run the strands between his palm and the bar. He looked up at Paul to see that he was okay, and then he took what time was needed to get the horse clean.

When they left the shower, the little horse shook her body and Ronny got Paul on a towel spread over the toilet seat and briskly dried his hair; he handed him another towel so he could dry those places that he could reach without difficulty. He was steadier than before, but when he rose to go to the other room he found the exhaustion in his legs. They felt like lead, and he was grateful for the bed when he got to it and could get his legs up and lie down. He was lying on his back, his eyes half closed but still awake when Ronny came back in. He had his kit with him, and after he sat down on the side of the bed he took things out of it and held them up so Paul could see them. He showed him a tube of first-aid cream, another of lanolin lotion, and a bottle of mercurochrome.

"Turn over. I'll get the back first."

He was as careful as he had been in the shower, and once he had the cream on and had used the mercurochrome for the raw places, he rubbed the bruises with lanolin. There was some deep pain, but it was not too much and the rubbing in of the cream felt good. After he had gotten Paul turned over again, he administered to the front of his body. Paul could see his hands at times, could see his head and face vaguely. And then things began to swim. He felt a bump on the bed and came back from what he knew was the edge of sleep. The little horse moved up beside him and looked down into his face. Her image was clear to him, but only for a moment.

"I'm going to sleep," he managed to get out in a whisper.

"Go ahead. It's okay. I'm almost done."

He woke once in the night and felt the sheet and the slight weight of the blanket over him. He was on his side and could see the edge of her mane, the curve of her head and her ears inches away from his face. He felt her haunches against his stomach and her spine against his ribs. On the other side of her head he could see the hair and the left ear of the other man. He shifted a little and felt his knee against the back of Ronny's thigh, and he pressed into it, moving his foot until it touched another. The horse breathed in deeply once, and he heard the whisper of her breath as she exhaled.

Chapter 16

In the morning he felt like a new man, like one who had literally risen up out of something that now seemed very distant, as part of another life, at least physically. He had new clothes. Ronny had gone out in the morning and gotten them, and when he opened his eyes at ten o'clock, Ronny was sitting in one of the chairs drinking coffee, the shopping bags with the clothes in them on the wooden table beside him. He had also found some alfalfa, and the horse was munching from the small pile on a newspaper in a corner of the room.

As he washed and shaved in the bathroom, Paul still felt the bruises and the cuts; he saw them, and some were still quite ugly, but he could move without difficulty, and the pain was something that he could handle. The clothes were very much the same as the ones Mary Grace had gotten him a while ago, and as he put them on he felt that what he had risen into was the thing he still had to resolve. He felt ready and anxious to get going, but he also felt a firming of resolve that made speed a relatively less important issue. When he came out and put the shoes on, he found that they fit him, and there was only a little pain left from the tightness of the farmer's.

After they had finished the breakfast Ronny had brought back with the clothes and were sipping a second cup of coffee, Ronny nodded at where the little horse was sitting, curled in one of the chairs.

"Hey, really, how about a few pictures of you and the horse?" he said.

Paul didn't like the idea, but Ronny was so direct in his asking and he had done so much for him that Paul didn't feel he could refuse. He nodded, and Ronny got up quickly and began preparing his tripod and camera. He had some lights for indoor shots, and he set them up to the side of the tripod. They were dim lights, just enough to illuminate the section of the room that he had chosen. He took some full-length ones, with the horse standing at Paul's feet, and he took some with Paul holding the horse. He finished with the horse standing on the table with Paul sitting on the edge of it beside her. It didn't take him long, and it was less of a burden than Paul had imagined it would be.

"You just want to have these, right? I mean you don't have plans for them."

"That's right. I won't show them to anybody, and if I ever do it'll be a while from now. I just want to have them."

They were packed and on the road again before noon. It was just over two hundred miles to Durango, but the road was not the best, and after they had gone only a short distance the sky darkened and it was soon raining hard enough that Ronny had to drive slowly. There were trucks along the narrow highway throwing up spray, and he had to keep the car well back of them in order not to be blinded. They talked some about the movie Ronny had remembered, and in the midst of that talk Paul was able to find a way of thanking him for the care, to say how much better he felt. He tried to say he thought he could get money to pay Ronny back for expenses, for gas and food, but Ronny waved it off, telling him not to worry about that now.

Ronny couldn't remember that much about the gathering at the house where the movie was shown; he wasn't even sure whose house it was. He did remember that there had been some Hollywood connections there, maybe some actors, the kinds you see in commercials and some movie executive types, nobody he knew or had seen before, but he thought he remembered snatches of inside talk, movie talk. And now that he thought about it, he didn't even know why his friend and he had been invited. The only connection had been his friend's acquaintance, and he couldn't think that that would be enough of a reason, given what they had seen and what Paul had added to the story. He did know that nobody had wanted anything from him; there had been no questions after the movie was over. Nothing else happened as far as he knew, or was concerned. Maybe there had been some private talks among people elsewhere in the house afterward. The party that followed the showing had been smaller than the one before, he thought. But really he couldn't say.

There was of course much talk about the movie at the party afterward, but he remembered it was the kind he could participate in, aesthetic movie talk, not anything that went beyond the picture itself. Maybe his friends in Durango would know something. They had been in and around Hollywood's fashion center for a lot of years; they might have heard something. One was a set designer, a Mexican who went back and forth between Durango and the states often; the other was involved in lighting, mostly big stuff that had to do with promotional stills and large outdoor scenes for magazines. That was Angie. He'd been at the showing with Ronny. He lived in Hollywood and was down here visiting for a few months. There might be others there too; he wasn't sure.

"What'll we do with the horse when we get there?" Paul asked. He told him the house was big, these guys were very good friends, and they wouldn't ask anything. They could find a place for her.

"We'll only have to stay for a couple of days. I really do have to stop by. You can handle that, can't you?"

Paul couldn't see any reason for not stopping. He certainly didn't want to try to continue on his own. There was still a way to go, and without Spanish and enough money he couldn't be sure he'd make it with the little horse. He wished Ronny were going through Chihuahua. He thought, now that he was beginning to be able to figure things again, that that was the place to go, to find Johnny.

"Did you ever hear of Abelardo García, some politician or other from Chihuahua?"

"No, I never did. But then I don't know much about Mexican politics. My friend in Durango will probably know about him; we can ask him. You want to go to Chihuahua, don't you? Hell, maybe I could swing up that way."

"No," Paul said. "You've done enough already. I'll go where you're going."

By five o'clock they were getting close to Durango and the rain was letting up. When they reached the small towns and villages at its outskirts the rain had finished, and the sun was back again, lighting the rain slicks on the highway and drying the drops on the Ford's hood. Before they got to the city, Ronny turned off to the right.

"The house is on the other side, but they said that it's better to go around."

They passed by farms and through a few small villages, making a loop around the city. When they reached the far side, where there were low hills, they entered a suburban area that Paul could see at once was very wealthy. The houses were on large, wooded sections of land. None seemed visible from any other. They were large, and most were set back, so that as they passed them they could only catch glimpses of drives, fountains and verandas through the trees. The streets were well paved, and the curbs were slightly sloped. There were no sidewalks and no cars. The street signs were low and tasteful. Ronny turned in at a drive that rose up sharply to higher ground, then leveled as it approached the house, a large sprawling affair, very modern, made of poured concrete with plenty of glass and a number of domed skylights set in its flat roofs. It had a broad porch at its center and two wings running off to either side. There was a black BMW parked in a small cul-de-sac to the right of the porch. Ronny pulled the Ford up to the stone steps that led up a few feet to the porch, and Paul could see through the glass door beyond right through the house to similar doors on the other side. He saw the trunks of large trees, chairs on a patio, and a diving board. He thought the trees might be eucalyptus, but he wasn't sure. In the middle of the passage that led from front to back was a large modern chandelier, and to the left was a chrome-railed staircase bending to a second story. Ronny got out and leaned in at the window.

"I'll tell them you've got a sick dog," he said, and then he turned and went up the steps and slid open the glass door and walked through the room and out the other side of the house. He stopped and turned to the left when he got to the patio, and Paul could see him smile and somebody come up to him with open arms. They embraced, banging each other on the back. The man was smaller than Ronny was, and

Ronny had to bend over a little to hug him. Another man came up and put his hand on Ronny's shoulder, waiting his turn, and when the first man was finished he and Ronny embraced as well. They stood close together, talking animatedly for a few moments, then Ronny turned and gestured toward the porch. The other men nodded vigorously, and one of them entered the house and moved out of sight to the left. The other stood with his hands on his hips, smiling, as Ronny came back through the house. When he got to the car, he leaned on the window sill again.

"Wrap her in the blanket; bring the alfalfa, and come with me."

Paul followed Ronny into the house, the little horse covered by the blanket in his arms. They went to a room, a small utility space that did not look as if it were in use. There was a glass bowl with water in it on the floor, and a large wicker basket with rags tucked in it in a corner. Paul put the bag of alfalfa beside the bowl, opening the mouth of it so that she could get to it.

"That's Ernesto for you; fastest man I know," Ronny laughed. The little horse went to the water and drank. Then she ate some of the alfalfa. Then she went and sniffed the bed and climbed into it, turning and testing it out. Before they closed the door she was curled in the basket, looking stoically at them.

It was Ernesto's house, but Angie, Ronny's Hollywood friend seemed very much at home in it. Paul learned that he had been in Durango for four months, living all that time with Ernesto. Ernesto was quiet, but very attentive. He saw to it that Paul and Ronny had rooms close to each other near the end of one of the wings. Both rooms had private baths, and there was plenty of soap, shampoo and shaving gear provided. He brought them each a cool drink, suggesting that they take them with them when they went to freshen up. Angie was larger than Ernesto, at least a head taller, but he seemed softer. He was very jovial and talkative, and unlike the extremely neat Ernesto his appearance was a little unkempt. Paul finished first. He made his way to the pool area, a tiled patio surrounded by carefully tended cactus and four huge trees that he saw now were not eucalyptus, though like them, and various colored chairs and pillows. A large wooden table had been brought out to the edge of the pool. It was covered with a white cloth, and it was set with china, silver and crystal. There was a centerpiece of fresh-cut flowers, roses and day lilies. There was no one there, but he heard voices from inside the house, and the smell of something cooking came out to him. It was beginning to get dark, and even as he noticed dusk's edge moving in, lights came on in the pool. The flat surface of the water was a pale rose color now that the lights lit the walls of tile. A few lights came on in the trees also, and the entire patio space was washed in a faint red hue.

He found them in a large and comfortable living room to the side of the open area where the chandelier was hung. Ronny was there, discussing something in Spanish with Ernesto, and Angie was leaning against the mantle listening to them. Each had a drink in his hand. Angie saw Paul first and smiled.

"Come in, Paul; let me get you something. What would you like? We've got most everything."

Paul told him, and he went to a wet bar that was a part of the teak wall unit and mixed a bourbon with water.

"Hey, Paul. Come sit," Ronny said, and Ernesto gestured to a chair in front of a coffee table that was large and made of glass. The conversation drifted. There was some reminiscing, but the three kept it to a minimum. Ronny had told them that Paul had been vacationing in Mexico City and that they had met there. Whether or not Ronny had suggested that their relationship was more than casual, Paul couldn't tell, but the unguarded way in which they talked suggested to him that they thought he was homosexual. Ernesto had never heard of Abelardo García.

"And that *is* a little surprising. I know many people in Chihuahua, and some of them are very political. I would have thought I'd heard of him."

"Maybe I have it wrong," Paul said.

Ronny talked about his pictures, mentioning some of the families that he had photographed and the interesting places he had found. Paul wanted to ask about Johnny Hotnuts, but for some reason he was not sure of he decided against it. Angie left the room from time to time to check the progress of the meal that he was obviously in charge of. The kitchen, judging by the aroma of food cooking, was just off the room they were in. Ernesto asked Paul how he liked Mexico City, and when he saw that Paul had little to say about it he told a story or two of his own about experiences he had had there. After they had talked for a while, Ronny managed to find a way of introducing the subject of the film and the little horse.

"My, I really don't know. I was a tag-along like you were. But what a coincidence. He's coming," Angie said.

"Here?" Ronny asked.

"Sure. To dinner. He really ought to be here by now in fact. We'll ask him."

"Ernesto, is he a friend of yours?" Ronny said.

"Not a friend. No. He's from Cananea. An acquaintance. We met in Hollywood, through you I think, Angie. He's in costumes. Why anyone would live in Cananea is beyond me. He called the other night. He's in Durango on business. Did he know you were here, Angie? He didn't seem surprised."

"I don't see how," Angie said. "Unless, well, from someone in Hollywood."

When Paul heard "Cananea" he stiffened slightly. It was very close to Naco. He'd spent that first night there with Mary Grace. That was a long time ago, or at least it felt like it. And this was the man Ronny had told him about, the one he hadn't liked too much. But there was no way that they could know about him here, at least he didn't think there was; it was coincidence, as much as Ronny's having seen the movie with the horses in it had been. There's been too much coincidence, Paul thought. And still nothing is adding up to anything. The only constant is the little horse.

"Those little horses were something else again. It was too much, really. Weird," Angie said. "Remember, Ronny?"

"There's more than you might know about little horses," Ernesto said. "I've never seen that movie, but I know there are others. But that's not the thing at all. There's other things, and they go deeper than movies, especially in some places down here, among some people anyway. There's stories and some history and maybe some real things going on at the fringes, things that could have trouble in them."

There was a sound of feet on the porch and somebody called out.

"That's Campos," Angie said, and he rose and left the room. They heard the sound of voices, and then Angie came back with the other man beside him. They all stood and Ernesto crossed the room with his hand extended.

"Campos, do come in."

The man was small, about Ernesto's size, but he was bulkier. He was dressed in a suit and tie, a little too formal for the occasion, and Paul saw the ring on his little finger as his hand extended to take Ernesto's. His hair was shiny, very black and very carefully combed. He had small lips and a narrow nose. The backs of his hands were hairy, and there was hair rising out of his collar at the knot of his tie. Still holding his hand, Ernesto moved to the side and introduced him to Paul and Ronny.

"Oh, of course, you know Ronny," Ernesto said.

"*Sí*, a time ago, I believe." His voice was high-pitched, almost a woman's voice, but without any lilt to it at all. His words were clipped, matter-of-fact, and there was no clear cadence at the ends of his sentences, as if he cut himself off a moment before finishing.

"*Sí, usted me ayudó mucho con mi español,*" Ronny said, and then, turning to Paul, "This is the man who helped me with Spanish."

"I was?" Campos said. "Well, it is kind of you to say so." Though Ronny had addressed him in Spanish, the man answered in English, and it was clear that he did not intend to speak Spanish with him.

They had a drink, and after Paul took his first sip he felt it going to his head. He had not had much to drink in a long time now, and though he liked the taste he didn't like the feeling, and he put his glass down on the coffee table and did not touch it again. Campos explained a little about his business in Durango. He was here mostly to look into fabric, but he was also doing some research into native costumes. He had found some old photographs that he liked, and he was planning a few day trips into the nearby villages, where he would see if he could get some first-hand shots. Ronny expressed interest in the photographic end of things, but Campos did not pick up the conversation and soon was sitting close to Angie, gossiping about people they both knew back in Hollywood. Paul didn't like Campos; he liked the others, but he found Campos's presence an intrusion and he was still troubled by the mention of Cananea. He wished the subject of the little horses would come up again so that he could gauge Campos' reaction to the issue, but he could find no good way of returning to the subject, even though Angie had said they could ask Campos about the film when he arrived.

Soon Angie got up and went to the kitchen. He was gone only a moment, and when he returned he announced that dinner was ready.

Ernesto ushered the other three out to the table at pool side, and Angie followed shortly with two bottles of wine, which he placed in front of Ernesto. When he returned he was carrying a large tureen of paella. It was dark now, but only a little cooler than it had been with the sun out. The rose hue on the lighted surface of the pool seemed brighter now, and the wash of its color extended to the table and beyond it to the trees. There was a rose edge touching the low growth in the yard even at a distance, and beyond it there was nothing but darkness. There were candles on the table, and their flames took some of the tint away. Still, the white cloth was faintly red, as was the sauce in the paella and even the white wine in the glasses. While they were eating, Angie brought up the subject of the little horses.

"Do you remember, Campos, a year or so ago, that private film showing in Eagle Rock, the movie with the little horses in it?"

Campos was sitting on the pool side of the table, leaning back a little in his chair.

"Yes, I remember. You were there too, I believe?" He looked at Ronny, who was sitting across from him.

"It was an interesting gathering there, but the movie was, I would say, a little theatrical?"

"Yes, I would say so," Angie said. "But we were wondering about the horses. Do you know about the source of the film? Who made it? Anything like that?"

"Ah, I know nothing really. But the horses, I believe they were brought in from Argentina. I remember that was the talk."

"I never heard of that," Paul said. "Horses of this size."

Campos looked at the end of the table. "Oh, and were you at the showing also?"

"No. No, I wasn't. I heard of the horses here, and from Ronny."

Campos continued to stare at him. "If you had seen the movie, maybe you would understand. There was some tricky photography. They may even have been small ponies."

Ronny blinked across at Campos, and Angie laughed a little. Then Ernesto spoke.

"Well, it is no matter. Angie, will you get the bottle that Campos brought?"

The bottle had been uncorked and was without a label, and Campos explained that it was homemade brandy from a place in Cananea. When he knew that he was coming and thought he might see Ernesto he had brought it with him. It was very fine and it would be a pleasure to share it with such good company. Ernesto thanked him formally, and Campos himself rose and poured the brandy. Then, when he was seated again, he lifted his glass and toasted Ernesto on his hospitality. Paul raised his glass, but he only wet his lips. When Ernesto toasted Campos on his kindness and on the quality of the brandy, Paul drank half of what was in his glass. Though a little too thick for his taste, the brandy was delicious.

A few minutes later, while they were smoking the cigars that Angie had brought out for them, Paul saw Ernesto lift his napkin to his lips. He was seated at the end of the table, and Paul caught the look of mild surprise in his eyes when he moved the napkin away and looked at it. It was flecked with blood.

"I seem to be bleeding," Ernesto said quietly and brought the napkin to his mouth again. Paul heard a scraping and saw Ronny rise up from the chair to Paul's left. He was seated beside Angie, but Angie was now under the table. Paul thought he was reaching for something he had dropped; he could see his back over the table's edge, but in a moment that too disappeared. Then he looked back at Ernesto. His napkin was now bright red, his head was shaking. Then the hand holding the napkin moved out from his mouth, pushed by the gush of the blood fountain behind it, and his fountain was joined by another coming from above it and splashing onto the rose-white of the tablecloth. It was Ronny's, and when Paul looked up at him, he was falling back, his left hand reaching toward Paul for help and support. Paul was halfway to his feet then, turning toward Campos. Campos had moved a little back from the table, but he was still sitting. His hand was moving inside his jacket.

"Be very still where you are," Campos said in his even, high-pitched voice as he brought the gun out. He had a smirk on his face and was looking directly into Paul's chest.

The table rose up a little and the silverware and the wine and brandy glasses tilted as Ronny's hand came over the edge and groped for a purchase on the cloth. He got a fold of fabric, held it for a moment, pulled the cloth over the surface, and then lost it. The glasses fell, one breaking and another rolling off and falling with a splash into the pool.

Campos' plate, still half full of paella, slipped into his lap, and in the moment that he looked down to see the fish and liquid staining his crotch, Paul was moving across the table toward him. His knee reached the salad bowl and his left leg hit Angie's chair and knocked it over. Then he dove at Campos, his chest banging into the tureen. Campos threw his right arm up into the air to keep his gun free, and Paul missed his wrist, but he was moving, and the force of his dive sent him into Campos, his head banging into his chin.

Then they went over, Paul, Campos and the chair, breaking the rose-mirrored surface of the pool in a tangle and with a loud splash. They were in the shallow end, and the chair got free and rose to the surface before either of them. Then Campos surged to the surface and struggled for footing. Paul had him by the lapels of his suit coat. He was still under the water, only his arms above it, and he jerked down and Campos came over hitting his head against the chair's seat as he went under again. Paul rolled and groped for his gun hand. He could see it coming around, moving toward his chest. He couldn't get it and settled for his throat. He wedged his fingers in at the shirt collar, his knuckles pressing, his fingers gripping the tie at the knot. Then he managed to get to his knees, to get his head above the water. He held Campos down, but again the gun came up out of the water, this time moving toward Paul's head. He tried to move his head, to dip it out of the way, but he was losing balance and had to jerk it back to keep from rolling over and losing his grip. He felt the metal barrel against his neck and heard the click. There was no report. Then there was another click and another. He began to count them, to wince less as they came. After a while the pressure of the barrel lessened and the clicks came quicker. At the end he turned and saw the arm and hand with the gun in it begin to slip and go down. The finger jerked at the trigger even after the hand entered the water. Then the whole body shook and vibrated for a while. And then it stopped and was still, and Paul released him and let him slip away.

He climbed the metal ladder and walked around the table without looking at it or at the pool and walked directly into the house and back to Ronny's room. He was shaking by the time he got there, and he wanted to sit down on the bed. Standing in the middle of the room, he took his clothes off. Then he went to Ronny's suitcase and opened it. He took out what clothes he thought he could get into quickly and dressed himself. Ronny's shoes were a little tight, bringing back the pain in the cuts and bruises, but they would do. When he was finished he closed the suitcase and put it by the door. He piled his own wet clothing beside it. Then he checked the room, leaving the camera equipment and selecting only the toilet kit. He looked around, checking the table and the bed. There were no car keys. He would have to go back to the pool again.

Ronny was lying flat on his back on the tiles of the patio, his eyes open and his head in a pool of blood. Paul could see Angie's body under the table. He tried hard not to look at Ronny as he searched his pockets, but when he found the keys and his wallet he went to the table and got a clean napkin and bent down and wiped the blood from Ronny's face and hair as best he could and tried to close his eyes with his fingers. The lids wouldn't go down, and finally he looked at him a last time and got up again. Behind the table he could see the chair bobbing in the lighted pool and the body of Campos, floating face-down next to it. He looked at him, at his slick hair and the slight billow of his suit jacket a little above the rosy surface of the water. He could see his hand hanging down, could even see the slight glint of the stone in the ring on his little finger. He looked hard and long, needing to take in this image of the man he had oddly killed. Then he turned and left.

He went to the room where they had put the little horse. She was no longer in her bed, but was standing to the side of it, alert and concentrated as if she had been waiting, looking at him when he opened the door. He paused when he saw her. She did not come toward him, but only stood there, her eyes open and unblinking. He stood for another few moments, and then he held his hand up, his palm toward her, and backed out of the room and closed the door again. When he got back to his own room, he took the blanket he had used to bring her in with and went to Ronny's room again. Then he stripped again and went back naked through the house and out to the pool. Campos and the chair were still bobbing in the shallow end, and the smell of slowly congealing blood was in the air. He went to the ladder and stepped in, up to his waist. He got to Campos and slipped his hands into the water and checked his jacket pockets. There was nothing there, but in his rear pant's pocket he found a wallet. He climbed the ladder, passed the bodies and the blood-soaked table and decking and went back to

Ronny's room and dried himself and dressed again. Then he took the suitcase and the toilet kit and the blanket and went to the front of the house and put them in the back seat of the car. He went back to the living room and sat down and emptied Campos' wallet on the glass coffee table. The wallet was only damp, and what was in it was hardly wet at all. There was a good deal of money, some credit cards, a driver's license and a few official-looking papers. Tucked in behind the bills was a folded piece of paper with two phone numbers penciled on it. There was a phone stand in the corner of the room, and with some effort he found a way to tell the operator what he needed. Both numbers on the sheet were for Chihuahua. He dialed the operator again and worked his way through getting the numbers from her. In a short time the first number was ringing. While he waited he noticed that the number had the letters o f beside it. There was no answer. Probably *oficina*, he guessed. He got the operator back again and asked for the other number. After two rings, a woman answered.

"Abelardo García, *por favor*," Paul said. There was silence at the other end of the line, and then *"Un momento."*

He heard muffled voices and thought he heard García's name spoken; then a man's voice came on the line.

"¿Quién es? Campos?"

"¿Es Johnny *aquí?"* Paul said.

Another brief silence.

"Who the hell is this?"

He took the phone from his ear and hung it up. Before he reached Ronny's room, he heard it ringing. He went back and picked up the receiver.

"¿Sí?" He said.

"Campos, *por favor*."

He thought it was the same voice.

"Un momento," he said, and put the phone down on the table and went to get the little horse.

━━━

When he had worked his way out of Durango and found the road to Mazatlán, he pushed the Ford up to fifty and drove west well into the night and early morning. He made it as far as a town called Guasave, a place near the coast and fifty or so miles below Los Mochis, a good-sized town on the Gulf across from the Baja. He found a place to stay and used some of Campos' money to rent a room. When he had the horse fed and settled in and before he went to bed, he sat down in a chair and smoked, thinking that he had better make some plans about his next move. He had tried to think while driving, but the images of the deaths behind him, most of all the one he had had a hand in, would not leave him. There was a phone book in the room, though there was no phone, but it was local and did not contain information about Chihuahua. He was not at all sure that the numbers he had called had actually been ones at the house of Abelardo García, if there was an Abelardo García. It was clear that both the woman who had answered and the man knew the names he had spoken, and that they were tied up with Campos. He thought the man could have been Parker himself when he'd first heard his voice, but he was sure when he heard it the second time that it was not. At first he thought that he would have to risk going to the house in Chihuahua. He had reasons to distrust Johnny, but he could not bring himself to distrust Mary Grace, and since she trusted Johnny he thought he would have to do so too. Still, something might have happened to him. The numbers might have been his and García's. Then he remembered Esperanza and the house in Naco. That was better, safer he thought, and he resolved to avoid Chihuahua and head toward Naco in the morning. It was close to six hundred miles. He would make it in two days and a little more; he would get there in the morning. The place was not so foreign to him, and he would have a little more of an edge. When he got in the bed the horse climbed up and moved against him. She felt heavy on his legs, but he was too tired to be irritated at the burden.

He started out late the next morning and pushed the entire day with nothing but gas stops, those few required so that the little horse could relieve herself and stretch. He managed to get fresh hay at a market in one of the villages off the main road, and when he stopped to let her run, he fed her. She didn't seem the worse for wear and remained a constant for him, the only evidence that prevented the turns and changes of the past weeks from seeming irrevocable. Though alert and awake, not sleeping as much as she had before, she seemed as placid as she had during those weeks spent at the lake house with Mary Grace.

At noon it began to rain, and he had to slow a little and take it easy. He thought he could feel the contours of Ronny's body in the seat he was in, and he missed him. He had been a help and a sanity, but like the farmer and his family had become another straw in the wind. There was nothing outside himself and the little horse that he could count on, and he tried hard not to anticipate anything from Esperanza. He tried to make a list of the ambiguities that lay behind him, but he found that he couldn't get past Ronny's story about the horse movie in Los Angeles. It was there that things got hazy, where Johnny and even Mary Grace became questionable. If they were the actors in that movie, then there had been many lies. Lies of omission, at least. But he did not want to speculate. Doing that hadn't helped him so far. He would have to wait and see what happened in Naco, and he began to visualize the town in his mind, to consider the practical matter of getting to the house without being seen and in safety. He couldn't be sure if they would have a line on Ronny's car, but he would just have to risk that. He didn't think they'd figure he'd go to Naco, not after those calls he'd made to Chihuahua.

Even with the rain and his late departure, he made good time, and shortly after dark he began looking for a place to stay. He was over a hundred miles below Hermosillo, but not much more than that, and he knew he could reach Cananea with ease by the following evening. He was tired and thought he'd better get his rest while he could. He found a place without much trouble, and by seven-thirty he and the horse were settled in. He was inland a little now, but when he went outside his room to smoke he thought he could feel the nearness of the gulf in the soft breeze.

When he got to Cananea it was dusk. He checked into a place, and when he had the horse in the room he went to the lobby and looked at the phone book. There were a dozen or more listings under the name Campos. Only one was a business number. When he called it he got a scratchy answering-machine message. The message was brief and in Spanish, and it was followed by what he took to be the same thing in English: *This is Campos. I am not presently in. Please leave a message at the tone.* Paul waited, and then spoke into the receiver.

"This is Paul Cords. Thank you for the pleasant evening. I can be reached through Pfeffer in San Diego."

He was sure that the voice had been Campos' and though he couldn't be sure that the message would get through, he expected that it would. He would find out soon enough. He ate at the restaurant off the lobby, and when he was finished he went back to the room and made a thorough check of Ronny's belongings. He could find nothing at all in the clothing, only a credit card receipt from a Mexico City hotel in the Zona Rosa. Next he checked Ronny's wallet. There were a few credit cards and more receipts, and there were a few scraps of paper with numbers and addresses on them, but that was all. He looked at the picture on the driver's license briefly; it looked nothing at all like Ronny. He didn't think taking the camera equipment with him was a good idea at the time, but now he wished he had that too. In addition to the clothing, the only thing he found in the suitcase was a small key; it was tucked in one of the pockets among some dirty clothes. He tried it on the suitcase itself, but it did not fit. Then he went out to the car and checked the trunk. There was a leather attaché case in it, and he brought it back to the room. The key fit. Inside was a photo album with a few loose pictures in a slit at the back. The album contained a series of eight by tens. They were all family shots, good ones Paul thought, and none were of Mexicans. The ones in the slit, about ten of them, were of more interest. The first few were pictures of men in casual poses, but the rest were candid group shots, all of them taken at the same place, on a patio in front of glass doors. In some, the edge of a pool was visible, and patio furniture. There were some eucalyptus trees at the edge of a yard beyond the patio as well. It was no place that Paul had seen before, but he had seen many like it, and he thought he could place it somewhere around Los Angeles, or maybe further south. People were holding drinks and plates of food, and when he went through the pictures he thought he could count at least thirty different people present. Then he saw Parker and one of the Mexicans. They were to the side of one of the shots, and were not smiling for the camera. He checked each picture again, but he could find no one else he recognized.

A good half of the people present looked wealthy, and a few of those in the pictures were Mexicans. He checked the picture with Parker in it again. He and the Mexican did not seem to be aware that their picture was being taken at all. Parker was smiling, half turned from the camera, and the Mexican seemed to be listening to him. He had no idea if the photographer, who it was clear from the quality of the shots was Ronny, had any idea who Parker was. He chose to believe that he didn't. He also chose to believe that Parker knew who Ronny was. Though he could construct nothing reasonable from looking again at the pictures he did think that he was looking at show-business people of some sort, and that many of them were homosexuals. Now Ronny fit in at least, though what it was he fit into was not clear.

That night she climbed on the bed and took her usual place with him, her body tucked into the curve of his own, her head against his chest. Before he fell asleep she grew restless, and straining to see in the darkness, he found her in the chair, preening, her muzzle moving over her belly and in her crotch. In the middle of the night he woke again and saw her eyes. She was still in the chair, but she was awake and watchful. He went to sleep again, and in the morning she was up and waiting, standing at the door.

They reached Naco early, shortly after seven in the morning. The town was just coming awake, and there were only a few people on the sidewalks, a few pickup trucks moving slowly down the dirt streets. He circled the town and came in from the back, down the road that led in from Parker's *rancho*. The Casa Blanca was silent. There were two cars parked in front of it. Those who have stayed the night, Paul thought; only one of the cheaper houses near the Casa had lights on. Two men, who Paul thought were soldiers, sat on the brief porch in front of it. One looked to be sleeping against the building; the other had a beer bottle in his hand. As Paul passed, the one with the bottle lifted his hand half-heartedly in a wave.

When he got the few blocks to the old Casa, he turned to the right and circled it. It was at the edge of town, and he could see it between the few houses beyond it as he went around. There were no cars parked in the drive and no lights in the windows. When he got back to the street on which the house was located, he parked in front of the house to its left and continued to watch for a moment. A light came on in what he thought was the kitchen. There was a dog in the yard of the house where he was parked, and when he got out he watched it carefully. It heard him, but it only lifted its head up and looked at him. Then it curled up again in the dust. He walked into the yard of the old Casa and moved beside the building to where he thought the back door would be. He thought he should remember the place better, but he was aware that he was unclear about it. As he passed the kitchen window he saw Esperanza moving behind the curtains. She was wearing a very fancy bathrobe with flowers on it, and her eyes opened wide and her mouth formed an O when she saw him. She looked beyond him for a moment, then opened the door and let him in.

"Joo are Pablo, no?" she said.

"*Sí*, Pablo," he said.

"*Dónde* . . . where is Mary Grace?"

"I don't know," he said. "Don't *you* know?"

"No, *Dios!* I don't know nothing!"

She got him a cup of coffee and a roll and got him to sit down at the wooden kitchen table. The morning sun was up fully now, and it washed through the curtains, casting soft shadows and streams of light in the room. She got up from where she sat beside him and got him some butter and milk. She sat again for a moment and then started to get up again. He reached to her arm before she rose, keeping her in her seat.

"Esperanza," he said. "Who is Abelardo García?"

When she heard the name she backed up slightly in her chair. It scraped on the floor. Then she went to the window and looked out. He was about to speak again, but when she came back to the table she held a finger up to stop him. She went to the front of the house. He heard the door open and then close again. Then she returned to the kitchen.

"*¿Donde está el caballito?*" she said.

He went and got the horse, carrying her back wrapped in the blanket. The street outside the house was still quiet, though he could hear the sound of horns and motors in the distance. Even though she expected it, Esperanza covered her mouth in wonder when she saw the horse. He put her down on the kitchen floor, and she hurried to get water and some vegetables from the icebox.

"I have alfalfa," he said, and he went back out to the car and got the sack; there was just a little of it left, but it still smelled fresh, and he thought it would be enough.

She stood and watched the horse eat and drink. She watched her closely and carefully; there was still a hint of surprise in her face, but he thought he could see something like satisfaction as well. Her look seemed odd, and he didn't understand it. When the horse was finished eating, she left the kitchen and began to move through the house.

"Come now into the parlor," Esperanza said, and she took their coffee, and they followed the little horse out of the kitchen. She was standing beside the couch in the living room when they got there. When they were seated, Esperanza looked around the room, then settled herself into the couch. Then she took a deep breath and turned toward him and began to speak. Her English was awkward, but she had enough of it so that he could piece together the story she told. As she spoke, she kept watching the little horse, and at times he had to call her attention back to the story. She tended to digress at times, and at times she spoke too quickly and drifted into Spanish, and he had to ask her to slow down, tell her that he was losing her. She had not washed off her makeup from the night before, and in the shadows of the room she looked a little bruised around the cheeks and eyes. The story was not all that long, but it took her a long time to tell it.

Chapter 17

Abelardo García appeared in Cananea about thirty-five years ago. He had a little horse with him. Word had it that he came from Colorado, from the mountains, and that he had come into a considerable sum of money there, but he was a teller of his own travels, and in his stories he had been in many places and had many experiences, so his real sources remained always in question. But the money was not in question. When he arrived he purchased a good-sized *rancho* a short distance out of town and proceeded to lead a life of leisure. He was only part gringo. He was big, with a light hair color, but his features and his skin were Mexican, and he spoke Spanish like a native. He was alone for only a short time, then he married a woman whose husband had died. They had two children, a boy and a girl a little younger.

The little horse he brought with him was a male, a palomino, and though the people who saw it linked it to the old stories they knew about little horses, they saw it more as an oddity than as anything else, and they were able to take it into their daily lives. Those who did not believe that such a horse was possible chose not to believe that it was real. They believed it was a trick of some sort, and in that way they took it in without any change. And indeed García held the horse back from the people for the most part. He branded it inside its thigh for safety's sake, but that seemed hardly necessary. His *rancho* was a private place, and only occasionally would people get a glimpse of the horse. He brought it once to the school to show the children and once he dressed it up in ribbons and showed it off at a fiesta. But he did not otherwise display it in public, and it was only the children who held it up as an object of wonder. People mostly shook their heads, transferring the oddity to García himself. There were a few superstitious people and sorcerers in the town who babbled on about the little horse and its dangers, but they were not taken seriously. García did things that the people of Cananea were unaware of for a number of years. He stayed private with his family and the little horse, keeping mostly to his *rancho* and only occasionally coming into town for supplies. Then things began to happen.

People began to think they saw more than one little horse when they passed the *rancho*, García began to hold little private shows, by invitation only, at his place. Well dressed men came to the town from other places to see the shows, and the rumor in the town was that they were sex shows of some kind and that they involved little horses. It might have been that there were two horses from the beginning, but the story likes to have it that there was only one; that way the coming of the second can be thought of as mysterious and a little magical.

García's wife began to look drawn, and in a very short time she wasted away and died. Then it was only Abelardo García and the children; they were teenagers, but he did not let them run with other children their own age. They went to school in Cananea, but they never lingered after school. He kept them close to him, out at his place. The boy was small and thin and witty, and the girl was very shy. They were Johnny Hotnuts and Mary Grace.

Things went on then without too much change, though the visits from outside increased, not more people but more often, and those who came looked influential; many were from the North, and it seemed that they came to Cananea and the *rancho* for more than just the shows. Then Parker came, and the beginning of the end began. Afterwards the story was that Parker came to revenge his mother, whom García had left with child, in shame, and with no money somewhere in Colorado, but his behavior afterward suggests that there was more to it than that.

It goes that Abelardo García was in the yard, in a kind of small circular pen with the little horses. There were two of them, a male and a female, and he was training them for some purpose with a whip. He was not striking them, but was using the whip by snapping it in the air and on the ground to get them to do things, to bring things to him and take things and put them in other places. He was not having much success with the female, but the male was doing all right. Johnny and Mary Grace were at the fence behind him, looking through the bars watching. Parker, who was only two years older than Johnny but a good head taller and thicker, came up behind them, and when they realized his presence they turned. He smiled and asked if the man with the whip was Abelardo García. When they answered that he was, he asked them again, and they told him that of course they were sure and that he was their father. Then Parker opened the gate that was in the fence beside them and entered the enclosure, moving up behind Abelardo García. The story has it that when he was close to him he spoke, and Mary Grace thought she heard the word *papa*. Abelardo turned his head around, startled, and looked back at Parker. They could not see Parker's face, but they saw his arm move from his side and saw the sun glint on the blade of the long knife before it disappeared into Abelardo García's back. Then Mary Grace and Johnny were grabbed from behind by the two men Parker had brought with him, and they were locked up for a week.

It was a takeover then, but a secret one, and Parker took up residence at the *rancho* as head of the household. Abelardo García was buried there, and word was put out that he had died of a heart attack. For the next two years, Johnny and Mary Grace were not seen in the town at all. People thought they saw one or the other of them when they passed by the place, but they could not be sure. The fact was that Parker deflowered Mary Grace, and subjugated Johnny as well. He also used them in shows with the little horses, and he used the pen he had killed his father in and his father's whip to train them like animals.

When it comes to the diamonds, Mary Grace and Johnny knew of their existence, but they had no idea where their father might have hidden them. But Parker thought they must know something, and he whipped them to get them to tell. He ransacked his father's belongings, and he even tried to trail his father back to where the source might be, somewhere in Colorado he thought, but he could find nothing. He knew his father had paid his way with the diamonds, and he thought for sure that he would find them at the *rancho*. The obsession of his frustrated search for them stayed with him, and even though he had considerable wealth and was gathering more through the little horses, he remained brutal with Johnny and Mary Grace; they were a constant reminder of how close he was to the diamonds, only words away he thought. And then Johnny escaped.

It was in the evening, and he had them in the pen with the little horses. He had been at them all day, raging about the diamonds. He was drinking and taking drugs, and he had beaten them and made them eat from dishes on the floor. He had sent his men away to town for more liquor and food, and he was alone with them, snapping his whip in the air, forcing them to trot with the horses in the pen. Though Johnny was smaller than Mary Grace, he guarded her, keeping her on the outside of him, between him and Parker, so she could move between Johnny and the circular fence. He moved them around and around in the enclosure, and in a smaller circle were the two horses, also running close together.

Johnny and Mary Grace were exhausted and stumbling, but the horses ran even in their subjection with a certain grace and dignity, a certain set of head that indicated that their integrity could not be contained or manipulated in any final way. And this enraged Parker further, and though in the past the long bullwhip had never touched Johnny or Mary Grace—the whipping he had given them had been designed not to hurt so much as to wear them down with dull and ongoing pain—this time the tip bit into Johnny's arm, cutting out a small piece of flesh. When it struck, Johnny reached for his arm and cried out in pain, stumbling and pulling up. And when he stopped, Mary Grace stopped beside him, and the two horses completed their circle and pulled up as well, facing Parker and standing between him and Mary Grace and Johnny. Then the female horse dipped her head once and stepped forward from where she was tucked in against the male's flanks and approached Parker.

When she reached him, he was towering over her, but her head raised and their eyes met. Then she rose up on her hind legs and put her hooves against his thigh. He looked down at her; he seemed ready to speak out, to yell at her and give her orders. Then he must have seen Johnny moving, because his head came back up, and he began to raise the handle of the whip, to bring the coil up from where it lay stretched out in the dirt. Johnny was halfway to the fence, gathering himself for his leap, when the horse sunk her teeth into Parker's thigh. He looked down in amazement. The coil of the whip came up, then fell back in the dirt. Parker shook his leg, but the horse, though lifted off the ground by his movement, hung on, and Parker looked from her dangling body to where Mary Grace was looking, at Johnny above the spikes of the fence and in the air. Then he was on a spike. It entered his stomach, and his body cupped around it, his head and shoulders on the far side of the fence and his legs kicking on the other. Parker twisted his body and tried to get the whip up again, but the little horse hung on and her hooves were now kicking at his groin. He doubled up slightly, and at the same time Johnny got his hands under him, gripping the spikes to his sides. His arms stiffened then and he pushed himself up off the spike that had impaled him, throwing his legs up and falling over the fence to the ground.

Finally Parker struck the little horse hanging from him with the butt of the whip handle; he caught her in the side of the head, and she fell to the ground at his feet. He tried to kick her, but she was up and away from him before his foot could strike, the motion of the missed kick throwing his body up off the ground. He lost his footing completely and landed on the seat of his pants in the dirt. Mary Grace saw him land and she saw Johnny running away from the fence, bent over, holding his stomach. Then the little horse was on Parker again, and it was all that he could do to keep her from his throat. When he finally got her by the scruff of the neck and threw her from him and struggled to his feet, Johnny was gone.

Later that night, after he had sent his men out in search of Johnny, Parker raped Mary Grace. He had raped her before, but on this night he was very cold and mechanical about it, and she felt she could remove herself from it, could take her mind elsewhere and avoid the experience of shame. His men never found Johnny, and it was only after two years had passed that Parker became aware of his public existence. He was working in small clubs, doing burlesque. He had not begun to tell stories. That was not to begin for a number of years. He was a man when Parker found out where he was, and he only attempted once to get him back. The man he sent out was found in the desert with a knife in his stomach.

He did make it as difficult as he could for Johnny. He had some influence with club owners and entertainment people, but it was not long before Johnny's popularity undercut his influence, and he found that he could make money in various ways from Johnny's appearances.

Three years after Johnny escaped, Parker closed the *rancho* and moved with Mary Grace to the place a few miles from here. She was sixteen then, and he quickly tired of her presence. She was in the way, and he sent her to the Casa Blanca, this house. The man who owned this Casa then owed Parker things, and he had him keep an eye on Mary Grace. But this was unnecessary, because there was nothing really that she could do. Parker was wealthy by this time, and there was no one who would take the word of a prostitute over that of a rich and influential man like him. And besides, she was strangely docile in her behavior. She served the owner well. She made no trouble, and she found a way of life here that she could live with.

———

Paul spent the next four nights in the old Casa Blanca with Esperanza. The night following the story of Abelardo García was a work night for her, and it was three in the morning when she crept into bed with him. She was freshly showered and cool, and her body felt good to him when she tucked it into his own. They rose at ten, and she made him a large meal of eggs and toast with plenty of strong coffee. That day he went through Ronny's belongings again, making sure he had missed nothing. He spent a lot of time with the pictures, even studying the family eight by tens in detail. He didn't learn any more from the shots of the party, though he thought he had memorized most of the faces by the time he was finished. He removed what clothing he thought he could use from the suitcase, and he put the case with the rest of the clothes under the bed. Then he searched the car. In the glove compartment he found a small address book. Most of the numbers were located in and around Los Angeles, and he put the address book with the clothes he planned to take with him. Ronny's wallet had very little cash in it, but Paul had a good four hundred dollars worth of pesos that he had taken from Campos. In the afternoon he went into town and bought a small knapsack, some shoes that fit him, a large steel hunting knife in a sheath, and a sling of the kind that women use to carry children on their backs.

Esperanza was off that night, and she cooked him a heavy beef dinner, with beans and tortillas. They spent the evening talking about how it was to work at the Casa Blanca, and she told him a few funny stories and some sad ones. She seemed resigned to her position, or rather he thought she seemed so much in the position that resignation, with its sense of loss, was not really possible for her. Still, there was an edge in her, in her talk and the way she moved with certainty, that made him wonder about her. He would have asked her about her life before the Casa Blanca, but he was so full of details and stories from the past that he could not bring himself to do so.

The next day he called Pfeffer. The pool secretary told him there was a load of mail waiting, most of it junk she thought, but that there was also a small package that had arrived by messenger; it was sent from Mexico, she said. He had made reservations at a motel in Bisbee before calling her, and he asked her to send the package there, special delivery, and to wire five hundred dollars to the same place. She asked him how his vacation was going, and though the question made him a little dizzy, forcing him to lean against the wall of the booth, he managed to tell her it was fine. Then he called the Bisbee motel and made arrangements for them to accept the package and the money for him.

On his third night, Esperanza had to work again, and he had the house to himself. He searched it, going through what he could find of Mary Grace's things. He could find nothing but clothes and jewelry and makeup and some money, which he left where he found it. There were no personal papers, no photographs or letters. The little horse went with him as he roamed through the house, and when he was finished and it was late she curled up on the couch beside him. He stroked her head and haunches, and without really thinking about it he ran his hand between her legs to feel the down at the inside of her thigh. Her tail lifted and settled, brushing his wrist, and then he thought he felt something. He reached with his other hand and lifted her legs so he could see between them, and there it was; though small and faint, he could make the letters out, the *AG* of the brand that had been burned into her hair and flesh.

She was at least thirty-five years old. She had been in the pen that day, and she had bitten Parker's leg. And Mary Grace had known this all along and had said nothing. But maybe that was all wrong and there were more horses and there had been some later brandings. In the story, though, García had died, and he did not think that Parker would have used his brand. But it was all from a story, and he was sure of none of it. He lifted her leg again and looked in and felt the faint letters. The burn had not been a burn or even a scar for a very long time. There was only a little that could still be felt. It was only there as a permanent discoloration in her skin.

The next day, when Esperanza was awake and up, he made plans for his departure. She told him where he could cross with ease. There were fences, but they were perfunctory only, and he would have no trouble. She would take him close to the place in the car, and then she would leave the car on the other side of town. He could walk back into town on the American side and get a taxi into Bisbee. The next night was not a soldier's night, so there would be plenty of taxis and he should have no trouble.

She dropped him at a place only a few blocks from the border crossing. There were shacks there, with their backs close to the river, but on the other side there was nothing but a metal grain storage shed with a few pieces of rusty machinery standing in the weather around it. The fence on the Mexican side was lower than on the other, but neither of them was high, and the river was no more than a trickle.

"It gets high sometimes; you can see the line there," she said pleasantly. It was a way of saying goodbye to him in his own language, or wishing him well.

"Goodbye, sweet Esperanza," he said, and he leaned back into the car window and kissed her full on the lips. There were two small children, a boy and a girl watching, standing beside one of the shacks, and they smiled as he kissed her. He adjusted the horse in the sling on his back. He had the knapsack across his chest, and he nodded and smiled to the children as he headed down the slope to the river and made his crossing. When he had gotten over the fence on the far side, he looked back; the children were still watching, but the car was gone. He thought he saw its dust trail rising toward the direction of the town.

⸻

The motel in Bisbee was small and very modest. There were radios in the rooms but no phones. But it was clean and neat, and when he heard the voice of the owner at the desk, an older man, he guessed that he was someone who had retired here, probably for his health, from somewhere in the Midwest. Though the man glanced at his clothing and the knapsack he now carried in his hand, he was sufficiently impressed by the package that had come special delivery and the wired funds that he asked nothing. Paul had folded the towel over the little horse's head in the sling, and what he carried looked to be no more than an inanimate bundle of some kind. When he got to his room and had freed the horse and unloaded the knapsack, he walked to the corner and bought a pint of bourbon from a small liquor and grocery store. The motel was a little up in the foothills above the town, on the old highway that was the main route through. It was a narrow and winding old road. There were few cars on it. The place where he had lived as a child was six or seven blocks below the liquor store, up a few more blocks in the hills to the side of the old highway. He remembered the store; it had not changed much, though the liquor section had been added on, and the candy in the old glass case inside the door had changed names and gotten smaller. He walked back slowly to the motel, taking in the half-remembered sights, the old houses, and the river that cut under the road, then followed along it, becoming a concrete wash, dry now, with a pipe railing along it. The store and the area where the motel was were not places that he had seen much of when he was in high school; they were attached to an earlier time, the time when he had lived here as a child, and he sensed that he might see the whole town from that nostalgic vantage this trip through.

When he reached the motel office, he went in and got some ice from the machine. Then he returned to his room and fixed a drink. The little horse rested on the floor in the corner in shadow. She rose as he entered, shook herself and went to the chair, climbed up into it and settled down. He got the small package and sat on the bed and opened it.

Inside were two sealed envelopes, one of which had his name typed across the front, and something wrapped carefully in tissue paper and held between two pieces of rigid cardboard. He opened the envelope first. There was a single sheet of paper inside and typed on it was the message: *There's money in Marble.* He turned the paper over and checked the envelope, but there was nothing else. The other envelope sent up a faint rose scent when he opened it, and when he withdrew the letter that was inside he lifted it to his nose and the scent was stronger. He looked at the signature at the bottom of the brief note; It was Mary Grace's name. The note said, *Pablo, I am with them. Please come.*

He realized that he had seen nothing of Mary Grace's handwriting and that he could not be sure that it was she who had written the note. The writing was crabbed, a little like his own, and seemed a little tortured rather than hurried. He put the note aside and reached for the thin, rigid packet and peeled the tape that held the boards together. Then he opened the tissue paper covering. There were two eight-by-ten glossy photographs inside. The sight of the first one startled him. It was too recent, and he couldn't believe that he had looked that way. He was sitting on the edge of a table, and the little horse was standing on the table beside him, her head slightly in front of his stomach and chest. They were both looking at the camera. The resolution was sharp and clear. Ronny had been very good. Paul could see into the depth of his own sunken eyes, the effort of his half-hearted smile, and could see some scratches on his arm where he held the horse. She looked well enough, her eyes clear and her head raised. The shot was almost full length, cut off only below the knees, and his body looked awkward and worn to him in his ill-fitting and unfamiliar clothes.

He got up and went to the bathroom and looked in the mirror. The sinking in his eyes was still vaguely there, but he thought he no longer looked so drawn and beat. He lifted his arm; the cuts and scratches were healing. Then he took off his shirt. He still looked a mess. The bruises were changing color as they healed; there were auras of green around some of them, but they were not too tender to the touch. The cuts were all scabbed over, and a couple had already shed a little. He thought he would have a number of scars on his body. He felt his buttocks, where the worst of them had been. There was a ridge of something that felt like callus, but when he pushed it it hurt faintly and very deeply.

When he returned, the little horse's head was stretched out between her hooves on the chair cushion. Her eyes were wide open, and she followed his movements as he came back to the bed. He picked up the other photograph. The shot had been taken from a greater distance than had the other, but the woman standing at the railing with the flat lake behind her was clearly Mary Grace, and the man off to the side and watching her carefully was the heavier of the two Mexicans that he had first seen at Parker's *rancho*. In a chair on the other side of the frame was the doctor, Gabriel. Mary Grace was standing stiffly at the deck railing. She was dressed in a robe and her hair was a little gnarled and uncombed, her expression blank. He remembered the shape of the deck as he had seen it from the underside, and he was sure the picture had been taken at the lake house where he had witnessed the making of the movie.

He dropped the photograph beside the other and looked down at them. Why Marble? he thought. And why did they think he would be sure to go there? They must have known that he would know of Marble; there was no mention of Colorado in the note, and the place was not a town and could not be found on map listings easily, if at all. Clearly they trusted that Mary Grace would draw him. What bothered him was that they were so casually right; the note and the letter, and the photographs too were so economically used to get him to come. The only way he thought he could mess with their expectations was to use time. They would probably have a way of finding out that he had called and had the package sent on. He had told the secretary that it was all right to give out that information, but under no circumstances should she say where the package had been sent. He could make Marble easily in two days; it was just under six hundred miles, and the roads would be fast and good between here and there. He decided he would wait, two days at least, to keep them hanging a little, give them time to wonder.

After he had put the photographs and the notes inside the sleeve of Ronny's album, he walked down into the town, got some change, and called the old Casa Blanca. It was eight-thirty and there was no answer. He ate dinner at a small, homey restaurant near the town center, and when he got back to the room it was ten o'clock. At first he couldn't get to sleep, but in a while she came to the bed and joined him, and soon after she had settled in against him he drifted off.

In the morning he waited until ten, and then called Esperanza again.

235

Her voice was sleepy when she answered. He asked her if she thought she could get a message to Johnny, and she said she thought so, maybe; she would try. He waited while she got a paper and pencil, and after he had given her the message, he asked her to read it back to him again: *P and MG in Marble. I'll be there, with the animal, soon.* He had Esperanza date the message, and then he thanked her and hung up. He wasn't counting on Johnny getting the message, and he had no idea what he would do with it even if he did. He recognized the perversity in his not explaining where Marble was in the message. He wasn't all that sure of Johnny, but he needed to send the message, to cover that base. After he had had a late breakfast, this time eating at the old Copper Queen hotel, he went back to the motel and took one of the cups out of the little horse's hooves and removed one of the diamonds, an average-sized one. While he was getting the cup back into place he noticed that there was only one stone, a small ruby he thought, still imbedded in the side of that hoof. He lifted the hoof up and noticed that the other places were closing over. In one place the tiny cup of the setting was protruding slightly from the surface as the growth of hoof wall pushed it out. When he touched it, it fell out in his hand, and with a little effort he was able to work the ruby and its setting out as well. He checked the other hooves, finding only twelve more stones still in place. Three of them came out easily. He had to work a little on a fourth, and he left the other eight. There were shallow circles of indentation on the hooves, some deeper than others, but there were many places where there was only the slightest hint of a setting. She was casting the gems out, and he imagined that they lay in various places on the twisted .trail behind him. She offered no resistance as he worked at her hooves, though she lifted her head up to watch him, following his hands with her eyes.

He entered the jewelry store at one o'clock. There were two women shopping, one of them going over silver patterns with a young salesgirl. A man in his mid-forties, in suit and tie, was showing the other woman some rings. Paul waited, looking into a glass covered display case full of bracelets. When the woman left, the man came over to him. He looked him over as he approached, and he was only a little distant, just a little brusque, when he asked if he could help him. Paul took the diamond out of his pocket. He had wrapped it in a pinch of tissue paper that he had torn from the photographic wrapping.

"Could you give me an appraisal of this?" Paul asked. The man spoke as he was moving a black, felt-covered square across the glass counter.

"There will be a charge. It will . . . " He caught himself after a quick in rush of breath when he saw the diamond.

"That's okay," Paul said. "Whatever the cost is will be fine."

The man took his eyepiece out of a vest pocket and lifted the diamond up between his thumb and index finger. He turned it toward the light, then put it down.

"We'll have to move it over here," he said, and Paul followed him around the counter to where he had a gooseneck light with a strong bulb in it. Again he picked the stone up, this time using a large circular magnifying glass and a pair of tweezers.

"Rough cut, but final split," he murmured. He looked at it, turning it for a long time. Then he got a scale, a small chrome and glass device from a drawer behind the counter. It was a balance scale, the weights extremely small and various. When he was finished, his eyes were swimming a little, a little moist from their effort. He braced a little when he spoke.

"Market quality, as is, before any final cuts or trimming and polishing, roughly eighty thousand dollars, ten thousand more or less. Finished and in the proper setting, a hundred and a quarter."

His voice was a little louder than he had intended, and the woman looking at the silver patterns and the sales girl as well looked over at them and blinked.

He did not need to count the stones again to know that what was at question here was a great deal of money, but he felt a need to get the terms as specific as possible, and when he returned to his room he removed the four cups from the little horse's hooves and poured the diamonds on the table. Though there was not much variation in size, he measured the one he had taken in against others to make sure that it was indeed representative, then he counted the lot. There were forty-seven of them, and even at the most conservative estimate this put their total worth at over two million dollars. After counting them, he didn't spend time looking at them, but loaded them back in the cups and inserted the cups back into the hooves again. The horse got down from the bed when he had finished and shook herself. It was three o'clock.

He had time now. There was nothing left for him to do until the next morning, when he would leave and make his way to Marble. Nothing had become all that much clearer, but he thought the diamonds now made a little sense beyond that having to do with Parker's specific past, whether he had the truth of it or not. Passion for his father's wealth was one thing, but the amount of the wealth tended to conventionalize the greed somewhat. The one real wedge he might still have was that they wouldn't know for sure, unless they had gotten it out of Mary Grace, that he had found the diamonds. He couldn't believe that she would let them know that. They would still not know why he had kept the horse, why he hadn't given it up to someone and freed himself. He remained, he hoped, an unknown quantity in some ways to them. This would make them worry, at least a little unsure. And while he too was unsure, about what was before him and how he might handle it, he did know what the goal was. He wanted Mary Grace, and he wanted the horse too, and he wanted, though he had not spent much time thinking about it, to kill Parker. The resolve had not left him. It was not a passion but a commitment. Though the fire at the farm and the death of Ronny helped cement it, he did not feel it as a need for revenge. It was just more of a certainty for him now. He was not certain that he could get it done, but he was certain that he would try to do it.

He sat on the bed for a half hour, and then he took a walk up the canyon in the direction of the divide where the Rockies would dip and descend a little and start down into Mexico. He walked along the railing beside the wash. When he had gone a few blocks he began to come to houses that he did not recognize at all from his childhood. These had only the mystery of his adolescence attached to them; he knew them from when he had returned to Bisbee to go to high school after his father had died. The ones below had the presence of his father locked into them. He returned, using the sidewalk on the other side, and when he got back to the motel it was still early, too early for dinner.

He got Ronny's photographic folder and brought it to the table. He put the pictures that had come through Pfeffer to the side, and again he went through the ones that Ronny had taken, starting with a cursory look through the eight-by-tens of the families and taking more care with the ones from the party. When he got to the one with Parker in it, he put it aside with the others and went through the rest of the party shots. He had taken some care with them before, and he found nothing new, though he studied them for a long time. When he was finished he took the one with Parker in it and lay it down along side the one of Mary Grace on the deck beside the railing. Looking back and forth, and even with Parker in the background of the shot, he could see the similarity. The set of cheek bones, the brow curve, even the turn of the nose were very close, and he thought he could see even a similarity in posture. He thought about the look of Johnny, closing his eyes for a moment to bring it up, and he thought he remembered a similar cast of skin color, a similar brow. The genes of Abelardo García, he thought. And then he glanced at the photograph of himself and the little horse that Ronny had taken. He took the picture and put it beside the other two, looking back and forth between them. Again, he was slightly startled at the way he had looked. The picture was almost too clear, too sharp in its edges. It was what he imagined a morgue shot might be like, vaguely remembering the look of the dead that he had tended in the Navy. After he had looked again at all three of the pictures with some care, he gathered them up together and put them back in the album fold and put the album in the drawer of the dresser. He checked the little horse, perfunctorily, to see that she was okay, and then he got his keys and left the room.

When he got close to the center of town, he turned to his right, up a steep and winding street that led into the foothills. He passed the statue of the Copper Man, a monument to the mine workers, and took the first left, passing a small grammar school that he remembered. He used to come down there from his house to play with his ball on weekends. After another turn to the right, the street flattened out, and all the houses were familiar. They seemed smaller, but there was not one of them that was essentially different, and as he passed by them he remembered how he had done the same thing on his way to school. At the end of the block, at a corner beyond which was a small square lined with little houses, was the house he had lived in, the place where he had been born. He had lived there until he was seven; then his father's work had taken them to Illinois. Then in a few years they were back in Bisbee again, in another house, and he had spent his high school years. When his father died, his mother had moved back to Illinois, her home, and soon he had found himself in the Navy.

There was a car parked in the street in front of the house, and he thought he could see someone moving beyond the front window. He went around the corner and saw that the toolshed behind the house was still there. Though the house had been sided and had a new shingle roof, the shed looked the same, weathered board siding and a corrugated tin roof. He went back to the front of the house and went in the gate and up the steps to the small porch and knocked at the door.

A woman about his own age, very pretty, with no makeup and in a flower print dress answered. She had a wide, open smile, and when he had gotten through his request, telling her that he had lived there over twenty-five years ago and asking her if she would consider letting him look around a little, she seemed very pleased and excited and let him in. Her husband was not there. He was working and would be home in an hour or so.

"Does he work in the mines?" Paul asked her.

"Oh, no," she answered, laughing lightly. "The mines are almost closed up now. Copper prices. Bob is a teacher, an administrator too; he's at the high school."

"I went there," Paul said.

"Did you! But I thought you said you were a child?"

"We lived here twice," Paul said. "Here up until I was seven. Then we went to Illinois. Then we came back, to another place the other side of town, in Lowell, and I went to High School."

"Oh, I see. Bob is from Denver, but I'm from the Midwest too, from St. Louis. We met in Denver, in college."

They had coffee and talked a little more, and in a while she could see that Paul was looking around the room, was less attentive to their talk, and she laughed lightly again.

"You want to look around?"

She took him from room to room, and though the furniture and the appointments were different there were things that he recognized. The bedrooms had the same wallboard, and the kitchen cabinets had not changed though they were painted a different color; they were stylishly old now. When he saw the little room in the back where he had slept, he looked in at the door for a long time. The place was now a storeroom, but things were neatly placed in it; he remembered where his bed had been, and when he looked into the closet he saw that the wooden doweling where his clothes had hung was the same. He thought he

240

remembered the indentations and scrapes in the wood. He asked her if he could see the shed, and she said of course he could.

"We hardly use it though, only store some garden tools there. It's a good building, I think. Sturdy. But Bob isn't much of a handyman; we hardly use it."

She let him out the back door, telling him the latch was open and if he didn't mind she wouldn't go with him. She had to get back to her dinner. Her husband would be home before long.

He had used the shed as a playhouse. In those days the yard was mostly cactus and sand, and what tools were necessary around the place had been kept in a wooden box inside the door. He had had a cot and some toys and a small table and chair in the place, and he had even slept out in the shed at times, his mother liking it that he was not afraid to do so, but always reminding him to lock the latch from the inside at such times. He vaguely remembered her coming out to check it, to make sure, when she thought he was asleep.

When he opened the door, he found that the room was not near as messy as the woman had suggested. There were not many tools, only a lawnmower, a few rakes and hoes, and a couple of tool boxes, and these were neatly placed along one of the walls. The rest of the room was empty. It had never been finished on the inside, and the walls remained as they had been, studded out and only covered with wallboard in the corner where his cot had been, the board there rising only half way up the wall. He remembered the look of the wall board, and when he approached it he thought he could see some slight discoloration where he had crayoned in some long-remembered figures of some kind. When he peered close, he thought he could see one of the figures emerge slightly, a small dog or some other animal. He looked at the ceiling, the ribs of tin, trying to remember how they had looked from his cot, but it was light in the place, and he could evoke nothing of what it must have been like to watch them before he went to sleep.

He checked as much of the floor as he could see, running his foot in the dust, but there were only old and recent scratches where equipment had been moved across it. Then he began to circle the room, running his hands lightly along the studs and two-by-four-braces that crossed between them halfway up the wall. On one of the braces, near where his cot had been, and at a place where the wallboard had been pulled loose from the stud it was nailed to, he found a slight bump, and when he picked at it with his nail it came away. It was a bit of hardened candle wax, no longer white but a dirty gray. He ran his hand up the stud beside it, above where the wallboard ended; it was rough, and he could feel nothing but the worn edges of the saw cuts. Then he checked below the brace, pulling the wallboard free of the few nails that held it so that he could get his hand in, and about four inches under it he felt something, a series of brief indentations. He squatted down, but the stud side was low and in shadow and the wall board prevented a good angle of vision, and he could not see in clearly. He got up and pulled the piece of board free, standing the section against the wall to his right. Then he squatted down again and leaned in between the studs, pressing his shoulder against the wall between them, his head at a level with the markings.

He took a match out of his pocket and lit it. There was something he could see there, possibly a fault in the saw cut, but it seemed too regular and complex for that, and he took his handkerchief out of his pocket and rubbed at the spot. The match went out, almost burning his fingers, and he had to strike another. Now the markings were more visible; they were letters, and he put his head against the wall under the brace, holding the match up close to them and his face, so that he could read them: *AG*, and below that, under a small *x*, *MC*.

He had a thought to rise, to get up from where he squatted, but he couldn't get his legs to work immediately, and he keep looking at the cuts of the letters in the match flame. Soon he felt the heat on his fingers and saw the dimming, and he turned his head slightly and blew the match out. The brace brushed his head as he rose. When he was on his feet again, he stood looked down where the candle had rested, the letters once again in shadow. The ones below the *x* were his mother's initials, Mary Cords.

They had come here in the evening, when it was dark, and used the floor or a blanket or maybe even some mattress or other. His father was away somewhere or was at work, and the romance had gotten to them, to her at least: the candle and the rough secret place. And who could know how long or how many times or exactly when. And afterwards, or possibly before, he had taken a nail or a knife and cut the letters in, in a place where they would not be seen, but where she could look at them if she wanted to.

He realized that it was another story, that he was telling it this time, and as he thought of it he realized that she at least had not been much more than an adolescent. She was in her early twenties, and García himself was not much older than that. And Paul's father had been much older, twelve years older than she was, already in his thirties and well placed in his position and his life. And he was stern and serious, and that could have made him seem even older to her, who had been taken from her home in Illinois to live in this foreign place. He might have seemed almost like a father. So why not, he thought.

He had probably been very exotic to her, half Mexican, mysterious, and on his way to places and involved in new experiences, danger possibly, and he would have told her stories about those things, ones that would have got to her; he was very good at stories. So why not? He came and went, and there were no expectations or sticky things to have to deal with, and then Paul was born, and that was okay too. And when he was old enough to use the shed, the memory was far enough in the past, but not so far that she could bring herself to scrape away the letters; it was enough to have put up wallboard, to make a place for his little cot, to leave the letters, but to cover them up, to leave the bit of candle wax. It came to him that he was glad he did not have, or want to have, children, and then he put the piece of wallboard back in place and pushed the nails back into the wood again with a chisel he found in one of the metal boxes. He felt that he was sealing up a kind of coffin, closing something off from view forever. But he had opened the coffin first, and its dead air had come alive again in the open air of thought, memory and new tales. There had been no real relics, but there had been the candle and the markings. And he now owned the core of the story and was responsible for it, for its telling, if only to himself, and for its consequences.

━━━

When he returned to his room, he took the three photographs out and looked at them again. The similarities between himself, Parker and Mary Grace were now unmistakable, and now he knew why he kept the little horse and why he would continue to do so. After he had put the photos back in the folder, he made a list of the things he would get the next day before he left. He knew it would be risky renting a car if they wouldn't take a cash deposit. He could use Campos' driver's license, the California one that had been in his wallet, but he hesitated to use his credit cards. He had Ronny's license and cards too, but that was at least as risky.

That evening he ate dinner in the dining room of the Copper Queen hotel, and afterwards he went to the bar. There was a mix of old men and a few young, professional-looking couples there. It was quiet, and he contented himself with overhearing the conversations between the bartender and what looked like a couple of retired miners. It was good to be listening to the lives of people who had no connection whatsoever to his own. It was ten o'clock when he decided to leave, late enough so that he thought he could get to sleep. That night the little horse curled at the foot of the bed, and the weight of her against his feet did not feel like a burden.

They were up at six, and by the time he had showered and eaten breakfast it was eight-thirty and he walked to the town center, to the car rental agency. Though he thought he appeared a little nervous, he had no problem using Campos' driver's license, and when they said they'd need a credit card number as security, he handed over two of Campos' cards. He parked the car at the town center, near the post office, and went to the store, a camping and army surplus. Then he made a stop at a drug store. He returned to the motel and settled up his bill, using cash, and then he got the little horse into the car and they left.

They headed south on route 80, and when they got to Douglas they turned and headed north into New Mexico. They were in lower country then, and the heat shimmered on the highway in front of them. He kept the windows closed and the air conditioner on, and she rested in the seat beside him. The road was wide and relatively straight, and he made good time, and it was just after two o'clock in the afternoon when he saw that Albuquerque was coming up. He cut off the road he was on as he approached it, taking the highway that skirted the city, and in another hour they were on the other side and heading in the direction of Santa Fe. The road was busier now, and he went slower. He kept a towel on the seat between him and the horse so he could use it to cover her in case anyone looked into the car as they passed them, or throw it over her when he stopped for gas.

When they got to Santa Fe it was late in the afternoon, and he found a motel close to the center of town. Before he unloaded what he needed from the car, and before he fed her and looked after her, he went to a general store and got a few things that he thought he might need later. When he got back to the room, he took her into the shower and bathed her, and then he brushed her out with the brushes he had bought. As he touched her he could come to no understanding of her age. She was firm and alert, and the only thing now that seemed to give it away was her eyes and his memories of her recent abilities, and those seemed more about skill and wisdom than years, though he realized that the latter might be a necessary condition for the former. There was no discernible gray on her, no sway in her back, and though he could feel that her teats were large and swelled under his touch as he dried her, their firmness seemed more a function of the stimulation than of any extreme maturity. When he had her ready, he fed her, and then he left her alone and went to a restaurant and had dinner. He spent the remainder of the evening organizing his gear and checking it.

The next morning they left Santa Fe and were back out and on the open desert road again by nine o'clock. They still had a good distance to go, and he did not stop for lunch, but got snacks at gas stops. By noon they were beginning to leave the open desert, to rise a little into the first foothills of the Rockies. The growth along the highway got greener and there were cooler breezes now, and he could open the vents and the windows slightly and keep the air conditioner low. He began to pass through places that were familiar to him. Somehow, in his travels for Pfeffer, he had bypassed most of New Mexico, but he had covered most of Colorado, and they passed on the outskirts of towns where there were hospitals that he had visited. He could not imagine that he would ever visit them again, and this did not bother him at all. That was another life entirely, one that now seemed of no use whatsoever.

He thought of his mother and *her* other life, realizing that she had managed to submerge it even before his birth probably. And maybe it had never even been another life, just a passing fancy, but he did not want to think of it that way and really suspected that it had meant something. It had meant *him* certainly, and that had always been there for her and before her. And yet, though he could manufacture the right explanations of her remembered behavior toward him, he really could not make them stick, could not inform them convincingly with this new information. His father had been stern and distant, but he had died while Paul was still too young and inexperienced to make any sense of him. He could remember no shift or change in him and no hint of a reason for the attitude behind his behavior. Though he had not treated him fairly, or in ways that he could now see as fair, he had been consistent in his distance, and there was nothing that could be said to be grudging. And as he thought of it he realized that it was all finally beyond understanding, and even were he able to speak to his mother, who was dead now too, he would not risk revealing it; it had been her business, and he was only the product of the business, and had no real rights in the matter at all.

And of his other father, the real one, there were only tales and stories, and he was as unknown finally as the father he had lived with for the short time they had been together. But there were a few things, the other products of the same kind of business. There was Mary Grace, and there was Johnny and Parker. Parker stood apart from the other two, and Paul also stood apart; their sources, in one of the tales at least, were similar. Most of all, there was the little horse. He reached over and touched her hoof on the seat beside him, thinking of his father's hands touching her there also. He could feel nothing. That had been, really, in history. But when he looked over at her, he saw her looking up at him, and then he did feel something, something he could not name and did not wish to try to name just then.

They were entering the beginnings of the town of Glenwood Springs. He went over a set of railroad tracks slowly; on the other side, to the left, was a large hot springs pool. It was full of the elderly, their heads bobbing on the surface of the water, steam rising in wet clouds into the air above them, obscuring their features, as their submerged and invisible bodies rotated their heads, their faces turning with the passing traffic.

PART IV

MARBLE

Chapter 18

Before he was able to recognize the turnoff, he was past it. He
had been going slowly, looking for it, but the brush and trees
had grown up in the years since he had been there, and they obscured
the mouth of the road and were no longer useful landmarks. He slowed
and pulled to the shoulder and made a wide U turn and headed back.
Once on the road he saw that there were some new houses, but only a
few of them; he guessed that no new ski slopes had been put in. The
stop he remembered, no more than a gas station and small restaurant,
was still there, but there were boards on the windows and grass growing
in the concrete beside the pumps. They had gotten coffee and a donut
for fifteen cents, but that was close to fifteen years ago; still, even then
it was very cheap and he and his high school friend had laughed about
it. A little past the place, only the foundation of the small abandoned
schoolhouse was still there. He had climbed through a broken window
that time and found an old clipboard with a child's scrawls on it: names,
hearts and letters.

Paul and the little horse had spent the night at the edge of Glenwood
Springs, no more than forty miles from Marble, and they were up and
on road again shortly after dawn. He had her on the seat beside him now,
and she kept her head up, watching the roadside through the window.
They had risen quickly, into the higher altitudes of the Rockies.

Two miles further down the road there was a parking area, railroad ties surrounding crushed stone. It had been nothing but a pull-off place when he had come here years ago, but now it seemed to mark the trail to Marble. Still, it was small and not well kept up; it was only late May, and he felt he could expect to be alone with her as they went up. He pulled in and parked against a tie. Then he let her out. She stood for a moment in the gravel beside the car, and then she stepped gingerly through it until she got to the trail's beginning, where the ground was hard dirt. She kicked at the dirt, then stretched herself. She looked back at him, then trotted up the trail and broke into a canter, her tail bouncing on her haunches. She looked good as she went around a turn and out of sight. In a moment she was back again, standing at the mouth of the trail waiting for him. He got his knapsack and his knife and kit out of the truck. Then he locked the car and moved across the gravel to her and they started up the trail.

The trail was wide enough for a jeep, but he could see that the tire ruts weren't deep and that there hadn't been much traffic. To the right, the mountain rose up from the trail. There was very little shoulder, almost none, on either side, and on the left the trail sloped quickly off into thick pine and aspen. He could hear the tree-muffled river, running shallow and fast to the left below them. She stayed with him, but like a dog would run ahead and linger back at times, sniffing at brush and wild flowers, nipping at bark, even dipping off the trail down into the trees, where he would hear her rustling. She held her head high and inquisitive and alert, her ears perked, and her tail stayed high also. After a half hour of gentle rise the trail steepened and narrowed slightly and began to straighten out.

The growth got lower as they approached timberline, and the strength and speed of the river increased its rush, becoming loud enough to require a raising of the voice to be heard over it. Though he had no one to speak to, could get her where he needed with gestures, he would have liked things to be quieter. Still the sound was more a term of anticipation than an irritation. If things had remained the same, he wouldn't be getting to where he wanted to be. He remembered the beauty of it, and he was pleasantly ready to see it again, especially after such a long time. He did not figure on an ambush, and at any rate he knew no other way to get here. The trail was vulnerable, but they did not know when he was coming. They could have guessed within a week, he thought, but he doubted that they would try to meet him here. The place was too risky, and though he would be easy they didn't know what to expect from her. He doubted that they would have the patience to wait here or want to risk the loss of her. Probably they'd aim for a more enclosed space, but one where there was no brush for her to run to, the quarry itself perhaps.

They came upon the opening of the trail and the river itself suddenly, at a place that he judged to be no more than five hundred yards from the turn-up to the quarry entrance. The river ran through a small high meadow of tiny wild flowers, columbine, daisies, black-eyed Susan, and many he could not name, and miniature pines. The river was low, no more than a foot deep, and rushing over rounded pebbles. But most of what was in it was not stone at all, but marble. It was full of marble. There were huge, two-ton obelisks set askew, some in places where the river dipped and deepened, and spray shot off them. Their sides that were against the rush had been smoothed and rounded by the water, looked finely polished, and their far sides held the saw-marks from where they had been cut out. In the shallows the rounded marble balls gleamed brighter than the pebbles, and as the river rolled them, they clicked against each other. The sun was brighter in the river; the marble reflected it and the rushing water threw its sparkles up so that the river seemed lit with a power stronger than the sun. The thin rods of marble, the broken chunks, the massive obelisks, the rounded balls and the pattern they all made was, as the light hit into them, another pattern, so bright that it made the eyes sparkle, and as they moved up to the edge of the river it was like looking into a kaleidoscope that was slowly turning.

He stopped at the edge, but she walked on, stepping carefully into the shallows, her hooves, now devoid of all but a few jewels, purely yellow among the marble balls and chips, solid yellow curves he could see through the perfectly clear water where she stood. When he looked up from them, he saw her tail and mane rise in the transparent spray at the river's edge, the breezy spray push changing patterns in the short hair of her barrel and shoulders. She was so small and close to the river's surface that the spray enveloped all of her, but her yellowness, the only color there among the various whites of the marble river, made her focal, her presence beyond any consideration of size or scale. The marble had been cut with care, and what was here were the cast-offs, the broken and mistaken pieces of an industry that had lit the stoops of cities. People stepped and sat on those stoops, and in a century wore the marble away from its hard edge to a kind of serviceable soft sculpture. And here the river had done the same with the leavings, taking them into itself, but not reducing them. What a strange and complex monument this was. He thought it stood for nothing. And she too stood for nothing; she was beautiful and unreachable, maverick, wild and aloof. But she was not unique, and she was therefore the possibility of something attainable. It was what she was aloof from that was not clear. She was a measure, but of what? That she was herself and so authentic, that was where the answer lay, but he didn't have the questions. He could only watch her as the spray enveloped her like a fixed and transparent moon behind which she dipped her head gracefully, touched her muzzle to the surface of the water and drank.

She came out, and they moved back from the river and started up the hill to the turn that would take them to the quarry. Here the trail was lined with slabs of broken marble, rusted cables looping among them, and indecipherable hunks of rusted machinery. The rubble piles were above his head, and the trail seemed narrower. She walked beside him now, her head still high and her eyes alert. And he was alert now also, thinking it was time to figure. Halfway to the top of the trail he stopped and picked her up and turned and started carefully up the pile of rubble to the right, above which was the mountain itself. In a few moments they reached beyond the rubble to solid ground, and he put her on her feet again, and they moved among the low pines heading for the crest, the hump that he placed at the top of the quarry entrance that would be below them when they got there. The rise was steep but the going was easy, and he was able to look around as they ascended. They were close to the top of the mountain peaks, though he could see a much higher snow-covered one off in the distance. The hilltops closer in were only slightly above them, all rising a little from what was a series of mountain valleys of low growth, moss slopes, and meadows of miniature wild flowers. He could see no structures, but he saw places where the ground was worn winding around hills and out of sight. A couple might have been remnants of a time when the quarry was working, but one seemed fresh, a jeep trail, and he figured it would be the one. Though he couldn't see the quarry entrance from where they were, he could see no fresh track heading in the direction of it, and he figured that meant that anyone coming there would be on foot.

When they reached the crest where the hill's hump was almost flat, he angled off to the left and headed for a thick and higher stand of pine, what he took to be a kind of brow at the edge of the top of the quarry opening. When he reached the place, he opened his hand and motioned for her to stay put and then moved in among the trees, edging out to where he thought the drop off was. The pines grew right up to the edge, but he could see the blue of the sky through the final ones, and when he got to them he spread the branches and looked over the edge and down. A hundred yards below him was the flattened place where the cranes and other heavy machinery had worked. It was a marble floor, still clean of growth, but now there was dirt scattered in places on it. Holding the trunk of a pine and leaning over, he could see down into the quarry itself, the gaping hole that started close to his feet and extended a good eighty yards below the floor at the entrance. He remembered how it was to stand at the lip of the entrance, the cathedral opening in the mountain had seemed to lean outward over him, the marble cavern pressing down from above. And below was the gigantic square hole, deep, and a good city block to its back wall. Leaning a bit further out, he could see the cable; it was still there. It was attached from the ceiling of the quarry, somewhere under his feet, and it hung still in the air beyond arm's reach at the lip, extending down in the dark where he could not see it anymore. He could see no one or any evidence of anyone, and he pulled himself back, his hand sticky with the sap from the pine when he released it.

When he got back to her she was waiting, still standing where he had left her, beside the pine seedling that reached almost to her crest. He motioned to her, and they moved down on the other side of the hill's hump. Near the bottom of the hill, and now with the quarry opening to their left, they came upon a large rubble mound of marble leavings that extended around the hill's side, and at the foot of it they found a grassy place with a few high pines and aspens staggered within it. He looked around when they got there. The place was slightly elevated, and by moving to the edge of it and stepping on a marble slab he could see the flattened area leading to the cathedral entrance just below his feet.

Thinking back, he knew that he had been only slightly less than reckless in the way he'd gotten them there. Though he knew no other way to Marble but the trail he'd taken, he could have stayed off the trail, working his way through the brush beside it. That would have taken much longer, but it would have been smarter and safer. Now that he was standing there, he felt restless and unsure. He didn't know what to do. He needed contact, but he knew no way to make it. There were higher elevations above him, and he knew they could be watching him. He could wait it out, but he wasn't sure of the best place to do that.

He stood looking at the quarry for a few moments, and then he turned and went to the grassy area behind him and picked her up and carried her back and over the marble pile and down the other side. When he reached the edge of the floor in front of the cathedral opening, he put her down, and they walked together over to the lip of the quarry. At the edge, the cable hanging down in space in front of them, they could see back and deep down into the quarry. When their eyes became accustomed to the dark interior, they could see the pile of marble rubble at the bottom, a long distance below them. The back and sides of the quarry were solid marble, and the marble was wet and glistening with water seepage. The quarry roof was marble too, and it hung and jutted over them. The cuts that the saws had made were less even and smooth than those on the sides, so that the whole roof looked precarious and ready to fall. The sight of it was both spacious and oppressive, and she pulled back a little from the edge when she looked up at it.

He knew that there was no reason to be standing there; they had nothing left to do but leave, go to higher ground, hole up, and wait, and when he looked down at her as she moved back a little, the encumbrance and the responsibility that she was to him rushed in upon him. He wanted to be rid of her; he didn't need this, didn't want it any more, and he wished she was gone. But he knew she would not go until in some way or other he released her, and he felt desperate because he didn't know yet how to do that. She snorted, and there was a brief echo of her snort in the quarry. Then he heard the sound of the motor.

The jeep came around the edge of the quarry hill the moment he heard it. He had enough time to think that the marble had prevented the sound from reaching them sooner. As he turned and saw it, it was pulling up, and its doors were opening. Parker and the two Mexicans and the doctor came out, running as their feet hit the ground. All but the doctor had rifles. She was pressed against his leg and shivering, and he reached down for her. When he came up with her he looked to his left where the marble pile was and saw he couldn't make it. He moved back from the lip of the quarry, seeing that they were getting closer. He had nowhere else to go. He took a few quick strides to the edge and leapt out for the cable.

It was heavy and when he hit it, it did not give like a rope. He got it in his left hand, and it swung heavily out into the cathedral space. He got his legs around it and brought her into him, holding her tight to his body with his arm, and caught hold of it with his right hand too. He could hear them coming behind him as he swung out almost to the middle of the marble room. He was surrounded by marble. He left the sunlight, but the wet walls gave off a light of their own. Before he began to swing back, he released his grip a little and began to slide, feeling the ribs in the cable rip at the flesh on his palms. He could hear them yelling and calling as he descended, their voices growing louder and more vibrant as the echo chamber of the quarry surrounded him. When he hit the slab at the bottom he stumbled but he did not fall. When he released the cable, he had to pull his hands free with some force, ripping more skin away. Scrambling over the slabs of marble rubble, he descended as quickly as he could. He could hear their voices echoing down from above him. Nothing made any clear sense, and he did not look up.

When he reached what he thought was the bottom of the quarry, his feet came to firmer ground and he paused and lifted his head, but he was well under the lip now, the marble hung out over him, and he could not see them. There was no more yelling from above, but he could hear the sound of feet on gravel, the steps exaggerated by the echo chamber that he was in. He had her tight under his arm again, his palm covering her belly; he could feel her breathing in his hand. And he could feel the wetness of his torn palm as well, the hair on her belly dampening with his blood. He turned around, felt the weight and swing of his small backpack, and reached up and pulled at the straps. It was dark, and he had to look up high on the walls of the quarry to see where the sun line lay, the space above it still wet and shining. The ceiling was a little darker than the higher walls, but still there were shadows and places of reflected light in it. It hung down oppressive and seemed ready at any moment to fall. He looked around at the dark shapes of the slabs of rubble. He could see that he was not at the bottom yet; there were darker places toward the middle of the quarry, possible passages among the slabs, and he began to work his way toward them, stepping carefully as his eyes became accustomed to the lack of bright, reflected light. He went deeper, coming to places where he had to turn his shoulders, adjust her body, to work between walls of marble that rose up tapering in toward each other above him. In ten minutes he was deep in a maze of passages. The walls brushing his shoulders were slick and wet, and he could smell the decay of dank moss. He had to pause often to make choices about directions. It was dark, but it had not gotten darker as he went down, and he could see pretty well. When he paused, he listened; he could hear nothing but water dripping, no sound but that of occasional brief bird twitters from above. Then he heard a motor starting and the sound of tires rumbling. The sound grew louder and then stopped; he heard the slam of a car door, footsteps again, sharp commands, talking from where he thought was the edge of the cathedral opening. He heard a heavy creak of some kind and caught his breath, knowing it was the hanging cable.

He went deeper, coming to places where he had to get on his knees and crawl through. At times he was not sure of his direction, did not know if the quarry opening was up behind him or ahead, was not even sure if it was above or below him. He feared for a moment that he was going in circles, that they would find him and that, in this place so separated from the life of the world, would go off half-cocked and kill him and take her. But he saw, as he pulled himself together, that whatever the circles might be, he was going downward, and he continued. In a while he knew that he couldn't carry her anymore. He was crawling through what he thought were holes in the marble, and the weight of her in this position was too much for him. He put her down on her legs in front of him, just beyond his pack, and reached to her haunches to urge her on. But she had stepped beyond his reach and all he touched was the strands of her tail. She didn't move off too far, and as he moved on his knees he could see the yellow wave in front of him. When it took him time to make a few feet, she would stop and wait, and when his cheek brushed against her tail she would continue before him.

Once he came to a place where the turns in the marble were like passages through a giant heart; he had to twist and turn his body, move one shoulder then the other through slick wet tubes. He had to bend at his waist, bring his knees through singly. He held onto her tail then, learning his direction from the way it pulled, like reins in his hand, his free hand running along the marble curves in front of him.

Then his hand slid from the marble and into the air. He pulled back, grasping the side lip of the opening. Her tail jerked free of his grip and he grabbed the lip on the other side. He feared for a moment that she was irretrievably gone, that what was before him was a chasm of some sort, but then he heard her wet breathing, a brief snort and snuffling a few feet off, and when he raised his face from the floor of the tight tube he was in, craning his neck back, he could see her a few feet below him, standing and looking up at him. There was some light coming from a source behind her and she was slightly haloed, her outlines hazy but lit like a vague fire aura. She bobbed her head once and snorted. Then he pushed his pack out and let it fall and reached to his sides and pulled on the lips, pushing outward as if he could open the marble mouth wider, and worked to get his hips free of the tube that had him locked snugly. His pants were soaked with water and slick moss remnants and when he came free from the tightness he popped a foot forward like a cork's first kick from a bottle.

His shoulders were out of the tube in the air now, and he reached to the wall in which the tube was exit, pressed against it, and turned himself over on his back. He searched the wall above for purchase, found juts in the marble, slight scorations, and was able to pull himself to a sitting position in the tube. There was no room to slide his legs out, so he had to follow the wall around with his hands, get himself facing downward again, bending at the waist. She stepped backward a few feet as his hands reached out to where she stood. He found he could reach the ground there, and on extended arms he walked forward until his legs cleared the tube; his feet walked down the wall below the exit, and he lay extended on his stomach on the ground. And it *was* the ground: dirt and moss with a few pieces of stone that he took to be bits of marble pressing against his body in various places.

He lay still for a while, breathing deeply, trying to force out the tension of the claustrophobia he had felt while working his way through the heartlike structure. He had not come anywhere close to panic in the tight, weighty spaces; his intent in getting away from them, the feeling that he was pursued, had driven him. But out in the larger space, even though he had no good sense of its dimensions, he felt liberated, and he sucked air that did not seem like his own fetid breath coming back into him again as it had in the marble corridors. Then he felt her breath on his head, in his hair, the kid glove of her nostrils, and felt her take a clump of hair in her teeth and pull gently but firmly at it, lifting his head up a little. She released him and then took another clump, gave another pull, a little harder this time. He rose to his knees and she moved back from him a step. Then he got slowly to his feet and looked around.

The opening in the marble wall behind him looked incredibly small when he saw it; it seemed no larger than his thigh, certainly not large enough for his body to have fit through. When he bent over and looked into it, he couldn't see far, and when he reached in he had to twist his arm awkwardly to make the first turn. Even then, he could barely get his fist into and around the corner, and when he extended his fingers they hit against marble and he could feel no opening beyond. It struck him that if they followed him, found and took the same pathway, they would have some difficulty. He withdrew his hand from the stone. Then he turned around to examine where and what he had come out into.

The chamber was small, possibly twenty feet high at its apex. Its ceiling was uneven like that of the cathedral of the quarry itself, but here the stone had not been cut; there were no saw grooves and no hard angles. What jutted down on him was rounded, as if formed by water, and there were recesses that looked like ascending tunnels and in some of them there was dim light entering that gave the chamber its dark glow. His eyes followed the curve of the ceiling down to the walls, then to the floor. The floor was circular, and the chamber had the shape of a large inverted cup over him. He saw that the little horse had moved away from him and was standing at the wall opposite his tunnel entrance. It was dark there, but he could see that she had that faint aura around her again. She was backlighted, and when he moved the few steps that he needed to get to her, he could see the low opening where she stood waiting. When he was almost to her and beginning to stoop down, she turned into the opening and disappeared. He paused, startled, but immediately he heard her hooves clicking a few feet from him, and he reached out and touched the walls at the sides of the opening, bent down further, his pack on his shoulders again, and crept in.

He was enclosed in marble again, but this time as he touched the sides and ceiling he found them warm and dry, and though he was stooped over he was standing, and in a few feet his hands could follow the walls to the ceiling well above him and he could stand erect. The passage was very narrow, and he had to move slowly, turning his shoulders at times to get through. It ran for what seemed a long distance on the level, turning very gradually, but enough so that though he could hear her very close in front of him he could not see her, and only occasionally caught glimpses of her tail and quarters ahead of him at a bend. It was lighter now, and though the walls looked tight and impenetrable and he could not figure the source of the light he welcomed it. The narrow floor in front of him was flat, solid marble and looked polished. Then the passage began to descend, gradually at first, then steeper, zigzagging in a serpentine manner. He could hear her hooves clicking in front but a little below him now; the sound they made had changed, the clicks were less rhythmic, a little awkward and hesitant, and he wondered why. He did not know how long he had been on them before the realization that they were steps came upon him. They were cut out of the marble and were shallow. They were well worn and they dipped in gradually toward their centers. He tried to imagine them as natural, as somehow worn in by water, even wind, but it was impossible. They continued on and down. They steepened, and he had to keep his hands pressed against the walls at his shoulders as he stepped down them, going deeper, following their single path and the sound of her hooves clicking in the distance.

He had time now to wonder where he was and where he was going. The narrow, steep stairway slowed her, and he had lost any anxiety about keeping up; she stayed at the same distance in front of him, still out of sight, and when he slowed to make a turn or to step down with care she slowed also. He didn't know how far or how deep they had gone, and he had no good sense of the direction or angle away from the quarry, but he guessed they were well away from it. He had little doubt anymore that the steps were manmade, but he couldn't see how the passageway itself could be; there were no tool marks anywhere, and the walls while dry now were very smooth, almost slick to the touch. It could be nothing but water, an underground stream of some sort. It had been found when the stream had dried up or diverted, and had been made of use. What the use was he could not imagine. But he knew that wherever he was he was better off here. He could not think that they could follow him; he was safe now, at least for a while.

He thought, remembering, that there had been the four of them, Parker, the two Mexicans and the doctor. He had seen weapons, rifles, but he thought he had seen them held very tentatively. They could not kill him and risk losing the horse. And he had held the horse and had been close to the lip of the cathedral entrance. So he was safe as long as she was in danger with him. And as he thought of it, he imagined that maybe they were as confused by him as he was by them. He, after all, knew why they would go to such lengths to get the horse back. One aspect of her potential was clear, and he assumed they'd know he'd understand this, would have figured it. The movies were worth a lot. And they had been training her and had already done well with the male. If they could be taught to carry roses, they could be taught to do other things as well. He couldn't be sure, even now, how rare the horses were, but all he knew suggested that they were important in ways that could not be clearly measured. And it struck him that two were much better than one; male and female could make them other horses, possibly. But what could they think of his actions? Why would he not give up the horse to some authority? How could he dispose of the horse for sufficient money to make worthwhile the drastic change in his life that taking and going with her had caused? He didn't think they could know all that was between him and Mary Grace. Even she might not know it. And even if they did, he couldn't believe that they were capable of seeing that as justifying his actions. They would have checked him out as thoroughly as possible by this time, but they would have found out nothing in his past or situation to help them. In a way, he felt he had them; his mystery was more profound than theirs. The only trouble was that at bottom there were still parts of it that were a mystery to him as well.

They must have been descending for close to a half an hour when the passageway abruptly straightened, the steps became shallower and the ground leveled out. He could see her a few feet in front of him, her haunches rolling, her tail hanging down, almost touching the floor of the passage. Then the stairs stopped completely, and they were again walking on a smooth marble floor. Then she suddenly went out of sight again, to the left, and he hurried a little to catch up, coming to a right-angle turn, a few feet beyond which the passage ended, and he stepped out of it into a large stone room, not marble anymore but what he took to be granite. Light entered somehow from above, and he could see the place clearly. Across the room he could see a bright opening where the passageway began again, an opening at least twice as large as the one he had just left.

The floor of the room was hard-packed dirt. It was a rough square, but the walls were curved slightly. He saw the bed and the small wooden table; they were set back in a natural niche to the right. There was a candle, half gone, sitting in a pool of wax on the tabletop, and when he looked around he saw more candles, sitting on rock protuberances at head level around the walls. She moved to the place where the bed was, looking over her shoulder at him, and when he went over to it he saw that the bed was fashioned of pegged wood, a straw mat in a kind of ticking serving as a mattress with a small clump as a pillow. He put his pack on the bed, found a book of matches in one of the little flapped pockets and lit the candle. Then he got out the canteen, a can of deviled ham and a good handful of alfalfa. He poured some water in her metal dish, and dropped the hay on the floor beside it. Some pieces stuck to his palm, and when he brushed them off he felt the lines of dried blood where the cable had ripped it. He fingered the lines; they were sore but not too painful, and when he opened and closed his hands they didn't feel like they would be much of a problem. He touched them again, feeling some wetness this time, and when he brought his fingers between the candle light and his face he saw the smears of blood on them.

While she drank and ate, he took a long swig from the canteen, opened the ham and ate it. When they had finished, he rose to pack things up and get started again, but when he stood his legs buckled under him and he fell to the bed and sat with his arms on his knees on the edge of it. He was tired and a little shaky. He had no idea what time it was or how long and far they had traveled. Before he could try to rise again she was up on the bed and already making her little circles before she curled herself, lay down, and settled in. She snorted softly, exhaling, and dropped her head down between her hooves. He reached down and touched her mane; then he turned and pulled his legs up and lay down with her. Before he fell asleep, he wet his fingers and reached out and snuffed the candlewick. As he did so, she inched her way up from the foot of the bed, stopping when she was in the cup that his body made, his legs pulled up and his back bent. She pressed back into him, her head just below his own, touching his sternum through his shirt. He reached to her, stroking her forehead and face; he could feel the pulse in the globe of her eye as his palm passed over it. Then he adjusted himself, found places for his arms, and moved his head for comfort on the rough fabric of the pillow. His left hand moved to her belly, and he held it in his palm; he could feel no more than a remnant of the incision he had made there so long ago. As he held her, he felt the quick heartbeat, and only after he felt a slight turning and a brief, soft kick did he realize that the beat was not her own.

Chapter 19

He awoke to the sound of water running, a soft, almost subliminal rush, broken at times by a kind of quiet sucking. When he opened his eyes and lifted his head, he saw that she was not there, tucked against him, and he felt her absence at the same time. He looked down in the cup where his crotch was and saw the bulge of his erection pressing against his pants. When he eased himself to a sitting position on the bed's side, his arousal left him and he squinted in the direction where he thought the source of the sound was on the other side of the half dark, rock room. He reached for his matches on the table and lit the candle. Then he got up stiffly and began to move. He found her at the other side of the room, in a slight indentation in the rock wall, a kind of alcove. The wall to her left was wet with veins of running water, and there was a kind of natural rock bowl formation in the wall at her shoulder, a brimming pool with veins of water running from it and disappearing down the wall to its right. She was drinking, snuffling softly between delicate gulps to get breath. When she heard him, she took her muzzle up from the water and turned slightly, looking at him. Her lips were wet, drops falling from them, and her tongue came out and licked them away. She dipped her head back and drank again. Then she lifted and shook her head and stepped back so he could get to the basin.

He knelt down and bent over, put his face into the water and brought his hands up and washed at his face with them. The water was icy cold; his face tingled when he brought it out. He cupped his hands in the bowl, lifted them and drank. When he got back up his eyes were more accustomed to the half light and he could see well enough. He crossed back to the bed, passing the opening in the wall that was a major source of the little light in the room, and stopped for a moment and gazed into it. It was tall enough so that he would be able to enter and stand almost erect. It went on for a few feet and then it curved gradually to the right. There was time enough for it, and he did not enter.

He went to his pack and got food for her. Then he emptied the contents of the pack on the bed. His knife was there in its sheath. He had two cans of deviled ham, a pair of socks and underwear, and a large blue-checked handkerchief. He put the meal kit and his medical kit to the side and checked the rest. He had a small pouch with a compass in it, a bar of soap, a waterproof can of matches, a length of nylon rope, and two brushes and a comb. After he had checked what he had, he stripped himself naked. She had come back and was standing beside him, watching. He took his tee shirt for a towel and the bar of soap and went to the rock bowl again and leisurely washed himself, soaping and rinsing his whole body, sudsing his hair even and brushing his teeth with a corner of the tee shirt and a bit of the soap. When he was finished he doused his face a few more times briskly and dried it on the now wet shirt. He was thinking of her pregnancy, was vaguely remembering Johnny Hotnuts' story and how he had awakened with an erection hearing her mouth moving in the water. He thought of Mary Grace and the distance he had traveled. But he was still traveling, his icy bath was holding his attention, and the thoughts were in the background, passing before his mind and leaving without his turning them.

When he was finished he went back to the bed and began to dress himself: clean underwear and socks, his shirt and pants, and then his shoes. Then he took the handkerchief and rolled it and tied it around his forehead as a sweat band. He sat down on the bed then and opened a can of ham, and ate it. He wished he had some coffee. Then he found a corner of the room and relieved himself, using the tee shirt to clean himself and leaving it as a cover over his waste. When he came back to the bed, she was standing beside it, waiting.

He got the curry comb and the brushes; one was stiff and he used this one to brush the gnarls and matted pieces of hair on her barrel and thighs. He combed her tail and mane, holding the hair in his palm and running the brush through it from above. When he was finished her tail was a silky fan again and her mane and even the brush at her poll waved in their natural way along her crest to her ears. He lingered over her, even scraping what debris he could find off her hooves with his knife. Then he lifted her up and laid her on the bed on her side so that he could get at the containers.

He still wasn't sure just how they had been fashioned or what the metal was, but he suspected that the rods holding them in were inserted in bone and that they went deeper than the coffin, probably into the short pastern itself. He found the small grooves, the little locks, and with the tip of his knife blade turned them. Then he put the tips of his fingers into the small indentations in the bottoms of her hooves and twisted, unlocking the cups from their sleeves. When he had all four out and resting on the table beside the bed, he turned them over, spilling the diamonds with small clicks in a little pile. They gleamed where they rested. He ran a finger through them, changing the way they refracted the light. He looked at them for a long time, thinking as he had thought before of other places to put them, places that might be better, safer. Then he shrugged and scooped them back into the containers and returned the cups to their sleeves in her hooves. If they caught him, it was possible that they would not know that he had found them. They wanted the horse as well as the diamonds. But more, he had gone so far now that he felt it had to be played out in this way. It seemed right and therefore the only way.

Okay, he thought, time to get on with this, and he rose and put his belongings back into the pack and lifted it to his shoulder. He took what remained of the candle stub and put it in his pocket. He looked down at her, then over at the opening in the rock. She seemed to nod then, and then she started across the room in front of him. He felt for his knife, touching its handle at his belt. When he looked to the opening, she was entering, and he followed her.

They were in the stone passage beyond the cave, and again she was out in front of him. He could stand erect, but the passage was narrow, and he had to turn his shoulders from time to time to get around corners. They were going down again, and again there were times when she was out of sight and times when he would catch only the gossamer tip of her tail as she went ahead. The light in the passage increased as they descended, and in a while the trail leveled again, the turns in the passage becoming less acute, and he could see her a good distance in front of him. He thought that the source of the light came not from above, in crevices in the stone, but from in front, and he thought he could feel a slight movement of air and could smell freshness.

In what seemed to him a good half hour, he came upon the opening. He might have missed it had he not been running his hands along the walls on either side of him as he moved along. The passage was bending in a gentle arc; she was a good thirty yards in front of him, but in sight in the dim light when his left hand slid from the stone and into absence. He pulled up and called out to her "Wait," and he saw her stop and turn back toward him. Then he motioned with his hand and she returned briskly.

He could only barely see his hand when he reached in and beyond the stone, but he moved his arm from side to side and above and he reached his foot out and found that the opening ran from the roof of the passage to the floor and was almost a yard wide. He got the stub of candle out and lit it. When he held it in the passage the flame moved a little, but when he extended his arm into the opening it held still. She stood back a little from him, waiting, and he glanced down at her. Then he turned his shoulders and slipped through into the other passage. It was tighter than the main one, and his pack caught and scraped against the stone as he went in. The candle lit the way, and in only a few feet the narrow passage forked off in a Y. He took the one to the left, but he had only gone in a little way when the passage branched off again. He stopped and then went back out. When he was in the main passage, back in the dim light, he blew the candle out and unhooked his pack and took it off. She watched him as he got the rope out of it. It was thin, but it was nylon and strong, and he had a hundred feet of it. He tied the end of it to a strap on his pack and put the pack against the wall of the main passage, a good five yards back, and against the same wall as the opening. Then he lit the candle again, and taking the coil of rope in his hand he played it out as he went in.

There were more branches as he went deeper, and he had to back track as the new trails ended in stone. She went with him, stayed well back behind him, but he could hear her hooves scuffing the stone floor. Though there were many false ways, the coil of rope kept getting smaller, and he knew he was making some progress. Then the rope petered out and he felt the slight fraying at its end. She was close behind him, and he turned and squatted, and after he had dropped the end of the rope on the passage floor, he reached out and stroked her back and the side of her head and pressed her a little, indicating that she should stay at the place where the rope ended. Then he went on alone. He came to one more Y, chose the passage to his left again, and when it stopped in only a few feet he returned and took the other. He could feel the candle wax dripping, hot on his fingers, and when he checked the flame he saw that there was no more than an inch of it left. Then his shoulder bumped against the stone as the passage took a sharp turn. He lifted his hand with the candle in it, scanning the wall at the corner, and when he had followed the turning, the passage ended, opening out a bit into a small cul-de-sac.

As he moved to the wall in front of him, lifting the candle, his foot hit something. He squatted down and reached out and found a flat bar of some sort, a kind of crowbar, but with a pointed end and a kind of hammer at the other. It was rusted, but the rust no longer flaked, and when he brought his hand away from it it was clean. Then he stood up again and lifted what was left of the candle and began to explore the wall. Most of the rock was smooth, but there were places where it had been chipped away, where some implement had been used to scrape and gouge. He put his fingers into the rough cracks and shallow openings, but he could pull nothing loose, though he could feel the scorations where the cuts had been made. He moved from the far wall, turning slowly to his left, the candle held up, and when he got to the far side he found the veins.

There were three of them. They ran from left to right, at an angle heading toward the floor. They were no more than six inches apart, and each was a good four inches wide. The flame of the candle caught the facets, and even in their rough, unmined state, the diamonds sparkled and looked wet. He was not sure they were diamonds; he hadn't thought those kinds of stones could be found in America, but he realized that the gouges that he had found along the wall had been places where the other veins had been cut out. He ran the candle up and down the veins, squatting again as he moved lower, and at knee level he found the letters, the *AG* chiseled carefully into the stone a few inches from one of the veins.

He felt himself dizzying slightly and had to put his hand back on the floor to keep steady on his haunches. It passed quickly, and he knew the shock had more to do with his presence there than with the discovery. He could not believe that he was not the first one in thirty-five years, at least that long, the first one since his father had stood and worked in this place. "You bastard," he thought, and felt his mouth curl in a smile.

But who had cut the steps? It had taken many more than one man. But as he thought of it, tried briefly to figure it, he realized that he would never know, unless knowledge came to him by accident, which he doubted, because he would not pursue it. This was as far as he had to go, and though it really explained nothing, it was literal source, and it was what lay ahead that mattered. His fingertips were encased in wax now, the candle no more than a hardening puddle, the flame sitting just above the nail of his thumb. He ran his thumb along the veins again, pausing only for a moment at the letters. Then he turned back to the opening. He felt the flame heat his nail, and he moved his hand to his mouth and blew out the candle and was in total darkness.

He called out to her, and she whinnied softly, and he felt along the wall and headed in the direction of the sound. He called again, and she answered, and with no false turnings he worked his way back to her, reached down and felt along her body to the ground and found the rope. He lifted it and coiled it as he moved, and before long he saw the light in the main passage. When he reached it, he put the rope away and got his pack back on. Then she went again before him. They continued on for an hour, slowly descending and leveling, and then they came to the end.

The passage had widened slightly, straightened and leveled out completely, and he could see the stone face where it finished a good hundred yards before they reached it. There was light entering from above where it ended. She reached it first, and the light made her coat shine again. She turned when she reached the face, looked back at him, then lifted her head into the light above her. When he got to her, he looked up also, having to squint a little initially. The light was no more than a glow, but he had been in half darkness for so long that it took some time for his eyes to get adjusted. High up above him, he could see a skeletal growth of some kind, branches with thick leaves on them silhouetted by the daylight that came through them from above. In a little time he could see better, could tell that it must be close to twilight or that it was cloudy. The growth spanned what he took to be a hole in the earth, the hole no more than five feet in diameter. Below the hole the walls tapered out slightly, the shaft widening, and a few feet down it straightened and descended.

He figured the opening to be close to a hundred or more feet above them, and as his eyes moved down, he could see that there were shallow steps of some sort cut into the rock going up, some no more than very shallow indentations, brief ledges. They went around the shaft in a spiral as they ascended. As he moved his eyes down and around the shaft, he saw that the steps ended a good twelve feet above the floor where they were standing, and that below them the shaft on all sides was smooth.

He wished he had taken the tool where the diamonds were, but when he went to the wall in front of him and touched it, he found that it was solid rock, and he doubted that even the tool would have been of much use. She watched his movements, followed him with her head, glancing up into the shaft toward the opening from time to time. He covered every inch of the wall, checking for any purchase, but he found nothing. Then, while he was checking, she went to the wall and lifted her forelegs and put her hooves against the stone, stretching her body upward. She looked up from where she was to the beginning of the steps and indentations above them. There was a shallow ledge at one place where the steps began, and after she had looked over at him, she looked up at it.

Maybe he could get her up to the ledge, but what difference would it make? Even if she negotiated the steps and indentations he would still be where he was. He couldn't think that she could go for help; it was almost comical to imagine. She saw him stand and consider; then she pushed up off the rock and snorted and went to the pack where he had put it on the ground. She nuzzled up under the straps and the fold, and he went to it and opened it. Then she got her muzzle down into it, and when she moved her head back she had the rope in her teeth. She pulled the end loose and went back to the wall and put her hooves against it again.

He squatted and took the coil of rope out of the knapsack, and as he did so she came back and stood beside him, the end still in her teeth. When he looked at her he thought of the roses she had refused to carry. He took the rope from her and tied it loosely around her neck, and then he lifted her up. He held her by her chest and her rump over his head. He could get her about four feet from the ledge, maybe a little closer than that. The first time she didn't make it, and he was lucky to catch her as she fell. The second time, he held her by the rump only. She was facing the wall, sitting on his hands, her hooves elevated above her head against the stone. He adjusted her until he had one of her rear hooves in each of his hands. He squatted slightly, and she sat back on his wrists, coiling her body. Then he thrust her up. She got a grip with her hooves, her rear legs hanging and her hooves kicking at the stone, and then he saw her shoulders bunch with the effort as she made the ledge. She stood on it; there was just enough room for her, and after she had looked down at him, the rope handing from her neck, she turned and tested the rock above her and started up.

It was slow going, and at times she had to pause for a long time and consider and change directions and position, but she ascended slowly, moving in an upwardly turning spiral. When she was close to the opening, his neck was getting stiff from the intensity of looking up and watching her. She was a few feet below the hole, where the rock tapered inward, and she was looking around and considering. He couldn't imagine how she could make it. There were no more steps or indentations, and the tapering meant that she would have to lean well back and jump up into space to reach the opening. She turned as much as she was able and then she was still, looking at something. He saw it too. There was a branch hanging down slightly into the space, a fairly thick one. Its leaves were green, and it might be strong enough to hold her if she could get to it.

He was still considering the possibility, moving into a position where he thought he would have some chance of catching her if she fell, when she made her leap.

He stumbled back to avoid the rope that rolled out from the wall and across the shaft as her body, upside down with her tail and mane hanging in the air, kicked away from the wall and headed for the branch. The rope almost touched his face, and he had to watch for its returning sway and watch her at the same time. He had his arms up. He saw her legs kicking and digging for a purchase on the branch. There were a dozen green leaves in the air, and then she seemed to be falling. But it was the branch giving a little, and then she was swaying, her front hooves locked over the branch, her body hanging down into space, the rope swaying in the center of the shaft. The green leaves descended at different speeds, and as the first one got to the level of his head, he saw her shoulders bunch again as she shinnied herself up and into the other branches and her body disappeared. Then the tail end of the rope was in the air and moving up. When it got to his shoulder, he wanted to reach out for it, to keep it from getting beyond and above him, but he fought against the urge and watched it stop when it was two feet above his head.

He waited for what seemed too long a time. Then he saw her head appear at the edge of the opening; it was almost obscured by the leaves and branches, but he could see it move up and down slightly and could hear her whinny softly. He reached above him and took the end of the thin rope and tugged at it tentatively. Then he took a turn in it, twisting it in his fist, and carefully lifted his feet up from the ground and let it support his weight. It held, and he reached up with his other arm and gripped it. He was hanging in the center of the shaft, and he wasn't sure just how he would get up the rope. Maybe he could swing across the shaft, kick off the wall and somehow get higher, but as he tucked his body slightly and started his first awkward swing, he felt himself begin to rise.

For a moment he didn't know quite what was happening; it seemed that places on the wall across from him were somehow descending. He straightened his body out in the first movement he would need to drop back to the floor, but when he looked down he saw that his feet were a good distance from it. Then his body began to turn slowly as he rose. He could see the abbreviated steps as his head followed them around in their turning ascent. He looked up and saw that he was approaching the branches, and he saw her head still there at the edge, and soon he thought he could see her eyes through the leaves. When the branches were no more than twenty feet above him, he realized that he better stop looking up. He had no free hand, and there were places where the branches looked pointed and a little dangerous. He tucked his head down then, pressing his chin to his chest, and soon he felt the first twigs hit his head, leaves touch his cheeks, and he was then in the middle of the tangle. His hands and arms were through and in the open air before his torso, and he felt the grips on his wrists before the hands that took his shoulders. Then he was sitting on the rim of the hole, his legs still hanging in the tangle of branches. He saw his knapsack on the floor below him; it looked like a small crumpled handkerchief, and then his head came up and he saw their rough boots and trousers. He recognized that they were darker than they might have been, and when he looked up and found their faces he could see the darkening sky behind them and he realized that the day had gone and that it was now twilight.

Chapter 20

They kept a low fire burning in a kind of shallow pit. It was roughly circular and very large, and the hot red glow of the embers cast light up a few feet above it, but only a few feet, and he could see figures on the far side, no more than shadows shifting in the distance. The moon was gone now, but there were stars, more than he thought he had ever seen, and the air was crisp and clear, but the fire warmed him and warmed the structure he sat against, a kind of sturdy but portable lean-to of some kind; he could see two more of them across the fire glow, beyond the shadow figures. He wasn't sure how many men there were. There were some women, but they didn't stay with him long. One in layered clothing, pants and boots, with a wool cap covering most of her hair, had brought him a bowl of hot stew when they had him settled. He had known she was a woman by the way she moved; she had had a different kind of grace and certainty than the men. Her cheeks were ruddy, and he had seen her eyes. He'd thought the meat in the stew was a kind of mutton. He could hear the sheep bleat all around him, and at times he saw them moving, shadowy figures also, with heads down and muzzles almost touching the ground, beyond all but the very edge of firelight.

The three who had brought him down from the place where the hole was had smiled when they'd helped him out, and the horse had stayed close to their legs, but on the other side of them. He was stunned to be back in the open again, and though he had managed a few words of thanks and reached for some that would make some headway into explanation, they had only smiled, and after an initial glance around him at the hill they were on and the lower hills below them and the sky, he had given up talk. The way down was clumsy and awkward. There was no real trail, and he had to keep his eyes on the ground. When the ground flattened out a little and he did look up it was already quite dark, and before he knew it the stars were fully out.

They brought him pants and a heavy sweater and a kind of parka. Somebody passed a cap along, and they left him alone in the lean-to while he changed. He couldn't stand up in it, but had to sit and shift his hips back and forth to get the pants on. They were short, but they reached the tops of his boots and they were ample in the waist, rough textured and warm, and they felt good against his legs. There were piles of blankets and bags that must have been pillows in the lean-to, and he saw some books leaning against each other in a corner, a few pots and utensils neatly stacked beside them, and some coils of rope and other implements that he could not identify. When he went back out, one of the men who had brought him down was waiting, and he motioned to the side of the lean-to, and when Paul had found a place to sit he went away. He was smaller than Paul, and maybe fifty years old, but he stood erect, and even under the layers of clothing Paul could tell that he was hard and fit. Then the woman brought him the stew in a metal bowl and a cup of something hot to drink. He wasn't sure what it was, but it had a hint of alcohol in it, and it warmed his stomach immediately. When he was finished he put the bowl and cup on the ground beside him and leaned back against the lean-to and looked up above the fire into the sky. The stars seemed constant at first, like fixed unfaceted diamonds, permanent and unblinking; then some began to blink, others to emerge and recede. The sky was covered with them, but as he looked his vision tunneled in on a specific clustering. It had a shape to it, both geometrical and figurative, but he could not make it out.

He woke with a start, his head lurching a little from where it rested against something, and his hand went to where the horse should be on the ground beside him, but there was nothing there, no bowl or cup. He had no idea how long he might have slept, but when he looked across the fire he saw that the light was the same, the shadows on the other side were still present, and he didn't think it could have been for long. He thought he saw her then, to the left beyond the glow, but when the figure came around the edge of the oval and closer to him he saw that it was not she or a sheep either but a small dog. It stopped when it found its place, got down and curled up. Then again he thought he saw her, this time among the legs of some figures standing off farther to the left, but he could not be sure about it. He was not sure of anything right then, but he felt no anxiety. It was not that he was too tired for it; it was just that it was not there. But then he did feel anxious for a moment: he had lost his pack. He felt at his waist for his sheath, but as he touched his belt he felt the foreign clothing, and when he tried to think back he could not remember feeling the knife in the sheath for a while. He heard sounds of metal against metal and the creak of leather and the mumble of voices and the constant bleating, and as he put his head back against the lean-to and looked again at the sky he vaguely wondered if there had been anything in the drink.

It was a gentle breeze this time that woke him, just enough to stir strands of his hair against his ear, and he came back to himself much more gradually than he had before. The stars had not changed, and when he moved his head from its resting place he could see that the fire was lower now, but still warming, and while the figures across it were fading shadows, there were still what seemed the same number, or close to it; the bleating seemed quieter, more like gentle snoring, and the mumble of voices had diminished.

"You've been here before, I guess." The voice was quiet and close beside him. It had an accent, like Spanish, but slightly more guttural, something European, but older somehow than that. He turned his head and saw the face of the man sitting beside him, almost against his shoulder. The face was half in darkness, but he could make out the features, the eyes and then the teeth as the man smiled; his look was like the accent, a mix of things, and old and hard to place. He had a somewhat floppy leather hat on, something like a small cowboy hat, and his hair was thick and straight, very black and roughly cut along his neck.

"Here?" Paul whispered, and the teeth flashed white in the dimness as the man smiled again.

"Well, not quite here, but close to here I bet, over at the quarry."

He was ready to answer, but he held back, wondering how the man could know this, that he had been here. Then it struck him that he could mean those times just days ago, when he had gone down the cable with the horse.

"Yes. Years ago," he said.

"Do you remember why you came then?"

He didn't remember. The question had not come up exactly. How Parker had known he would know the place, that was a question that had come up. Now there was this man and this other question.

"Hold on, I'll get us something to drink," the man said, and he rose to his feet with no seeming effort at all, like a man getting out of a straight-back chair, and went around the edge of the fire.

=====

He had been in his junior year of high school in Bisbee, in the second semester, when his father died. It was the year before, when he was a sophomore, that he had been going to Naco. When his father died his mother had mourned him, but that had ended pretty quickly he thought, and she had wanted to go back to Illinois. But he had wanted to stay, to finish high school where he had begun it. He did not have many friends, only two fairly casual ones, and he was uninvolved in school affairs, but he wanted something to hold onto, some continuity when his father died, and he had insisted that they not leave until he graduated. He thought he remembered that she had fought against this a little; there were vague memories of difficult days. But he could not tell how much of the difficulty had to do with his response to his father's death, how much maybe even to do with Naco and Mary Grace, though it had been close to a year since his involvement with her. God, he thought, it was my sister who had my virginity.

His mother had given in and they had stayed, and he could remember how his mother brightened once her time of mourning was ended, how she seemed younger, and how she had taken a clerical job in town and developed friends and gone out a lot. It was as if she was going to stay on in Bisbee, was beginning to carve out a separate life of her own there. But she seemed restless too in her new energy, and as he worked to remember things he realized that the analysis he was giving to them was beyond any final verification, was a construct of the kind one would give to a fiction. He had some facts, but they were few; the rest *was* a fiction, and as he recognized this he vowed to try to stick to the facts.

He thought he remembered that it was no more than a week before the spring break, his senior year. They would have almost two weeks off, one before and one after Easter Sunday itself. They had no real plans for Easter; it was hard to get excited about the holidays since his father's death, and though he had given some thought to a gift for his mother, he had no real expectations. Nor did she seem to have any; he thought he remembered that they had not talked about anything having to do with Easter Sunday at all. Then, a week before the break began, she had suggested that he take the trip to Marble. He had wanted to do some camping, had mentioned it a long time ago, talked about heading up into the hills a few miles from Bisbee and spending a few days there. That it was only a week before the holiday came back to him strongly as he thought about it. He had not thought of it then, had been too excited about the release from home and about the length of the trip, too busy with lining up his gear and his friend, with bus connections to Colorado, with the wonder that she should let him go away so far. He thought he remembered that she had gotten on the phone with the parents of one of his friends, had convinced them that they were old enough, they'd be all right, it would be good for them. Then he thought he remembered all of it, thought he could almost remember her words.

Someone had told her, she said, that it was a beautiful place, an old marble quarry. There were pieces of marble all over the place, beautiful, and a river filled with it, huge pieces of marble that the water washed over. And the place was very high up in the mountains. This had been the mildest winter they'd had there in years, really almost warm, she had said, and no snow. There wouldn't be crowds of skiers in the area.

She had a map, she thought, in a book. And the quarry itself was immense, marble walls and ceiling. She had gotten the map out, and he remembered that it was not literally *in* the book, but was folded and tucked between the pages. He could almost visualize it, could almost see her hands opening it and spreading it across the kitchen table. It was large and well worn and cracked at its folds, and she had spread it out slowly and with care. He remembered it showed main roads and trails and a broken line that was the trail up to the river and the quarry itself. Then there was an insert at the bottom of the map that was the floor of the quarry. This he could not remember too well. But he remembered she did not give him the map to take, but that she made a rendering of it, complete with insert, a tracing he thought. And he remembered her brief disappointment when he returned from the trip and told her that he couldn't find a way to get down inside the quarry. There was a cable, but he didn't think it was safe. She had wanted a bit of marble from deep down in the quarry itself, but he had brought her a nice piece that he had found in the river. At first she seemed unmoved by it, seemed disappointed in knowing its source. But it was not long before she had placed the piece on a table in the living room, and he remembered that when they got back to Illinois she had put it on the mantle, prominent at the end of the room.

It had been just as he was leaving to get to the bus that she had asked him to bring her the piece of marble from the quarry bottom. She had asked it somewhat coyly as he remembered, and maybe she had caught herself in her coyness, because she had laughed and winked and turned her head away in the asking, and as if to justify it in some way she had said, "there's money in marble, you know," and as she said the words her eyes went a little out of focus as if she was seeing things that were happening or had happened elsewhere, as if the words had been said in some other place or time, as if they were a private joke or saying, and then she laughed again, and when she came back to where she was she looked at him, trying to force her expression away from something that was not in the room with them. She couldn't quite make it, and he remembered how strange she seemed to him as he kissed her and said goodbye to her at the door.

"I can't really figure out what she expected. Maybe it was only the piece of marble, something romantic, something from what he had told her. But there's the map. I can't think he would have told her about the diamonds, not from what I know now. She said, *there's money in marble* though, and I've heard that since then."

The man was back, seated beside him again. He had handed him a tin cup, a toddy of hot whiskey and water with a little sugar, and Paul had told him some of how he had come to be here before. He thought it was late now, possibly close to midnight. The breeze was constant now, but not too cold, and the stars were white and as clear as crystal. He could still hear voices and bleating, but there were no sounds of movement, no activity beyond conversation.

"They're not diamonds," the man said. "They're only quartz, some other crystals, and fool's gold."

Now Paul had more to incorporate, more changes, and another narrative to construct.

"What about the steps?" he said, "the room, the crowbar, the initials?"

"The steps are one thing," the man said. "The rest? Well, that's something else altogether. Would you like another drink?"

"No," Paul said. "This is fine. Do you know what time it is?"

"It's ten," the man said.

So it wasn't twelve, and there were no diamonds, and the steps were something else. But the diamonds in the hooves were real enough, and she had said *there's money in marble, you know,* and Parker knew those words and could not have gotten them from her. And the initials under the brace in the shed were real, and so was the little horse. Where was she? He wanted her with him, but he was not worried about her exactly, not at all. And the strange accent. Somehow, she was familiar and comfortable here. She had walked close to their legs when they brought him down.

"You're Basque, aren't you," Paul said.

"That's right," the man said. "You know the horse is pregnant?"

"I know it," he said. "But I don't know what to expect from it."

"That's something," the man said.

"Do *you* know what to expect?" Paul said.

"No, *Dios.* I don't know nothing," the man said. He whispered it, and it was a mimic of Esperanza's voice when she had said the same thing. It was yet another twisted change, and Paul could do absolutely nothing with it at all.

"There's someone you got to talk to," the man said, and he got up from the ground with the same ease with which he had risen the last time, and again he went around the fire's edge and out of sight.

Paul wondered what it would be this time, and then as his eyes followed as the man faded into shadow, he saw the horse coming around the edge of the firepit toward him. The fire made her glow on one side, and when she flicked her tail and her mane rose from her neck as she walked toward him they were like yellow flames dancing above and behind her body. Her eyes sparkled like hard stone as she approached, and only when she got beyond the edge of the glowing coals did she become halfway conventional again. She walked up and stood before him. She had been brushed out, and her mane and tail had been combed. Her eyes were as clear as the night sky, and she looked vibrant and extremely healthy, wide awake and alert; her ears were pricked and her nostrils tested the air. He lifted his hand and motioned, and she dipped her head once and then moved to his side and found a place for herself and settled in. But she did not settle as if she were there for any extended time, and when he touched her skin it felt taut and ready under his fingers. He touched her muzzle, feeling the breath in his palm and her soft nose, but in a moment she moved her head away, and though she looked up at him, he could see that she was watchful, glancing across the fire and into the darkness as if she could see things in those places that were invisible to him.

They sat there for a while. He was waiting for the man to come back, and though she was alert she did not really seem to be waiting for anything at all. While he waited, he went over what things might now be getting settled. Things in some ways were getting clearer, and in the ways he was thinking of it the only thing that was not all that clear yet was Johnny and the one who could have been Mary Grace in Ronny's story about the movie. But then he came up with other things: the diamonds, the house across the lake, the pregnancy of the little horse. He knew these were the smaller things and that he brought them up to keep away from the larger things that he might remember, and he felt himself drifting into disorientation again and he pulled himself up short. He was surprised how easy this was to do, and he began to understand that the ease had something to do with his own past and not with the stories and the changing matrix of events in them. He felt himself coming from his past now, coming out of it; it was a kind of fiction, and it was people who made fiction, and it didn't make much difference if it were one's past or a story about the past of others. He looked down at the horse, noting again how erect and tensed she was in her sitting, how alert and contained, and then he realized that he was sitting in the same way beside her.

The man came back in a while and reached his hand down to help Paul to his feet. He took his hand, and when he was up he felt that he had not needed it. He was a little stiff, but as he followed the man around the fire's edge he did not walk as if he were. They went to a lean-to on the other side of the fire, and the man lifted the canvas flap that hung across its opening and stood aside so that Paul could enter. He had to duck down a little to get through the opening, but once inside he could stand erect.

The lean-to was larger than the other one had been, and when he looked up to the cloth roof, he saw that there was an opening in the middle of it and he could see a large piece of the starry sky framed by the opening. He felt something bump against his calf, and when he looked down he saw that it was the muzzle of the little horse, who had entered behind him. She moved past him then, and when he looked where she went he saw the man sitting on a stool in a corner of the lean-to, working with a pot, what looked like a coffee pot, over a small burner. The place, like the other, was full of blankets and pillows, and here there were books and other implements as well.

"This is Álava." He heard the voice of the other man behind him. "He wants to talk with you some. I'll be back later to help you get bedded down." He heard the shush of the flap fall back over the opening behind him, and then the man looked from his tinkering with the pot and the burner and smiled. The horse had settled in beside the man's stool, curling herself on a pile of blankets. The man rose a little from the stool, pushed it away, and sat down on the blankets beside the horse.

"There. We'll have some good coffee soon. Seat yourself. There's a place over there ought to be of some comfort. Your name is Paul they tell me?"

"Yes. Paul Cords." He went to the place the man had indicated and dropped down among pillows, bags and blankets.

"That's an interesting name, Cords," the man said.

"Álava is interesting too," Paul smiled. The man laughed, nodding his head.

279

"Not around here, it isn't. A place name, just a name. Cords is probably the same for you."

"I'm beginning to wonder," Paul said. "García seems to make more sense to me these days."

"Ah, García," the man said. "Now that's a name. I know a story about a García that it might be good to tell you."

Paul was about to answer, when Álava pushed up from where he sat and checked the coffee. It was ready, and he poured Paul a full cup from the pot.

"We don't most of us use milk," he said. "But I can get some, and sugar too, if you want it."

"No. This is good," Paul said, and Álava moved back to his place beside the little horse. When he was seated, he reached out and stroked her, and she rubbed her muzzle against his wrist. He looked over at Paul then, and he must have noticed something in his posture.

"It's all right. You've been with her a while. I won't hurt her."

Paul felt himself relax from a tension he did not know was in him. He must have been leaning forward slightly, and he sunk back a little, feeling the muscles in his arms and stomach loosen.

"Yes. It has been a while," he said. "I'm sorry."

"Don't be," the man said. "I can understand it." Paul saw the deep lines in the man's face as he turned again toward the horse and stroked her, and when he turned back he could see that the man was much older than he had first thought. He had the size and physical vigor of the other man, and this had fooled Paul initially, but now that his eyes were growing more accustomed to the dimmer light on the inside of the lean-to, he could see that his hair had considerable gray in it and that it was quite thin. When he glanced at his hands, he could see the tendons and the veins in them and the way the fingers were knotty and twisted a little with age.

"Oh, yes, I'm pretty old," Álava laughed. "But still young enough for most things."

"I didn't mean to be staring," Paul said.

"Old enough, though, not to be bothered." He laughed again, and this time Paul smiled and laughed with him.

"But it's the story," Álava said. "That's why I wanted to talk with you."

He only took a moment to adjust himself where he was sitting before he began, and for Paul, who had heard so many stories now, the preliminaries were a brief comfort to him. They all did this, or had done at least something like it, as a way of getting ready to begin. And it was also a way of losing time before they left time, a way of doing that formally, which Paul began to think was necessary because there really was nothing formal about it at all; it was not an exit into something else. It was the here and now. Even Ronny had done something similar, though his telling had been the least story-like of all. He hadn't known he was telling a story, Paul thought. He thought he was providing facts and information. Still it was a story, and in a way there seemed nothing other than that now at all.

Chapter 21

M y people came here from the South over a hundred or more years ago. When I say south, I mean way south, below even Mexico, some even further down than that, and when I say here I mean the United States and the trip all the way up as well. Some dropped off along the way, assimilated, and became Mexican. Esperanza is one of us; you may have gathered that. There's no immediate family connection, but she knew to look out for the horse. Thus we have known about Parker for quite a while. There were other horses too. Some stayed on with groups who dropped off in Mexico on the way up. But the groups were smaller, and as they assimilated and lost our language, outside greed got to the horses, and the ones there got captured or killed, and I don't think there are any more in Mexico at all. When the people I was born out of got here, I mean right here, they had two horses with them. It took until I was close to forty for the mare of the two to give foal; she managed it twice, a male and a female, and then she and her partner died. To get it straight, that was around nineteen-twenty; I was forty years old; I'm now seventy-five. It was around nineteen-twenty that Abelardo García came here as a young man.

I think in the beginning, and I'm not sure how far back that is, the little horses were used for sheepherding. They are very intelligent; I'm sure you know that by now, and I suspect that they were good at it. But as we left our places where our numbers were large, my thinking is that forces of culture from the outside got to ours, and the horses took a kind of stand against that. How gradually and in what ways that might have happened, I really can't say, but I can say how the horses we had here acted. They stayed close to our children, protecting them, and in odd ways instructed them. It's too much to go into, but by the time I came in contact with the little horses it is clear to me they had not, for a long time, been sheepherders.

When I was born here, and even when I was forty here, though things were beginning to change a little then, the land up here was free and open. We had plenty of grazing room and no problems, and even with the coming of the marble quarry we were left alone to our own ways and devices. Some of that has changed. Now it's a trade off. We get this land as long as we spend some time in the summers grazing on the ski trails at resort places, a trade off to keep the trail grasses low so they'll be ready for the winter season. And some of the people you see here don't live here all the time, but live in houses down lower, with wives, and children who go to school. It was different thirty-five years ago, about the time I guess that you were born. Close to it anyway. This is the story.

Abelardo García came one day to the place where we were grazing our sheep, not far from here. He had a knapsack and a donkey with a few supplies on it, and that was all. We took him in. He seemed pleasant, and even at his young age he had a lot of stories to tell. They were not braggart's stories; they seemed real, and he told them with a lot of flavor. He was with us for quite a while, and for a time it seemed that he might stay longer, might even stay permanently, though that would have caused problems. We don't go much for outsiders. We kept the horses out of his sight, but in a while it got difficult to do so, and also it began to seem a little foolish. He was even beginning to pick up pieces of our language. Though I think English was his first language, he was fluent in Spanish, and he had great facility. I think it was the way he gave himself to our language that seduced us. Oh, he was good company, inquisitive in a proper way, and a little laughable too. He helped with the sheep, but at times he would wander off in the hills exploring. That was all right with us; though he was pretty good with the sheep, he did get in the way a little. Incidentally, he never even came close to messing with the women who were here, though I think there were some who might have wanted that, and I think that made us feel comfortable with him as well.

In his wanderings, he found the shaft where we found you. We already knew about it, but as a joke we didn't let on to him that we did. He was very excited, and he roped himself down the shaft and explored the tunnels below. When he came back, he told us stories about the cut steps. They were wonderful stories, really, and even though we knew about the place, the steps and the rooms, when he told about them it was almost as if we were learning about them for the first time. He had a way with his stories. The elders among us had used the rooms as hideouts in the old days, in the middle and late nineteenth century when we first came here as a people. There was just a little problem in the beginning. This was the Old West then. We were initially seen as interlopers, and hideouts were good things to have available. The steps had been there then. They are probably ancient, and there is no way to know about them now. When the marble quarry was cut in, it was suspected that the tunnels and steps would be found, but they never were, and I suspect that it was only when the quarry fell into disuse and ruin that a passage from it into the tunnels and rooms opened up somehow. Some of our young men have explored the quarry for openings. There have been rumors for a long time that they existed, but they, to my knowledge, never found them. I think you're the first one who did.

At any rate, Abelardo García kept at the place; he went down often, and every time he had another story to tell. What he didn't tell about was his diamond find. One day one of the people from our group went down and found it, found that he had been working at the veins. We knew they were there. There are in fact more of them there. But we also knew that they were nothing, quartz, crystal, and fool's gold, and we had a little secret laugh that García should be working them. We kept the secret, and we felt a new suspicion. He was keeping something he thought major from us, and we began to distrust him and to notice what now looked like greed in his eyes. I think we were getting ready to ask him to leave, when he left. That was after we let him know about the false diamonds. He told us he knew they were false, that he hadn't mentioned them because he assumed that it was nothing at all to speak of. He said he liked the idea of learning about mining veins by working them, and that he also liked the idea that somebody else, someday, would find his mark on the stone, his initials, and maybe even a tool, and would wonder about it. He was hard not to believe; he told a very good story. And I think we did believe him, but that a new sense of him came to us from the strange deception that he thought to foster on some future. Though any fool should know there are no diamonds in the Rockies, the idea was disorienting and it seemed almost immoral, that he should wish to foster such a deception. Oh, not too seriously immoral, but the light way he treated it seemed too light. It was no small game to contemplate, this twisting of history in the earth, to be contemplating in the way he was, too gleefully.

It may have been that our discovery of his mining and his story about it played some part in his leaving, but there were a couple of other things, probably more important things, as well. There was the matter of the real diamonds and the matter of his past. Of his past we could find out little. He had plenty of stories, but we could never make them into a central story that would tell us in some way who he was. He was always moving in the stories. Some were in Colorado, but others were in Arizona, and there were a good number in Mexico too. Then we found out about the real diamonds. I saw them when the bag broke and they fell on the ground. I remember he was slightly startled as the sack broke free of its tether on the donkey's back rack. But he hid it quickly, and as he picked up the stones in a leisurely way, he laughed and joked about the false diamonds and how they would make for some good jokes, maybe, in the future. I knew they were real the moment I saw their glitter where they fell. I was alone with him when it happened, and I let it pass, but I knew that I had to talk to the others about it, and I did so that night.

In the morning he was gone, and so were the two little horses. I don't know how he came by those diamonds, but I knew that there were a lot of them and that they were valuable. They were not from the mine, but from something in his past. I knew from his stories that his past was impossible; it was only a story of a past, made of awkward and ill-fitting parts, and I knew that there was no answer to the diamonds at all. The horses, however, were not from a story, and though they had no working value to us, we experienced the loss of some great value when they were taken.

It took a long time to trace him, but we kept at it, using what people in Mexico we had contact with, our people, even those who had assimilated. We used our language. Even those taken in had mostly still preserved it. There was no getting at him though. Any way that could be figured would put the horses in danger and be no good to us, and when he died, suddenly and a bit mysteriously, we kept information about the son flowing back to us. The information was hazy and uncertain, but the thread was there. The movies were public, and we were able to trace them out West, to Los Angeles. There was one where the little horses were tethered and led out in some ritual of some kind; that was the one I believe in which he used stand-ins that looked like his brother and sister. This Parker seemed almost the realization of the vague twisted darkness that we'd begun to note in García before he left us. Esperanza kept us up on the location and activities of the sister. Of the other, the younger brother, he was public, and once he began telling the stories about the little horses we learned of him. And we learned of his house, the one he called the house of Abelardo García. It was a joke of the kind his father might have constructed, but it was healthier, a kind of righting and remembering of what he knew was his past. Then you came into this. It was Esperanza again who let us know, a few days ago, that you had one of the horses. We were somewhat amazed to find you heading for Marble, and we decided to wait it out. We were ready to come and get you at the quarry, when another thing amazed us. We didn't know Parker was here too, and you were going down into the quarry before we could find a way to reach you. You didn't come out, and we figured to wait as long as we needed to and then go down, but we put some men at the opening you finally did come out of just in case.

Part of it has worked out, I guess. We have the mare. We'll have to see about the stallion. You came into our story of this like a knife out of nowhere, one cutting into the strands that connected the elements. I think we've still got most of the pieces, but I'm not sure how they'll fit together in the future. Odd that you should come upon Abelardo García's false fortune and be convinced by it in the way he wanted, but it's a good thing that we were here to correct that and make it accurate.

We know where they all are and that they've got the stallion. We're trying to figure a way to get him back without injury. Maybe you can help us. Maybe that's why you're here.

===

He slept that night in the lean-to with Xavier, the man who had taken him to Álava, and a few others. They slept very close together, among the blankets and the pillow sacks, and it was warm enough inside so that they left the flap of the lean-to open, and Paul could see the stars.

He wondered about the Basques, about the tribal stories of the little horses. Álava had been there for only part of it; he had been with the horses here in Colorado, and that was fact that Paul trusted, but the rest was a story handed down, part of a people's history, and Paul could only think of it as like some of the other stories he'd been told, permutations of tales that could well be myth. And even that it might be a people's history was not certain. Álava spoke of the splitting and assimilation over the years, and the source of the story could well be local, its beginnings only here and from no larger context. It could have been Abelardo García himself who took the story south. He could have been the tale and the teller of the tale at the same time. He'd had the real horses, and who could know what he'd told Johnny and Mary Grace and what they'd overheard. He was a good teller of tales, Álava had said. Still, there was one thing, at least one; there was the farmer and his reconstructed model, a real skeleton and a hoof cup. That had been fact too, and he could see no way that Abelardo García could have had a hand in twisting it. But then he thought of the quartz, crystal and fool's gold, of his thrill when he'd found the place of his father's source of riches. He was still thrilled by the thought of it; he had stood in his father's footsteps there, in the place of his strange contrivance. But even when he'd reached that real source, that bedrock of the journey, he'd been tricked by him, and had he not heard the real truth from Álava he might never have known it.

That night the little horse remained with Álava, and though it was the first time in a long time that Paul had slept without her, he really didn't miss her. He had things to think about, but he was tired and he did not think of them for long. He felt a sense of well-being when he was bedded down among the other bodies, but he was sleeping before he had any chance to savor it.

In the morning they let him sleep, and he was awakened by the sounds of pots and pans and by the smell of coffee. A woman brought him a cup in the lean-to. He thought it was the same woman who had brought him the stew the night before, and when she handed him the cup he smiled at her in recognition. When he had finished the coffee, he got up and went out into the air. It was crisp, and though the sun was already bright he saw the dew on the bits of moss growing among the rocks, and he knew that it was still early. He stood in front of the large, shallow firepit; there were ashes now, but there was still some pleasant heat rising up from it, and he could see the waves and a few thin wisps of smoke moving in the air over its surface. There were four lean-tos on the other side of the pit and four on his side. The place was like a miniature valley, no more than a hundred feet in diameter, a place of low-growth moss and grasses set in a shallow cup of rock. Boulders rose on its perimeters like the configurations at the edge of a crown. The sheep were nowhere in evidence, and the camp was almost empty. He heard children talking, and then voices of women from one of the lean-tos across the firepit, and an old dog looked at him from where it sat, close to the dying embers. Then he saw Xavier throw back the flap on one of the lean-tos and come out. He guessed it was the place where Álava bedded, and he smiled at Xavier as he approached.

"Hungry?" he asked as he got to him, and before Paul could answer he touched his arm and led him to a small stone basin at the edge of the encampment. There was a towel and a bar of soap ready, and he left him alone while he washed up. Before he left, he pointed to a place out of sight of the rock basin.

"Over there. You can relieve yourself if you need to. I'll wait breakfast for you in Álava's place."

Paul stripped to the waist, and when he felt the pleasant wash of the clean air on his chest he removed his pants as well. He had been too long down in the dark and then in the night, and the day and the fresh air seemed to clean him even before he began to wash. Before he was finished, he thrust his whole head under the water in the rock basin. Then he cleaned his feet, legs and crotch, and sat on the stone beside the basin and dried himself. He was still tender in some places; he had to shift his buttocks to find a comfortable position, one that did not cause his deepest bruise to hurt. But his feet were much better, almost completely healed. After he had dried and dressed and relieved himself, he went to the lean-to. He could smell the bacon cooking before he got there.

Though they smiled at each other and nodded in appreciation, they ate in silence. The little horse ate with them. There was a metal bowl off in the corner with food in it that Paul could not identify, and she ate heartily from it, coming up, as a dog might, for gulps of air. When she was finished she went to another bowl from which she lapped up water. They ate eggs and bacon and thick black bread, and when they were finished Álava toyed with his coffee pot, poured three cups and handed one of them to Paul. Then he leaned back in the blankets and pillow bags and crossed his arms and looked at him. His age was clearer now in the brighter light, but his wiry fitness was clearer too. Xavier sat to the side, between them, and waited for Álava to speak.

"Last night, while we were talking," he said, "I told you we know where they are."

"I remember that." Paul said.

"They're still there."

"Where are we?" Paul asked.

"Not far," Xavier said. "They're up on the highland. We're on the other end of that highland. It's no more than two miles or so."

"How many are you?" Paul said.

"We're twelve men."

"But you see we can't really help you, not really. Not until after," Álava said. "They want you, and they want the horse, and they figure you came this far and that you'll keep coming. So they're waiting in a good place. They'll see you coming. But if they saw us too, I don't think they'd stay around. They have the stallion with them. That was risky, and a little desperate, but a possible way to the mare, maybe the best way. They think you want the woman, that that's driving you. I figure they've got much of that right."

"I *do* want her," Paul said. "I want her away from him."

"We can give you what you need," Xavier said. "A good rifle, whatever else."

"I need a knife," Paul said. "A good one."

"We've got that," Álava said.

"I have to show you something first," Paul said, and he got up and went to the little horse. She had finished eating and drinking and was resting beside her drinking bowl, her head up. She was alert and seemed to be listening to the conversation. When he got to her, Paul stroked her and touched her face and muzzle; then he turned her over on her side, and using the handle of the fork he had used to eat his breakfast he twisted the notches and removed the cups and poured the diamonds out in a rough pile on the blanket beside her.

"That's Abelardo García's work," Álava said, shaking his head and laughing when he saw the cups and the diamonds. "Only he would think of something like that. Those are the real ones. But they aren't all of them. There were twice as many at least in the bag that broke."

"There could have been other horses," Paul said, "and other cups. I saw a place in Mexico; there was a man and a farm, and there were remnants of that."

"I see. And why not?" Álava said, still shaking his head. "I wouldn't put it past him."

"Whose are they?" Paul said. "They're worth a fortune."

"The heirs," Álava shrugged.

"But they're in your horse," Paul said.

"But not of the horse."

"I guess they're mine then. And Mary Grace's and Johnny's and, I guess, even Parker's," Paul said.

"And do you want them?" Álava said.

"What I want is Parker. I want to put an end to it," he said, and he scooped the diamonds up and put them into one of his pockets. He left ten stones lying on the blanket.

"You've missed a few," Xavier said.

"For bed and breakfast." Paul smiled.

Álava laughed and nodded. "Okay," he said. "Done."

Chapter 22

He felt the press of the bag that held the diamonds on his lower spine as he moved down among the rocks and split boulders, twisting along the narrow, rough trail. She was behind him, not far away, and though he could not see her he could hear her hooves clicking among stones from time to time. The little bag was fixed through slits to his belt. He could have left them behind, in safe keeping, but it seemed proper not to, and they had shown a kind of approval of this through their silence and the way they quickly got the bag for him. They got him a small telescope that fit into a tubular container that he attached to his belt also, and on the other side was the broad-bladed knife. It had a leather handle, and it was tight against the side of his waist, locked in with a leather thong. It rode lightly in its sheath, and it did not impede his movements. They got him better-fitting pants and a rough cotton shirt and a hat with an abbreviated brim to keep enough of the sun out. The sun was getting higher, but it was not glaring. It was to the side now, and it only warmed his left shoulder a little. It must be close to nine, he thought, as he moved below the camp.

In a while they reached flatter country; the narrow trail petered out in low grasses and mosses and small flowers, and she was able to move up beside him, to walk close to him, almost at heel. They were going through a series of miniature meadows, small shallow bowls of low growth among rocks. Each one was a little lower, and as they descended he could see the jagged bare rock structure he was heading for; it seemed to be rising higher, and when they reached the final meadow and were almost at the base of it, it no longer looked like cathedral spires at eye level; he could see that it was jagged and sheer, but he could now see that there were crevices in it, places where with a little care a man could climb. When he got almost to the base and looked up he could see that it rose to hundreds of feet in places and that at the peaks, where the sky began, it was a running wall of jagged stone. He looked down at her, and then he moved off to the left along the rock face, heading for the opening. They were in the shadows that the wall cast, and it was cooler.

It took them close to an hour to get there, and when they found it he stopped and took her into a deep crevice in the rock face, and they rested. He had bread and a piece of cold mutton, and a small canteen of water. He ripped open the bag of food that he had for her, and they both took their meal. When she was finished, she preened only for a moment. Then her head came up, her nostrils scenting, and she was ready to go. He reached out and touched her, but she bumped against his hand only briefly and then moved her head away. Then he was ready too, and they headed down the rock face toward the opening.

The place began as only a wide fissure that moved into the rock at an angle and narrowed a little as it went deeper; it was open clear up to the sky, and when he stood at the entrance to it and looked up he could see the blue that the jagged spires cut into. The markings they had told him of were clear enough, and he lifted her up and started in. In twenty feet he was past the first turn, but the ground was a rubble of fallen rock and stone, some of it that had to be climbed with hands as well as feet, and he reached her forward and put her on the rocks in front of him and then climbed up beside her and lifted her again, carrying her forward to the next obstacle. They were in the rock for a while; the shadows were constant on the stone, but there was plenty of light from above, which he checked occasionally. The sky was a cloudless blue where he could see in among the towers of rock high up above them. Then he saw light on the stone face up in front of them, and still carrying her he headed for it, moving upward steeply for a few yards. When he got there he could see most of the valley.

They were at the mouth of a small crevice opening in the side of the rock face. Below them the face descended for a long way until it skirted out a little and ended in the valley floor. He could see that though it was steep there were ways down. She moved a little under his arm, and he realized he was squeezing her and he put her down on the stone ledge beside him. And then he rose and looked back, trying to take in as much of what was before him as he could manage. The valley was an immense oval; its floor from this height a mix of low, rolling hillocks, flat places like green carpets, and occasional piles of stone. A few thin fingers of streams meandered across it. The whole of the valley was contained in the crown of jagged rock towers that he was in the far end of. The other end must have been a good mile away at least, and when he stared at it its massive spikes and spires looked two dimensional against the blue sky behind it. On either side of the oval crown, the rock was the same, and it was only when he looked close to the sides of where he was standing that the weight and mass of it became evident. He thought he saw an animal, then two of them, move on the valley floor and come to a thread of stream and then stop. They looked like rabbits or very small dogs, but when he squinted and looked very long and carefully he saw they had antlers, were probably elk, and only then did the true size of the place become apparent. He moved his eyes down to the stone skirt below him and up it a little. There were two pools of water far down, one below the other, where the stone face came out in brief terraces. He realized that they were good-sized lakes. When he looked back at the valley the animals were gone, but he could now see that the trickles of water were streams and that the piles of rocks were large hills and that the green carpets of flat growth were extremely large, as big as football fields.

Then he remembered the telescope in its leather tube at his waist and he took it out. It didn't help much. The place was too big for it to make much difference, but he scanned the valley and the rock face for as long as he could concentrate on doing so. He felt he would have seen something, someone, had it moved enough, had it been there, but he thought too that they would have to move quite a bit and that he would have to catch them at it. Besides, he thought, they would be tucked down and out of sight. He wondered if anyone could see him were they looking to do so.

He stayed in the crevice with her for a long time, taking the whole thing in and considering. He could stay there and wait, but he knew even as he thought it that it would accomplish nothing. Not even if they came out and showed themselves would it make any difference. Finally he would have to go down, and so would they. They couldn't risk picking him off somehow, with a rifle; the place was too big, and she could most probably get away. And even if they didn't think she could get away, they couldn't risk it; they had come too far for that now. He wondered briefly if all his considerations were silly and overly dramatic. Maybe no one was there at all; they could have gone away. But then he saw the brief flash of pinpoint light at the other end of the rock oval. He brought the scope up quickly, but he could find nothing but the crown of rock. Then he put it away and lifted her up again and started down.

It took him twenty minutes to reach the first lake. It was set totally in rock, almost a miniature version of the contained valley, and when he got to where the stones touched the water he found he could see deep into it, could see fish suspended as if in crystal. It was perfectly still, and he dipped his hand in and drank the icy water. Then he moved around it, still carrying her, and climbed over its rock rim and descended to the second lake. Before he got there the rocks began to give way in places to mossy trails, natural ones where rain had washed through to the earth and wind had seeded. He put her down then, behind him a little, and avoided the crown of the second lake and headed for the edge of the valley's floor, passing through moss trails in the rock's skirt and beside alluvial fan-shaped spills of pebbles and rock ground into sand. Then he came to the last bits of protection, the final rocks and crevices, and looked back at her. And knowing it was foolish now to hesitate, he slapped his hip lightly in signal and stepped out into the edge of the valley and walked away from the shadows the mass of the raw rock behind him cast, and in fifty yards he was free of it and in the mild sunlight. He felt the touch of a light breeze now as the valley opened beyond the rock.

She walked beside him again, almost prancing, her head and her tail up, and when he saw her he pulled himself more erect also. He touched the knife handle and the sheath's thong. As they went out into the valley, he could see there was a place far ahead to the left where the rock crown ended briefly and then started up again. It was almost as if a piece of crust had been broken off at the edge of a deep pie. It was a strange fault in an otherwise perfect configuration. He was a good way out in the valley, at a place where moss covered the ground and the ground was almost flat for a good hundred yards on each side when he heard her voice, or at least the first echo of it, before it moved out and around the massive rock rim, finishing or fading only when it reached the far end of the oval. It was his name only, "Paul" this time and not Pablo, and it was no yell across great distance, but a call from his left, a little above the floor of the valley and not from far away.

He stopped and turned, and he was not really surprised that they were so close, only a few yards up in the rocks at the valley side, no more than a hundred feet from him. He could see them clearly in the thin air, could even see their expressions. The two Mexicans flanked her, one slightly behind her and a little higher, the other holding her arm. Gabriel, the doctor, was a few feet off to the side, pressed back into the rock. Paul almost laughed when he saw that he had a suit on, even a tie; strands of thin oily hair hung down on the side of his face, touching his ear. He would count for nothing.

But the two others would. The stockier one at her side holding her arm had a rifle in his hand. It hung down below his waist, held under the chamber on a balance. The other had a pistol, and was pointing it at him. Their postures seemed uncertain, but their looks were not.

"Paul," she said, this time almost in a whisper, and as he saw her white teeth as she smiled the word echoed again, briefly, along the rock face. He checked where the horse was beside him and then moved toward them for twenty or more yards. He could see they were watching her, checking the possibilities, and he pulled up before he got too close. There was open and unencumbered space between them now, but they would have to get the few yards down from the skirt to begin to get at her, and he knew they couldn't be sure of it, and would not try yet.

"Where's Parker?" he said, and there was no echo at all this time.

"Do you want her?" the one a little above her said, and he moved the pistol and pointed it at Mary Grace. He smiled briefly, as if he was sure of his position, but his smile crumbled. Then the other one spoke.

"Never mind Parker. We can make a deal now, can't we?" The "we" echoed out a little, repeating itself, insistent. Paul thought it would be the only way. He had no reasonable plans and he had known it would come to something like this in the sense that he couldn't have planned. They weren't giving him much, and he would have wanted Parker in it right then. But he didn't have him, and he had to take what he did have, though he had no real idea what to do with it even when he spoke.

"Sure. A deal," he said. "Let her go to the side, and we can deal."

"Do you have the diamonds?" Gabriel whispered. "Did you find them?"

"Shut the fuck up!" the one behind Mary Grace said sharply, and the echoes were distinct this time.

"Come down," Paul said, and the two looked at each other and nodded. They did not release her to the side but held her between them as they climbed down out of the rocks. They kept their eyes on the horse, holding Paul in the corners of their eyes as they came down. When they reached the edge of the valley floor he had moved toward them, and they were no more than twenty feet apart. He realized that he had not loosened the knife thong, but knew that he could not risk it now. She was wearing a dress and she had sandals on her feet, and he guessed that that had been a good way to keep her from bolting if she had the chance. He saw that her bare legs had scratches on them, but he saw too that her face was not too worn. She didn't look all that tired, and there was a hard resolve in her eyes. There was something new there too, not just the recognition of one she had not seen for so long, but something shy and pristine. He thought he probably had a look of the same kind in his eyes. There was nothing for it now, for either of them, no possible undoing, and if incest were a word to name and mark them in some way, he knew it was certainly not one that they would find a use for, nor was it part of their looking at each other. It had all been much richer than that could be, and he thought what he recognized was a deepening of commitment in her look, something simply familial, and in that way prior to any event or complication. They were both shy, even in their difficulty, but the shyness seemed to him no more than a right reaction to the newness and the power of their basic link.

When they reached the flat beyond the rocks they stopped, and the one holding her arm released her and brought the rifle up to his side. It was still held loosely, but it could come to the ready quickly. They stood looking across the space at each other for a moment, and then the one with the rifle, the thick, stocky one, spoke, glancing once at the other, then looking hard at Paul.

"This is the way I figure it. You had to carry her most of the way down. The only possible way out for her is that cut down the line, but we can head her away from that. I can shoot your leg easily, man. The deal is you hand her over now, and the diamonds too, and then we let you go."

"Where's the stallion?" Paul said, wanting to keep him talking. "And where is Parker?"

They could have seen that he was looking behind them a little as they talked, but Gabriel was there, and that would account for it. The fact was that he couldn't help himself, and in a crazy way he couldn't help it because all of his effort was given over to working at not smiling, even laughing. He was dressed madly, in a tremendous sombrero and a flower-print shirt open almost to the waist. His jeans were baggy and too long for him, the cuffs rolled to the tops of a pair of tooled climbing boots, palomino in color, with scallops at the ankles. He had that pencil-thin, painted mustache on; Paul could see the ridge of the scar on his belly when he turned, and as he crept down through the rocks behind them, he raised a finger to his lips to indicate that Paul should not give him away. And when he smiled at the joke of even asking such a thing as that, Paul felt the laughter begin to rumble in his chest. The horse saw him too, but she gave no sign. He was to the side of where Gabriel was, the whip was snaking through the rocks behind him, and he flicked it a little as he worked his way down, making sure that it did not get caught up. Gabriel was watching them, but Paul could see that his eyes were beginning to get ready to wander as the one with the rifle spoke, and the horse must have seen this too because she moved a little from where she stood close to Paul, drawing Gabriel's eyes back with the slight motion.

"This is not fucking funny!" the one with the rifle said. "Never mind about Parker and the other one. What the fuck are you laughing at!"

He could see that the laugh was pulling their attention then, that it was keeping Gabriel interested as well, and he let it go. It began to echo out, and then the whip uncoiled and straightened behind Johnny and began to roll forward. And even before it got there, Paul was moving at them. He saw the rifle come up quickly, then saw the man turn to the other as the whip hooked his neck and he yelled and was jerked back. The horse peeled off from his side as Paul moved, and he caught a glimpse of Gabriel's mouth drop open as he saw her go, and then Gabriel twisted his head back and saw Johnny in his sombrero, leaning back on the heels of his silly yellow boots, the whip taut in the air. The rifle was almost back at him when Paul reached the man, but he was moving with good speed then, and as he hit into him with his shoulder he saw Mary Grace's fist strike into his Adam's apple.

Then he was rolling on the ground with the man, catching glimpses of Johnny on the other, of Mary Grace dancing and shaking her injured fist, of Gabriel between two men coming down out of the rocks. Then he was not rolling. He was on his back and the Mexican, whose strength was too much for him, was on top of him and had him by the throat. He managed to get the knife out and across his belly, but before he could thrust it forward they pulled the man off him. He saw Xavier and five others. They had the three of them sitting on the ground, had their weapons in hand. He saw Johnny smiling and nodding under his ridiculous hat; he had his arm around Mary Grace, and in the space left between their bodies he saw the little horse in the distance coming back. He got up and moved to Mary Grace and Johnny, but before he got to them he heard the call.

There were too many words in it, and they had to listen intently and wait so that they could gather what was said out of the echoing, to go back and construct it after the last echo faded. It said something like, *I'm coming down now, brother.* The source of it was at the far end of the oval valley, and they all turned and squinted, searching the rock face in the distance. They looked for a long time, in complete silence. Then there was something coming down from the far skirt and entering the valley. Paul raised the scope to his eyes and found him. He saw the small stallion, and behind him and up a little in the rocks the figure move down with hands on stone and legs spread and reaching for purchase. He was like a spider, but when he reached the edge of the valley his limbs gathered into his body and Paul saw that it was Parker.

The stallion was well in front of him, but he saw through the glass that Parker's hand came up, and they heard a brief undistinguishable syllable. He saw then that the horse pulled up, turned and went back to where Parker was and came to heel. They began to walk toward them then. He thought Parker had something in his hand, a weapon of some sort, but he wasn't sure of it, and he lowered the scope. Then he raised his hand and called out to the horse, and she came to him. He looked at Mary Grace and Johnny. There were still standing close together, arms around each other and faintly smiling. They turned toward each other and then looked back at him and nodded. Then he turned from them, and he and the little horse set out down the center of the valley.

===

They had to pass by cairns of stone and a few rocky mounds, and there were two shallow streams when he had to pick the horse up, step from one small boulder to another above the skimming rush, and put her down on the other side. He never lost sight of them in the distance, and once beyond the few easy obstacles the ground changed again to a gentle roll of grass and mosses. There was nothing between them now of consequence, no places in which to pull up and take a stand, and they were approaching each other down the valley's center with the side of the oval crown too far on either side for any thought of heading for it. He could almost see what Parker wore now, and he thought he could see hints of the stallion's mane and tail. When he looked down at the little horse beside him he suspected that she was aware of him too. What breeze there was moved toward them; they were downwind from them, and though she might not see him yet, or see him clearly enough, he saw her nostrils open and vibrate a little and he guessed she was beginning to scent him. She moved out just a little in front of Paul, but he whispered and she backed up. She didn't turn around to do it. He saw the muscles in her shoulders bunch, her steps shorten and her legs lift higher in a prance, and she was almost stepping in place when he got beside her again. Then she released herself a little, staying now just a bit beyond his leg. He didn't think the stallion had seen her yet, but he thought he could discern its extended neck, its head thrust forward a little, as if it saw the beginning of something it might recognize, but was not sure of, and was straining to see better.

It was when there was three hundred yards between them, and he could see that the object held across Parker's chest was a rifle, that he was sure that they were both aware of each other and certain about it. He heard a deep, guttural sound come out of her and saw her rise on her back legs, her forelegs lift a few inches off the ground and kick at the air for a moment. He thought he saw the stallion do something similar in the distance, and saw Parker's head turn to the side toward him. He wondered what he would do when he got to him, what Parker himself would do. He thought he knew what ought to happen, but what he realized now as a climax was taking too long to develop, and he was beginning to feel the node of resolve that had been pushing him for so long begin to shift and come away from its place in him. Parker looked so harmless out there. There was only the fact of the stallion, her counterpart, and his too in a way, to focus the resolve he knew he needed. Then he saw Parker's head cock and move a little to the right. They were getting closer, and Paul recalled the gesture; it was the same half-quizzical one he had seen behind the camera, and he felt he was coming back to readiness again.

But it was not Paul that Parker was looking at this time; it was something else, and when he turned his head he saw it, its massive, pillowed bulk that filled the single break in the rock crown of the oval and seemed almost stationary there. It was not stationary at all, though, but moving very slowly, squeezing through the opening. He could see under it as it pushed into the valley, could see how the moss on the ground got greener as the aura of its wash wet it. Then, in what seemed too long a time, it cleared the crown completely and was free and solid in the valley and moving toward them. He realized that he had stopped, and when he turned his head he could see that Parker had stopped too. Paul felt the breeze come up on his cheek, and when he looked down at the little horse he saw her mane lift up and her head turn from the cloud and look toward Parker and the stallion.

The cloud was like a quilted dirigible, a huge blimp, a three-dimensional cartoon figure, but it was not so large as to be beyond comprehension. He felt his stomach tighten, a sound come to his throat that was both a sound of fear and a laugh at the silliness of being afraid of a cloud. But it seemed ominous in the way it moved, as if there were silent motors in it, or a mind of some kind, and because it was purely white and as thick as cotton, and because he was standing there, in a perfectly clear and sunny day, he had no idea whatsoever of how to address himself to it, what could possibly be appropriate action or the lack of it. He realized that he was freezing in his gazing at it as it moved, and he jerked his eyes away from it and looked for Parker and found him.

Parker was looking back and forth from the cloud to where Paul was, and when Paul looked at the cloud again, he saw it rotate slightly, still slowly, like a massive oblong ball of some kind, and saw that it was now headed toward the very center of the valley, moving toward the acres of space between him and Parker. He felt the breeze shift slightly until it was touching him full in the face and guessed the passage of the cloud, down the center of the valley to the other end behind him, up over the jagged towers of rock at the crown's far end. Then he was aware that she was moving and that he was too. And as he walked forward, he could see the stallion quit Parker's side and trot ahead of him. He thought he saw Parker gesture, his head move in speech to call him back, but then the cloud's expanse entered the space between them; its body rotated, and it settled in its path, moving directly toward him now, heading slowly for the valley's end behind him.

He dropped to his knees, then to his stomach. The cloud was a few feet above the ground, and he needed to find if he could see under it. He couldn't. As it got closer, no more than a hundred yards away now, he could see that its thick aura of mist reached the ground opaquely, and he could see no more than a few feet into it, just bits of green color rising as the moss was soaked. He saw her reach it, in her brisk trot, and enter it, and saw her inside the edge of it for a moment, but then she dissolved. He got back to his feet, and when he was standing again it had almost reached him. He leaned forward slightly, bracing himself, anticipating a blow of some kind, but there was nothing but mist and a slow drenching as it got to him, and then he was inside it. At the edge of it he reached for the knife, but all he felt was the empty sheath.

It was like being in a cool steam bath. He could see, he thought, about ten yards all around himself, but the distance didn't remain constant. The clouds inside the cloud thickened and dissolved slightly, were constantly changing as the whole of it moved slowly over him. He stood still, and then he saw the horizontal lines in the mist, the tracings, and heard the muffled sounds of the firing, sporadic and arbitrary and only a few yards to the left of him. He hit the ground and rolled and reached for the knife again, and though he wanted to get to his feet and do something, find the knife or do something else, he fought against the urge and stayed down.

His cheek was in the grass and moss, his head turned to the side and below the various level lines of the tracings. Then he saw a bulk of some kind, and he held his breath. In a moment he saw how low the bulk was, how small, and he exhaled as he saw her moving toward him in the mist. She had her head down, her legs slightly bent, and there was something in her mouth. She was only a few feet from him when he saw that she had the knife. It was held crossways in her mouth, the wet leather handle darker now and the oiled blade beaded with drops of dew. She brought it up to him, came almost to his face, and then she lowered her head, opened her mouth, and rested the knife almost delicately on the ground. Then she turned and moved quickly away and was gone. Then he heard Parker speaking.

The words were totally without echo now, were fractured completely in the cloud, and he had no idea at all what they said or where they were coming from or how far away they were. Then, much quicker than he had imagined, he saw him. He was off to his left, no more than fifteen feet away, almost a silhouette, one leg before the other, standing and leaning forward and peering into the cloud. Paul was afraid to rise. If he heard him when he was halfway up he would have no chance at all, he thought, but he knew he had to rise, had to go for him. He pushed in one motion to his feet, stirring his space in the cloud's body, and he saw the stir of mist roll out from him and get to Parker as he reached his feet. He knew, as he saw Parker turn toward him and bring the rifle around, that he could not get to him. Parker saw him then and saw the situation, and Paul saw his teeth shine through the clouds of mist. He held the rifle pointed at him, but he did not fire, and as Paul squinted he could see that Parker squinted too and leaned forward a little. He wants to see me better, wants some connection before he does it, Paul thought. It's like when he did it to García, did it to our father, he needed to let him know who it was first. Paul wanted something similar, but he did not make any move to get closer. Then, in a thin pocket of mist, he saw his face, and saw it was the same as he had seen beyond the wooden scaffold and the donkey's haunches and the tripod. His hand tightened on the wet leather handle of the knife, and he thought he saw Parker see the knife, and then he saw his head jerk down, and saw the stallion on him.

It was like an image from a story. The stallion had him by his thigh, and he was looking down at it and shaking his leg, almost tentatively. Paul saw his leg come up, and saw the stallion come completely off the ground, its hooves kick against his boot and ankle above the bright green of the wet moss. Then he saw his right hand come free of the rifle, cut down through a puff of cloud and strike the stallion's head. It fell free and rolled, splashing in the dew. Then it was on its feet and back at him again, this time locking its teeth higher, near the hip. Paul was moving then, and he saw Parker's fist rise up high above his head. Then he saw her coming.

Parker was slightly crouched, but still she was very high in the cloudy air. Her hooves were moving as if she were swimming, and her mane and tail were dancing. And then the cloud billows behind her were turning rose colored, and her mane and tail were like rose flames. He saw her lips curl back as her hooves reached Parker's shoulder, and behind her he could see the vague figure of the stone crown through the cloud. The sun was on it and it was in the cloud too now. And then he saw her head come down, her teeth sink into Parker's throat. The whole side of her head was rosy, and then the brighter red was gushing, washing over Parker's collar and down his chest. Paul reached him when he began to fall. He had the knife up, but there was no place to send it. He dropped to his knees as Parker hit and saw the stallion go and saw the mare's mouth open as her head turned and she too moved away. Then the last mists of the cloud passed over them, and he was on his knees at Parker's side.

His eyes were wide and he was looking up at him. He could see his teeth again, this time bright in the sun, and he saw the pump of bright red arterial blood as it washed over his neck and shoulder and flooded into the still bright green of the wet grass. He brought the knife up high in the air over his head, looked into Parker's eyes, and then he brought it down, burying it to the hilt in the moss beside Parker's head. Then he reached out and grabbed at his neck, pressing his palm into the jagged wound to stop the blood. He saw it ooze out between his fingers, and when he looked at Parker's face again he saw his eyes glazing. He pressed deeper, wanting to bring his gaze back, to focus his eyes in his own again, to get something that he realized could not be there. But he was beyond returning, his pupils thin and washed wide across the milky surface. He looked away, and then he saw the horses going down the valley. They were trotting close beside each other, their manes and tails pure palomino yellow now in the sun and breeze. Beyond them he saw a figure at the skirt of the crown and he knew it was Álava. Still pressing into Parker's neck, he turned his body and looked behind him. The cloud was climbing, pressing into the skirt of the crown now and rising toward the crest. He saw them moving toward him, just the two of them. They moved away from the larger gathering, and though he could not see them distinctly yet, he knew by Johnny's size beside her and by his sombrero that it was they. Then he saw Johnny's arm come up, saw the sombrero rise, and heard him call out. The hat went very high, and when it reached its peak it seemed to hang there, free of everything, in the pure sunlight. He pulled his hand away from Parker's neck and got to his feet. He raised his own arm then, and turned his blood-soaked hand palm out and waved it at them.

Chapter 23

They roped Parker's body down through the opening and the shaft and buried him in the chamber where Abelardo García had carved his initials beside the veins of false diamonds.

"Wasn't the floor stone?" Paul said, and Xavier told him it was just some surface rock with dirt under it; they got him deep enough and got the stone back over him. It was a good place and it would be all right.

Xavier and some others took Gabriel and the two Mexicans into Glenwood Springs and turned them over to the police. They told them they had found them in the high country and that they thought they were fugitives of some kind. They gave the police their weapons and a piece of paper they said they had found on one of them. The paper had the names of Ronny's friends on it and the address in Durango.

"Without Parker they have nothing," Johnny said. "We won't hear from them again."

By the time it was all over it was almost dark, and they were invited to Álava's lean-to for dinner. The five of them sat among the blankets and pillow sacks and ate hot stew and drank coffee. The horses lay close to each other, close to Álava, and the body heat of all seven of them kept the lean-to warm. The flap at the top was open as it had been before, and the stars were out full again, as bright as they had been. They talked, haltingly at times, but they got things said. Johnny had cleaned his mustache off, had changed into rough outdoor clothing and Paul could see he'd washed the grease from his hair and that it had some curl in it now and stood out a little from his head. He sat beside Mary Grace, who was also in long pants and boots now and wore a sweater. As they talked, she touched Paul from time to time, putting her fingers on his arm or his thigh, pushing a strand of hair away from his cheek. Johnny's gold tooth had been a false cap and was gone now, his smile even and white.

"She's pregnant," Paul said. "Look at them." The stallion had his head resting on her rounded stomach, as if he were listening for the heartbeat of the foal.

"Is she?" Mary Grace said, a little hesitantly.

"It was only a story," Johnny whispered. "She'll be okay."

"We'll have another horse soon," Xavier said, and Álava nodded and smiled.

"I don't know how he knew I would know about Marble," Paul said.

"I'm not sure of that either," Johnny said, and he looked over at Mary Grace, who shook her head. "But it was our father who told us about it, talked about it in stories, and he told him that much too."

"How can that be?" Paul said. "He killed him before he could talk to him. He only said 'Father' or 'Papa' or something."

"Oh, that's Esperanza's story, isn't it?" Mary Grace said. "That's not exactly the way it happened."

"He didn't die," Johnny said.

"After he had knifed him and he didn't die, they tended to him a little and locked him up in a room with a little water. They locked us up too and wouldn't let us see him. Then they went through the house. We could hear them do it, and when they did let us out in a few days the place was a mess from the searching, and they made us straighten it up. We knew where he was and we knew he was still alive because they went in there at times and they talked about it. I think Parker tried not to let us hear the talk, but he was in a rage very soon and couldn't hold it back and keep his voice down. He was looking for something and he wasn't finding it, and he was trying to get it from Father.

"Then there was a time when they searched the house over again. They must have spent close to a week doing it I think. And at the end of that, Parker really became enraged, and I think it was then that he started beating us, wasn't it, Johnny? And then one day one of them went to the room and Father was gone."

"He was just gone," Johnny said. "I don't know how he got out or where he went, but I think we both figured it must have been north. He had citizenship, and that would have been a good place. We never heard a thing again, at least not until I heard something, and that was only a few years ago, when our brother came."

"Our brother?" Paul said.

"That's right." He raised his hand to keep Paul from further questions, and then he rose to his feet and stepped gingerly among the blankets and pillow sacks and left the tent. Paul turned to Mary Grace, but her look told him that he must wait.

"There was another horse," she said. "One was born before Parker came. We were very little then, and I remember how we played with it. It wasn't there for very long, though. I have no idea where it went, but maybe it was the one the farmer showed you. Maybe it was that skeleton."

"That sounds possible," Álava said. "And it could have even been that Parker somehow had a line on that one, something to explain how he came to the farmer's house and burned it. Something other than that he was following you."

"I don't know," Paul said.

When Johnny returned he was carrying something under his arm. Paul could see the edges of it and he thought he vaguely recognized it, but he could not place it. Johnny went back to his place and sat down, cross-legged on the pile of pillow sacks, and then he took the object and placed it on the blanket in front of him. Paul recognized part of it then. He saw the curled edge of the horse drawing, a line and the letters of a legend at the end of it. It was tucked between the pages of a magazine, and he knew he had seen that before, too.

"It was only a few years ago, and I was working a club in Matamoros. That's below Corpus Christi, near the border at Brownsville. You were in Corpus Christi in the Navy, weren't you, Paul? Maybe you were even there at that time."

"I *was* in Corpus," Paul said. "I don't know the time."

"At any rate, he came there one night. The place had women, and he was alone, and I think I picked him out during the show because he was having nothing to do with the women at all and seemed uncomfortable at a table all by himself. I could see he wasn't laughing at the jokes and figured he had no Spanish. It was a weeknight, a rather out-of-the-way club, and I think he was the only gringo in the place.

"It was after the show, when I was sitting at a table and talking and drinking with a couple of women, when he approached me. I remember he stood there, awkwardly beside the table, not interrupting, but waiting to be recognized. I'm sure he was relieved when he found out that I spoke some English.

"He handed me this magazine, and he said he came there with it because he'd found my name in it. My name's still there, penciled in the margin. Yours is there too, Paul, and so is Mary Grace's. And there are other things too, little notes, scratches and things. The only things

I've been able to make out thought are the names. The notes aren't very clear. There are a couple of other names there too, and one of them, the man said, was his. He said the magazine had belonged to the man he thought was his father. The man had died in San Diego, in the Naval Hospital. He said he wasn't really all that sure that he was his father and that was why he'd come down to Matamoros to find me. He wanted to find out what he could.

"And I lost him. I couldn't make the connection at all at the time, and even though he pressed the magazine on me, told me to keep it, I missed out with him. I thought it was a sailor's souvenir of some kind. I'd played Tijuana often, and that was the way I connected it. And he was awkward and quite unsure himself. And so he gave me the magazine, and after we'd talked a little and he saw I couldn't help him out, he left. He was our brother, but it was a long time before I figured that out."

He lifted the magazine up and gestured with it as he came to the end of his talking. Then he reached out and handed it across to Paul. The folded horse drawing was tucked between its pages.

"Is there somewhere? . . ." Mary Grace asked.

"He can go to the other lean-to to look it over," Álava said. "We can have a little brandy and wait a while. It's still early."

===

He sat on the blankets in the empty lean-to. It was one beyond the firepit from Álava's, and he had passed the fresh flames rising and warming the side of his body as he'd moved around the fire's edge to get to it. Xavier had pointed it out, and then left him. It was cooler now, but there was little breeze, and the lean-to was comfortable, and he could see the canvas of the wall glow in a rose color as the fire warmed and illuminated it.

He opened the magazine to the page the horse drawing marked and saw the faint pencil lines in the margin. He glanced at the printed prose. It was an article about diamonds, one that discussed the quality of stones and their identification. He read a few lines. The sentences were stiff and a little odd, like something translated awkwardly from another language. When he tilted the page, he could make out Johnny's name in the glow from the rose wall, and then he saw Mary Grace's and then his own, Paul simply, and below that he saw Mary, not Mary Grace but his mother's name, with no Cords following it, but García: Mary García, a very common name. Then he saw the other one, the one he had expected: Taunton.

He wondered if it was García who had named him, had told his mother to name him Paul. He thought it probably was. But Taunton? He remembered that day on the ward, the day the curtains had lifted in the sea breeze, and he remembered Taunton and the woman in the small garden beyond the window. Nasty Jack was lying in the solarium only a few feet from where they sat, and Paul stood watching them. And Jack was Abelardo García, and was their father, his and Taunton's, Mary Grace's and Johnny's, and Parker's, too. And the woman was Taunton's mother and was like his own mother, a woman with a secret, and they two, the sons, *were* the secret.

He had been a secret to himself he thought for a very long time. And he imagined, with some longing, that the same had been true of Taunton. Their father had been a sailor in another life, and there had been many ports, landlocked, and some perverted.

He wondered about Jack's wife at the hospital, the small woman who had thanked him. At least he had tended his father in his dying, and though García had tricked him with the story when he was Jack, that was something. And it was he, Paul, who had aided him, had got the swelling out so that the story could be told.

He picked up the horse drawing and looked at it. He remembered the legends and how he had studied them, and though they were no clearer to him now, he did not think of them as something to be deciphered and understood. They now looked simply artful—they looked like a kind of celebration, and not a message. They had been parts of a presentation of a texture of a past, and it was the simple rendering of the horse itself that now drew him. The legends stood as a kind of fence of language around it, but they did not touch it. It was an empty outline; it just was.

The horse rendering had been tucked in at page one hundred and seventeen of the magazine; that was where the diamond article was and where the names and other marks had been penciled in. The diamond article was the last piece, and he fingered back from it, glancing at the old advertisements and elegant typography, and on page sixty-two he found the story.

Some of the facts were what he remembered them to be, and he remembered how he had only briefly thought it odd that it had not been the same story that Jack had read to him. He wondered if it would have made any difference at all had he looked carefully through the magazine and found the names and markings. It may have made some difference, but he wasn't sure it would have. He had read the story, after all, and though he remembered parts of it, reading it again he realized he had missed the core of it completely. It was no simple romance, was not the circle to a happy ending he had thought it before . . .

THE WOMAN WHO ESCAPED FROM SHAME

There was an end to the talking, and it seemed a presence. And for a while there was the faint smell of pomade in the room, marking his absence. A horse with a bird on its back: a palomino and a Cardinal. It was too red, and her hand went to her cheek where the slight flush had risen under her makeup. It was cool now, and she knew it had receded beneath the rose dusting. The horse was across the wide gravel drive, standing and looking in at her, the bird perched on its croup in the sun. Then its tail lifted, and the bird lifted and twisted like a small flame and darted away. It had been too red, and she wondered with an odd smile if he had planned it. Now that it was over with, it was as if he had planned everything: the lawn and the shaped trees, the small squares of garden, the drive's curve, the slant of sun, the bird on the horse's back, had planned it through a cool magic, a magic made mostly from money.

"We've lost all of it," he said. "Every red cent." And then he had said other things and had moved around the room as if he were looking for places to stand, now behind her and now to the side, places where he could find some posture that would come before loss and thereby negate it. She could go live with her aunt in the city. She could try to find work. It would be shameful, but no one need know it. Then he had left her, still looking for a way he had once walked as he went to the door.

Fire, when she was a child, a red flame under her dress; she could see her father's elbow in the shine of her leather shoe, his large hand holding her whole knee. And above it the small scab, and his finger just touching it. "Does it hurt; is it still painful?" "No, Papa," and her eyes moving, to small window and oak door, and telling her she should be moving also.

It did hurt, but the hard sheath was already forming. His hand was large, but awkward and too hesitant and gentle for her own good. "Papa?"

Now the horse watched her. There was a picture of her dead mother on the wall at the window in a perfunctory frame. Her mother watched her, and the horse lifted its head once and nodded. Then it lifted its front hooves from the gravel and wheeled slowly, presenting its rump and tail, and walked from the drive into the yard, a place it should not go, but without malice, and touched into the grass carefully, injuring nothing, and beyond its head in the distance she saw the gates opening and the wagons and vans entering. When the horse got to the middle of the yard, it turned again and looked at her and then looked up as if searching for the red bird.

"Buy me a fine-toothed comb made of bone. Get me a new bridle. Bring me a bird in a copper cage and someone to feed it. I want gloves, a new hat, a gold thimble, a diamond ring. And if you see anything you think I might like, even a little, buy it for me. Give me money and a pearled purse, and now that I think I am old enough, silk stockings and crinoline slips; have somebody do needlepoint at the hems. And hankies with red birds on them, and a gold buckle and a pin for my bodice, and get me a tooled leather saddle, and put a horse of my own under it. Buy me the best perfume and oil."

When she was old enough she came out. There was a formal dance and young men and girls wiser in some ways than she was. But she was concerned with her new dress, the cut of her bodice, her jewels and her purse and the scent of animals in her perfume, and what the girls had to tell her was not heeded or heard. Her mother had nothing to tell her; she sat with her father, watched her with a vacant smile. And she watched the young men, measuring them, most especially the one her father had picked out for her. Later, he came calling, brought flowers and appropriate gifts. Her mother nibbled the candy; her father sat with the young man in the smoking room. The scab on her knee was gone now, and the skin over the place was a little thicker than before.

Sitting in a square garden in the evening, checking the weight and taste of the young man's stickpin; the pomade was different and more fragile than her father's was, the hand smaller, sweat in the palm rotating her floating patella. And over his shoulder the horse stood off in the trees looking at her. She took his hand then and spread her knees a little; he trembled; she almost had to laugh at him. He was so expectant, and she knew there was nothing up there for him.

In the picture her mother wore a heavy coat; it was winter. A small pill of a hat, and below it her short hair and no scarf. Her neck rose like a column of alabaster; she had prided herself in it. There was a thick diamond pendant at her throat, tight in a wide cuff of diamonds. Her father had liked her neck that way, had made it a showcase. Her makeup was perfect. Cut off at the shoulder, her image filled most of the frame. It was a black-and-white picture, and though she was dressed for the weather it had been taken inside and against a white wall. Her eyes were wide open, and she was smiling, presenting her neck. To the right was the window, and the wagons and vans. The horse turned again, following them with his eyes as they approached the house. The bird sat on the stone wall in the distance, the size of a candle flame.

"A rose-colored scarf to wrap around twice, four strings of pearls, a fine leather harness. And if you go to the west end there's a small shop, and in the back is a small locked case with a little box in it, wood and gold leaf, useless, expensive and pretty; bring it as well. And some new shoes, four pair, and whatever else you would like for me. I've enough pretty underthings now, unless you see something. I need someone to dress me, the right clothes for riding."

She knew that the young man thought he had her where he wanted her; he had his hand on what he thought was her, wet, but flamelike and ready. Already she wanted the ring she had felt against her knee, a large diamond. He gave it to her, vaguely thinking that it sealed something. Her father watched them carefully. When the three of them were together, he stood at an awkward distance, arms at his sides, stone-faced. Her mother was failing in illness; she thought she knew things.

Evening again: not in the square garden this time, but in the room with the small window and oak door, a room that had once been a stable, altered into a private place for four years now, but with the faint smell of the horse still in evidence. A bed, two chairs and a lamp, a dead bolt; there were pictures of horses in gilt frames on the walls, wooden walls that kept the room dark. And it was the same touch again, only diverted by her and controlled. What disgusted her was the young man's pleading when she thwarted him. "Wait," she said. "Oh, why? I can't," he pleaded. And to stop him she took his face in her hands and moved her own face to it; then she ran the very tip of her tongue, featherlike, over his lips in a slow circle. His hand stopped trying, only his eyelids trembled. She held his head still and could feel only his shallow breath in her mouth. Later, he gave her his silver cigarette case. It was no use to her, but it was pretty and thin.

The horse turned again and headed for the oval garden that lay in the very center of the broad lawn. The vans and wagons were getting closer, but the horse ignored them now. It was prancing slightly, its haunches rolling dancelike as its hooves rose higher, shining in the sun. The garden was a showplace, roses set in perfect rows, pruned, artificial and even. There was a low iron fence, filigreed, surrounding the oval, a miniature and useless gate. The fence rose only to the horse's cannons, and when he reached it he stepped carefully over its spiked tips, then moved to the center of the garden, turned and looked at her. The roses came only to the horse's knees, and she could see what she thought was a fine rosy powder rise from their petals as his legs struck against them. This was her father's garden. Her mother had brought no roses into the house from it. It was the first thing visitors saw when they entered the grounds. There was a gardener who did nothing but tend it. From the corner of the windowframe, she saw her father moving, trotting, his hands up and palms out. He crossed the gravel and entered the lawn. She could hear the wagon and van wheels crunch in the gravel now. Her father moved quickly but hesitantly, his arms fixed in the air, hands moving slightly forward, gesturing to keep the horse from movement as he got closer to it. The horse stood still, up to its knees in the roses, watching her father now, and then she saw its neck sway slightly and dip down, and when its head came up it was looking at her again.

Her father was no more than thirty feet from the low oval fence when the horse dipped its head again and then rose up on its hind legs. Then it came down and was kicking and wheeling in tight circles. Then the uprooted roses were rising around its turning body, petals like small flames in the air. She saw her father come to the miniature gate and stop. Then she saw his right fist shaking, and then his arms fell to his sides suddenly. Beyond him the horse kicked and wheeled and the devastated roses filled up the air. Then the horse stopped turning, gradually, and steadied. When it came to rest it was facing her father. It extended its neck, bringing its head only inches from where her father stood, and then she saw its lips pull back from its ivory teeth and thought she could hear it braying.

Her father's head fell to his chest then, and the horse pulled itself perfectly erect, the mass of its chest thrust forward. A light breeze lifted its mane and stirred the hundreds of rose petals that still hung in the air. It turned its head slightly then and looked at her, and through the window she could see its nostrils flaring. Then it nodded to her, and she felt her eyes faintly burning. It turned then and stepped over the iron fence with the same grace with which it had entered. She watched it head for the stone wall, its tail rise, beautiful and yellow in the air behind it as the rose petals drifted down to her father's feet, and it picked up speed.

Her father stood at the fence of his rose garden for a long time, then he turned and walked back toward the house. The servants were loading the vans and wagons. She saw her mother smiling at her from the picture, as she heard the door open behind her and smelled her father's pomade again. He came up to her and told her that he had informed the young man of the situation and that he would not be back again. Then he reached for her hand as she rose and took her to the wooden room. This time he was less quick with her and more thorough, and somewhere in the middle of it she knew that it would be the last time. He looked at her, something he had never done before, and there was something below his gaze that she didn't understand until later. There was his large hand again, his pomade and his sweat, and there was the end of it in a rush that she felt no part of.

That night she found the horse in a low meadow of willows and old oaks near a lake at the far reaches of the land. They called it a lake, but it was really no more than a small pond, the limbs of the trees at its bank hanging and extending over it. It was a place she and her brother had come to often, when they were no more than children. She remembered her brother had done a strange thing there, had drowned a newborn colt. She had not been there when he did it, but she had an image of him standing in the pond to his waist, his arms straight and vibrating as he held the colt down. That had broken things between her brother and her father, and now her brother was gone.

There was a full moon, and the horse stood among trees on the far side of the pond in the branch-filtered light like a pale gold statue, but when it moved, its head turning to look at her, the gold flowed in its skin like liquid, like gold blood, and she saw there was nothing hard or mechanical in it. She moved to the edge of the pond then, and sat on a thick, low limb and put her head against the tree's trunk and watched it.

She heard its low snuffle, heard its hooves click and rustle in the brush, and then she saw it moving and coming around the pond's edge toward her. She was tensed a little; she realized her hand pressed too hard against the branch she was sitting on, but when the horse cleared the obscurity of the thicker growth and reached the open space she could see all of him; he was no longer mysterious in any way, and her grip relaxed. He was prancing slightly as he approached her; his head was high, and she could see the root of his tensed tail, the fan rising slightly behind him. He came on slowly, looking at her, and when he got to her he lowered his head and looked directly into her eyes. He moved his head forward, curling his lips back slightly. Then she felt his sweet breath on her cheek, the softness of his muzzle, and the hard bone of his square teeth under it.

It was surely because he could not speak and tell lies, because he had destroyed the garden. Because of the quiet wash of his tail against her knees, she remembered how it was to ride him. She threw her garments down, like puzzle figures in the moonlight, because he had pure expectations. Because of handfuls of his mane. Because he wore expensive tooled leather as if it were nothing. Hanging under him, she felt strong and protected. Because of her picture, large, in his eyes. She wanted nothing from him that he could not give her. Because when he left her he looked back at her without shame. He had put his large head in her lap, and she had felt his eye pulsing against her palm.

In her first month in the city, her aunt died in a fever. She was told that her father had headed South, something to do with horses, and could not be found. She had a brother, but she didn't know where he was. She found a job in a dress shop in a good section of the city. She was smart about clothing.

The women came to the shop dressed as if they needed no clothing at all. They would meet there, acting as if they were surprised to be meeting. Some dressed for their arms and shoulders and made selections accordingly; there was one, like her mother, who dressed a perfect neck. And there were breasts and ankles and elegant ears, and she could see the men in carriages across the street waiting with cigars in their teeth. Sometimes a man would come in with a woman. These were not wives yet, but *trainees, she thought. The men would nod or shake their heads faintly, and the women would make their choices accordingly. She would help them, behind curtains, and in the farthest of the dressing rooms, out of earshot, they would pinch her and laugh and confide. In the closer rooms, they would wink and mime. When she saw them in their underwear, she saw that they were all the same, thin-skinned but with a kind of hard, transparent gloss over it. They stood and turned in the same ways, and they dressed themselves with the same proficiency. He came into the shop with a woman when she was in her second month. When he came back, in a week, he was alone.*

She was in her third month when he married her. He had wealth, but it did not move her. She did it out of need for respectability and the basic comforts. He bought her things, but she asked for nothing. She liked him well enough, but she knew it was a trade off, was essentially economic again, and she was at enough distance from that now to feel shame. He returned her to her proper station. She had a house again and servants, and had she wanted a horse he would have gotten her one. He asked nothing more of her than the young man and her father had, and though he was more experienced than the one, he was less powerful than the other, and with him she found herself in a kind of limbo. She did what he wanted, which was very little, and when he touched her and took her she was somewhere else. She told him she was pregnant in a few weeks. Hearing it, he smiled and proceeded to turn away from her. His eyes started to glisten. He began to prepare a room, and he spoke only of the coming future.

Then she was in her ninth month, and he was waiting for three more. Their house was a little out of town and not unlike the one she had lived in before, but there was no picture of her mother on the wall. She was the mistress now, and though she felt the sense of the circle—that her husband, like her father, would like to hang a picture while his thoughts were elsewhere—she was not thrilled, saddened, or moved in any way by it, but only watched her stomach and the new roses rise in her husband's garden. He was alive in what he thought was his virility as he watched her, and in the evenings he went elsewhere. He was powerful in the associations in his life, and there was no talk or sign from the servants or others that she was aware of. If there had been, she wouldn't have cared. He watched her and he watched the preparations of the room.

And in the twelfth month the child came; it was an easy birth. She bore it in a room to the side of the one he was watching. When he saw it for the first time, it was in her arms. It was a boy, and it had blond hair, but its skin was dark and swarthy, like her father's, and its eyes were wide open. He saw its face, and not hers, over her shoulder when he entered the room. The child's pupils were clearly focused, and it was looking up into her face. She didn't turn when he entered, nor did the child's head move. He stood back and watched them, and in what seemed a long time to him he saw a faint tightening in her shoulders and knew she was aware of his presence. Then she began to turn, and he was not sure just what to anticipate when he saw her face . . .

When Paul turned the page, he found he was reading something else, something about entertainment, a review of some kind, about an actor or a comedian. He looked into the spine and saw the jagged edges where the last page of the story had been ripped away. He looked back to the last few sentences and read them again. They told him nothing about what might happen, really nothing at all. The possibilities were open and as such seemed vacant. He tried to remember how the story had ended when he had read it after Jack had told the other one to him in San Diego, but that was so long ago now, and all he thought he remembered was that the ending had been circular. He didn't trust that, though, didn't trust his memory much at all. Jack was my father, García, he thought. He had missed the drowning of the colt in the pond completely, and even now he could not figure it. He was left with the image of the woman beginning to turn, and that would have to satisfy him. He thought of her with the child in her arms. Her look would be peaceful or powerful. But possibly it would be distant, shameless, beyond modesty. But it was only a story.

He closed the magazine and looked down at the worn cover, the faded illustration of a woman in the middle of some gesture. There had been other figures, and words, and the magazine's title across the top. They had all faded away now, and there was nothing that he could make out. The woman faced out at him, and though she still had features, the wearing of hands and transport and weather had removed all remnants of expression from her. She was alone there, gesturing for some reason that could never be clear.

"What will you do?" Paul said. "Will you go back?" He had returned to the lean-to where the others were and had handed the magazine and the illustration back to Johnny. Johnny had winked at him, and when he turned to Mary Grace she had let her hands fall, palms up in her lap. He knew then that the story was Abelardo García's if it was anyone's and that there would be no good answers to it.

"I won't," Johnny said. "I'm retired now. I'll go back to the house that Abelardo García built, the one I gave his name to. You remember? You were there," he said to Paul.

"It's yours, then," Paul said.

"It's mine. And it's yours too when you want it."

"And you, Mary Grace?"

"I'll go with Johnny. I'm retired too." She laughed. "It's finally finished."

He wanted to ask what it really was that had freed them, but he knew he had the answer in himself; he wasn't going back either, not to Pfeffer, not to anything. He had Ronny's address book, and he would go to Los Angeles; there were things to clear up about that movie, the party in the story, and he wanted to find out more about Ronny too, to put that part of the thing at rest for himself. And then there would be San Diego and the Naval Hospital. He would try to find out what he could about Jack and about Jack's wife, Taunton's mother. He wanted to know how his father had gotten there. And then there was the farmer, and the skeleton, and the burning house. But the last thing, and that would begin in San Diego too, would be Taunton and the start of his search for him.

"You have the diamonds," he said.

"If you would come with us, Pablo, there'd be no need to mention that," she said.

"I'll come," he said. "But I need a while."

"I know," she said. "So do I."

"We'll be there, Brother, when the time comes," Johnny said, and though Paul was not yet ready to hear himself called that, he knew he would be soon; he felt he already welcomed it.

He turned and saw her rise as Johnny spoke. She moved to the door of the lean-to and pulled the flap aside. Paul could see the bright, low stars in the frame of the opening. She turned then and looked at Johnny and then at him, and he realized he had not held her eyes for a long time now, but before he could find what he needed in them she had moved through the starlit frame and into the night.

"She didn't know you were her brother. Not until Parker told her, after he'd brought her here. She told me about it when you were in the cloud. I don't know how Parker found it out, or when, but he had a mother too, like yours, and maybe the explanation is there somewhere." Johnny shifted on the blankets, his hand brushing the tail of the male horse. The two were tangled in a pile, but their eyes were open. The female looked into the stars through the opening in the roof. Álava was smiling, watching them.

"But we knew García was our father, Parker our brother, and these were things we held in private. But of course you're in that privacy with us now."

"What about the horses, the brand, and the diamonds?"

Paul watched the horses move apart and rise together. The male nuzzled the neck of the female, and they both shook themselves and stretched. Then Álava got up and went to the flap on the lean-to and pulled it aside. The horses turned their heads, and Paul could see the starlight shine in their eyes. Then they moved, close against each other, to the opening, and they too disappeared into the night.

"We knew about the diamonds, but it was never much of a matter to either of us," Johnny said. "You'd have to understand about Parker, what he put us through. I'm not sure *I* understand it yet, but now there's time for that. He was the one obsessed. When you were in the cloud, our sister told me about our father's trick, about the hoof cups. I don't know when Parker found them. That was the first I'd heard of it. And yes, she knew about the horses and the brand, knew more about that than in those movies. That was private too then, our family privacy."

_____

He stood to the side of the firepit, facing it, and watched the heat waves twist in the air over the flames. They rose almost to his shoulder, and he could see the shadows of lean-tos waving beyond them, and beyond that the low rock crest at the edge of the encampment. Where the waves ended, the air was rose tinted, and above that was the clearer air and then the thousand hard jewels that were the stars. The sky between them was black, but even as he watched it it began to lighten, and the stars, though still brilliant, began to recede.

When he lowered his head again, he saw her. He wasn't sure just how he knew it was she. Her clothes were neuter, layers of muted-colored garments, baggy pants, a loose sweater, and she wore a hat. She came beyond the pit on the far side and moved to a slight rise of rock at the encampment's edge. She didn't see him. When she stopped, the stars were all around her. He thought he knew her by the way she moved.

What is the real story? he thought, knowing that even if he could find it out it would take a long and careful time. They were brother and sister, but the name for what they had done seemed really of little consequence in the face of everything else. And as he thought of making love to her, though the hair rose on his arms, he thought less about the incest than about the few times that they had truly touched each other.

He watched her. She stood at the crest with her back to him. And then he saw her arms move out a little from her sides and saw the figures of the two small horses. They came together from below the crest and moved up to her, one standing on each side of her, facing out as she was, their heads alert at her knees. He felt the fire's heat press into him, felt the gentle breeze and saw it in the yellow waves of the horses' tails and manes and in the edges of her hair below her hat. The horses stiffened beside her, and the female lifted her left foreleg and pawed once at the rock.

And then he saw the broad curve at the edge of the full moon as it rose up beyond them. The sky lightened and the stars receded, and the moon filled half the sky as it rose, and in what seemed only a moment it was all there. He could see the details of its craters. It was round in the sky, and he felt he could almost reach out and touch it. Then her arms came up from her sides.

Her hands were open and palm up, and she seemed to be reaching out to hold something, possibly the moon itself. The horses saw her movement, and their heads came up to watch her. He thought at first that she was doing something that could have great significance to him, to his understanding of the cost of escape and what was escaped from. But he had seen so many enigmatic gestures, those on charts and magazine covers, or heard them in stories, that he despaired at ever understanding what she might be doing.

But then he saw, quite suddenly and clearly, that it was no ritual or obscure thing at all. She was merely stretching, getting kinks out, feeling the freedom in her body, enjoying the crisp air and the grand sight of the moon.

Her arms moved above her head. She took her wrist in her palm, and he saw her back twist a little as she loosened her spine. Then her arms came down to her sides again and she shook them briefly, and then she just stood looking into the sky.

It was only after a long while that she turned around. He saw the horses turn with her, then saw the smile on her face. The moon hung huge behind them. Neither she nor the horses saw him, and he made no move at all to interfere.

━━━

They slept that night in Xavier's lean-to; he left it to them, and stayed with Álava. He left the two horses with them for the night as well.

Mary Grace slept between them in the common pile of blankets and pillows, and the horses, curled against each other, slept at their feet. It was warm under the blankets, and they drifted off quickly. Sometime in the night Paul woke to hear her crying, and when he turned over and faced her, he saw that Johnny was awake also and that he was stroking her arm and shoulder and brushing the tears from her cheek. When she felt his movement, she turned her head toward Paul, and he could see that she was smiling and that her brow was smooth and relaxed.

They stroked her, and she touched each of them, and they moved closer to her. She turned on her back, and their arms crossed over her, and they pressed their hips against her hips and kept their heads close to her head. She could see the stars up through the opening. Their arms gripped her tightly at first, but soon they felt the tension of wakefulness begin to leave her, felt her breathing become deep and steady. Then they relaxed also, moving their arms a little until Johnny's arm was against Paul's, his fingers touching his elbow. Paul felt his fingers move. Then his hand found a place above his elbow, on his upper arm, and settled there. He heard his breath steady and grow deeper also. Then Paul was the only one awake. He could feel the breathing of the horses, the way it gently moved their bodies against his feet. He felt alone. But it was a good feeling; he felt freed of everything within it. And he knew, at the same time, that he was no longer alone, was on the brink of a new beginning. And he thought, as he fell asleep: this is our happy ending.

Chapter 24

There was an end to the talking. And then, on the way back, there was Marv in the prow again behind me, steering me and mumbling intermittent things we could not understand. At least, I couldn't make them out, those fragments of English, but when he fell into Spanish he was making sentences, questions and assertions, although it was clear he was talking to himself.

"It's about Connie, and another woman; things about Mexico too and I think his car and belongings." Morales faced me from the stern; the sun was going down, and I could hardly see his face, could barely pick his voice out of the blanket cowling his head.

"His Spanish is improving by the minute," he whispered, and I thought he laughed.

And there was an end also to the past. The Navy and the tissue bank were no longer behind us as markers, as places of preservation. I knew this because of Marv, because after two more days in La Púa with the women he found his resolve, and there was not another word about Kansas, Sally or San Diego. He smiled, blushing a little when he told us, but the two weeks of sun had moved his farmboy burn to a deeper tan, and the blush seemed only a formality, as did his laugh, and when he spoke Spanish there was a new veil of reserve, a hardening in his round, farmboy face, something I knew I could not penetrate at all, at least not in the old way. It seemed to me he even moved differently now, stood more erect, had lost a certain swing in his arms. It was not that he didn't talk as he had or joke in the same way, but that now there was something behind what had seemed transparency of consciousness; there was another consciousness, and it was totally opaque.

Connie had made what calls were necessary, and they would drive south to La Paz and there get the ferry to Mazatlan. And if the ferry wouldn't take the car, he would leave it there. It didn't matter. Then they would head down below Mexico City, into Oaxaca where her town was. They would leave on Friday. I would close his apartment in San Diego when I got back there, send his things on, and do the same for Morales.

By Tuesday it was clear that Morales was failing again and that the dip was deeper than before. The chalk was back in his face, closer to the surface now, and he wasn't eating or moving around much. I saw Marv's face harden when he looked at him. Before his expression would have been open in concern. But it was no hardening against him; it was recognition, and he leaned over the bed and put his face close to Morales and whispered to him in Spanish. Morales nodded, managing a feeble smile. Verta sat on the bed, dabbing with a wash cloth at his brow. Marv and Connie called his father, and when they came back they told Morales that he would be there on Saturday. Morales nodded again, and then Marv turned to me.

"You'll wait with him?" he said. "We won't be here."

"I'll stay," Verta said.

"I'll wait here with him," I said.

And that was it. And when Friday morning came, we ordered breakfast in Morales' room. We all knew it was our last meal together, and I think each of us tried hard to rise to the occasion. Connie had the best of it; she was on the brink of something monumental in her life, and she laughed and told things about her family and her town. Marv laughed with her, touched her occasionally, and when he was able to make connections he brought me into the talk and tried even to bring Morales in. He had a few things to say about the Navy, told a few operating-room stories, and joked about his poor Spanish. I tried to join in. I think I mumbled a few things about Mexico. Verta was no help at all. She seemed already in a kind of mourning, and we had to force ourselves to make it into a sadness only about parting. Morales said almost nothing. He smiled and laughed a little at things Marv said, but he seemed to have run out of words and energy at the same time. What he did say sounded hollow, bits of talk rising from his hollow chest. I think we all felt relief when the meal was ended.

Marv got up and went out when the coffee had cooled. He had parked the car outside the window of Morales' room, and we could see him loading their belongings into the trunk and back seat. Connie stayed in the room with us, and she tapped on the glass once to get Marv's attention. When he looked up, he smiled and waved his fingers at her.

In a while he was finished and he came back in. He seemed a little shy, but he stood very erect and only his head hung down a little. He was smiling, but his smile seemed fundamentally reticent. I felt we had already parted when he moved up to me, grinning broadly, and took my hand and hugged me.

"Take care, Marv," I said, and he released me, and I turned to Connie and held her for a moment and kissed her. When she turned away from me and went to Verta, I saw that Marv was leaning over Morales again, and though I could not understand what he was saying, I could hear him whispering. And I think when he was finished that he kissed Morales full on the lips, but his head was turned away from me, and I could not be sure of it.

Verta and I went to the window and watched them drive away. Connie was leaning out, smiling and waving, but before the car had gone out of sight behind the building she had brought her hand inside and rolled the window up.

"They're gone," I said, but when I turned to the bed I saw that Morales was already sleeping.

Early the next morning, we packed his things and got a taxi and took him to the small airport in Loreto. We found a chair and put it in the sun outside the little terminal and helped Morales into it. Verta draped him with his blanket, but when she put it over his head he lifted his arm up, and I helped her tuck it in around his neck. We were silent for a while. We stood flanking him, looking up into the vacant, cloudless sky. Then we heard the distant droning, and in a few minutes we saw the small plane. I felt something at my sleeve, and when I looked down it was Morales tugging at it. I bent over so I could hear him. He swallowed, wet his lips and shook his head weakly, clearing his throat. His eyes blinked, and though they were watery they sparkled a little in the sun.

"Don't worry," he said. "You know the story. I'll be all right."

I didn't know what he meant exactly, but I didn't think he was right about one thing. He wouldn't be all right. At least I didn't think he would, but even as I thought of it I knew I wasn't really sure.

I don't know what it was I expected, but when his father appeared in the small hatchway of the plane he seemed smaller than he should have been. He had a hat on, and when he came down the few steps and made the ground I could see that he was shorter than Morales was, lean and wiry, but bent slightly with age. His hat was a cowboy hat, but it was tooled and painted straw and it looked like a small sombrero. He had a thin mustache, and I could see a loop of thin gold chain at his pocket. He wore pointed-toed boots, light in color, wellworn under a fresh shine. He blinked at the two of us as he approached, and we moved away a little when he reached Morales and the chair. He didn't have to lean over much to talk to him. They only talked a few moments, both nodding, and then he gestured behind him to the plane. Morales raised his hand then, and I went over to him and leaned down. I was a little shocked to see how his face had brightened, how a new blush rose from under the chalk.

"My father says we can go right now; they only have to fuel up, and then we can go."

"Right," I said. "Go on."

"That's it," Morales said.

Verta carried his few things, and I helped his father get him to the door and up the steps. As he passed through the hatchway the blanket fell from his shoulders, and when I reached down and caught it and then looked back up he was well inside, where it was dark, and I could not see him at all. His father turned to me before he entered, and he smiled a little bleakly and extended his hand.

"*Gracias,*" he said, and then he paused for a moment and spoke again, his face brightening a little, his thin mustache tipping up. "My son will be all right," he said. "Soon. He'll be as right as rain." And he took my hand then and squeezed it and blinked and smiled, and then he turned away from me and went inside. The windows were opaque, and we could not see their faces in them.

We waited until we could not longer hear the drone of the engine, and then we waited a little bit more, looking up into the empty sky. Then Verta looked at her watch.

"Time to go?" I said.

"*Sí,*" she answered, and we turned back and went to the small terminal, where the taxi that had brought us out waited. We drove to the bus station in silence, a silence we were not uncomfortable with. Verta spoke only once.

"Do you think he will be good again?" she said.

"Yes," I said. "His father will see to it."

I stayed the night in the motel, and in the morning I ate a large breakfast, and then went into Loreto, feeling some need to explore what was there. Time enough for San Diego; there was time enough to get to the records at the Naval Hospital. Through the lazy late morning and early afternoon I went into shops and felt fabric and lifted wooden, carved figures of small animals and bought a postcard with a picture of three men watching bucking horses at a rodeo. I ate an early dinner in the town, and when I got back to the motel it was still light, and I went out and lingered on the beach. The light was failing, but I could see the island we had gone to, and along the curving shore toward Loreto I could see the tentative appearance of electric lights.

It was that time, just as the day has ended and before the preparations of early evening have begun, when the world itself can seem to come to rest, and I like all the others exhaled and felt the pause before the intake of the next breath, the one that would get me going again into something else. The lights along the Baja seemed feeble and without intention. Probably they were the ones that had been left on all day, by mistake, and had stayed on invisibly in the bright sun. Now they swelled as rooms darkened, and soon they would be joined by others, the ones that would light the way of involvements into the evening. But that was not yet, not yet. And as I stood there, even the water of the Baja seemed to come to moratorium as light left it and it flattened and became lakelike. I wondered how far Marv and Connie had gotten, would they have any trouble with the ferry at La Paz? Then I thought about Verta. She would be on another bus by now, after a layover, on her way north to Ensenada. And even Morales, I thought; he'll be home by now. Everybody was going somewhere, and some were probably getting there or had already arrived. I brought the breath back in then. It tasted clean and sweet and had a faint scent like roses. But that lasted only for a moment, and then it was all over. I went back then and packed my things and headed out.

TOBY OLSON was born in Illinois, but spent most of his life in California and New York City. The recipient of National Endowment for the Arts and Guggenheim fellowships, he has published numerous books of poetry, most recently *We Are the Fire*, and two previous novels, *The Life of Jesus* and *Seaview*, which received the PEN/Faulkner award in 1983. He currently lives in Philadelphia and Cape Cod with his wife, Miriam, and teaches English at Temple University.